When Desmond goes off to college, he allows himself to be more open about his attraction to men rather than the secreted-away experiences he's had in the past.

As Desmond grapples with the pressures and expectations society forces upon him, while trying to understand what his heart is telling him to do, he is initiated into a high-class gay underworld and attracts the attention of an influential—and potentially dangerous—closeted businessman.

Set in the fictional coastal town of Oakvale, New Jersey in the mid-1970s—a decade of alternative eroticism, experimentation, and promiscuity—*When Love Calls Your Name* follows Desmond as he discovers who he is and who he is expected to be.

WHEN LOVE CALLS YOUR NAME

LBJ HarrisA

A NineStar Press Publication

www.ninestarpress.com

When Love Calls Your Name

ISBN: 978-1-64890-431-8

First Edition, December, 2021

Also available in eBook, ISBN: 978-1-64890-430-1

CONTENT WARNING:

This book contains sexually explicit content, which may only be suitable for mature readers. Depictions of alcoholism, cheating, domestic abuse, homophobia, and sexual assault (on page). No HEA.

This book is dedicated to my brother from another mother.

I did it!

Rest in peace my friend and may you continue to watch over me.

Lorenzo "Tony" Fletcher III

October 22, 1956 – September 19, 2016

Part One

A Summer to Remember

Interlude One

Graduation

"Fantasies, friends, and foes…they are the realities of our lives."

Desmond Cameron Dawson

Fantasies. What teen doesn't have them? We're taught that boys' fantasies revolve around lust, while girls dream of love and romance. As a young man, I certainly fit that mold. And while my boyhood fantasies came true—to an extent—they evolved somewhere along the way, from lust to love. Moreover, they ended up clouding my judgment so completely and ruling my heart so firmly that they changed my life forever.

That evening, thoughts raced through my head as I stepped onto the field at the Oakvale High School stadium. The band played "Pomp and Circumstance" from the stands, and I wondered to myself, *How many times have I sat up there, playing this same damn song for past graduates? How many times have I watched others walk the full length of this football field and wished it was me?* Now it was my turn!

I scanned the stands for my family, but the crowd of faces was a blur. Carla—my senior-year sweetheart—was by my side, and she had never looked prettier. Now, it had taken a little manipulation on my part to get her there next to me, but it had been worth it. Or so I thought.

The day couldn't have been more perfect. *Ask, visualize, claim it, and it will be so.*

At the height of the day, it had climbed to eighty degrees: warm enough for us to catch a swim at the Ocean Club. Around four in the afternoon, a light breeze cooled the air down to seventy degrees. The glowing full moon peeked over the eastern horizon, the sun not yet having set, far to the west, with a cool pink and blue salutation. High above, the heavens were a dome of sparkling diamonds. The stage was set. My high school graduation had arrived.

My name is Desmond Cameron Dawson. I am a Pisces, born on March 19; the middle of three children. My older brother is Calvin Vincent Jr., aged 25, whom we called Vinny. He attended law school at George Washington University in DC. My younger sister is Nina Nicole, who was to be a freshman at Oakvale High that upcoming fall.

I had what was known as bougie parents (upwardly mobile Black people), who achieved their success ten years ago. They decided to move us away from Newark, New Jersey, to this white, ocean-side town called Oakvale. It was just off the Garden State Parkway, halfway to Atlantic City.

Calvin Vincent Sr. and Mildred Nicole (Cal and Millie to each other; Mom—*or, endearingly, Momma*—and Dad to us) owned a small but prosperous advertising firm, with the original branch in Newark and a newer one here. Business was good—so good that my folks had achieved upper-middle-class status. They were good United Methodists too, raising their children in a predominantly African American church. We kids were acolytes; we sang in the choirs, did youth ministries. If you're a United Methodist too, you know the drill.

So, what the hell were we doing in good old Whites-ville, USA? To hear our parents tell it, they'd moved us down here to ensure we'd get a good education.

And speaking of education, isn't it funny, the things that run through your mind at milestones in your life? For instance, standing with my fellow seniors, waiting to march across that field, I thought to a time when—only five years old—I had been so sick I was unable to start school with the other kids my age.

I'd spent a year visiting over a dozen specialists, undergoing every test conceivable, trying out all sorts of medications—all to no avail. My illness had been so bad, making me weak to the point where I couldn't get out of bed even to go pee, that doctors had finally given up hope, telling my parents the devastating news they would likely lose their youngest son at some point that year.

Momma wouldn't accept it—not at all! She prayed long and hard—feverishly hard—and God answered her prayers. Miraculously, some weeks later, I had a full recovery. From then on, she would always tell me I was her prizewinning fighter.

I skipped from this memory to a present one—to what I considered my second major accomplishment of my life (after surviving my illness). Imagine this, if you can: I was about to become the first African American in my predominantly white high school to graduate at the top of my class. First out of three hundred and ninety-six students! Yep—I beat all those white folks to the top of the list! And despite being in law school, my brother Vinny hadn't come close to matching me in the brains department: he graduated high school forty-fifth out of three hundred and fifty.

My parents were proud of me, to say the least. Their crazy-acting, late-blooming middle kid managed to get his shit together and come out on top. Top of my class, awards in French, history, and politics, captain of the debating team, top track athlete, and in the marching band, to boot. Momma cried tears of joy when the guidance counselor called to give her the news; Dad couldn't stop calling our relatives to boast about his boy.

You want to know how hard it was to become valedictorian? Well, I knew for a fact the girl who finished second to the top hated me with a passion. Miss Dirty-Blonde-Bombshell-With-Glasses had worked her ass off for every top grade she earned. But as for me? By the time grade nine rolled around, I'd figured out the game. From that point onward, I found all this school shit straight up easy. Yeah. I'm one of those kids.

To an outside observer, everything in my life looked pretty good, right?

The truth was, I couldn't wait to be done with it. I was ready to leave this small, meddlesome, dysfunctional community that would have chewed me up and spit me out without even blinking an eye, had I let it.

It was all good, though—I was on the verge of being done and had a foolproof plan to get out of here: I'd aced all my courses in school, gotten involved in the "right" extracurriculars, and scored 1600 on my SATs. And halfway through my senior year, I found out I had been accepted to some pretty prestigious universities, most of them with full scholarships: Princeton, Yale, Harvard, Temple, and Dartmouth.

Not wanting to be too far from Momma but needing to put a bit of distance between me and Oakvale, I chose Temple University in Philadelphia—an hour and a half down I-95. Temple had a great communications and journalism program there—rated one of the top ten programs in the country. I'd decided I was going to be a television correspondent, and come September, I would be taking my first step toward television stardom!

But back to graduation day. That ended up being a condensed reminder of the things I wanted to forget about high school, beginning—and not ending—with the memory of Samuel Garrison, an unexpected fantasy *twist*.

I guess I need to explain some things before I go on.

Samuel Garrison. My best and oldest friend in all of Oakvale. He and I had both been having…*problems* with our girlfriends that whole year. We'd ended up talking and consoling each other for much of that time. And before you ask the all-important question of who was getting poontang and who wasn't: well, I was the less fortunate.

Samuel and I spent a lot of time barhopping during that year as well. Two years prior, they had lowered the legal drinking age to eighteen. We had died and gone to heaven, my posse and I—they turned eighteen at different points during our senior year, while I had reached the drinking age the year before. And believe me, they didn't miss a beat trying to catch up to me. We quickly established some favorite watering holes we took girls to, but we also reserved a spot for gents only.

Every Friday night, we would sneak out to this strip club called The Cabaret. We couldn't get enough of the place. Well, at least, Samuel couldn't.

Back to the posse—there were four of us who went through Oakvale High School together: Matt, Samuel, Michael, and me. We all played trumpet in the band together. We ran indoor and outdoor track. Two of us were on the yearbook committee. Matt and I acted in school plays together. We may as well have lived together, we spent so much time in each other's company.

I was the oldest of our group and the only brother. Did that make me feel uncomfortable at times? *Yes!* I was the butt of Samuel's too-frequent racist jokes, and as I look back now, he was a real redneck. Yet there was more to him than that.

When I moved to Oakvale, I was just an average seven-year-old kid. I didn't know anything about racism or prejudice. All I knew was that I wanted a friend—someone I could simply play with. Samuel was that person.

The day we moved in, I sat on the curb outside my new home, "staying out of the way of the movers." Across the street sat a little boy, watching me. We stared at each other wordlessly for quite a long time. Finally, he yelled across the street, saying, "My name's Samuel; what's yours?"

I called back, "Desmond."

Then he surprised me by saying, "You wanna be friends?"

And not wanting to seem overly keen on the idea, I said, "Mmm…okay."

He stood up, looked both ways, and ran across the street. He held out his hand and I mine. We shook. And then he hugged me. It felt really strange, like a spark arcing between us; from that moment on through high school, we were essentially inseparable.

Despite being close, Samuel and I didn't attend the same school until high school. His parents didn't care much for public schools, so he attended St. Catherine's Catholic School until the end of eighth grade. The Catholics didn't have a high school, so he had no choice but to transfer to Oakvale High for ninth grade. I introduced him to Matt and Michael, and just like that, he was one of the boys. I knew from then on, high school life would take me and him to another level. And it did.

Interlude Two

Caught in the Act

What can I say about Samuel? A skinny, beach-blond, too-good-looking-for-his-own-good white boy. He had sun-kissed wavy hair and crystal-blue eyes. His cheeks had a hint of peach fuzz and his lips were broader than most guys'.

In high school, he grew into a six-foot-one-tall young man with broad shoulders and a natural six-pack. He reminded me of a young Bill Bradley. His thighs and legs were as thick as a basketball player's…probably because he was the all-state point guard for our division.

For all his looks, though, there wasn't much going on up in his head. Don't get me wrong: Samuel wasn't stupid; he just wasn't very book smart. Good with his hands, though; he liked fixing cars and making things out of wood; auto shop and industrial arts—these were his favorite classes.

The four of us got jobs at a local restaurant during our junior and senior years. Samuel and I parked cars; Matt and Michael waited tables. The owner of the King's Palace was Mr. Wayne Simpson, a former football and track star at Oakvale

High. He always hired varsity athletes, cheerleaders, and even band geeks to work during summers and off-seasons.

The patrons were all wealthy socialites, and if you gave the men a firm handshake and told their wives how nice they looked, you were sure to get a five-dollar or even a ten-dollar tip. More, if the husbands were drunk enough.

We could not have been happier, the four of us—money in our pockets, good friends, and hormones raging. We were at that point in our teenage lives when we listened to our cocks instead of our heads. And what did our cocks want? A fast car and a virgin girl. Every teen boy's rite of passage begins there, ending in conquest or defeat.

First, you needed a car: swift, shiny, and sexy. Perfect for a girl to lose her virginity in. Hoopties didn't cut it unless you were an auto mechanic. Next, you needed the girl: snatch her virginity and, in the process, lose your own. After that, the game carried on, pulling as many virgins as you could, remaining true to the physical realm and not being sucked into that tedious emotional abyss. These were the adolescent tests that would really prove you were *the man.*

I was no different from the rest. I just wasn't as skillful as some of my peers. Samuel had skills. With those beach-boy looks and perfect body, he pulled girls in like flies to flypaper.

And that's how our senior year got rolling. Work, drinks, cars, poontang. Rinse and repeat.

Then, one unforgettable night in mid-October, my life took an interesting turn. It was harvest festival weekend, and we were at school playing for the football game. June—Samuel's girlfriend at the time—was the drum major for our school band. She was built like Ann-Margret and had the looks to match. She and Samuel—first trumpet in the band—made for an enviable couple.

Well, early on in the game, Samuel had leaned over to me and said, "You know Mandy Watkins, the captain of the baton-twirling squad? She's been dropping hints she wants to jump my bones. She passed me this note before the game." Mandy was the resident band slut. It was well known throughout the locker room that she would let you feel her up if she liked you. All the band guys wanted a piece of her, though she only gave it up to football jocks.

I unfolded the piece of paper covered in curly pink writing that Samuel had pushed into my hand. *I'll be waiting for you in the drum closet after the game. Take a look behind you when you get in the stands and see what will be waiting for you.*

As we read this, Samuel swiveled around to look at Mandy, who was seated with the other baton twirlers on the bleachers up and behind us. I looked around too. Mandy gave the impression of enjoying the game below but must have been watching out the corner of her eye for Samuel to look back. With a sly twist to her lips, she nonchalantly spread her legs. She wore no panties under her short skirt, and the pink lips of her pussy were there in plain sight. My eyes popped, and I searched around to see if anyone else had noticed; most eyes were on the game. I shook my head and faced forward. *Man, Samuel has all the luck!*

"Maybe I'll get a two-for-one deal—a blowjob and some fingers in that cunt!" he said in my ear. I looked over to see a huge grin on his boyish face.

After the game, Samuel, June, Carla, and I were walking out to my car from the drum closet. We were the last ones out.

Mr. Carlson–the band director—had instructed us to close the door behind us, as it would lock automatically.

As we approached my car, Samuel turned to June and said, "Oh man, I forgot I was supposed to drive Mom to Aunt Kelly's after the game today." Turning to me, he added, "Dude, would you mind giving June a ride home?"

This was my cue. I turned to Carla. "Okay if we drop June off first?"

She shrugged her indifference, popping a stick of gum in her mouth, and the game was in play.

Samuel gave June a long, wet kiss, his tongue driving into her mouth like his life depended on it. "I'll call you later, babe." He took off the way we'd come. The girls and I climbed into my car. Carla and June started talking about one of the cheerleaders while I tried to find some good tunes on the box. Suddenly, June gasped.

"Damn! I forgot to put my baton away. I'll be right back." She jumped out of the car and rushed off, her baton under one arm. I hadn't quite registered that, so I asked Carla over my shoulder, "What did she say?"

"She said she had forgotten to put her baton away," my girlfriend replied between blowing a bubble and chomping noisily. "I hope she has her key."

I swiveled my head around fully, the radio forgotten. "What key?"

"Didn't ya know? Mr. Carlson gave June a key to open up the drum closet on Saturdays so he didn't have to come early to weekend practices."

Shit! I yanked the car keys from the ignition and leaped out, sprinting the way we'd come, screaming June's name. I was too late. By the time I arrived, June was standing in the open doorway, frozen. As the inside of the closet came into view, I spotted Mandy, down on her knees, Samuel's slick hard cock in her manicured hand.

Our arrival must have broken the curse, because June let out a savage shriek, throwing her baton toward Samuel and Mandy, then ran back toward the car, hyperventilating, tears starting to draw streaks of mascara down her cheeks. The baton had caught Mandy squarely in one eye; she'd collapsed to the floor, writhing around, mewling in pain.

I barely noticed. My eyes were fixed on something else…Samuel's still-hard cock.

When I finally broke my stare, I met Samuel's eyes. Clearly he'd seen me watching. A smirk shot across his face. *Shit!* I thought to myself for the second time in as many minutes. What was I doing? More importantly, how could I justify staring at my best friend's piece when there had been a smoking-hot girl down on her knees right next to him? A cold sweat broke out on my brow. This was going to end badly.

Carla had come up behind me at that point, in time to see Samuel buttoning his pants and Mandy sitting up, nursing her eye. Carla blew one bubble, grabbed me by the jacket, and yanked me away, propelling me in the direction June had taken off.

We caught up with Samuel's girlfriend in the parking lot a few moments later. She was bent over—one hand on the side of my car, gasping for breath. Carla did that stuff girls do for other girls when they're in that state: stroking hair and whispering and shit. Once June calmed down enough to stand up straight and breathe normally, Carla suggested we take her out to the diner for some coffee.

It took Carla two hours to convince June that Samuel wasn't worth losing her mind over. Carla kept nudging me to say something, but I had no clue what to say. June had known about Samuel's reputation before they'd started dating. Matter of fact, she'd stolen him from *another* girl in pretty much the same way.

Impressively, June had managed to keep Samuel on the hook for a lot longer than most girls. Until tonight.

What went through my mind during those two hours, though, was…well, you can guess by now: Samuel's piece. I had just caught a glimpse, really: long enough, though, to have seared an image into my brain. It was big, for starters. Big, and erect, with loosely curled blond hair surrounding the base of his shaft. Still wet with Mandy's spit, and…and…*beautiful.* There it was. I thought my buddy's hard cock was beautiful.

Eventually, we took June home and saw her to her door. Carla told June she would be home all night if she needed to talk. Then we left for Carla's house.

"You knew Samuel was in there, didn't you?" my girlfriend said after a few minutes of silent driving. My first reaction was to lie my ass off.

"No way, baby! I had no idea he'd be in there!"

She looked at me with knowing eyes. We rode the rest of the way in silence. When I parked the car in Carla's driveway, I leaned over to kiss her good night. I was met with the back of her head and a mouth full of hair. As she opened the door, she said, "Nah. If you want a kiss tonight, go find that dog you've been hanging out with." She closed the door and walked off.

Gnashing my teeth, I rolled down the window. "Well, if you feel that way, maybe I ought to go get me some of that same action Samuel got."

"Do as you please, but after you finish, make sure you check for crabs," she tossed over her shoulder without missing a step.

When I got home, I went straight to my room and flopped onto the bed. *This was a crazy day,* I thought. And still I was stuck with that image going around and around inside my brain. Samuel's penis. The head, a glistening pink mushroom; the shaft, skinny, lean, and veiny. I swear it must have been around eight inches long.

As I lay there, I realized I had my own piece in my hand, unconsciously stroking myself to fullness. As it grew, I imagined comparing our cocks side by side. (I'm pretty sure mine would be bigger.) I wondered what the sensation would be to have some girl put her lips on it. (Carla was still holding out.) The idea of a tongue sliding up and down the shaft of my penis had me rock-hard and twitching. A couple dozen strokes later, I was about to shoot my load, when there was a quiet knock at the door. I scrambled to pull my shorts up when I heard Momma's voice. "Desmond, Samuel's at the door."

Samuel? Now? Why the hell is he here? Is he going to say something about me staring at him earlier? The cold sweat I'd experienced when he caught me looking was back. *I'll play it off if he mentions it,* I decided. And if he pressed me, I'd tell him to fuck off. I'd play it real macho. "Okay, Mom! Tell him to come up!" I thought for a moment and yelled out again, "Actually—tell him I'll be right down."

"Okay, dear."

My erection wasn't going down fast enough, so I threw on one of my oversized jerseys and ran downstairs. Samuel waited at the bottom. As I reached the last step, he leaned in close and whispered, "We need to talk." He turned and walked out the door onto the front porch. I joined him a second later, after adjusting my penis one last time.

"What am I going to do about June and Mandy, man?" He was staring off into the night as I came up next to him. *Maybe he's forgotten about me staring at his piece?* The thought didn't make me feel any less nervous, though; I *knew* he'd caught me looking. "You want to get out of here for a couple hours?" He still hadn't looked at me. I couldn't come up with a reason to say no; after all, it was only 9:30 p.m.

I went back in and poked my head into the living room. "Mom? Dad? Samuel wants to run down to the diner and get something to eat. Do you mind if I go out for a few?"

They looked at each other with that look parents give each other; then Dad responded. "If it's just to the diner, that's fine. Be back by midnight."

"Not a problem." I blew them a kiss and ran outside. We jumped into Samuel's '69 Chevy pickup and roared away.

As we drove, I fought to banish the image of Samuel standing in the closet with his pants down around his knees, that monster piece, hard as rock, protruding from his patch of curly blond hair, between those muscular legs. It got so vivid I felt myself getting hard again. I tried to play it off by listening to Parliament-Funkadelic on the radio and focusing on the cars going by. *Why isn't he saying anything?*

I suddenly noticed we weren't heading in the direction of the diner. "Hey, what's up? Where we goin'?"

"Relax, dude," Samuel replied. "I got a couple of brewskis, a joint, and the perfect place to get totally fucked up." I was up for that. A joint would take the edge off my nerves. We continued to drive in silence. I resisted looking over at him.

Is it possible he didn't catch me looking at his cock? Well, I certainly wasn't going to bring it up myself! When he was ready to talk, I would listen and take my cue from what he said.

We drove out to the Ocean Club, where our families were all members, and parked behind the double dumpsters in the back of the clubhouse restaurant. Samuel told me he had done this before and assured me that while we could see between the dumpsters, no one could see us. He pulled two six-packs from the back seat and a joint from inside his jacket.

As we sat smoking and drinking warm beer, he finally began to talk. He described having the resident band slut take care of his piece, up until the point when June opened the door.

"Man, I almost shit myself when she burst in on us! I gotta make it up to her, dude." Though Samuel had never said it out loud, I knew June kept him on a very short leash. It wouldn't be easy to convince her to forgive this transgression.

In no time, I was ripped. And all the talk about how it felt to have Mandy go down on him had made me extremely horny. A lull fell over the conversation right when Chaka Khan and Rufus's single, "Tell Me Something Good," started to play on the radio.

Man, with the rhythm of that song adding to the sexual tension in the car and the high from the joint, I was feeling...well, I didn't quite know. It sure was something new, though.

My head bobbed to the music, when I caught a motion out the corner of my eye. He had his hand in his pants and was stroking his giant bulge. I froze. For the second time that day, I found myself transfixed. Without glancing at me, he whispered in a low growl, "Yo, man—you think you could help a fella out?" He turned his head, staring at me with eyes I'd never seen on him before.

Fear as a hot flash shot up and down my spine. *Is he really asking what I think he's asking?* I wasn't so stoned I didn't know what I would be getting myself into. Samuel slid toward me along the bench seat and reached his free hand up behind my neck. He ran his fingers through the soft curls of my Afro. I pulled away, leaning into the car door.

"Hey, man, what the fuck's up with you?" I slurred. "I'm not gonna… I don't wanna… Why are you doing this?" I blinked, struggling to regain clarity of mind.

"You'll enjoy it, trust me." He continued to stroke my hair, his own words sounding sort of distant. "I saw you, Desmond. I saw the way you stared at my Jimmy, man. You couldn't take your eyes off him. Your eyes were tellin' Jimmy you wanted to give him a try. And don't think I didn't notice you watching me get myself off just now."

He leaned in close now, turning my head and forcing me to meet his eyes. "Look, Desmond, it's perfectly natural. Dudes our age do this shit all the time. Try it out. Come on. Trust your buddy, Samuel."

Samuel's hand went from a gentle stroke to a tight grip about the back of my neck. My instinct was to resist—to push him roughly and call him out. But, at the same time, some part of me, from the unplumbed depths of my psyche, told me this was exactly what I wanted to happen.

And so, I relaxed into it. Samuel pulled his hand out of his jeans, unzipping them. A thrill ran through me as I saw he wasn't wearing any underwear, and his hard cock practically leaped out of his pants. It looked bigger than when I'd seen it from afar, in the closet.

"Go on, Desmond. Suck on my Jimmy until he spits. You can do that for me, can't you?" His hand at my neck drew me down, closer and closer to his erect penis. I breathed in, smelling his musk. The strong aroma of his groin invaded my senses, awakening an instinct I hadn't known before. I closed my eyes and absorbed his cock into my mouth, letting my lips guide me. My mind blanked. My body twitched with pleasure. My mouth and tongue explored Samuel's shaft, up and down rhythmically, in time to the music on the radio.

I lost myself to the taste, gently savoring the flesh as you would the meat on a rib bone. A mental image of myself enjoying my best friend flashed through my mind. *This is insane!* His intoxicating aroma drew me back in, even as his groaning urged me on to pleasure him more. Strong fingertips firmly kneaded the back and top of my scalp as he pushed my head down onto him—deeper, deeper, deeper. Further and further inside me, Jimmy went.

Samuel's hips bucked once, then twice, and he plunged his shaft down my throat. I resisted the urge to choke as his cock pulsated against my tongue, against the walls of my throat. His gasps of ecstasy intensified as his load started to explode inside me. I moaned and gagged but took it all. There was no hesitation in me. No doubt.

The pulsing slowed, as did the torrent of his cum. The vise grip on my head relaxed, and I drew my mouth off his still-twitching shaft, the taste and smell of him filling my senses. Instead of sitting up, I laid my head against his lap. Without looking down, he stroked the side of my face. The sound of our labored breaths filled the car. And I wondered if something as erotic and amazing as this could ever be spoken of afterward.

Apparently, it wasn't over yet.

Samuel drew me up. He reached across me to trigger the seat recline, and I dropped back with a bang. I didn't know what would happen next, so I lay there, still panting lightly. His hand fumbled for my pants button, unfastening it. He unzipped me, and with both hands, he pulled my jockey shorts and my shorts down. I hiked up my hips, and he jerked the shorts down to my knees. Exposed, my snake began to pulsate.

Through the gloom in the car, I saw a smile crossing Samuel's face as he whispered in a husky voice, "Look at that delicious piece of dessert you've been hiding inside those pants. Damn, man—you're as big as I am. I'm just sorry I didn't think of this sooner." And, with that, he descended upon me, his tongue hungrily licking the length of my shaft like a popsicle. His lips melted over my head like warm chocolate oozing over a mound of soft ice cream.

Samuel worked my snake like magic, stroking it with his thumb and forefinger from the rocks at the bottom of my tail to my dark mushroom head at the top. His tongue teased me as my snake danced in his clutch. His rough hand and firm grip drove me mad.

As he had done to me, I slid my fingers through his soft, wavy blond hair. On instinct, I grabbed a handful of that corn silk, forcing him to go faster and deeper on my snake. Within seconds, it felt as if venom was being drawn in from every corner of my body toward my snake's head and my entire being vibrated. Like the venom from a cobra bite, my orgasm coursed through me, rushing through my cock and into Samuel, filling the inside of him. I forced him to take one last thrust, knowing I had filled the walls of his throat with the warmth of my injection. A low, long sigh escaped from the depths of my soul. My best friend had claimed his prize.

We zipped ourselves up and drove straight home. We spoke not a word. I was in a fog; my whole body floated in that seat, next to him. I think I even drifted in and out of sleep because, when we reached my house, Samuel was shaking me awake, whispering, "Last stop—all nonvirgins disembark here." He smiled. "How you doing?"

"Okay. I guess," I muttered. He reached over and cupped my chin, forcing me to look at him.

"I never want to do this with any other dude but you. You hear me?" And then he stroked my cheek. *What does he mean? Will we be doing this again?* In that moment, I was ready to do it again. And again, and again. Well, maybe not *right* then, because I could barely get myself out of the car. Samuel got out and came around to open my door. He guided me with his arm around my waist to the front door, his fingers digging into the front of my hips. Right before I opened the door, he reached over with his other hand and grabbed my piece, squeezing it gently but firmly. "Remember, this belongs to me now."

Without responding, I slipped into the house and closed the door, glad to see everyone else had gone to bed. There was no way I could have explained my state to my sister, much less my parents. I stumbled up the stairs and collapsed onto my bed. I descended into sleep, lulled by swirling visions of Samuel and our hard cocks.

The instant before sleep overtook me, a chilling thought washed through my mind: *Am I gay now?*

Interlude Three

Betrayal

That night was the first of many to follow. Whenever Samuel and I could find an excuse to ditch the girls or Matt and Michael, we did.

June and Samuel made up a week later. Samuel put his Jimmy to work getting her back. As it turned out, Samuel had been banging June all the previous summer and all during the school year; she couldn't get enough of him and decided she needed to have even more.

During our private time, Samuel told me about the sex he and June were having. I couldn't get Carla to do any more than let me finger her, and those times seemed fewer and further between. She would tell me she wanted to wait until she got married. Her mother had told her if she ever got pregnant, she shouldn't bother coming home. All I could think of was, *Isn't she concerned about what* I *need?*

Luckily, fooling around with Samuel really took the edge off. Each time I was with him, it felt great. He and I were into the basic stuff: blowjobs and jerking off together. We never crossed the line into kissing or doing the "nasty," though I often wondered what it would be like.

I admit to being a bit jealous of June. She enjoyed Sam in a way I could not. Knowing he wasn't with any other guy satisfied me, though—even June couldn't say that! I knew he still had other girls on the side.

As good as it felt to be with Samuel, feelings of guilt began to creep up on me after we'd finished. *I'm committing a colossal sin*, part of me would think as we cleaned ourselves up, and I knew God would be reaping his punishment on us both before long.

Another part of me longed to seek out some advice. I just didn't know who to turn to.

I had a pretty cool relationship with my dad. We would go on long walks and talk about almost everything. Talking about sex with other guys was a line I was too afraid to cross with him, though. I didn't want to think about what he would say or think.

Momma: she was pretty cool too. But there was no talking to her about *that* type of guy stuff. We did talk a lot about girls. She never came out and said she disapproved of me dating a white girl, and she didn't try to stop my relationship with Carla either.

Momma would drop hints about Black women and how there were a lot of good ones out there. "The problem is all those trifling Black brothers who won't even give a sister a chance!" she'd say. To me that signal came through loud and clear. I have to say, though, she always made Carla feel like she was one of the family.

★

Graduation was quickly approaching, and our prom only a couple of weeks away. We'd come up with great plans for that night. In the back of my mind, I hoped Carla and I would finally go all the way.

Matt, Samuel, Michael, and I pooled our money and rented a limo for the evening. The plan was to get dressed at Matt's house and get picked up by the limo there. Then we'd make the rounds back to each of our homes for family pictures. From there, we'd go to the Palace (Mr. Simpson had graciously invited all of us for hors d'oeuvres) before heading to the official supper and dance.

The senior prom was being held at the Oakvale Tennis Club and Spa, situated right on the ocean. The hall we ate and danced in had a glass wall overlooking the Atlantic. Doors led out to pathways leading down to the beach. There couldn't have been a nicer venue for our high school send-off.

Perhaps because this was one of our last nights together, the mood in the room was a true lovefest. Everyone was hugged-up at the tables and on the dance floor. There wasn't a slow dance that went by where most of us almost graduates weren't bumping and grinding our dates.

The prom went well into the next morning, after which the whole class was invited to Marsha Brook's parents' beach house for a catered breakfast. They really knew how to throw down: white-tableclothed banquet tables were covered with everything from Belgian waffles with strawberries and powdered sugar, a selection of dim sum, little smoked-salmon quiches, mimosas, and Bloody Marys to more standard fare like bacon, sausages, eggs, hash browns, toast, fresh fruit, and steaming-hot coffee.

It couldn't have been a more perfect night. Except for what happened at the tail end.

At one point, we were sitting on the patio at Marsha's house, stuffing our faces with platefuls of the catered food. Samuel and June were sitting in a lounge chair, with Samuel behind his girlfriend. He was stroking her arm and whispering into her ear. As overtired as I was, I could still clearly see June's body language: she was *not* reciprocating Samuel's romantic overtures. In fact, she was looking more and more irate by the second. Finally, she shoved her elbow into his chest and wheeled around to face him.

"Hell no, you won't be getting this piece of ass today!" She stood up, hands on her hips, ignoring Samuel's gestures to keep it down. "I'm tired of you looking at other girls, and I'm tired of putting up with you going limp on me after a few minutes. I'm ready for a real man!"

The patio had fallen absolutely still. Every last eye out there locked on either Samuel or June.

Samuel had dropped his head. He'd gone all white and looked like he was crumbling in on himself. My heart ached for him—far more so than I thought I could feel for a friend—and I wanted to reach for him.

June spun around and walked over to Delvin Wicks, the power forward for the basketball team, and a brother. She held out a hand to him. He looked around at his circle of friends with a bemused look and, with a shrug, stood and took June's offer. She guided him across the patio, disappearing into Marsha's house.

The spell broke after they walked out of sight: the patio erupted into whispered gossiping. In the midst of it was

Samuel. He blinked twice, grabbed his jacket, and bolted off the patio toward the beach.

I leaned over to Carla, giving her a quick peck on the cheek. "I'm really sorry, honey. I gotta go after him. He's like—" She cut me off with a hand and a roll of her eyes.

"Sure, of course you do, Desmond!" She looked at me, her eyes softening. "Go to him," she whispered.

I nodded to Matt and Michael, grabbed my own jacket, then ran down to the beach after him. "Sam? Samuel!" The rising sun shone in my eyes, so I couldn't see which way he'd gone. I squinted, looking left and right. *There!* Down the beach several hundred feet, I spotted a silhouette walking past a beach cabana. "Samuel!" I ran after him and grabbed his arm as I got close.

"What the fuck? Get your hands off me!"

"Sam—it's me! Are you all right?"

He snorted. "Yeah. That bitch and I were over anyway."

"So you're not going after her?"

"Won't have to. You'll see. By graduation she'll be back on her knees, begging for it. Anyways, she's not what I want right now." He glanced around, grabbed me by the shoulders, and pushed me against one of the cabana posts. "I want you," he whispered.

Before I could reply, our lips locked. *He's kissing me!* Sam's lips were moist; I tasted Jack Daniel's and maple syrup on them. Those smells, along with the smell of him, drew a deep sigh from me. With just an instant of resistance, I let his tongue slip inside and probe the inner caverns of my mouth, feeling a warmth rise in me. My snake stirred—and sought a release from my tight dress pants. I reached for Samuel's piece; it had already risen to the occasion.

While making out, Samuel had unbuttoned his shirt and ripped his tie off. He was working on unbuttoning his pants when I grabbed his hands. "Here? Out on the beach? What if someone sees?" My eyes drifted down to his open shirt. His nipples were standing up in the cool morning air. Sam shook me off, pulling his dress pants down.

"Who's gonna see us here? And who cares anyways?" I didn't need more convincing than that. Not with his naked torso just inches away, drawing me in.

I leaned my head into his neck, breathing him in. I used my teeth to gently bite the skin where his neck met his shoulder, sucking lightly. I let my tongue travel slowly down his pecs to his nipples and began to kiss and nibble at them.

A moan escaped from Samuel's lips, and his hands ran up through my hair, massaging my scalp. He pulled me up to his sweet lips. Grabbing me by my shoulders, he drew me closer. Passionately he kissed me until I gasped for breath.

His hands moved down to encompass my whole body, mashing me to him. I was so lost in our kiss I didn't realize my feet were off the ground. Sam took a few steps into the cabana and dropped us to the paneled floor, both of us laughing breathlessly. We rolled and stopped with his body on top of mine. *What is he doing? Where is this going?* The desire I felt overwhelmed me; I didn't resist when he started to ferociously unbutton my clothes, stripping me like a pro, kissing my flesh that had been left naked as he went.

He lifted off me for a moment, throwing a pair of cushions from a wicker love seat onto the floor beside us. He spread his jacket over the cushions, signaling I should lie on it. We kissed again, Sam moving down to kiss my neck, my chest, and my nipples. It was my turn to moan—I think it came out more like a whimper—and rubbed my hands over his shoulders and in his hair.

"Turn over," he said in a husky voice. Without thinking, I did, going face-first into his jacket. The aroma of his sweat filled my head as he licked and kissed the back of my neck. He traveled down my spine, continually licking, nibbling, and kissing every part of my back. His tongue leaped down to my thighs, sliding up into the hairs of my behind, making me gasp, and then he kissed his way upward again. His Jimmy followed the path his tongue had just laid, rubbing between my thighs and over the crack of my behind.

I knew what he wanted, and I knew I wasn't ready for that. I firmly reached behind me and grabbed Jimmy in my hand. I rolled over, facing him once more.

"What's wrong? Don't you want me, Desmond?" His voice dripped with lust. My own voice caught in my throat.

"Sorry. I'm sorry, Sam. I'm not ready to try that, man!" Samuel looked down into my eyes, seeing I was serious about not going that far. He sunk down on top of me, his naked torso, thick legs, and inflamed groin hot in the morning chill. Undeterred, he kissed me, deeply and more passionately. Of their own doing, our pulsating manhoods began grinding together, eliciting groans from each of us.

It didn't take our teen bodies long to brim with ecstasy, then overflow with searing streams of our semen. Barely had we finished than our bodies urged us for more, recharged again. We made love three, four times, unable to quench our lusts.

Finally, though, our bodies—overtired from a night of partying—demanded rest. As the morning sun strengthened, we lay wrapped about each other, spread out on Samuel's jacket in the beach cabana. Sweat coated our bodies, and our chests heaved from the marathon of orgasms we'd shared. The events from earlier that morning had been forgotten; we were the only two people in the world.

A gentle snore signaled Sam's level of exhaustion. I lay in the crook of his arm, a warm smile creasing my face. *Could making love to a woman ever be as powerful and intense as this?* I wondered. As I gazed at my lover, I knew this was right, for this moment in time. I felt satisfied, not guilty, which was all the confirmation I needed to know this was not a mistake and I wasn't a freak of nature.

In my wildest dreams, I never imagined men could make love and feel drawn to one another so naturally and completely. Then another thought crossed my mind: *What if I had let Samuel fuck me? What would I have felt then? Will I ever be ready to go that far with him?* I had no answer for that. But, for right now, as we lay naked in each other's arms on this beach, with the sun warming us and the ocean serenading us, all was good.

After tidying up the cabana and dressing, we decided to go straight home instead of back to Marsha's house. I figured Carla was gone by now anyways. I had no regrets about not getting it on with her. Samuel had said what he really wanted was me; I realized I felt exactly the same way with him.

As we walked off, we didn't realize we had not been alone on the beach that morning. Someone had been there with us, watching with angry, jealous eyes.

★

We met up with Matt and Michael that afternoon for a swim, then visited our favorite bar for drinks. We were all still exhausted from last night, though Matt was especially quiet. I figured he was still suffering from too much Jack Daniel's.

Once we were at the bar, though, he began to drink way more than normal, even going so far as hogging the joint Samuel had brought with him. By the end of the night, I knew something was wrong. Matt barely stumbled from the bar before puking his guts out onto the parking lot.

We took him back to my place and called his mother to let her know he was staying the night at my house. My parents and Nina had gone down to Washington for the weekend to visit my brother Vinny. Michael, Sam, and I were in my kitchen feeding the munchies when Matt came out of the bathroom looking like he'd been hit by a Mack truck. No sooner did we start to tease him than it all came out.

"You *ass*holes! Why, *why* did you do that to me?" He looked over at Samuel. I thought I saw tears starting to form. "What the fuck's wrong with you? Don't you have a heart?"

"Man, you're fucking wasted!" Samuel shook his head. "That's the last time we let your ass drink and smoke at the same time!" Michael and I laughed. Matt was less amused.

"I saw you. I saw you guys fucking in the sand. I watched you for hours this morning." *Shit—exposed!* Fear shot through my body, and I broke out in a cold sweat. Matt pointed an unsteady finger at Sam. "You told me I was the only one, Samuel!" He leaned into the doorframe, looking not so steady.

"Shut the fuck up, Matt. I don't know what you're talking about. Why don't you go sleep it off on the sofa?" Samuel refused to meet my eyes. My fear threatened to overwhelm me; I felt the tingling of nervous sweat in my armpits.

"What's he talking about, Desmond?" Michael asked.

"Look how drunk he is, dude," I bluffed. "He doesn't know what he's saying." But our secret was out. *And, apparently, ours isn't the only one.*

Matt staggered into Samuel's face and yelled, "You're a fucking faggot! Go on, admit it. Tell Michael what the two of you were doing last night!" He started beating Samuel on the chest, sobbing openly now. "Tell him what you did last night! Then tell him how you told me I was the *only* one!"

"You want to talk about queers and faggots, Matt? Why don't you tell Michael how many times I fucked you up the asshole, bitch!" Samuel swatted Matt's arms away. "And how much you loved having me in you! How each time you screamed like a bitch, begging for more! Do you want me to show them how I take your bitch-ass right here?" Samuel grabbed Matt by a wrist and spun him around, slamming his crotch into Matt's rear end.

By this time Michael's mouth had dropped wide open. "Would somebody tell me what fuck is going on here?" I stood frozen to the spot, expressionless, watching Samuel roughly hump Matt.

"Matt saw me and one of my hoes on the beach last night, and I guess he thought it was Desmond; she just happened to be Black! He must have thought—"

"Yeah, Matt must have thought it was me," I added, glaring at Sam. He still refused to meet my eyes.

"No!" Matt bucked Samuel off and wheeled to face us. "It was the two of you; I *know* it was. I saw everything." He looked at me, tears running down his face, lips quivering. "I saw him kissing you and undressing you, Des! I saw him on top of you!"

My emotions were a tornado inside me, even as I kept my face blank. Anger swirled with guilt; I both hated and empathized with Matt in that moment. As for Samuel...

Sam reached out and grabbed Matt by his shirt, drawing him in. Before Michael or I could react, he punched Matt in the face. "I was with one of my bitches, and if you don't stop saying it was Desmond, I'm going to fucking beat the shit out of you!"

That was the line.

I stepped in between, pushing Samuel away from Matt. "Okay, okay, that's enough! Look at him, Sam!" Matt had slumped to the floor, holding his face in his hands. "I'm gonna put him in my sister's bed and let him sleep it off. Michael, help me." We pulled Matt up and guided him upstairs to Nina's room.

As we climbed the steps, Matt kept muttering, "*Why? Why did you do it?*" I ignored him, as well as Michael's probing looks. We rolled him onto the bed, tugged off his sneakers, pulled the covers over him, and closed the door.

As we got back to the kitchen, Samuel was shoving a handful of chips into his mouth. None of us said anything while he chewed and swallowed. I heard the clock in the hallway ticking as things grew awkwardly quiet.

Michael finally broke the silence.

"Okay, guys, what the hell did he mean? What was all that 'you said I was the only one' shit?" He looked the two of us over. "What the hell's been going on with you guys? Have you really been fucking Matt?" he said to Samuel, and then to me: "And have you and Samuel been getting it on too?"

Samuel got right in Michael's face. "Shut the fuck up, man, and don't pay any attention to that shit Matt was saying!"

Michael shoved Samuel away, keeping his fists clenched, ready to strike.

Yet another line was drawn.

I put myself between Michael and Samuel, holding a palm out to each of them. "I've had enough of this shit for tonight! Get the fuck out of my house, okay? Both of you, get the fuck out!" I was yelling now, shaking with unresolved emotions. Without saying a word, the guys picked up their stuff and stumbled out of my house, going their separate ways. Standing in my doorway, I watched them disappear into the night.

Except Samuel didn't quite vanish.

He slowed to a stop under a streetlamp, sort of hunched over. Even angry as I was, I saw the hurt he carried—the indecision. After a moment, he turned toward the house. Seeing me in the doorway, he jogged back. As he neared me, he slowed, holding his hands out. Confident Sam had vanished—this one looked like a lost puppy.

"Look, man, don't believe a word Matt says, all right?"

"And what about what you said? Have you been fucking him?"

"I told you, Des—it's me and you, dude. You hear me? You gotta believe me!"

"I... I *have* to? And when were you going to try again to fuck me? Graduation? Was that your plan? Was I just another notch on your belt?" I sneered at him; half his face was lit by the yellow porch light, the other half lost in the gloom. "Yeah, I thought so. All you had to do was drill my hole and your belt would have been complete. You've already fucked my mind up, but that wasn't enough for you, was it?" I was almost spitting with anger.

Instead of recoiling, Sam took a step nearer to me. His hands twitched. *He wants to reach for me,* I realized…and I wanted desperately to pour my body into his open arms. I resisted, though, thanks to the pain I still felt inside. I shook my head and crossed my arms. His shoulders drooped a bit.

"I'll call you," he muttered, crestfallen. "We've gotta talk this out man, okay? Desmond? Okay?"

"When hell freezes over," I said through gritted teeth and slammed the door in his face.

The moment the door shut, my knees began to buckle. I slid down to the floor. *How stupid could I have been?!* What made me think that if Samuel would cheat on his girlfriend, he wouldn't do the same thing to me? *How could he do this to me?* I thought, realizing bitterly that Matt had been saying the same thing only a few minutes earlier.

I lay down on the cold, hard floor, taking in a shuddering breath. I shocked myself when, with my exhale, I whispered, "I love you, Sam."

I'm as bad as those stupid girls who cry and paw over him when they find out he's cheated! Despite this realization, I cried out, "How, Sam? How could you do this to me?" I kept repeating it, beating the tile floor with my fists and sobbing myself to sleep.

The next morning, I jerked awake, moaning in pain at my sore neck and back. The floor had definitely not been good place to sleep. I dragged myself into a hot shower and threw on an old pair of sweats. I fixed myself some bitter coffee and was shoveling in some tasteless cereal when Matt stumbled into the kitchen.

"How's your head?" I asked him.

"Which one?" he asked. "It feels like I have three or four. But more specifically are you talking about the one the booze got to or the one Samuel's had?"

"I see there's nothing wrong with your memory."

"Yeah, you don't forget when someone shits on your face! Especially when it's your friends. So, did you and Samuel have fun laughing at me behind my back?"

"I wasn't laughing at your back, Matt. I didn't know about you and Samuel. Do you think I would have been with him, had I known?"

"Knowing he was with June never stopped you, did it?" he retorted. *That point goes to Matt.*

"Look, dude, I think we've both been dogged by the master of all dogs."

"And you're just gonna sit there and tell me you're not pissed about it?" Matt's voice was cracked and raw, and he'd grown all flushed. I took a bite of my cereal.

"Oh, I'm pissed, man. I'm just not going to make a fool of myself over someone who isn't worth it." I turned over a mug and poured him a cup of coffee. "If you want to tell me how you and Samuel got involved, I'm listening. But if you're going to be a little sissy and sit there crying about how he did you wrong, then that's pure bitch shit and I ain't got time for it." I pushed the mug toward him. He picked it up without a word; his gaze had gone far away.

"I thought he really cared about me, Desmond. He told me I was the only one." He chuckled bitterly. "That my piece belonged to him and only him." I chuckled too. *I've heard that line before.* I'd have thought Samuel would be more original, but then again, it *was* Samuel.

"This was his piece, you know," Matt whimpered as he grabbed his cock through his pants. I winced. *Damn, this boy fell hard for Sam's shit.* Matt noticed my look. "I didn't see you pushing him away on the beach yesterday—you bought his shit too, Desmond!" That set me back. It was true, and it hurt. I realized I wasn't angry with Matt.

"I'm sorry, dude. I guess I'm annoyed for being as big a fool as everyone else he's fucked over. I should have known better." Our eyes met; after a moment, Matt gave me a small nod.

After a few silent sips of coffee, Matt opened up.

"It started about a month and a half ago. We've been messing around ever since." One day after track practice at the end of March, he and Samuel found themselves the last two in the boys' locker room. They were showering, Samuel fully lathered up under his showerhead, right next to Matt.

"I was rinsing my hair when I glanced down at his dick. He was rock-hard. I couldn't believe how big it looked, even covered in soap. And I couldn't take my eyes off it, until I heard Sam laugh. He'd been watching me watch him." Matt turned off his shower and retreated into the locker area. "I got dressed really fast, trying to get out of there. I wasn't fast enough."

Matt had walked out of the school, finding Samuel waiting for him by his car. "He convinced me to go out and have a drink. We had a few, smoked some weed, then drove to the Ocean Club. There's this spot—"

"Behind the dumpsters. I know the spot," I said, my stomach boiling.

"Oh. Right." Matt described the encounter he and Samuel had shared, which sounded awfully like our first time together. He continued to tell me how, within a few weeks, Samuel had convinced him to agree to fuck. "I was really nervous. But once he was inside me—" Matt squinted; his cheeks had gone slightly red as he dropped his eyes. After a moment's embarrassment, he continued. "After Samuel was inside me for a bit, it felt really good. I mean *really* good, Des." His head came up and he met my eyes. "Does that make me…gay?"

"I don't know. Maybe it just means you like the feeling of a dick in your ass," I replied, trying not to think about it too much.

I didn't reciprocate with a story of my own. I figured it would do little to soothe the anger and betrayal I saw Matt was still feeling. In fact, he and I agreed it would be best not to talk about what we had done with Samuel anymore. Not with each other, or anyone else, for that matter. As far as our friendship was concerned, it remained a bit frosty from then on.

After that night in my kitchen, the four of us quickly grew apart for the remainder of the year. Michael tried a few times to get a story out of me, but I just shrugged it off, blaming Matt's ramblings on alcohol and weed. Matt and I avoided each other, by silent, mutual agreement. As for Samuel, he and I didn't speak at all, and that was entirely my choice. I caught him looking at me at school or at work, but I would never meet his eyes. I turned the other way whenever I saw him approach me.

I realized for me, at that time in my life, friendships were the most sacred relationships I had. Samuel had crossed a line and violated that trust.

Call it idealism, call it naïveté, but I would have done anything for my homies—and I thought they'd felt the same about me. That had been my mistake.

These were not my homies. But I guess I wasn't their homie either. I'd also crossed a line, thinking that sex, and getting caught up in the emotional moment, was a part of our bonding process.

I realized now, for some men, that wasn't the case. I hated myself for being so naïve. For allowing myself to be used.

As it turned out, Samuel was the only one of us who passed the teen male rite of passage. His conquests were many. Matt ended up being just another virgin piece of booty, and I got caught up in his sexual games.

While I couldn't bring myself to talk to him, much less look at him, in the back of my mind, I wanted answers. I wanted to confront him and ask, *Why me?* I needed to know if our relationship was any different from all the others—male or female. And, without admitting it out loud, I clung to the belief that our relationship *had* been different and Sam hurt *just* as deeply as I did.

★

All that aside, I started this story reminiscing about fantasies—sexual ones.

So, let's get back to that. I can say with certainty I never anticipated the one I got caught up in. But did I enjoy the ride? Hell yeah. I have no regrets about the sexual exploration Samuel and I did. In fact, having listened to Matt's tale, part of me felt disappointed I hadn't agreed to go all the way with Sam. But he and I were on separate paths now. We'd cross paths again, not as friends but as foes. (But that's a story for another time!)

Something felt incomplete with my own fantasy. It wasn't only about lust for me anymore. That much I realized. I just didn't quite know what I was missing yet.

Oh—what about graduation, you ask?

It came and went. We marched across the sports field, got our diplomas, had a celebration, then went home. Don't get me wrong; I enjoyed the hell out of that day. I made a great valedictorian speech, partied hard, and closed that chapter of my life.

And now you're probably wondering what happened with my girlfriend Carla. Here's the short and skinny: I am a Black man living in a white man's world, while she was a white girl—the forbidden fruit. Her daddy surely never approved of our relationship, as polite as he always was to me.

Yeah, the writing had always been on the wall for the two of us. I knew it, and so did she. We had a great time at our graduation party dancing and hugging, but there was no sexual attraction left between us. We broke it off in the first week of summer. No hard feelings on either side. Which was surprising yet unsurprising at the same time.

Breaking up with Carla was the best thing that could have happened to me; it left me open to what was to come later that summer. It left me open to find the true gift of love waiting for me right around the corner.

Finding my Angel.

Interlude Four

Angel

I quit my job at King's Palace and decided to chill for most of the summer. My mother volunteered at the soup kitchen run by our church. I started helping her once a week, which made her happy. Our relationship was evolving as I grew older, and I liked where it was going—I really enjoyed and cherished the time I spent with her.

She asked me a few times why she hadn't seen the guys around much, but after I told her we'd grown apart, adding I wanted to build new friendships once I got to Temple, she stopped pressing me about it. But I knew she didn't buy my story. A mom knows.

One afternoon she got a call from another church in our district. They asked her if she could fill in for a month at their soup kitchen while another member was out on maternity leave. She agreed and asked me if I would help too. I still had nothing better to do, so I agreed. Not only was my college already paid for, but I was also getting a monthly allowance from the savings bonds my grandparents had invested in for me. It wasn't like I needed to work.

This other church was thirty minutes from where we lived. We arrived early one morning and introduced ourselves. One of the regular volunteers agreed to show us around.

Before long, I was ready to jump in and help serve food. They put me at the bread station, making sure everyone passing through got a serving of a buttered roll. Farther down the line, a girl passing out utensils caught my eye. She was a sister with a natural beauty from her hair to her feet. I knew it sounded cliché, but she was what you'd call classically beautiful. She had a Jayne Kennedy look going on, and I couldn't take my eyes off her.

At first break, people headed outside. I followed them and spotted the girl sitting on a bench, reading a book. I decided to go over and talk to her. I introduced myself and asked if I could join her. She nodded and smiled but didn't respond with her name. I saw this would be an uphill battle, which only motivated me more.

For the time being, I settled for making general conversation, trying to tease responses out of her. After about the tenth random thing I said, something finally sparked her interest: "I graduated number one in my class, and I'm attending Temple University in the fall."

She lowered her book and turned to me with an intrigued look, saying, "So I guess that makes you pretty smart, doesn't it?"

"She speaks!" I cried, throwing my hands in the air. She laughed, blushing a bit. "Does she have a name?"

"I'm Angelique Janelle Ferris. Angel for short."

"Nice to meet you, Angel," I replied, extending my hand. Her hand felt delicate and soft, but she shook firmly. "What brings you to St. Matthew's United Methodist Church today?"

"This is our church," she replied, retrieving her hand. "My mother volunteers here, and I help her out sometimes." Angel spoke softly and without pretense. I really liked how her face lit up when she smiled.

All too soon, our break was over, but I knew I had to talk with her more.

"Are you doing anything after this?"

"Ask me after we're done." And with that, she dropped her book in her bag, stood up, gave me a smile, and disappeared into the church hall. Speaking with Angel put a bounce in my step that hadn't been there since prom night. I knew there was something about this girl.

For the rest of the day on the line, I couldn't take my eyes off her. I knew I'd made an impression on her because I caught her periodically glancing over at me with a smile. We had some serious chemistry going on.

At the end of the day, I sought Angel out with my mother in tow. I knew what I was doing. If Momma got a good feeling from her, I knew she was the one. However, Angel had one-upped me: a woman was standing there with her. Apparently, I would have to pass *her* mom test. I walked right up to her. "Hi, Angel, this must be your mom."

"Desmond, this is my sister Valerie." Both sisters looked at me with matching arched eyebrows. Boy had I ever stuck my foot in my mouth. Just as I thought there'd be no recovery from my gaffe, Momma swooped in to save me.

"Hi! I'm Mrs. Dawson, Desmond's mother. And you are?"

"Angel Ferris, ma'am; this is my sister Valerie." At this point a woman who looked the same age as my mom walked up to us. "And *this* is my mother, Mrs. Francis Ferris," Angel indicated as she cut me a look. We all exchanged handshakes and smiles, but I still wanted to crawl into a hole. Seeing my discomfort, Angel gave me a way out.

"Could you excuse us?" she said to the moms and her sister, reaching for my hand and pulling me toward another part of the room. "You don't do this much, do you?"

"Do what?"

"Talk to girls. Flirt. Date."

In my most macho voice I replied, "I've dated a lot!" She looked at me without a word. My bravado crumbled a bit. "A little?" Still, Angel didn't say a word. "Okay. Maybe once or twice."

"You're a brother with some sorry lines, Desmond. 'I'm the first in my class'?" She mimicked me from earlier, with a smirk. *Shit*, I thought, *I really messed this up.* "Is your invitation for tonight still open?"

"Tonight?" My mind struggled to process what she'd asked. With a jumble of extra vowels, I managed to blurt, "Yes!"

"Where should I meet you?" she asked with an amused look. I blinked. *Damn! This girl moves fast!*

"You don't want me to pick you up?"

"No, I'll meet you. Wherever you want."

Here I was, valedictorian of my class, struggling to keep up in a conversation with this cute girl. *What can I say that will impress her with my charm and wit?* Frankly, that boat had sailed. The best I could do was pass the buck back to her. "Is there somewhere around *here* you like to go to?"

She thought for a second. "Yes, there's a community dance my mother is chaperoning tonight in Mayville. That's the next town over. It's very easy to get to; two miles down the highway." Angel gave me the address and the phone number of the community center and told me she'd meet me there at seven.

With a wave over her shoulder, she walked away. Before reaching her mother and sister, she turned and gave me a bombshell of a smile. I was so blown away I didn't notice my mother standing behind me. Her hand touched my arm and I jumped. "Angel and her family are very nice, don't you agree?" she said. Then, with a wink, she headed to our car.

Later that evening, I showered and threw on a pair of khakis, a polo shirt, and my Adidas sneakers. Before heading out, I stopped to say bye to my parents. As I kissed my mom, she turned to my father. "Desmond met this wonderful Black young lady today." My dad put his paper down and raised his eyebrows.

"Is that who you're seeing tonight?"

"Well, yeah. But it's no big deal." I felt my heart pounding in my chest. Momma and Dad exchanged a look. I could tell they were holding back smiles.

"Well, have a good time, son," Dad said. I waved and darted out the door. *That's weird*, I thought, loping toward the car. *They didn't give me a time to be in.* It almost felt like the beginning of an episode of the *Twilight Zone...*

I arrived at the Mayville community center around 7:15 p.m.; I always like to be fashionably late to things. My rule was never be first (you don't want to look desperate to be there), but never be last (you'll look like you're trying to make a grand, dramatic entrance). I walked around searching for Angel but didn't see her. I stopped one of the volunteers and asked if she knew Angel or her mom.

"Oh, you must be Desmond! I'm Mille Peoples. Angel called and said she and her mother would be late, but she wanted me to make you comfortable and see if you'd like to help out." I wasn't sure what I could contribute, but I saw no reason to refuse.

"Sure! No problem. What do you want me to do?"

"Do you know how to dance, Desmond?"

"Ahh...I know a few moves?" *What kind of dance is this?* Mille smiled.

As it turned out, this was no ordinary dance. Every Wednesday night, a group of mentally handicapped adults got together for a dance and social. I was fresh meat for every handicapped girl in the hall, which didn't make me very popular with the handicapped dudes. Every girl in the place smiled and winked at me as I approached the dance floor. From the looks all the dudes were giving me, though, I was pretty certain they wanted to take me out back and kick my good-looking ass.

I ended up dancing for two hours, getting passed around from girl to girl. After a while, time passed in a blur. I didn't even notice Angel coming in.

I was in the middle of a dance with this large girl who kept locking her hands behind my neck and pulling me close. I locked my arms out straight, hands at her waist, smiling nervously. At that moment, Angel walked up and tapped the girl on the shoulder. "Hi. He's my date tonight. May I please cut in?" Clearly reluctant, the big girl loosened her grip and, with a clear attitude, allowed Angel to take her place. She went off mumbling some foul words, but I'd already forgotten her, unable to focus on anything but the woman in front of me.

Angel looked beautiful. She had on a flowery summer dress that showed a little cleavage in the front and cut low in the back. I knew I had a goofy grin on my face, but I couldn't stop myself.

"I'm so sorry I'm late, Desmond. My grandmother got sick and we had to take her to the hospital."

"Is she okay?"

"Yes. She is now. Mom is staying with her but told me to come to the dance."

"I'm glad you did," I admitted, somehow smiling even wider than before.

The rest of the evening was magical. We danced. We talked. We laughed. It all felt so right. So natural.

Angel admitted, even though she'd mocked me about it, the thing that impressed her most about me was when I admitted to being first in my class. "It's as if we share the same experience. My high school is mostly white, and I graduated first in my class too!"

"So, you didn't think I was just bragging?"

"No! Until you told me, I thought you were just another boy trying to get into my pants!"

Of course, that's exactly what I wanted to do with her, but I tried not to show it on my face and kept my mouth shut.

"There was something different about you, Desmond. You're not like other brothers I know. You seem more open to your feelings. More sincere. That's why I agreed to go out with you." Then, with a smirk, she added, "It helped that my mom and my sister liked you too."

The dance ended at eleven. Angel took me to a little diner not far from where she lived. As we talked, the feeling we'd known each other all our lives grew. We seemed to fit together naturally. Somewhere inside me, I knew this woman was the one.

But with only three weeks left of summer, how could I secure my place in her heart?

At about one in the morning, Angel told me she had to get home. I sighed, and she laughed.

"What's wrong, Desmond?"

"Have you ever met anyone who you just feel so comfortable with?"

"Yes," she replied, too quickly. I caught my breath. Had I misjudged what was going on here? She looked away, going distant for a moment. Then she turned to me, looking me square in the eyes. "I met him today."

Man! If I were a rocket, I would have shot through the ceiling in that instant. We settled our bill and walked out to her car.

"Can I see you again?" I asked as she opened the driver-side door. She turned to me, looking quite serious.

"Oh, yes." My heart fluttered wildly in my chest again. "But I'm leaving for Howard University on the twenty-seventh. That's three weeks away."

"That's the day I leave for Temple too," I declared.

"Then we'd better make the best of it." She tilted her head to one side. "I help Mom out at the soup kitchen every day. You can stop in and see me if you like."

"That's perfect—Mom has promised to help out there for the next month. I won't miss a day!"

She glanced down at her car, then back at me. A moment of silence passed between us; then she leaned forward and kissed me on the lips. Her lips were full and soft, not at all like Carla's narrow, bitter, white-girl lips. I breathed Angel in, wanting this to last all night. It was so intense I must have blacked out for a second because, when I came to, she'd climbed into the driver's seat and fastened her seat belt. She started the engine, gave me a wave, and drove off. I couldn't do anything but stand there and wonder how I had gotten so lucky.

★

For the next three weeks, Angel and I spent as much time as we could together.

On our second date, I went to her house and met her dad. Man, was he scary! Mr. Ferris was a career army man: six and a half feet of lean, mean muscle. His only expression seemed to be a stern stare. When he shook my hand, I thought he would crush it. But I knew what this was all about.

When I was growing up, my dad used to always tell my brother and me, "You can tell a real man by the strength of his handshake."

So, I squeezed back as hard as I could.

Her dad and I talked for a good half an hour before Mrs. Ferris and Angel came in to rescue me. I must have passed his test; he seemed pretty cool with me after that.

In the days after that, we shopped for college supplies together, saw a couple of movies, went bowling, spent a day at Great Adventure… You name it, we tried to do it in the days we had left, knowing our time together was short.

All too soon, August 26 had arrived.

Angel and I decided to do our goodbyes that evening, not wanting to stress out what would already be a stressful day for both of us tomorrow.

We chose to go to the beach that night. We strolled along the water, finding a spot to lay out a blanket and enjoy a picnic supper. We got to watch the sun go down and the full moon rise over the ocean.

I caught myself thinking about the last time I'd been here, watching the moon set and sun rise as I lay in *his* arms. Before I went too far down that rabbit hole, I looked over at Angel, focusing all my thoughts on her.

Sitting on that blanket with Angel in my arms was all I needed in that moment. I felt very protective of her, wanting nothing more than to hold her and share the rest of my life with her.

It was too soon to make commitments like that, though. I knew. We were both going off to college *tomorrow*, and who could tell what would happen to us when we got there? As Angel nestled in my arms, she gazed up at me and asked, "A penny for your thoughts?"

"It'll cost you a dollar; a thousand percent inflation, you know." We laughed, and then I turned serious. "How do you feel about me, Angel?" She looked away.

"I'm not sure I know how to answer that."

"Okay. Let's try this: do you like me?" I reached down and stroked her cheek.

"That's a silly question to ask."

"No, I mean it, Angel. You make me feel like I've never felt before. I can't explain it, but you do. I need to know what you feel before we leave tomorrow."

Silence settled over us for a moment before she answered. I looked deep into her eyes and she into mine. I knew then what she was about to say. "I'm falling in love with you, Desmond, and I thought I would never say that to an eighteen-year-old boy, but I know I am. And it doesn't matter if you feel the same way or not. I've been trying to deal with it the best way I know how, but I'm having a hard time. I know you'll be leaving tomorrow, and at some point during the year you'll find someone else. And I'm just trying to process that."

I didn't know what to say. She'd expressed everything that had been on my mind and more. I pulled her face close to mine and kissed her gently on the lips, finally finding some words.

"I've fallen in love with you too, Angel. And I'm afraid of you finding someone else too. I never make any promises I can't keep, so I'll say, yeah, there might be someone who comes into my life. But what I do know is this: I don't want to lose you."

We made a pledge then. A pledge to *see other people*. We decided that if our feelings remained the same for each other after this first year of college, we'd plan a future together. That was enough for now.

We spent the rest of the evening on that beach, locked in each other's arms, locked in each other's gaze. This woman—this *Angel*—had lifted me out of the darkness I'd fallen into at the end of the school year, after I lost my friends and lost my way.

Angel had saved me from myself and gifted me with a magical, angelic summer.

Part Two

A Whole New World to Explore

Interlude Five

New Home—New Friends

The car ride to Temple University was long and quiet. Dad focused on the road, Nina had her head stuck in a book, and Momma kept looking out the window with this faraway look in her eyes.

I could tell Momma wasn't taking my going away to college very well. I wanted to ask her what was on her mind, but I knew better than to open that can of worms. Instead, I kept my mouth shut and looked out my window.

Temple University is in the heart of North Philadelphia, just outside of Center City. The neighborhoods around the university weren't exactly appealing to an upper-middle-class suburban boy accustomed to lavish homes and wide, lush lawns.

Sitting in that car, I began to wonder what I'd been thinking, electing to come here instead of Harvard or Princeton. *Well, I'd better get used to it—this is home for the next four years!*

I knew Momma was worried too; she'd made her feelings about me living on my own crystal clear from the moment I received my college admission letter. "Maybe we could move closer to Philadelphia so you don't have to live in one of those awful rooms," she'd suggested more than once. Nothing I said could deter her.

"*Mom*! Vinny got to live by himself when he went to college!"

"Yes, but you're my baby boy." Then my dad would try to calm her down.

"Millie," he'd interject in his stern, patriarchal voice, "the boy's got to find his own way, and this will be a fine experience for him." She'd look at him and shake her finger.

"Oh, hush up, old man. That's my baby."

"Fish gotta swim, baby birds gotta fly." Dad would chuckle and go back to his paper or his news. "Give him a chance, Millie; give him a chance. He'll do just fine, you'll see."

The twenty-seventh of August was when all new students had to report for dormitory room assignment and freshmen orientation. We had the campus to ourselves, with the exception of the jocks in football camp and the older students running orientation.

My dorm was pretty cool; I'd pulled a spot in one of the coed ones. When Momma found out, she flew into a Flip Wilson-as-Geraldine mode. "Oh no, no, no," she started, hand on her hip, head twisting, and finger wagging, "I am not sending you to college for wild, drunken sex parties in those coed dormitories!" She shook her finger at me. "I know what goes on in those types of places. No, no, no!"

Needless to say, Dad had my back then too, giving her his favorite line: "Fish gotta swim, baby birds gotta fly!"

She gave me a pointed look, saying, "You better fly your ass back down to that post office and swim your skinny little body through those letters and find that application. Fish gotta swim, birds gotta fly my ass. You've lost your mind, child!"

See, I'd mailed my acceptance letter before telling Momma about it.

"Millie, he and I have already spoken about the matter," Dad said. (We hadn't. With the look she gave both of us, I thought I'd have to swim to the post office; Dad snuck me into the garage later on for that chat to cover our butts.) "Desmond will be very focused on his schoolwork. Don't you worry."

Upon our arrival at Temple University, we parked close to my assigned dorm. We all got out of the car and went in. I signed in, collected my dorm key, then found my room—only to discover my new roommate had already been there and claimed the bed and dresser closest to the window.

His bed was neatly made—military-grade. I snuck a peek through his drawers: underwear and socks in the top drawer, shirts and pajamas in the next, jeans and shorts in the bottom. Everything squarely folded and perfectly positioned inside.

I knew this roomie relationship was on a fast track to hell.

No sooner had we gotten the last load of my stuff up to my room than in walked this prepster, followed by his Donna Reed mother and Raymond Burr father. The four of us turned and said, "Hi!" at the same, even while sharing covert looks. I could tell we had come to the same conclusion, but we played it off nicely.

Momma did her Hazel-the-maid thing by unpacking my clothes and putting them away in my dresser. Believe me when I say she was perpetrating a fraud. She hadn't done this for me in years, but I knew she wasn't going to let Donna Reed outplay her.

Dad and Raymond Burr talked about work, politics, and their respective sons. I couldn't tell who had the upper hand until Dad came out with, "And Desmond was the valedictorian of his class. He had a full-paid academic scholarship to Princeton, Yale, and… What were the other schools, dear?"

"Dartmouth and Harvard." Momma had moved on to making my bed and didn't even look up.

"Yeah, those two. Oh, and of course here at Temple." With those fighting words, I knew it would be safest if I excused myself and checked out the rest of the dormitory. I figured I could find out more about my roomie later, after our fathers' one-upmanship was over. I signaled to Nina, and we went for a walk.

We returned a short time later. My roomie and his television-perfect family had left. The two strangers in my room had turned back into our parents. The time had come to send them and my sister packing and start the next phase of my life.

Before they headed home, we had dinner at Winston's, a bistro in the heart of the city. While waiting for our meal, I couldn't help noticing two men seated at the table next to us. Obviously they were more than friends. Interestingly, both men were brothers: a Black version of Laurel and Hardy.

One might have been a modern jazz dancer, from the way he dressed. Plus, he was tall and wiry. Not skinny, but with no fat hugging his bones. He had a large chest I thought was going to pop right out of the tank top stretched over it. His jeans looked like he had been poured into them. He wore his hair short, with tiny curl wisps across his forehead, and his face was clean—no mustache or beard. His skin color was the color of caramel candy.

His friend couldn't have been more different. He looked as if he were a member of a theater production crew—what you'd call "burly." His skin was the color of a Milk Dud. He had a full bushy beard and a nappy Afro. His chest was enormous too, but he carried more thickness around his waist.

What gave their relationship away was the tall brother's mannerisms. He kept running his fingers across the short curls hanging over his forehead, brushing them back periodically. When he wasn't doing that, he sat listening to the other man, with his elbows on the table, chin perched in the palm of one hand, long fingers cupping his cheeks.

Our food arrived, and we dove in. While I ate, I couldn't stop staring at the two men. The whole persona they were giving off fascinated me. Momma—sitting where she could see them too—had picked up on it as well. "Cal, Cal," she whispered, motioning for my dad to lean in. "Look at those two men behind you. Are they...well, *you know*?" She made a swishy hand gesture. "*Funny*?"

My father raised an eyebrow and casually turned about. He just as casually turned back to his plate, nodded, and mumbled through his food, "Yep."

She carried on in a stage whisper. "I knew it. They dress differently." She pursed her lips. "I know they have a right to their ways, but decent people shouldn't have to be subjected to it."

Nina—who couldn't resist the temptation to ask ill-timed, awkward questions—blurted out, "What ways do you mean, Momma?"

"Never you mind, girl! Be quiet and eat your dinner." My mother fanned herself with her cloth napkin. She swiveled to me, adding, "And you stay away from perverts like that, you hear me?"

"Yes, ma'am." I kept my eyes on my plate. *Am I one of those perverts?* I wondered, struggling to push images of me and Samuel away.

We finished dinner and walked around the city. One reason I'd chosen Temple was because of how much I liked Philadelphia. I'd always felt at home here. It wasn't as fast-paced as New York City or as dingy as Newark. For me, Philly truly lived up to its name: warm and inviting—it was truly the City of Brotherly Love.

The sky grew dark, signaling I needed to get back to my new home.

When I got out of the car in front of the dormitory, Momma couldn't contain herself anymore. Tears started to roll, and the hanky came out. I hugged her tight, swallowing a lump in my throat.

"It's okay, Mom. I'll be all right." She kissed my cheek and ran her hands over my face.

"I know, I know." She had more to say, but it got caught in her throat. With one last hug, she retreated into the car.

I turned to my sister. She was on the verge of tears too, though she fought them back.

"Don't go in my room. I'll be visiting in a few weeks to check on my stuff." She stuck her tongue out at that, then rushed in for a hug.

I turned to my dad last. Illuminated by the lamps outside the main entrance, his eyes were rimmed with tears, even though he sported a huge smile.

"I'm so proud of you, son," he said hoarsely. I felt tears welling up in my eyes. Then he did something he hadn't since I was about six years old. He pulled me into a bear hug and kissed me on the forehead. I squeezed him back, cherishing this moment. After a few breaths, he gently pushed me away, nodded, and climbed into the car.

As they were pulled away, Momma and Nina waved frantically. I waved back, keeping it up even after their car had faded into the distance.

I stood there with mixed feelings, glad the dark hid my face. I turned toward my new home, slowly walking through the doors, and entered into a new phase of my life.

I knew from the beginning I wouldn't be very receptive to my Caucasian roommate, and I didn't care. I guess I blamed him for all the feelings of betrayal I felt toward my friends back home. Through the grapevine I found out Samuel told Matt that hooking up with me had been a mistake and that Matt was the one he really wanted to be with. From what I understand, Matt bought the story, hook, line, and sinker.

Matt believing the lie hurt more than Samuel telling it. I knew what to expect from Samuel; he treated guys and girls the same way: like shit. I'd been open and honest with Matt that night, but he chose to believe Samuel's story. *What did I expect?* Clearly, the boy was head over heels in love with Sam, and I guess he was still getting what he needed.

Good riddance. It didn't matter anymore. I wasn't there. I had a fresh start. This time, I vowed to build relationships with brothers and sisters of my own kind, after my own heart.

Freshman orientation was the perfect time to start new friendships. In fact, it turned out to be mandatory: in short order, I'd made four new friends.

Early that first morning of orientation, all freshmen were assembled in this huge gymnasium. We'd each been given an index card with a colored dot and number on one side. The orientation leaders told us to find the person with the same number and color as we had on our card. We looked around at one another in disbelief. There were hundreds of us freshmen—how the hell were we going to find our match?

As frustrated murmurings grew, one of the leaders spoke up: "Now I know you all are wondering how you will accomplish this." Grumblings of agreement followed. He held up a card and said, "As you can see, there is a building name written on the opposite side of your card. You've all been given a map in your orientation bags. Now if you can't figure out what to do with that information, please hand your card to one of the counselors at the door. You can head to your room, pack your bags, and enroll in another institution. Thank you and happy trails to you."

Well, obviously, I wasn't about to quit. So off I searched. It took a while, but eventually, a few of us "blue-dot" people found one another. We decided to go off as a group to find "Meden Hall, lecture room 24"—written on the back of our index cards.

When we got there—a typical classroom with the desks and chairs stacked against one wall—our task became a little easier. There were about fifty of us with blue dots; it was no problem finding your "number partner" from there.

My partner turned out to be a guy named Antonio. He had transferred from Lincoln University, an hour the other side of Philly.

I could tell Antonio wasn't into the fun and games by the bored look on his face, not to mention the comments he made under his breath about how stupid this activity was. I wasn't looking forward to being his partner if this was going to be his attitude for the rest of orientation.

Little did I know he would become a lifelong friend and have an enormous impact on my life.

At the same time Antonio and I found each other, two brothers were standing together close by. We exchanged introductions; their names were Brian and Phillip.

Brian was a freshman like me. He came to Temple because it's what his parents could afford—at least that's what he told us then.

Phillip, a freshman too, made it through the doors thanks to easy financial aid for residents of the Commonwealth of Pennsylvania.

The orientation group leader called us to attention, indicating we would start the next exercise in ten minutes. He was another brother named Kyle, who turned out to also be our residence hall director.

After we'd found our partners and had a chance to get to know each other, Kyle came to the front and spoke. "Welcome. As you can see, you have all passed your first test here at Temple U. Congratulations. Give yourselves a hand." We all (except Antonio) gave ourselves a round of applause.

"Now, if you would all grab a chair and make a circle, we'll begin the first session. Make sure you are next to your partner." When we settled down in our seats, he spoke again.

"By the end of this session, you'll figure out why you were selected as a blue dot, why you were matched with your particular partner, and whether or not you have what it takes to continue here at Temple U." No one said a word, but I could tell we were all feeling the same nervous tension.

"In our first exercise together, I want us to begin the bonding process," Kyle continued, at which Antonio sighed.

"This is some ridiculous shit," he murmured. I ignored him. Kyle must have heard, though.

"I can tell from the look on some of your faces you are not feeling this. Well, my answer to that is 'tough shit.' Everything we will be doing over the next three days will help to make your adjustment to university life a smooth and safe one. Heed my words." He paused, looking at the freshmen faces around the hall. "Take a look at the person to your right. Now look at the one to your left." We did so, all of us silent except for another loud sigh from my partner.

"One of those people will not make it to graduation with you. In fact," Kyle said, raising his voice, "by the end of this school year, one-fifth of you will be gone. And it might come down to how much support you have from the people in this circle. So let's get started."

Something tightened in my stomach. *Is that true? One-fifth of us?* From the looks I was seeing in the eyes of those around me, I wasn't the only one thinking this. *Well, it won't be me!* But I wasn't so sure anymore. This wasn't high school. I wasn't valedictorian here. "All right," Kyle continued, "in our first exercise I want you to tell us your name, where you are from, something about your family, your major, and something in your life that hurt you. Because this is our first exercise, I will start us off. From now on, though, we'll be drawing numbers to see who goes first in other activities. Are there any problems with this setup?" He paused for a second, waiting for anyone to speak up. No one did.

"Okay, my name is Kyle Elliott. My family lives here in Philadelphia, in a neighborhood called Germantown. I was the lone man in a house of five women—my mom and four older sisters. I am a senior in the communications and journalism major, and I will have my own morning radio program some-day soon. My dad left us when I was three years old. I never saw him again until a year ago.

"And there you go. Short, sweet, and to the point. For now, that's all I want to know. There will be time to get to know one another better in our other sessions. Believe me, be-fore these three days are over, you'll have plenty of time to re-veal yourself if you choose. Let's have a volunteer to go next."

Phillip jumped right in without missing a beat. "Hi! My name is Phillip Michael Garvey. I'm from the west side of the city—Philly, I mean. I went through some pretty rough schools, and I'm the first person in my family to go to college." He stalled there until Kyle reminded him what else to say.

"Oh yeah, I'm the oldest of seven children; I've got four brothers and two sisters. My major is journalism, and I hope to be a reporter for a major newspaper someday. Um." Phillip paused, blinking. He seemed reluctant to add any more.

"It's okay, Phillip," Kyle said softly. "The people around you are going to become your closest friends. You don't have to hide anything."

"Okay. So, my hurt... Well, my mom is an alcoholic—*recovering* alcoholic—and a drug addict. That's all."

"Thank you, Phillip." Kyle gave him a wide smile, then asked for another volunteer. Brian—sitting next to Phillip—raised his hand.

"I'm Brian. Brian Carter Harris. I'm twenty. I live in West Chester. I'm an only child. My dad is a minister for the Pentecostal church. I took a couple years off after high school to work with my dad and the community. My major is communication. I hope to be a minister myself one day. My hurt? I guess it's being an only child. I never knew what it was like to have a sibling to share growing up with. I spent time by myself a lot of the time."

Other freshmen shared who they were until it came to Antonio's turn. By now, he was so unimpressed with this activity you could pretty much see the contempt rising off him in waves.

"I'm Antonio Lawrence Savileo. In case you can't already tell, I'm biracial. That means my mom is Black and my dad is Italian."

I faced Antonio while he spoke, *really* looking at him for the first time since we'd met a few minutes back. He verged on being short—about five foot seven. He wasn't skinny; I made out his sprinter build underneath his tight shirt and pants.

He'd paused, looking over at me with his piercing hazel eyes. I averted my gaze, wondering if he'd seen me checking him out. If he had, he gave no sign.

"I live with my brother and my mom," he continued. "My asshole father is in jail for attempted murder." A few people gasped at this news; Antonio curled his lip at their reactions.

"Oh, and yeah—I got thrown out of Lincoln University for being a faggot. You know, a homosexual—gay. Anyone got a problem with that?" Silence fell over the room until Kyle moved things forward.

"Okay, thanks for sharing, Antonio. Who's next?" I had my hand up before realizing it. Kyle nodded at me to go ahead.

I gave my name, my family history, my major—all that stuff. When it came to my hurt, I chose what had happened last spring.

"I had a group of white friends. I thought we'd be close for life, you know? Well, they all turned out to be phonies. So, I'm looking forward to making some new, *real* friendships here." *And speaking of new friends...* I turned to Antonio, adding, "And I'm not a faggot, but I don't judge a person for who they love." Antonio lifted his eyes to meet mine. I couldn't tell what he was feeling, but he didn't sneer or roll his eyes, so that was something...

Lunchtime arrived shortly thereafter. Kyle gave us directions to the dining hall and sent us on our way.

As we were leaving, Antonio stormed off by himself. Phillip, Brian, and I grouped up. While we walked, we heard other small groups talking about Antonio.

"I know him from my neighborhood," Phillip revealed. "Yeah, he can be a real asshole, but he's cool. I didn't give a fuck what he was as long as he didn't inflict it on me."

We saw him ahead, still walking alone. As he noticed us approaching, he made a face but slowed to let us catch up. I sensed there was going to be a confrontation between us, so I took the initiative. "Look, man," I started, "I can't say I understand your lifestyle—"

"So why the fuck are you in my face?" Antonio snapped. I pressed on.

"Because I believe in coming to the table clean. If you can drop this shitty attitude and just be a person, well, maybe we can find out enough about each other to be friends. Plus I'd like to get to know a few people who'll still be here at the end of the year!"

He stared at me coldly. "What makes you think I want to be friends?"

"Hey, you don't have to; I'm just putting it out there. Like the man said, 'You have a choice.'" I extended my hand. He looked down at it and then at me. For a moment our eyes locked. An understanding passed between us. I guess you could call it a truce. Antonio shook my hand and turned to the guys.

"What about you mofos? Are you with him?" They expressed their assent, extending their hands, and we took off for lunch.

In the dining hall, we sat off by ourselves. I caught other members of the blue group staring at us. I guess Antonio made for good gossip. It didn't matter to me—he'd earned my respect for his straightforwardness and honesty. Plus, I had a feeling he would be one of those at my side come graduation.

Four young ladies approached our table with their lunches—three sisters and an Asian chick. "These taken?" asked one of the sisters—a bit on the heavy side.

"No," I replied. "Join us if you want." Then Antonio chose to get a dig in.

"Careful, homosexuality can be contagious and dangerous to your health."

The sister looked at him, arching an eyebrow.

"Oh, don't you know? We were all inoculated before we came to school." She extended her hand toward him but snatched it right back. "You don't bite, do you? I sure do hate biters." Antonio sneered, ignoring her hand. She shrugged, reclaiming it. "Your loss."

"Hardly," he muttered. *Enough of this,* I decided.

"Ladies, Antonio may not have manners"—I threw him a look, which he ignored—"but the rest of us do." I offered my hand. "I'm Desmond."

"I'm Karen Stewart," the heavyset sister replied, shaking my hand.

"Nice to meet you, Karen. This is Phillip. That's Brian. And I guess you now know Antonio."

"This is Dianna, Melissa, and Myling." The girls each nodded in turn, smiling at us. Karen looked at Antonio and said, "Let me guess: God killed off all the other gay brothers, leaving you to fend for yourself. That's why you're such an asshole, right?"

He looked at her and fired back, "I just come at life real, sister. I am what I am, and I don't ask for anyone's acceptance. I just want them to leave me the fuck alone."

Karen didn't miss a beat; she fired back with, "I don't give a shit who you fuck as long as you don't fuck me over. How's that for real?"

Antonio squinted at her and uttered, "Fag hag."

"Drama queen," Karen retorted. The rest of us sat there in silence. *This is awkward, and not how I'd imagined making friends on my first day of collegiate life.*

Karen and Antonio managed to shock all of us by breaking out into laughter. The mood around the table thawed, and we enjoyed our first lunch together, cementing our fledgling friendships.

Interlude Six

Rescued

The orientation sessions prepared us for the work that awaited in our majors. Kyle explained what our professors would expect from us. He stressed the rules and regulations of the school. Most importantly, he talked to us about safety. The how-to-stay-alive tips for a not-so-safe city.

My orientation group explored the culture and climate of the school, as well as our differences and similarities. We discovered it was no accident how we were grouped and paired. The questionnaire we filled out way back when we applied to Temple had been used to match people with similar interests and fields of study. From there, the orientation groups were paired with upperclassmen from matching schools of study. That's how Kyle came to be our leader.

I made it through orientation, and what Kyle said turned out to be true to the last word. By the time it was done, I'd grown close to everyone at the table from that first lunch. We became one another's support base, getting one another through the good times as well as the bad.

That fall, the eight of us found ourselves in most of the same classes, which helped when it came to studying for tests and writing papers.

All work and no play wasn't the MO of our grouping, however. In Pennsylvania the legal drinking age was still twenty-one. But if you think that stopped us, think again! CEPTA, the city's transit system, allowed us to get around—even into Jersey. We could also depend on Myling, who had her dad's car, as long as we anted up gas money.

The ladies spent most of their free time shopping. If there was a sale, they were there. If they weren't out looking for specials, they were in one another's room doing hair or painting something on their bodies.

Phillip and Brian loved to shoot hoops and were always looking for a pickup game somewhere or settling for some one-on-one. They tried to get me to play, but basketball was not my thing nor Antonio's. Instead, Antonio and I shared a love of jogging, cycling, photography, bowling, and playing cards.

Well, all eight of us enjoyed playing cards and bowling. So when there was nothing else to do, we would gather in someone's room and have these marathon games of spades or bid whist.

All in all, life during my first fall term at Temple U was pretty good.

Even my roommate wasn't that bad. As I'd suspected, though, he and I were like night and day. I would wake early and go running. By the time I got back he'd left, and stayed out for a good part of the morning. I'd shower and meet with the crew and be gone for most of the afternoon.

I'd often go for a run in the late afternoon, too, and find my roommate's friends hanging out in the room. So, after my shower, I spent most of my time in Antonio's or Karen's room—those were the two from our group I grew closest with, seeing as we were in the same dormitory.

Karen shared a room with a white girl who rarely slept there. By late November we found out why: she spent her nights with her English professor. She and Karen had worked out an arrangement where, if her parents called, Karen told them she was at the library. Karen would then call the professor's house and let her know. Karen didn't mind, because this gave her a big room to herself. Quite naturally that's where you'd most often find us. Because Antonio was openly gay, the school accommodated him with a single room—a small one (I would say a little bit bigger than a closet), but it was his and his alone.

I enjoyed running for a couple reasons. First, it gave me an excuse not to be in my room. Second, it just made me feel good.

I wore a pair of satiny Nike shorts and either my Temple U tank or sweatshirt, depending on the temperature outside. I carried small weights in either hand to get an extra workout.

Kyle had taught us to always let someone know where you were going and what time you would be back. We were also encouraged to always travel with a buddy if possible. Antonio and I would meet somewhere along our route and either run together or just check in.

Antonio liked running for a few reasons too, primarily because it helped with another of his habits—getting a piece or two with random guys. It would be an understatement to say Antonio was very sexually active. He had a ton of spots near the Philadelphia Art Museum in Fairmount Park where he met his men. I didn't want the gory details, but I did want an idea where he would be in case something happened.

One particular evening in late October, Antonio and I had done our normal check-in with each other before going off on our respective routes. We started out a bit later that day—the days at this time of the year were beautiful, but the nights came quicker.

I had on my usual outfit of tank top and shorts, warming up once I got running. Antonio had taken off to one of his usual "spots." As I ran, clouds rolled in, and it felt like it might start to rain. I decided to turn back a bit early and find Antonio to see if he would head back with me.

He always ran along a wooded path before disappearing in the bushes. I hadn't been on it before but ran down it then to find him.

As I got deeper and deeper along the darkened path, I heard rustling. I slowed to a walk, calling out Antonio's name. When no response came, I kept going, calling out his name periodically. The rustling sound grew louder, and I realized it was coming from behind me. I turned around and got the shock of my life.

A huge silhouette of a guy bore down on me. I couldn't make out any features—probably because he wore a ski mask. I also noticed the outline of one arm was longer than the other—he was holding something. As he got close, I made out the outline of a knife, which he brought up and pointed at me.

Without thinking, I turned to run.

Another figure had appeared on the path in that direction, though, and before I could react, his hand smashed into my face. I found myself on the ground, the little weights I held scattering in the dirt.

The breath had been knocked out of me, and the whole side of my face buzzed. Fear like I'd never felt surged through my body as my two assailants drew closer. I wasn't a wimp—I could have handled one of them, I figured, but two of them, with a knife between them... *I'm in trouble here.*

Another thought struck me—*Where is Antonio? Have they gotten to him already?!*

The guy who had landed the sucker punch grabbed me by my upper arm and yanked me to my feet. The one with the knife wrapped an arm about my neck, pulling in tightly. I clawed at his arm, even as the first guy slammed his fist into my stomach. The air rushed out of me, and I groaned in pain.

"Looks like we got us one of those preppy Temple boys," the guy in front of me said, leaning his masked face in close. I heard a *click*, and he brought his own blade to my face. I turned my head away from it, starting to taste blood where I must have bit my cheek. Switchblade guy sniffed at me noisily. "Mmmm... this one smells like a faggot."

I began to shiver—from both fear and from the cooling sweat on my body. *What do they want? Am I living my last few moments?* I wouldn't go without speaking for myself, though. "Look, man, I don't know what you want, but you're not going to find it here." The only response was a fist in the face again. Blood now ran freely from my mouth; it leaked from my nose too.

The two of them laughed. The guy holding my neck raised his knife, waving it in my face. "Look, pussy boy, when we want you to say or do something, we'll tell you." I smelled beer and stale cigarettes on his breath, almost making me gag. The arm about my neck tightened. *Gotta stay calm. Can't let fear take over.*

I cursed myself for not following Kyle's advice. *This is why they teach us this at orientation…*I thought bitterly. I wasn't ready to die. I needed to figure out how I was going to get myself out of this mess.

The man holding my neck leaned his head over my shoulder. "You know what we do to pretty little bitches like you in the joint? Hmmm?" I caught a whiff of his body odor mixed with Aqua Velva. "We have lots of fun with them!" His raspy voice grated in my ear, even as I felt his hand squeeze my ass cheek.

"Ooh! This bitch has got some ass on her! And firm! I like it firm." He started to knead my butt as his partner laughed coarsely. And then I got an erection.

What the fuck?! This is no time for shit like this to be happening! I thought frantically. My body didn't seem to care. My life was at risk, and here I was, getting turned on. My dick must have pulled my shorts tight, because it drew the attention of the guy at my back.

"What's this?" He reached around and grabbed my hard cock through the fabric. "Damn! This boy's gettin' all hot on us!"

"Oooh! Let's see what he's got!" his partner exclaimed, reaching out with his blade. The sound of fabric splitting reached my ears, and my sliced satin shorts slid down my legs. The air chilled my ass and my cock, but not enough for my erection to fade. In fact, it continued to throb with heat.

I didn't know what to think, to feel. This was surreal.

"*Damn*, will ya look at the piece this bitch is packing!?" The guy ahead of me waved his knife at my dick. "Boy—you some sorta porn star or something?"

"Let's see whatcha packin' topside," said the guy at my neck as his blade worked under my Nike tank top. In a flash, he sliced upward, my shirt flapping open unnaturally. More cool air rushed over my torso, brushing at my nipples and the light curls of hair that had developed on my chest. His partner whistled through his mask.

"Oooh yeah! Look at that chest, and those cute little nipples. We got us a whore here, boy-ee." He ran the dull side of his blade down my abs, pushing the tip into my belly button. I sucked my stomach in.

He brought it up and stroked my nipples. Tingles ran through me, and my cock lurched. *Shit! Why do I have to be enjoying this?!* I tried everything I could not to give off any sign of pleasure. *Think of the danger I'm in!!*

It was hard, though—no pun intended—to process these warring feelings. More than anything, I needed to come up with a plan. I knew if I didn't do something soon, I wasn't going to walk away from this alive.

At that point the man in front of me shut his knife, shoving it in his rear pocket. He reached down with one hand and fiddled with his belt. "Yo, bitch—you ever suck a dick?" He unbuttoned his pants, unzipped his fly, and reached into his boxers. He pulled out what looked like a pink cucumber, which flopped over the band of his underwear. "See, bitch, we got a little sumthin'-sumthin' in common, you and me—we both packin' Magnums." He stroked himself to a full erection, humming away.

The guy behind me tightened his grip on my neck. He must have put his knife away too, as I felt his free hand run down my sweaty back toward my ass. Without pausing, he pushed a finger through my crack, probing at my hole. He was thrusting at my bare hip; I felt his piece through his pants. Apparently the three of us were equally well-endowed.

As all this was happening, a thought struck me: *This is my chance.* I might not get another. With his knife away and his buddy giving himself a hand job, I could at least disable one of them and hope for the best with the other.

Before I could act, the guy in front called out, "Yo, dude—push that bitch's face down here and let them big lips of his work this." He held his penis at the base, pointing the head toward me. "And, bitch, if you bite, I'll cut you up till yur mommy don't recognize ya."

As they forced my head downward, I heard a rustling in the bushes off to one side. Whatever that may have been, it was the cue I was looking for. I drove one elbow into the gut of the man behind me as hard as I could, even while reaching around to grab his shirt. As he groaned, I flipped him over my hip.

Out of nowhere, Antonio burst onto the scene, swinging a thick branch at the man pleasuring himself. The *whack* of wood striking his skull rang through the forest, even as I stumbled to the ground, having overbalanced myself in throwing the other guy. My hand came down on one of my running weights. I gripped it instinctively, a growl bursting out from between my teeth.

I'd found my anger.

I whirled to my first assailant, who'd risen to his feet. His hand reached into his pocket and he withdrew his knife again. I slammed my weight-bearing fist right into the middle of his face. He groaned in pain but caught me around the neck with his free arm. We started to roll around the forest floor, him struggling to bring his knife to bear.

Peripherally, I was aware of Antonio swinging at the other guy with his makeshift club. The masked guy blocked a blow with one arm, even as he got his own knife back out.

I'd never wished death upon another person in my life. At that moment, though, my sole goal was to hurt these bastards, bad! I rolled up to a crouch as the masked guy I faced brandished his blade. My bare butt struck something—Antonio and I were back-to-back, facing these two knife-wielding masked men. Lights flashed at us, and loud rustling emanated from around us.

"POLICE! Drop your weapons and get down on the ground! YOU! With the masks! GET ON THE GROUND!"

The arrival of the police stunned me into inaction. I blinked as flashlights bounced blinding beams throughout the forest clearing. Someone had his arm around my shoulder—Antonio. One of the police approached us—a brother, I noticed despite the gloom—and placed a hand on my forearm. "It's over, son—you're safe now. It's over." I blinked, unable to find the will to respond.

In short order, my assailants were de-masked and handcuffed by the other police officers—four of them in total. The two men were dragged off through the woods, protesting loudly about their rights and shit.

I'd fallen to my knees. I hugged my arms to my chest and rocked back and forth, hyperventilating. Wet tears streamed down my face, and I sobbed with each exhale. The police officer who'd first approached me knelt, placing a warm hand on my shoulder, pulling my naked body into his arms for a hug. "You're okay, man. You're okay. You did good. It's over. It's all over." He nodded to Antonio; between them, they got me to my feet, collected my stuff, and led me out of the forest.

At the ambulance, the paramedics wrapped me in a blanket and got me inside. I grew frantic for a moment, looking for Antonio, finding him right behind me. He climbed into the ambulance and sat across from me, holding my hand while the paramedics took my vitals.

They took me to the hospital. I sat on a metal-framed bed behind beige curtains under bright fluorescent lights, wrapped in a blue blanket. Antonio sat next to me, rocking back and forth with me, hugging me close.

As I became coherent enough to talk to, they asked me if I'd speak to a reporter who happened to have been in the ER as I was brought in. "No! No way! This isn't gonna make tomorrow's front page!" I declared emphatically. *I don't want any publicity—I don't want this getting back to my folks,* I thought as Antonio calmed me down.

Once the ER doctor declared me free of injuries and not requiring any further tests, he allowed Karen and Kyle to come behind the curtain of the cubby. I guess Antonio had called them when we first arrived.

Karen wrapped her arms around Antonio and me, crying into our shoulders. Kyle squeezed my arm, saying nothing. This outpouring of support and love choked me up, and fresh tears stained my cheeks. These were good tears, though. Antonio smiled at me over Karen's head, giving me a small nod.

The police officer came back in, asking how I was feeling. I mumbled something, and he nodded. "Gotta tell you, Mr. Dawson, not sure who was more scared when we got there— those thugs were pretty shook up. You both did quite a number on their faces!" Kyle and Karen smiled, as did I, though it made me wince from the pain in my own face. Antonio, I noted, didn't smile.

"My name is Officer Johnson, by the way. Mr. Dawson, do you feel up to telling me exactly what happened out there? If not, I understand; we can do this in the morning when you are rested." My breath became a bit unsteady for a moment, and Karen spoke up.

"Yeah, maybe you should do this in the morning, Officer Johnson."

"No!" I exclaimed. "I don't want to do this in the morning; I want to do it now." I told Officer Johnson what had happened point by point. When I got to the part where my assailants sliced off my clothing, Karen started to sob again. Kyle pulled her into a hug. I was determined to keep my composure.

When I finished, Officer Johnson turned to Antonio and asked him to repeat what he'd told him earlier.

"I heard Desmond calling me as I was running with a friend. I veered in the direction of his voice when I heard those guys talking. I stopped and could just make out Desmond in the clearing with the two of them. When one of them pulled a knife on him, I sent the guy who I was with to get help."

Officer Johnson interjected, "The guy who flagged us down."

"I guess so." Antonio rubbed his eyes and continued. "I looked for a rock or stick or something to bash their heads in with. I found one and started to get close to them as quietly as I could." Antonio's voice cracked and he stopped. I reached over and put my hand on his.

"When the one guy put his knife back in his pocket, I figured I'd better act fast. And the rest is history." He glanced at me, and I at him. Not a word passed between us, but we knew what the other was thinking.

Officer Johnson finished writing in his notebook. "You two gentlemen were lucky tonight. Not many people make it through something like this unscathed. With your statements and the doctor's report, I'm sure we'll be able to put these guys away for quite a while." He put his notebook and pen in a shirt pocket.

"As a brother, I'm very proud of you. Both of you kept your heads and acted wisely. Can I say it won't happen again? No, I can't. I will tell you this, though: I have a son a bit younger than you fellas and—God forbid—if this ever happens to him, I can only hope he'll be as brave as you two were tonight."

He reached into another pocket, pulling out a small card. "Here's my name and number, gents. If there is anything I can ever do for either of you, please don't hesitate to call." He reached his hand out, shaking both of ours. With a nod and a smile, he walked through the curtain.

We looked at one another without speaking, when the ER doctor came back into the cubby. "Okay. Officer Johnson says you are free to go, as long as you're feeling up to it. I see no reason to keep you here overnight, Mr. Dawson. But I'll write you a prescription for some painkillers. Due to the trauma and bruising to your body, you'll likely be in some pain by the morning. You'll need them over the next couple of days to help you to sleep."

I nodded. "Thanks, Doctor." Turning to Kyle, I added, "Take me home please."

"Gladly." He took the prescription slip from the doctor. Karen excused herself as Antonio helped me off the bed and into some of the extra clothes Kyle had brought with him.

We caught a taxi to the dorm. As we were about to head to our respective rooms, Kyle spoke up.

"I should let you know—you guys will have to talk with the dean of students about this. Probably even the university president too. It's mostly a cover-their-ass move."

"Yeah, figures," I replied. Kyle hesitated before saying more.

"As resident hall director, Desmond, I think I should let your parents know what happened and that you are okay. The caveat is you are a legal adult, so the decision is yours."

"No, I will tell them when I am ready."

"Well," he replied, "if you'd died, I'd absolutely have to let them know... Are you *sure* you don't want to let them know tonight? As I said, it's your decision and I will respect it."

"I'm sure." I looked at Karen and Antonio. "Listen, guys, as heroic as things turned out tonight, I don't want anyone to know about this. I want to remain anonymous. I don't even want the rest of the gang to know. At least, not all the details." I rubbed a hand over my eyes, overcome with fatigue. "I want to put this behind me as fast as I can..." *Though I know I can never undo what happened!* "So, promise me, promise me, please!"

They agreed. Both Karen and Kyle offered to have me stay in their room; Antonio overrode them both. "I got this." Wishing me good night, the other two walked off.

We got to Antonio's room and I collapsed on the bed. I closed my eyes for a few seconds, and when I opened them, he stood before me, holding out a glass of bourbon. In his other hand, he held a joint. I sighed, sat up, and accepted the drink.

He sat beside me on the bed and lit the joint. We drank and smoked in silence. I was still numb by what had happened, and even in my stupor, I saw Antonio had been affected too.

Finally, though, I felt the need to bring this up: "You didn't tell the police the whole truth tonight." Without answering, he got up and, with his back to me, stared out the window. After a moment, his shoulders begin to heave as he sobbed silently. I went to him, wrapping my arms around him from behind and laid my head next to his. He grew still within my hug.

"I heard you calling me as I was about to finish off the guy I was with. I figured you'd turn and go back to the road to wait for me." He drew in a shuddering breath. He laid his head on my cheek. "When I didn't hear you call anymore, I figured that's what you had done. Still…something didn't feel right."

Antonio turned his head under my neck. "I jumped up and ran to the last spot I heard you calling from. And there you were, with those fuckers. The guy I hooked up with came up behind me and almost shit his pants. He was freaking out, so I slapped him and sent him to get help. I found that big branch I had and eased toward where you were." His body began to shake, and I held him tighter.

"I saw and heard everything they were doing to you, and I wanted to kill them. I wouldn't have been able to live with myself if…" He started to cry again.

I held him until his tears ran their course, rubbing one hand over his shoulders and through his hair. He turned to face me, looking at me with his tear-stained hazel eyes. There was no signal, no warning. We leaned in and kissed.

All our fears and desires rushed into that one slow, passionate kiss. Excitement grew in both our bodies as we moved closer and kissed more deeply. I still hurt from where the thug had punched me in the mouth, but it didn't matter. We kissed with an urgency that no pain could stop.

Where are we taking each other? I thought, even as my hands explored his back, and his, mine.

Finally, Antonio pulled back. "Desmond," he said in a voice thick with emotion. "You need to know...to know I love you. I loved you from the first day of orientation when you called me out." He shook his head, holding me out at arm's length. "I know I am going to kick myself in the morning for saying this. As much as I dreamed of this moment...this is not the right time."

He covered my mouth as I tried to object. "I know we both think we need this right now, but I think I need a best friend more. You've become a brother to me, Des. If we did this now, if we slept together...it would change our relationship forever." He pulled me close again, and we rested our foreheads together.

"I just found someone I can trust with my life and a person I would be willing to give it up for. I don't want to jeopardize that." His lips quivered as he added, "But...if you *really* want this, I'd be willing."

I brought my closed hand up, lifting his chin with my knuckle. I looked deep into those enticing light-green eyes of his.

I knew he was right.

Knowing he was right and trying to understand what I felt, though, made me dizzy. *Will every man I feel something for reject my affections?* Then, another thought surfaced. *If I wanted a relationship with a man—a real relationship—how long would it take for me to find the right one? Would I know him when I saw him? Would he know me?*

Stroking his cheek with my thumb, I said, "You know, Momma warned me to stay away from boys like you. She said you were a bad influence. I love my momma, but I think she was wrong." I kissed him again, passionately, as we had before. "I want you, Antonio. I want you so bad. But you're right. Our friendship is too important." I looked at his bed. "But…do you think I could still stay the night? I just…I just need someone to hold." Antonio reached down and took my hand, leading me to his bed. We undressed—I piled the clothes Kyle had given me on the floor—and we climbed under the sheets of his twin bed. I laid my back against his chest, and he wrapped his arms around me, and like that, we drifted off.

Right before falling asleep, a vision flashed through my mind—the thugs, bearing down on me with their knives. I must have tensed up, because Antonio rested his face against the back of my head and held me tighter. He whispered into my ear, "It's okay, Des. I got you. They can't hurt you here. They'll never hurt you again."

I reflected on how tonight could have turned out very differently. I counted myself one lucky brother and fell asleep in Antonio's arms.

Interlude Seven

Parental Intervention

I spent the next day hiding out in Antonio's room, only creeping out to use the bathroom. I wasn't ready to face the outside world yet. Not with the pain I felt, both inside and out. I couldn't move without wincing, and I couldn't close my eyes without seeing those masked faces... Thank God it was Saturday—I had nowhere to be.

Karen and Antonio stayed with me, leaving when they saw I needed time to think and rest. I'd crawl back into Antonio's bed, going between fitful periods of sleep and jerking awake in a cold sweat. Every time I woke up, though, one of them would be there to reassure me.

Saturday night came, and I lay huddled against Antonio again. I never wanted to leave his room. It had become my haven. No one could hurt me here.

Karen and Antonio respected my wishes and only gave the news to the members of our group. They were told Antonio and I were attacked by two masked guys but were able to fight them off. There was a short piece on the news and in the paper the next day. Thank the Lord, though—nothing in the report would lead anyone back to us.

Kyle looked in on me, telling me I could talk to the dean and the president when I felt ready. They just wanted to know I was okay. Kyle also passed me the name of the university's psychiatrist in case I wanted to talk to her. I figured I'd pass on that. I hadn't actually cried about this incident, nor did I feel the need to.

That Sunday afternoon, while I lay in bed, there came a knock at Antonio's door. No one from the dorm knocked, so I figured it was one of Antonio's "pieces." I grumbled, pulling on some shorts. Antonio had assured me I'd have complete privacy.

I shuffled to the door, calling out, "Who is it?" The voice that answered was not who I'd ever have expected.

"It's Dad and Vinny." Hearing my father's voice triggered something inside me. My vision blurred. I lunged for the door, flung it open, and threw myself into my dad's arms. "Wow!" He recoiled, catching himself. "If I knew you were going to be this happy to see me, I'd have visited a long time ago!"

Another voice spoke up. "Do I get some of that welcome too?"

"Vinny!" I pulled my older brother into the hug. The men in our family rarely hugged, so I knew this was taking them by surprise. "Where's Mom and Nina?"

"They're at home," Dad said, shooting a look at Vinny.

"Well, what's the occasion; did we win the lottery or something?" Something hit me. "Hey, wait. How did you know where to find me?" My mood soured as two guilty parties revealed themselves from where they'd loitered down the hall. "You guys called my *parents?*"

"Look, Desmond," Karen said, coming closer now she was found out. "We were worried about you. You need your family at a time like this, so I called your dad." Frustrated, angry, and worried, I retreated into Antonio's room. Everyone followed.

"Does Mom know too?" I asked, turning to Dad. "Are you two here to pack me up and take me home?" I looked into my dad's eyes as he opened his arms once more, beckoning me toward him. I fell into his embrace and just lost it. "I'm so sorry, Dad, I'm so sorry!" I said as I blubbered, hiding my head on his chest.

"It's all right, son. It's all right." He rubbed my back, guiding me to the bed, where he sat beside me. I looked around; Dad must have waved everyone out—we were alone.

We sat on the edge of Antonio's bed for an hour, me crying on and off, Dad holding me and kneading my shoulders and neck. By the time I regained some composure, I looked at him and said, "This is the man you sent away to college: look at me, crying like some sissy…"

"Now, look here, Desmond Dawson," he began, his voice getting all fatherly on me. "I don't know all of what you went through, but from the little your friends told me, you are *no* sissy." He held me by both shoulders, making me look up at him. "I am so very proud of you, son. And I am very glad you are safe and alive." He pulled me close again, tightly.

"Okay, I'm going to call your brother back in. And when I do, you're going to tell us what we can do to help."

"You already have, Dad, just by being here."

Dad and Vinny took me out for supper at a sports bar near the train station, and I gave them an...*edited* version of the story. I didn't go into the thugs' sexual advances or my reaction to them. I told them masked men had attacked me, that Antonio came to my rescue, and that we beat the shit out of them until the police arrived.

"Looking back, Dad, I'm finally thankful for all those years of self-defense courses you made us take!"

The expression on Dad's face grew thoughtful. I guess my opening up about my experience was about to trigger him to open up about our family's past—something neither Vinny nor I had known about.

"Boys, your momma and I always said the reason we moved to Oakvale was to give you and Nina a better education. That wasn't the only reason." Vinny and I shared a look, putting our forks down. Dad took a long swig of his beer.

"One night while we were still living in Newark, your momma and I were walking home from the bus stop. Out of nowhere, this guy came at us and grabbed Millie. He held a knife to her throat." Both Vinny and I sat dumbfounded, our mouths hanging open.

"He wanted our money, and your momma obliged him, giving him her purse. We were lucky that night; all he took from us were the contents in that purse. We got to keep our lives.

"Millie and I made a decision that night: whatever it took to move our family out of Newark, that's what we were going to do. I made another promise to your momma: I'd make sure you children knew how to take care of yourselves; that if ever you were faced with a similar circumstance, you'd know what to do." Dad closed his eyes, bringing a hand to his forehead.

"Then I got the call from your friend this morning, Desmond. I didn't tell your mother. I thought it was best I come check on you by myself. I told Millie I wanted to bond with my sons today. Luckily, your brother had the day off—I wired him a ticket and told him to meet me at the Thirtieth Street Station. And here we are."

"Did Mom buy your story?"

"I think so. And if she didn't, she's chosen not to let on, bless her." Dad reached across the table, grabbing my hand. "Son, if you want to pack up and come home with us tonight, there's no shame in that." Vinny nodded at me, echoing Dad's words. I loved them both for that. But I knew I was going to stay. Having Vinny and Dad there to remind me how strong I was reinforced my desire to stick it out for myself.

We moved on, enjoying the rest of our supper. We talked about home and even joked around like old times until we had to take Vinny to the station for his eight o'clock train.

Vinny and I shared a moment when Dad went off to call Mom and pay the bill. My brother told me if I ever needed him, for any reason, to just pick up the phone and call. "But don't call collect." We both laughed, throwing our arms around each other again. He grew sentimental on me. "I love you, bro. Couldn't imagine not havin' you around."

Dad returned and we headed out to the train station. We walked Vinny to the gate for the DC train. As he boarded, Vinny looked down at me. "Stay safe!" I nodded, waving as the train pulled off.

Dad drove us back to Temple and walked me to my dorm. We sat on a bench outside for a while, watching the stars. I told him I had another bit of information I needed to tell him and I wasn't sure how he was going to take it.

"Tell me, Desmond. I'm happy to have you alive—there's not much you could tell me tonight that would change that!" We shared a smile.

"Well, it's like this," I said. "Antonio is gay." Dad nodded slowly, staring off into the night. Then he turned to me.

"Are you and Antonio...you know?"

"No! No, it's nothing like that!"

"All right!" he said, raising his hands. "So, he's just a friend?"

"Yeah. He's one of the crew. We all met on the first day of orientation."

"But he's...special to you?" Dad held my eyes. I met his gaze, saying nothing. "Look, son, only God has the right to judge whether a man's life is moral or not. For me, I don't understand homosexuality...but I have no reason or right to judge unless they do something to harm my family." He put a hand on my knee. "In my eyes, this guy Antonio is all right. He was there when you needed him. He risked his life to help you. You could not ask for a better friend." I nodded, not trusting myself to say anything else. Dad cleared his throat.

"You know, Desmond, we're going to have to tell your mother about the attack." He looked at me, wincing. I winced back.

"Can we not tell her right away?"

"Not right away. She'll have to be told at some point, though."

"You know she'll freak. She'll want me to pack up and come home and go to Rutgers or Monmouth College!"

"Yeah, she might, at that," Dad agreed with a nod. "Look, son, I've never held anything back from your momma; I couldn't if I tried. But you put your mind at ease—I think we've got some time. For now, this will be the Dawson men's secret."

We shook on it and headed inside.

When we got to Antonio's room, Dad did something un-expected: when he saw Antonio, he shook his hand and gave him a hug.

"Thank you for saving my son," he said as he hugged my friend. He and I went to find Karen and Kyle; he thanked them for their help, too, and said goodbye.

Before he got into his car, he hugged me again and kissed me on the forehead.

"You hang in there, son." He got into the car and turned to me before shutting the door. "Oh, and enough moping about that boy's room in your underwear. It's past time you got your ass back to the realm of the living!" I chuckled and agreed, waving as he drove off into the night.

That night is one of my best memories with my dad. It reminds me of why I love and respect him as much as I do.

Thanksgiving arrived, and I headed home. Dad was true to his word—no mention of the incident had gotten to Momma's ears.

I got a chance to see Angel while I was home. I told her an edited version of what had happened to me, swearing her to secrecy. She was worried for me, but I put on my best macho face, assuring her everything was fine.

Seeing Angel and my family was a perfect reset to an eventful autumn. By the end of the weekend, I was more than ready to get back to Temple.

I returned to school on Monday, ready for the last three weeks of school and finals leading up to Christmas. What I wasn't quite ready for was what took place in the middle of all this: the trial.

We'd learned from Officer Johnson that my assailants were neo-Nazi skinheads. I also learned I'd broke my assailant's nose and even busted his jaw. Antonio's guy suffered a fractured skull. Neither of us were too sorry about that.

I found out from the prosecutor that the two of them had been in prison twice before for assault and attempted rape. If they were convicted this time, three strikes meant they'd be out!

I sat in the courtroom during the entire trial, enduring the looks of pure evil from my assailants. Antonio, Karen, Kyle—and even my dad—were with me the entire time.

At the end, the judge convicted them both, and they earned twenty years behind bars, without parole. I listened to the sentencing, a tension I didn't know I'd been harboring releasing all at once. At my side, Karen sighed aloud, hugging me tightly.

Back on campus, Antonio noticed something was up. I relayed to him how I'd been worried when the defense attorney had asked me if I'd felt any arousal during the attack.

"I told them no…but I was lying. I actually did." Antonio placed a hand on my shoulder.

"It's over now, Des," he whispered. "Put it out of your mind."

★

With that chapter barely over, it was time to stress out again: final exams.

I got back into running, but never alone anymore. Where Antonio used to go off and do his own thing and meet up with me afterward, now he stuck to me like glue.

Back in the dorm, I couldn't seem to find any private time. If Karen wasn't finding excuses to study with me at night, Kyle was there just to "hang out."

Dad grew a little overprotective too: he started calling twice per week, sometimes three. He and Momma would "pop down" Sunday afternoons for surprise visits, saying they were in Philly to do some shopping. I knew everyone was concerned for me, but it wasn't long before I was feeling completely smothered.

The week of finals I sat them down: Antonio, Karen, Kyle, Dad, and even Momma. (It didn't take long to figure out Dad had finally confessed everything. Momma agreed not to reveal she knew, as long as she got to come to make sure her baby was safe.)

So that Sunday morning I called Dad to confirm he was going to make one of his "surprise" visits. I told him to send Nina to a friend's house that day rather than bring her. I did not tell him why. I then arranged for Karen, Antonio, and Kyle to meet me around one in the afternoon in my room.

At exactly 1:00 p.m., everyone showed up at my door. This was the first and last time I put my foot down, throwing my roommate out. He didn't object, especially when he opened the door to find a bunch of brothers and sisters staring at him—in fact, he couldn't get out of there fast enough.

I invited everyone in and made sure they were comfortable. Momma hadn't yet met Antonio or Karen, so I did introductions, watching my mom's face when I presented her to

Antonio. Her arched eyebrow told me what I wanted to know: she'd been given the lowdown on my friend already.

"First off, Mom—I know Dad told you about the attack." Turning to my dad, I added, "It's okay, Dad—I know she must have tortured you for it. Believe me, I know how persuasive she can be!" He and I chuckled at that; Momma did not.

"Now, here's the deal, family. The attack happened months ago, the trial is over, the perps are behind bars and will be there until I'm almost forty." Everyone nodded—how could they otherwise? Facts were facts.

"What I need you to know is that I'm fine. I'm not sad, I'm not depressed, I'm not broken, I'm not suffering." I looked around at each of them. "I love the attention I've gotten, but enough is enough. I've got exams this week, and I can't concentrate with all of you badgering me all day long!"

They tried to cut in, each in their own way, but I cut off all attempts to interrupt me.

"Here's the deal: I'm fine, really. The perpetrators of this deed are behind bars, and they've thrown away the key. I am not broken, and I've proven I won't break. I love all the attention you're giving me, but you are driving me to want to share a cell with my assailants. No, Mom," I said, forestalling her raised finger, "I am not taking any questions. Love you all; I am going to the library to study for my finals. Bye!"

And, with that, I quickly bolted for the door and down the stairs, feeling pretty good about how that had gone.

Sure enough, things went back to normal after that. I saw Karen, Kyle, and Antonio only when I wanted to see them. Dad was back to being himself. Momma, though—now that she didn't have to use Dad as an intermediary—decided to do her own calling. Her first call was to let me know in no uncertain terms what she thought about what I'd said in my room that afternoon.

"I don't know who you think you are, but I'll tell you who I am: your mother. I am a card-carrying member of the Mothers' Club and have rights and privileges over all my children, *forever!*"

"Yes, Mom."

"That means when I have questions, you give me answers!"

"I know, Mom" was the only reply I could make. That was my momma; I guess I should have known she wouldn't have had it any other way!

Interlude Eight

Antonio's Story

Exams came and went. I aced them, so there's no need to go into them.

With exams out of the way, Christmas holidays were almost upon us. The crew and I celebrated the successful completion of our first semester by partying hard that final night and walking back to the dorms together as the sun rose the next day. After a few hours' sleep, we shared a midmorning brunch in the cafeteria and went back to the dorm lounge to exchange Christmas gifts before parting ways for the holidays.

What we didn't know was Kyle's prediction of us losing classmates would come true sooner than we thought.

I noticed Antonio sitting quietly during the gift exchange; afterward, I caught him sneaking back to his room before everyone else left. The rest of us said our goodbyes, leaving me and Karen in the lounge.

"I've still got Antonio's gift," I indicated, holding up a wrapped present.

"Me too. Sneaky bastard slipped away without anyone noticing."

"I've gotta pack, but do you wanna meet by his room to see what's up?"

"Deal," Karen said, adding, "Make it a half hour. And don't even *think* of being fashionably late." I laughed and headed up to my room to pack.

Thirty minutes later, I lurked on Antonio's floor, waiting in the corridor outside his room, with Antonio and Karen's gifts still inside my bag. No Karen. I waited for ten minutes. Just when I decided to head in myself, I heard the elevator ding and Karen appeared around the corner. I made a dramatic gesture of looking at my watch.

"Well, *look* who ended up being fashionably late!"

Karen flipped the bird at me.

"Whatever. You probably just ran up the stairs this second." We smirked at each other, heading for Antonio's door. I heard a voice coming from his room as we approached. No, not a voice, but crying. We exchanged a look, and I knocked tentatively. The crying cut off immediately.

"Who's there?!" He didn't sound like he wanted visitors.

"It's me—Desmond. And Karen. We came to say goodbye."

"I thought you tired-assed groupies already said your goodbyes."

Karen rolled her eyes and pushed me aside. She was going into her annoyed Black-woman routine.

She hit the door with her closed fist, shouting, "Look, nigga, if you don't get your pale ass off that bed and open this door right now, I'm gonna kick it into the next century!" She backed the attitude off a bit, adding, "Look, Antonio, just let us in. We're worried about you."

She and I shared another silent look, hearing footsteps approach from within. The knob turned, and the door swung in, revealing Antonio in nothing but a pair of boxers.

"That would be some kick, bitch," he mumbled, turning to walk back to his bed.

"You know I woulda done it too; why else did you open the door, dairy queen?" Karen pushed into his room and bore down on him. I dropped the bag of gifts by the door and rushed between them to stave off any more aggression.

"Okay, you two, 'tis the season to be jolly and all that, remember?" I gave them each a big, fake smile. Antonio snorted while Karen gave me the finger. "Well, fine—scratch on this, both of you!" I declared, pointing at my ass.

"If I wanted to suffer insults, I'd go home for the holidays," Antonio declared.

"Wait. You're not going home?" Antonio ignored my question, rolling his wet eyes.

"You came to say goodbye? Fine. Goodbye. There. Done." He sniffed, wiping the back of his hand across his nose. "Now go home to your Christmas trees and your turkeys and your presents and shit." He slumped down on the edge of his bed. As one, Karen and I approached, sitting on the mattress to either side of him.

"Come on, Negroes—don't you understand English? Do I need to put it in sign language for you?" Antonio pointed at me and Karen in turn, then gestured dramatically at the door.

I leaned in close, wrapping an arm around his shoulder. "We aren't going anywhere until you tell us what the fuck is bothering you, so cut the shit and come out with it."

Antonio closed his eyes for a moment, pushed up from the bed, and retreated to his favorite spot by the window. He took a deep breath, crossing his arms across his chest.

"It's nothing, guys. I just don't do Christmas well." He welled up again, despite his obvious attempts to hide it. Karen went to him, trying to give him a hug. He waved her off, wiping his face. "No. This is stupid; I'm all right, guys. Please leave me alone."

Karen crossed her own arms, squaring off in front of Antonio. "Look, drama queen, it's obvious there is something wrong by the shitload of tears coming down your face. Now, if you can't trust us after everything we've been through, who can you trust? So, bitch, you're gonna tell us what's up!" I couldn't see her expression from where I sat, though Antonio wore one of resignation. He wiped the tears from his cheeks and told Karen to sit down with me. He pulled the chair out from his desk and sat facing us. His face slackened, a faraway look coming to his eyes.

"I told Desmond I came out during my junior year of high school, after I turned eighteen. What I didn't tell him was why or how it happened."

★

Interval One: A Past Christmas Revisited

My father worked construction and my mother worked at a dry cleaner's in town. Dad had been out on disability for months, and the checks he got didn't match the money he was accustomed to bringing in.

He was a violent son of a bitch at the best of times. You can imagine how he acted when he wasn't making enough money to make ends meet. Or when he got drunk. Which got more and more frequent after he stopped working.

Back when he still could work, we only really had to worry about two nights per week: Fridays and Saturdays. My brother Carlos called Dad "the weekend drunk." After he had his accident, he drank every day.

He started to go into fits of rage for the smallest, stupidest shit and smack my mother around. He would beat us kids at the drop of a hat too. We learned real quick to stay out of his way. We also learned not to talk around him either, because that would set him off even more.

But there was something about Christmas that would change him. For the whole month of December, he became a different person. We would go out as a family and get a real tree, spending hours decorating it and the whole house. He'd drive us out to Rockefeller Center to see the decorations. We'd go back to the Italian neighborhood in Harlem where he grew up and visit our grandmother.

Dad didn't get along with my mother's side of the family, because they knew how he treated her. Still, at Christmas, he'd drop us off at Mom's parents' house on Saturday evening after we'd gone gift shopping, then pick us up on Sunday to have dinner at his mother's house before we went back to Philly. My grandmother could cook her ass off. Amazing Italian dishes with all the fixin's.

So, yeah—December used to be the happiest month of the year for us. We all looked forward to it. We were a real family, for a while.

He had his accident in April of '72. I was a freshman, and Carlos was in seventh grade. I remember coming home from school one day and finding my mom bawling her eyes out. I thought he'd beaten her again. I went to her and helped dry her tears.

She calmed down enough to tell me he'd fallen off the scaffolding at work and was unconscious in the hospital. They were not sure how extensive the damage was, but they believed the swelling in his back meant he'd ruptured a disk in his spine. They'd told her he might not have any feeling in his legs anymore.

With him being unconscious, though, they couldn't tell much. We could do nothing but wait for him to wake up.

Between you and me, I hoped the bastard wouldn't ever come out of it. I couldn't tell my mother that, because, despite how he treated her, I knew she still loved him. Why else would she stay?

(Antonio paused, shaking his head at the memory. Karen nodded in understanding. I didn't—I wasn't exactly able to relate. Momma and Dad argued, sure, but there had never been any physical violence in their relationship, not like Antonio's parents.)

He came out of the coma a few days later, going through seven months of physical therapy to regain the use of his legs. Even after that, the doctor wouldn't let him return to work until after the New Year. Being stuck at home with nothing to do drove him mad.

During that same summer, I had my first sexual encounter.

I liked riding my bike through Fairmount Park and would spend hours exploring every inch I could. Early that summer,

I found a section of the park where men seemed to just hang around. I got curious and kept going back there until I figured out precisely what took place. And, believe me, I eventually saw it all there—everything you could imagine in your wildest porn dreams!

(Karen turned her nose up at this; I nodded, my thoughts slipping to me and Samuel before I blinked them away.)

Eventually, I got brave enough to hide in the bushes and whack off while watching other men go at it. I couldn't get enough of the place.

Then one day early that fall, it was my turn. I'd biked to the park after school and was crouched down behind a bush watching these two freaks get it on. I had my dick out, just whackin' away. I was about to come when I heard someone behind me. In a panic, I turned around. There stood this god-like man smiling down at me. I scrambled to get my pants up, when he said, "I'm sorry. I didn't mean to interrupt you." He grinned at my state of undress, adding, "And please don't stop on account of me. I'm enjoying the show!"

I didn't know what to do; I just squatted there, frozen, my dick going limp from shock. He looked down at my shrinking erection, asking if he could help. I didn't think about it; I nodded. He nodded too, getting on his knees in front of me. He pulled my pants down, leaned over my crotch, and took my piece in his mouth.

(Karen shuffled a bit on the bed beside me. I glanced over, catching her lift her eyebrows wryly. Antonio didn't notice; he was lost in his recollection.)

Fuck, the things that man did with his tongue were sinful. It didn't take me long to pop another erection and keep it for the duration. This guy had me panting and moaning and pounding my fists in the dirt. I didn't care who heard me at that moment.

Then I came, shooting my load directly into his mouth as he sucked me dry.

I leaned on my elbows, struggling to understand what had just happened. The guy raised his head and said, "Wow, that was good. Do you wanna try it?"

"I've never done it before and I don't know what to do, but I'm willing to try."

The guy laughed, unbuttoning his jeans. They dropped past his knees, and there it was, standing at attention, right in front of me. A throbbing white shaft surrounded by a thick bush of reddish-brown hair, which continued down his legs and up his abs. He had a beard and mustache the same color, as well as the straight hair on his head. He looked like Kris Kristofferson; even had the same build.

Well, I got close to his dick and caught his musk; just smelling him got me hard again, even though I'd only come less than a minute ago.

He told me to take one hand and grab the shaft of his cock while licking the head with my tongue. I visualized how he'd done it to me and tried to do the same. I knew it was working when he began to breathe heavily and moan as much as I had.

I remember, his dick was like the thin part of a baseball bat and as long too.

(Karen snorted at this. "Hey, shut up," Antonio said. "It's my story, not yours!"

"Whatever, homo. Just keep going." They sneered at each other before he carried on with his tale.)

I couldn't wait to put it in my mouth. I opened wide, breathing in as I dove down, feeling it slide between my teeth. I looked to see him close his eyes and heard his moans and growling. I bobbed my head up and down, taking him further and further inside me.

He spoke to me with this deep sexual voice that made me bob even faster and deeper. I gagged suddenly, pulling back. Before I could withdraw all the way, he grabbed my head and forced himself back inside me.

(*"Just like a fucking man," Karen grumbled. I said nothing, sensing a growing need to adjust the stirring in my pants. I noticed Antonio's boxers were looking a bit fuller too, for that matter.*)

I thought I was gonna throw up. Before I did, he backed off a bit, shooting his load straight down my throat. It went down like a thick milkshake and kept on coming. I pulled off him, hacking and coughing, wanting to bring his semen back up. The deal was done, though—it was already in my belly. And part of me loved knowing I'd swallowed all of it.

I'd done it. I'd had my first sexual encounter, and I'd loved every second.

"Thanks, kid. I gotta get back to work." The god-man pulled his pants up. "Listen—I can be here tomorrow at the same time, if you wanna do this again?" My cock jerked. *You'd better believe I would!*

I nodded my head; not that I needed to. My expression and my dick's reaction were answer enough. He gave me yet another of his gorgeous grins, finished buttoning his pants, and disappeared along the path toward the parking lot.

I sighed, slowly pulling up my jeans, until I became aware of my immediate surroundings. Hidden in the woods around me were a bunch of perverts, all leering. They must have been watching as the white guy and I went at it; I hadn't noticed them until now.

I zipped up quickly, hurrying down the path I'd come from. I reached my bike, jumped on, and didn't stop pedaling until I got home.

I walked in the house to find my father sitting in his favorite chair, watching *Gilligan's Island*. He looked up long enough to say, "Where the fuck have you been?"

"Nowhere, Dad," I muttered, hurrying to my room.

I flopped onto my bed, smelling onions, garlic, and basil wafting into my room. Mom always cooked with those three ingredients, no matter what she made. And I knew it would always taste great.

I sighed, interlacing my fingers behind my head. Visions of being with the gay guy in the park ran through my mind. *Damn, he was fine.*

I realized I hadn't even gotten his name.

And then another thought hit me.

Was I now gay? Was I one of those faggots and fairies that my father screamed at from the car window as we drove down South Street?

What if he finds out what I did? My whole body tensed at the thought of his reaction. Mom rescued me from my thoughts, calling us to supper.

I sat to the right of my dad; Carlos sat to his left. We did this deliberately so when Dad got into one of those evil moods of his, we could be his targets rather than Mom. The worst he could do to her was hurl a piece of food or sometimes the salt-shaker.

I ate supper in silence while Dad drunkenly summarized his daily television programs for us. He *used* to talk to us about work; all he had to talk about now were *Beverly Hillbillies*, *Get Smart*, or *Gilligan's Island*.

When I'd had as much of his bullshit one-sided conversation as I could take, I asked to be excused. My mother glanced at me.

"Is there anything wrong, dear? You haven't said a word since you got home."

"No, I just got a lot of schoolwork."

"Yeah, that's right, boy," Dad said, needing to give his two cents. "You don't wanna be a low-class dumb shit like your mother and me, do ya?" He sneered at me, something dark and green stuck in his teeth. "You wanna be one of those smarty-pants motherfuckers livin' up in Society Hill!"

Mom came to my defense as she always did. "Leave the boy alone, Tony." To me, she added, "You go ahead, dear. I'll bring you some dessert as soon as I do the dishes."

"Yeah, get in yer room and put that brown nose of yours into them books!" He turned to Ma. "Carol, you keep babyin' that boy of yours, he's gonna turn into one of them faggots from downtown. You mark my words, woman."

"No, he's not. He's going to turn out fine." Mom ruffled my hair. "Go on, Antonio. I'll be in later." As I walked to my room, I wondered if Dad had known about me all along.

I had a wet dream that night: in the park, sucking on giant alabaster dicks. I woke with a start, sticky and spent. When I couldn't get back to sleep, I got up, cleaned myself off, and stripped my sheets. I managed to get breakfast and leave for school before my dad even lifted his head off his pillow.

I couldn't stop watching the clock. I sat there in my last class of the day, staring as the hands slowly ticked toward 2:00 p.m. Time had deliberately slowed down just to drive me crazy.

The bell rang and I launched out of my seat, headed for the L train. I didn't get off at home; I took the train to a bus, which got me to the park twenty minutes later.

As I walked along the path, I passed men who gave me long, lingering stares. They must have recognized me from yesterday. None of them were my guy, though.

I walked up and down the path for a few minutes, getting antsy at the unwanted attention. I was about to dart when I heard a voice call, "Hey, over here!" My white guy crouched in the clearing where we'd met yesterday. I hustled over.

"Man! I was getting worried you weren't going to show!"

"I'm here on time—it's you who's early!" He smiled; he had nice teeth.

"Yeah—I took a bus. Only took me twenty minutes."

"I'm glad you came."

"Me too." We stood staring at each other for another couple seconds before our hormones took over. He'd brought a blanket, which made things a little more comfortable in the bushes. Though, honestly, I didn't care—just so long as I could be with him.

We both came almost immediately. After, we talked before he headed to work. His name was George, but he didn't want to share last names, which was fine with me. He told me he was thirty-two—almost twice my age; two years younger than my dad—and married with three children.

We agreed to meet daily in the park around 2:30. He would take a late lunch from work, and I'd keep catching the bus to get there. We also agreed that if one of us hadn't shown up by 2:45, the other one would leave, and we'd try again the next day.

Like clockwork, we began to meet at our spot. Monday through Friday; rain or shine. We were having—what I thought at the time—sex for men, either in the woods or in George's car if it was raining too hard.

Gradually, he and I talked more. Instead of rushing off after we finished, we'd linger, drawn to each other's company beyond the physical.

I still made sure I got home before Dad roused from the stupor of his afternoon drinking binge. It saved me from explaining "where the fuck" I'd been.

On Mondays, Wednesdays, and Fridays, Dad had physical therapy at 4:30 at a clinic down the street from us. I'd go with him to catch him if he fell while walking with his cane. I didn't mind this task too much; I'd come from having sex with George an hour earlier, my mind filled with thoughts of him. Whatever cruel shit Dad muttered at me would go right over my head. We'd make it home by six, just in time for one of Mom's great dinners.

Fall weather came, and it grew less comfortable for George and me to do our thing in the woods. Strangely, we'd built a type of father-son relationship I wished I had with my own dad. I learned George worked in construction like Dad, though I never told George about it. And he never pried.

George and I were able to talk about almost anything, as long as it didn't cross into our families or where we lived. Those were his only parameters.

One day in late October, we were finished with our business (he'd taught me how to 69, and boy—did we ever work that one!) and were spying on two other men in a nearby clearing. After pleasuring each other orally, one guy turned the other around and started to fuck his ass. The guy getting fucked moaned loudly enough for the entire park to hear. I don't think I've ever heard someone express such ecstasy. I got hard again in about five seconds flat.

"Man, Tony—doesn't your guy ever take a rest?" George asked, grabbing my shaft, still slick from my earlier release. I laughed, leaning my head into his hairy chest.

It was about time for George to go, I knew, with a weird pang in my chest. I looked up at him and on impulse asked, "Have you ever been fucked by a guy?" He smiled.

"Sure!"

"Did you enjoy it?"

"Yep!" He laughed again, then turned serious. "You goin' somewhere with these questions?" When I shrugged, he pressed me. "You want to try that?" He nodded toward the other clearing. I didn't have to think; I just nodded.

"Yeah. But only if it's with you." We shared a smile. George looked down at his watch, then kissed me on the forehead.

"You got it, champ; someday soon maybe we'll give it a whirl." He eased up from where we'd been sitting and dressed. I looked to where the two men still lay—one on top of the other—and visualized how it would be with George.

November came, and we still met regularly. By now, though, it had grown too cold to do anything outside. We'd hang out in George's station wagon, trying to take care of business while *also* taking care not to get caught by the police, who patrolled occasionally.

We were sitting in his car the week after Thanksgiving when I laid my plan on him. George had told me that during December, work would be slow and he'd have more time to spend with me. I knew my dad had an appointment with the Social Security office during the third week of that month to settle some matters before he returned to work. He'd be there all day.

Mom and Carlos caught the train at 8:00; she rode with my brother to school, then carried on to the next stop, where she worked. Dad would go with them on the day of his appointment.

I'd cut school, wait for everyone to leave, meet George at the park, and bring him back to my house.

I pleaded for him to take the chance, reminding him of the promise he made. He reluctantly agreed.

★

Interval Two: Take Me I'm Yours

Our big day, December 19, 1973, was the day I truly lost my virginity and gained my manhood.

The night before, I made a plan to fake being sick. That way if the school called Mom's work, I had a legitimate excuse for being at home. Seeing as I rarely got sick or missed any school, Mom bought my performance hook, line, and sinker. The next morning, when I kept up the sick routine, she made sure I was comfortable before she left for work.

"I'll call you around eleven to see how you're feeling, sweetheart," she told me before heading off with Dad and Carlos. I waited a few minutes before jumping out of bed to call

George, assuring him I would still be meeting him. Everything was lining up according to plan. My excitement grew.

I left the house and met George at the appointed time.

"Are you sure you still want to go through with this?" he asked me, for the umpteenth time, in the park parking lot. He stroked my hair as we sat next to each other in his AMC Matador station wagon. "Once we take this step, things will never go back to the way they were before." He couldn't have been more right.

When we got to my neighborhood, I had George park his station wagon around the corner. We came through the alley separating us and the houses behind ours, then in through the back door.

When we got to the living room, George took a moment to look around before spotting our family picture from last Christmas on the wall unit. He gestured, asking, "This your family?" I nodded. He looked again, squinting and cocking his head to the side. Suddenly, his expression turned sickly. "Shit! No, you gotta be shitting me! This is your dad?" He pulled the picture off the shelf and pointed to the only white guy in the picture.

"What's wrong?" I asked. George took several breaths before replacing the picture and dropping to the sofa.

"I don't know if I can do this, kiddo."

"Why not?" I replied, my voice cracking. "No one's gonna show up, I promise!"

"Antonio, your dad and I work together. *Worked* together," he corrected himself. "We were on the same scaffold the day he fell. I remember him whistling and shouting at some woman. He didn't see the crane swinging toward him. I yelled at him to watch out, but it was too late. I watched him fall twenty-five feet to the ground, thinking I was witnessing a man die." He put his head in his hands.

I stood there a moment, not sure what to say. Then I did the only thing I could think to do. I reached down and grabbed his wrist, pulling him to his feet. I led him into my room, turned toward him, and unbuttoned his shirt.

George said nothing, stroking my hair as I removed all his clothes. Seeing him fully naked for the first time, I was pleased to see he was hairier than I'd imagined. This stoked a fire in me hotter than any I'd experienced with him yet.

He took his turn undressing me. First, he pulled my tank top over my head and raised arms. Dropping that to the ground, he smiled and took a deep breath of my body. He gently worked my sports shorts over my hips until they slid to my ankles. I stepped out of them even as he began pushing my tighty-whities down, the waistband drawing my woody down until it snapped free.

We both giggled. I leaned into him as he pulled my socks off last. We stood there motionless, next to my bed, unabashedly taking in the view of each other's body for the first time.

George broke the spell first, cupping my chin. He leaned in close, his breath caressing my face, and kissed me gently. He started on my left cheek, lingering for a moment as his lips caressed the soft skin there. He moved to the opposite cheek, holding the kiss even longer. He kissed my forehead and all the way down the bridge of my nose. When he reached my lips again, he pulled me in close. My lips parted of their own accord, welcoming the gentle probing of his tongue.

We'd never kissed like this before; our kisses had always been rushed and furtive—afterthoughts with our pants around our ankles, hidden among the bushes. This new level of sensuality made me light-headed, so much so my knees buckled. I felt his smile through my lips as he caught me. I wrapped my arms about his neck, and he lifted me effortlessly. Our kiss broke finally; he rubbed his nose across my cheek, whispering, "There's no turning back now." He laid me on my bed.

I settled back, catching my breath as he explored every inch of my body with his tongue and his lips. He traveled down my neck and my chest, stopping to worry at my nipples, tasting and retasting as he went along. All I could do was moan at his ministrations—a moan that came from a place of primordial need, deep within my teenage body.

He kissed my shoulders, working down my biceps and my forearms, treating each of my fingers to a long bath with his tongue. I shivered as I watched him do this, my dick painfully hard, throbbing in tune with my racing heartbeat.

He let me take over, and I matched what he had done to me.

Back and forth we went, exploring each other's body, stroking, kissing, licking, until I could take no more teasing. George must have sensed this, as his tact changed. He straddled me, his muscular, hairy legs pinning mine to the bed.

"You ready?" he whispered in a husky voice. I nodded, feeling an aching need. George reached down to his pants on the floor, drawing two objects from his pockets.

"What's that?" I whispered, eyeing a small bottle that read only "rush."

"You'll see," he answered as he rolled me on my side and pulled my leg up, exposing my ass. He twisted the cap off the other object—a small squeeze bottle—and squished some clear thick liquid into one hand. My heart pounded fiercely in my chest. I felt my blood pumping away in my ears as his lubricated, rough, construction-worker fingers worked their way along my ass crack, circling around the entry point.

"George," I moaned as his index finger began to dig away at my virgin hole, the cold lubricant quickly warming up with my body heat.

"It's all right, baby. I'll go slow." Even still, when his finger slipped past my sphincter, I hissed and clamped down on my butt muscles. He kissed my shoulder and withdrew the finger, waiting for me to relax again. I nodded or groaned or something; then his finger was back at my hole. He slid in a bit farther, and I didn't tense as much this time. "That's it, Tony—you're doin' great," he whispered as his finger penetrated to the second knuckle.

When he drew it out, I glanced over my shoulder. "No, keep it in there!" The presence of his finger in my ass felt...*really* good. George chuckled and said not to worry; I understood why a second later. Before his finger popped out, he reversed direction, thrusting back inside me, right up to the last knuckle this time. I cried out at the intense feeling, even as he withdrew his digit again, to repeat the action. "Oh my God, oh my God!" I heard myself saying as he continued to plunge into me with his lubed index finger.

"Want to try a second finger?" he asked, pausing mid-thrust. I nodded, and he withdrew completely. As he applied lube to his middle finger, I shamelessly rocked my hips into him, wanting to feel him inside me again. He laughed and obliged, and after a moment's discomfort, he was back at it with twice the girth.

I think I lost track of time for a bit because, the next thing I remember, he'd removed his fingers to apply lube yet again. I craned my head around, and there it was. The masterpiece my mouth had so often tasted in the park and my fingers had so frequently caressed in the front seat of his Matador. George had slathered lube all over his erect dick until it glistened in the morning light of my room. *Damn, it's big*, I thought. He must have seen something in my eyes, because he reached for the second little bottle.

"Take a deep sniff. It'll make things feel even better," he said. I shrugged and took a breath of the fumes from the proffered bottle.

"Smells like bananas," I said, wondering what it was supposed to do.

"Really? I always thought it was more like apples," George replied, taking a sniff for himself. The bottle disappeared. He leaned close to give me a kiss on the lips, and we both focused on his dick again. It sunk between my ass cheeks, pushing firmly against my hole. "Take a deep breath and push out, baby," he instructed. I did that, even as a warm rush filled my head.

"Wow," I muttered at the sudden chemical high. He nodded and pushed. His cock forced its way past my hole. I focused on not tensing up; the light-headedness I felt seemed to help. His rod filled me up, never seeming to end, and I found myself wiggling for more of him.

"Easy, easy, baby. Just let your ass get used to it first." A few breathless moments later, he was finally rocking back and forth inside me, and it felt amazing. I can only describe it as a mix between intense pleasure and deep pain—a pain I wanted more and more of.

George collapsed on me, flattening me to the mattress, and intensified his rocking. I shoved my head into my pillow and screamed wordlessly in exceeding ecstasy and in delightful pain. "Is this what you wanted, baby?" he said hoarsely in my ear.

Without thinking, I lifted my head and yelled out, "Yes! Yes! Fuck me, George, please fuck me!"

My cries seemed to urge him on; his thrusts intensified, and he moaned rhythmically, saying, "Give me that ass, baby—give me that ass." He rode me hard, slamming into my boy butt skillfully. My bed squealed and rocked like never before, but my cries and his moans were all I heard. It was like heaven and hell had gotten mixed up: feeling so good I couldn't take it, hurting so bad, needing it to never end.

Like a gunshot, George shouted out my name, exploding inside me. His dick throbbed deep in my ass; I rocked my hips toward him, squeezing on his piece with my sphincter, not wanting to let him go. As my butt shoved back and forth onto him, my erection scraped across the sheets of my bed; before I had a chance to control it, I erupted just as George had seconds before, spraying my lava across the creases of my sheets. Never had I come with something in my ass before—the sensation was out of this world.

Exhausted, we lay there: George on top of me, his softening cock still deep inside my teenage ass, and me, spread-eagled, not caring that I lay in the sticky remnants of our lovemaking. Both of us were panting softly, lost in a postcoital glow, unable to utter a word.

Eventually, I stirred as he whispered in my ear, "Are you all right?" I half groaned, half laughed, nodding my head in confirmation. "Was it everything you had hoped it would be?" I nodded a second time, letting myself drift off yet again.

When he finally rolled off me, reality (in the form of a cooling sticky mix of sweat, lube, and lovemaking) asserted itself.

"Eww. I need a washcloth."

"Why, 'cause of this?" George asked, collecting some of the wet cum off my backside and wiping it on my cheek. I swatted at him, grossed out, but he narrowly avoided the swing, rolling off the bed.

("That's disgusting," Karen muttered with a shiver, seemingly unimpressed with that part of Antonio's story. My piece was throbbing painfully in my pants—it obviously felt otherwise.)

After washing up in the bathroom, George wrapped his arms around me and asked, "Are you ready for you turn?"

"My turn for what?"

"Did you think I was going to let you sit there and have all the fun today? I want that Italian sausage inside me!" He pointed to my dick. It twitched at the attention.

"Right now?" I usually recovered quickly, but that first orgasm had left me spent. Even with my teenage endurance, I wasn't sure I was ready. Luckily, neither was George.

"Ha! No, not right now. How about you get me some orange juice and a sandwich? *Then* I'll be ready to take you on!" The mention of food triggered my own appetite.

"You got yourself a sandwich!" I sprang from the bed. "Oh." I stopped at the doorway to my room. "What kind?"

"How about ham and cheese?"

I danced around the kitchen like a fuckin' bitch in heat. I made two sandwiches and filled two tall glasses with OJ. If Mom asked why I drank all her juice, I'd tell her I needed the vitamin C to recover from my cold.

I loaded everything onto the tray we'd used for Dad back when he first came home after his injury. As I was about to pick everything up, the phone rang. I glanced at the kitchen clock: it was 11:30. Even a half hour late, I knew it was Mom.

Anyway, I was glad she called late; a half hour earlier and she would have totally blown the moment. I answered the phone with my sickest "*hello?*"

"Hey, baby. Are you feeling any better?"

"Yeah, Ma," I replied.

"You don't sound any better; why don't I come home? I'll make you soup."

"No!" I blurted in a not-so-sick voice. I cringed at the silence that filled the line for a good five seconds.

"Okay, then. There's some Campbell's soup in the cupboard if you get hungry. Remember to turn the stove off when you're done."

"Oh, by the way, Ma"—back in my sick voice—"I finished off the orange juice."

"That's okay, baby. I'll bring some more home for you. See you this afternoon?"

"See you, Ma."

"Love you, baby; hope you're feeling better soon."

"Love you too, Ma." I hung up before she could add anything else.

Mom's caring voice messed with me. I didn't like lying to her. I snapped back to the present when I heard George call out.

"What happened to my sandwich? I'm dying of hunger in here!"

"Don't die before I get my turn!" I grabbed the tray and balanced it, heading toward my room. I walked into my bedroom, kicking the door shut behind me with my bare heel. George lay spread-eagled on my bed, hands laced behind his head. *I have my own personal god, right there*, I thought, getting hard at the sight of him. A sheet covered one leg to his waist; the foot of his other leg dangled off my mattress. I carefully set the tray on the bed beside his leg, handing him his plate. He was about to take the first bite of his sandwich when he caught me staring. He withdrew it quickly.

"Is there something wrong with my sandwich?" He turned it back and forth, eyeing it closely. "Did you poison it?" I laughed.

"Nah." I took a bit of my own sandwich, smiling as I chewed. He snatched it out of my hand, passing his sandwich to me. I shrugged and ate his instead. He winked, digging into mine.

Over the next half hour, we talked and laughed as if we were the only people in the world. It was a nice feeling. I could have stayed in bed for the rest of my life, being near him.

Our conversation, disappointingly, shifted to less pleasant topics. George informed me it would be hard to see him during Christmas holiday. His wife wanted him to spend time working around their house, fixing things he'd been putting off for months.

I told him I understood. Deep down, though, I wished he were free and single with no obligations other than keeping me sexed. It was a nice fantasy. The reality was I needed to be content with what I had. We finished our lunch, and I set the tray and glasses on the chair next to the bed.

I settled beside him, and we started back into slow, gentle lovemaking. After a few minutes of kissing and rubbing our bodies together, I rotated around into my favorite position: 69. Over the summer I'd learned how to use my mouth and tongue to really get George fired up. In no time at all, I had him moaning and groaning and shoving his cock down my throat.

I pulled off him without warning. He looked at me with smoky eyes.

"What's wrong?"

"Get on your hands and knees," I ordered. A wide grin broke out on his face.

"Sure thing, boss." He got into position, passing me the lubricant. "Go easy on me to start; been a while since I bottomed."

It was my turn to explore his ass, and what an exploration it was. I placed the lubricant on my finger as he did and began to rub it through the forest of hair that lay between me and my quest for "manhood." I found my target and shoved my finger into his hole. With that came a gasp of pain.

"Whoa, boy! Go easy!"

"Sorry!" I exclaimed. "I'm new at this, you know?"

"I know. Go *slow*," he reiterated. I withdrew my finger and tried again, slower this time. I pulled out almost all the way, then sunk in again, a bit deeper. I loosened him this way until it felt like I was pushing into a warm peach pie. I added a second finger and, after a bit, a third. I knew I was doing it right when he moaned, much the way I did when he was sucking me off. George's moaning was deeper, though—more resonant. Like a real man in heat.

Withdrawing my fingers, I grabbed for the bottle I'd taken a sniff from, tossing it to him. He took a deep draw and offered it back to me. Again, I held it to my nose, breathing deeply. From the other bottle, I squeezed out some lube and worked it all over my throbbing cock. He knew the game; he was ready.

I shuffled closer, pushing my erection through that bushy crack, seeking the entry point. Lubed up as we both were, it didn't take much searching. The head of my cock penetrated an inch into George's hole, drawing a moan of pleasure from him. I pulled back, then pushed into him a bit harder. I repeated this, each time sinking deeper and deeper into his man-hole.

The chemical rush overtook my body as I plunged into him, right down to the root of my cock. We sighed together as I bottomed out. His ass was warm and juicy, and I had a sudden vision of a kid riding a pony.

"Oh, yeah—take all of me inside you," a voice said, full of lust. *My* voice! I hadn't consciously said those words—they must have come from some deep instinct I'd held inside until now.

George was eager to oblige. "Fuck me, Tony, fuck me!" He pushed his ass into my crotch, my dick digging a bit deeper into that dark, hot place. "Yes, that's it—you're in me so deep! I love you inside me like that! Go on, fuck me, now, Tony!"

Hearing him call my name with such lust, looking down at our joined bodies—I nearly came again on the spot. I squeezed, like when I needed to stop peeing, willing myself to cool down a bit. After a few seconds, I leaned over his back, wrapping one arm around his stomach.

And then I fucked him.

I pulled out and thrust back in, throwing the weight of my hips into it. George screamed but didn't stop me. I rode that pony. Harder and harder I thrust into him. He moaned and screamed my name, clenching his butt muscles tight around my cock as I invaded the depths of his hole.

Neither one of us heard the jingling of keys in the front door.

(*"Oh shit!" Karen blurted. "I know where this is going." Antonio just nodded, a sad, resigned look on his face. I ached for my friend, even as my Jimmy ached from his story.*)

I knew I wouldn't last long, riding him like that, with his sphincter clenching around my dick. I felt my climax build even from that first thrust. My second orgasm of the day washed over me, like water bursting through a dam. I exploded powerfully inside him, my cock twitching out of control. Beneath me, George laughed and cried—from the sudden pulsating of his ass, I knew he was busting his nut across my bedsheets.

We both were heaving and panting heavily, drenched in sweat, when my bedroom door burst open. I spun my head about, coming face-to-face with my father. "Mad" didn't begin to describe his expression. He looked from me to George and back again. His hand clenched into a fist.

"What. The. Fuck. Is going on in my house?" He took one step forward. George swore beneath me. Dad looked at George again, blinking. "*You*!? What—" He shook his head, his eyebrows drawn together. "No. NO. You fuckin' faggot. You dirty fuckin' queer! What have you done to my son!?" His teeth were clenched, as were his fists. My dick slid out from between George's ass cheeks, shrunken and shriveled in mortal fear.

"Dad," I breathed, not sure what else I might say.

"I'm gonna fuckin' kill you, you son of a bitch!" he said to George, ignoring me.

"*Dad*!" But words would not stop him. He lunged for the bed. I scrambled forward, placing myself between him and George. Dad slammed into my chest, and we both recoiled from each other's momentum. My legs tangled around George's and in the sticky bedsheet. Dad regained his balance and leaped toward George again. I propelled myself off the bed, wrapping my arms—still slick with sweat—around him, sending us both toppling to the floor.

Dad flipped me around, pinning me beneath him. "No son of mine is gonna be a faggot, you hear me? I'll kill you too, before you turn into one of *them*!" His fists began to pummel me.

I couldn't move—my feet were trapped on my bed, tightly wrapped in my bedsheet. I used my arms to protect my head as Dad hit me anywhere he could. "NO! SON! OF! MINE!" He cried, with tears of anger streaking down his cheeks.

George was there then, pulling Dad off me. Dad elbowed George in the gut, twisted around, and landed a punch in his neck. George gurgled in pain, stumbling out of reach.

I knew then that Dad wasn't joking. That punch had been meant to kill George.

"George, get out!" I yelled, grabbing at Dad's wrists. I was too wet with sweat, though; all I did was redirect his attention on me.

"No!" George said through a damaged windpipe. He held one hand to his throat, using the doorframe to pull himself up with the other.

"George, please!" I cried as Dad caught my jaw with a left hook. "You need to go, NOW!" Our eyes locked for a moment; he was broken with indecision.

"Antonio—" he croaked.

"I love you," I said. His face crumpled, tears bursting free from his eyes. "Now, GO!" I turned back to Dad. I had to give George time to get out. So I fought back.

I stopped trying to grab his wrists; instead, I showered him with my fists, mirroring the abuse he had poured onto me. Peripherally, I saw George grab his clothes and bolt out the room. I brought my knee up, catching Dad in the groin.

"Oof! You ungrateful fuckin' punk!" I used that moment to slide out from under him, trying to get to my feet. Out of nowhere, Dad's fist caught me under the chin, sending my head backward. Stars filled my vision. A door slammed somewhere in the house. *Good—George made it out!* I blacked out for a moment.

I regained my senses, finding myself lying on my back. Dad had gotten to his feet and was glaring down at me with utter hatred in his eyes. "First, boy, I'm gonna beat the *shit* out of you. I'm gonna make you bleeeeeed," he said, almost conversationally. "Then I'm gonna kill your faggot ass." He undid his belt, ripping it out from his pant loops.

I crab-crawled backward. *Gotta get away.*

He reached down, grabbing one of my ankles. I managed to kick free, but he snatched it again, holding on with his freakishly strong grip. His other hand rose behind him, belt grasped firmly.

I barely felt the first lash. The shock of the situation probably shielded me from it, as well as all the punches I'd endured. The second and third lashes stung. Real bad. I grunted, jerking this way and that, trying in vain to avoid the thick, cruel leather.

I won't cry! I held tightly to that thought; there was no way I'd give Dad the satisfaction.

With my free foot, I kicked at his grip, breaking free at last. I rolled to my feet, preparing to land a few punches. Before I could settle into a fighting stance, he slammed into me, sending me flying into my bedroom wall.

The room spun. Pain exploded from one side of my face as his fist drove into my skull. I slumped to the ground, straining to maintain consciousness. I heard footsteps fade away, then grow louder again.

Dad stood over me, one booted foot on either side of my prone form. Something cocked. I knew that sound well. He'd fetched his forty-five.

I canted my head back, unable to bring anything into focus. *I'm about to die*, I realized, not sure if I cared.

"You disrespect me, bringin' that shit into my home, boy? I'm gonna put a bullet through your head, you piece of faggot trash!" I jerked as I heard a deafening *bang*, waiting for death to take me. *Shouldn't it hurt?* I wondered, trying to decide if I'd felt the bullet go through my brain. Something heavy crashed down beside me. I thought it looked like Dad but couldn't be sure; things were getting muddier.

"Goddamn bastard, not my baby! I'll fuckin' kill you before I let you hurt my baby!" Mom cried out, something long hanging from her hand. *Carlos's baseball bat?* With that last thought, unconsciousness took me.

("Holy shit, Antonio. I'm so sorry," I said. I looked down at my hands; they were shaking. I wanted nothing more than to reach out and hit his father for saying those things, for hurting him the way he had.

"How can a father do those things to his child?" Karen asked. Her cheeks were stained with tears. "Oh, Antonio!" She sobbed, rushing to him. As she wrapped him in her embrace, Antonio and I shared a look over her shoulder. I shook my head, not trusting myself to say anything else. Karen collected herself, sniffling. "What happened next?")

★

Interval Three: Never Forget

I opened my eyes to a familiar face in an unfamiliar room. Mom sat in a chair next to my bed—a hospital bed, obviously. I smelled a strongly antiseptic scent with my first breath. Mom was flipping through a dog-eared issue of *McCall's*, not stopping on any one page for very long. Something alerted her to the fact I'd awoken, and she put the magazine on a side table.

She rose out of the chair and settled next to me on the bed. She took my hand in hers, stroking it gently. "If I'd known you getting sick was going to land you in hospital, I might have called ahead for a better room." I blinked up at her, giving a wan smile. She tried to return it but failed. "Oh, Antonio," she whispered, squeezing my hand.

As consciousness returned, so did my aches and pains. My head felt as if I'd been hit by a Mack truck. I brought my free hand up, finding most of my head wrapped in bandages.

"The doctor said you were lucky. You have hairline fractures in your skull and your spine. You could have lost—" Her words choked off there as her face crumpled. "Oh, my baby!" Tears poured down her cheeks. She kissed my hand, repeating "my baby" with each sob. I lay there, letting her settle, saying nothing.

"He said it will all heal fine, with time," she continued when she'd collected herself. She smiled and squeezed my hand again.

"Dad?" I managed to stutter. Her smile disappeared. She wiped each cheek with her free hand.

"Your father is in a coma again," she stated matter-of-factly.

"You hit him. With Carlos's bat." She nodded.

"Right as he pulled the trigger. Bullet went wide." Her eyes went distant for a moment. "The doctors are watching him, waiting to see if he'll come out of this one."

I knew with sinking certainty the bastard would wake up. I just knew it.

"I want him to die," I whispered, looking at Mom. I know she heard; I saw it in her eyes.

"You push all that out of your mind right now, Antonio." She straightened my sheets, tucking them under my chin. "When you're feeling stronger and are up and around...we'll talk." She gave me a brave smile. "For now, your ma's just happy she's got you back." She leaned down and kissed me on both cheeks, the way she had when putting me to bed when I was younger.

She rose and walked to the window. She placed her palms together, bowing her head. "Thank you, Jesus," she whispered, "for saving my baby. Thank you, thank you, Jesus." I closed my eyes and drifted to sleep.

I stayed in the hospital for a couple days until getting a clean bill of health.

I woke up during my second night there, aware of a shadowy figure in my room. It didn't look like Mom, and I panicked until it resolved itself into George. Still too doped up on medication, all I could do was reach out to him. His familiar rough fingers interlaced into mine, and he covered my face in kisses.

"I'm so glad you're alive, Tony!" he whispered. "I'm so sorry—I didn't mean for any of this to happen!" I nodded, clinging fiercely to his hand. His voice changed. "I…I can't see you anymore, Tony. But I wanted you to know…I love you too." His lips kissed mine, and he retrieved his hand and slipped away into the shadows.

(Karen was biting back tears. Admittedly, I had a lump in my throat too. I wondered if I felt as deeply for Angel as Antonio and George had clearly felt for each other. How would I feel to lose her under similar circumstances? I shied away from even considering it, feeling a new appreciation for what Antonio had suffered through.)

Mom and Carlos came to pick me up; we took the train and a taxi to get home. I tottered to my bedroom, pausing as I crossed the threshold. My bed was neatly made, and everything had been tidied up. No evidence remained of that day.

Mom followed me in, helping me undress and climb into bed. The doctor said I still needed rest for the injuries to my head. I didn't fight it; for the past few days, I'd been getting awful headaches that only got better if I slept.

I shut my eyes, willing myself to relax.

When I woke, Mom was making supper. Carlos came in, and we played checkers. He kept looking out the door and back to me. He obviously wanted to talk.

"What?" I asked, jumping one of his pieces.

"*What*, what?"

"What do you wanna know?" He looked out the door one last time, licking his lips. Then he leaned toward me conspiratorially.

"What the fuck happened between you and Dad?"

"What did Ma say?"

"She won't tell me hardly anything." Carlos moved a piece, putting it in danger of being taken. I didn't clue him in. "When I got home, there were police cars and an ambulance outside. Mrs. Ronoli was waiting on the street. She said Ma told her to bring me to her place until they all left." I jumped another of his pieces. He made no notice.

"When I came home later, your room…it was like a tornado had gone through!" He looked at me. I swallowed. "Ma said Dad tried to hurt you real bad."

"He came home drunk," I blurted, the story forming on my lips. "He beat me and shot at me with his gun."

"He's such an asshole. I hate him, Tony. I hope he never wakes up." My brother bit his lip, fighting tears.

"Yep," I replied, taking another one of his checkers pieces. "Looks like you still suck at this game too." He gave me the finger, our brotherly competitiveness lifting our moods.

Mom brought dinner into my room for us to eat. We chatted and laughed well into the night, even playing a couple board games we hadn't pulled out in years.

It was nice not having Dad there. I knew Ma and Carlos felt the same way.

I never really got into church, but that night, I prayed to God, wishing my father would never come home again.

As the days went on, Mom never once asked me about what had happened that day. I was thankful for that. I owed her my life, though, as well as an explanation…one day soon.

Christmas Day came quickly after that. Carlos and I were up early (as always), tearing away at our gifts. Santa (okay, Mom, actually—I'm not that naïve) always wrapped our presents in all sorts of different kinds of paper and bows: this year was no exception. The base of our tree looked like a picture from a fancy catalogue.

Mom woke up, made herself a cup of coffee, and sat, watching us go from gift to gift, ooohing and aahing. We were happy. We were relaxed. Unafraid to be goofy; unafraid to say the wrong thing. I couldn't remember a time like this ever in my life.

Then the phone rang.

I remember it was 7:30 a.m. Carlos and I had gotten ourselves cereal and were eating it on the living room floor, talking about our gifts. Mom was sitting in her chair, looking idly out the window.

Somehow, we knew it was the hospital. Mom answered. They told her we had to come right away. I hoped it was because he'd died. Of course, he hadn't. Dad had to ruin our special day.

When we arrived, the nurses told my mom that Dad was waking up. He was mumbling and moving his head but hadn't yet opened his eyes. The staff figured if he heard familiar voices, he might awaken fully from his coma.

We entered the room, hearing the strange mumblings we'd been told about. It wasn't words—only guttural sounds. They'd cranked his bed up so that he was seated. His eyes were shut, head lolling back and forth. I stood at the foot of his bed.

As if he knew I stood in front of him, his eyes popped open. Just like they do in scary movies. His muttering stopped. He stared right at me and uttered in a sinister voice these unforgettable words:

"My son, he became a 'man' today! And I had to kill his faggot ass for it!"

Then he turned to my mother and said, "You see, he fucked the joy right out of Christmas." He blinked slowly, then closed his eyes. They wouldn't open again until mid-January.

I stood there, not daring to move. I heard some shuffling of feet, though no one spoke, not the nurses or the doctor who'd come in with us.

The devil visited us that Christmas Day, speaking through Dad, and erased any joy of the season I'd ever feel again.

The doctors convinced us to wait around for most of the day to see if Dad would wake again. We wasted our whole Christmas sitting outside his fucking hospital room.

We returned home around 6:00 p.m. Mom fixed us a light supper—nothing like the Christmas dinner she'd had planned.

The day had devastated her. She cleaned our dishes and straightened the living room while my brother and I retreated to my room. We didn't speak a word about what Dad had said. No one dared.

When it was time for bed, Carlos went to his room, and Mom came to kiss me good night. She gave me a faraway look as I lay there in bed. "I don't know what the devil did to your dad for him to say those words...but ain't nobody, and I mean nobody, gonna ever hurt my babies. Not as long as Carol Lee Maybelle Johnson is alive."

She kissed my forehead and ran her smooth fingers across my face.

After Christmas, Ma started going to church on a regular basis.

Dad had never let her go while he'd been home. He'd always say, "There are more sinners in church than there are out. Why would you wanna give 'em yur time and money? I don't want you or my boys anywhere near yur nigger churches."

She didn't fight him; in return, he left her alone those Sunday mornings when she watched the Reverend Price on television.

She joined a Baptist church in North Philly, even convincing me and Carlos to attend every other Sunday.

As I said, it was mid-January when Dad woke again. This time he opened his eyes and became completely conscious. Strangely, though, he didn't speak a word. We'd been told this could happen. I was just sorry it hadn't happened the first time around.

Anyways, the doctors called, but Ma refused to go back to the hospital and refused to allow him back in our home. Granddaddy Johnson helped Ma pay for a lawyer, and as soon as they declared Dad well enough to be released from hospital, the lawyer made sure he was transferred behind bars until his trial for battery and attempted murder.

Before the trial, the lawyer had me tell him what had happened that day. I told him the same story I had told Carlos: Dad came home, drunk and angry. He just started to attack me and then got his gun out. After that, I didn't remember anything. The lawyer got a doctor to say I had some type of traumatic amnesia and had blocked the whole incident from my mind.

Because my dad never said anything in his defense, it was an open-and-shut case.

We attended the sentencing in June. As we sat in the courtroom, the judge looked at Dad and said, "Before I render my sentence, Mr. Savileo, is there anything you would like to say to this court?"

Of course, Dad chose that moment to speak, as clearly and plainly as he had that day in the hospital. He turned and stared at me.

"My son, he became a 'man' today! And I had to kill his faggot ass for it!"

He sought Mom out in the benches and added, "You see, Carol, he fucked the joy right out of Christmas."

The courtroom fell silent, just as everyone in that hospital room had months ago.

The judge arched his eyebrows. He broke the silence a few seconds later. "Antonio Nicolas Savileo, this court finds you guilty of attempted murder and reckless endangerment of your wife and children. It is the opinion of this court that you be sentenced to the maximum of twenty-five years in the state prison with no chance of parole."

As the judge's gavel struck the block, I jerked. Emotions swirled within me. I'd never endure his abuse ever again, but the truth of that day was still hidden from people who deserved to know it.

That evening the three of us prayed for a better life, now that the nightmare of living with Dad had ended. Ma told us we shouldn't hate him, and if we prayed, he might finally get the help he needed.

Later that night, after Carlos had gone to bed, Ma and I were sitting in the living room watching television. After our show ended, she walked over and turned the set off. She sat down next to me, and I felt her eyes on me.

"Antonio Lawrence Savileo, it's time you and I had a talk." I sighed, leaning my head on the sofa. I couldn't meet her gaze. "Now, I know what you told them lawyers, but I'm your mother, and I know you don't have any fancy illness that made you forget. So, I'm asking you, right here in the eyes of God, tell me what happened between you and your father." I squeezed my eyes shut, wishing I could be anywhere but there. *What do I say? Or, more importantly, where do I start?*

The beginning seemed like a good place.

"You know that park, Ma—the big one by the river?" Her eyes narrowed, but she nodded. "Well, I started biking around there last spring…"

Sentence by sentence, the story came out. It got easier as I went. I glossed over any sexual details; I knew Ma understood the gist of it, though, by how her shoulders slumped as the story progressed. I talked about how George and I spent more and more time together and how I invited him over that December day.

When I started to describe how Dad walked in and attacked us, my voice broke. I tried to finish, but the words stuck in my throat. Ma just nodded furiously, pulling me in close to her.

She laid my head between her enormous breasts and stroked my hair. "Oh, my sweet baby. Why the Good Lord has placed the burden of this lifestyle on you, I surely can't say. I never thought one of my boys would go through this." She grabbed me by the shoulders and straightened me up, forcing me to meet her eyes.

"But you listen, and listen well, Antonio: no matter where life takes you, God will never give you more than you can bear. I don't ever want you to be ashamed of who or what you are."

I nodded, blinking as my eyes blurred from tears. "I want you to make something of yourself," she continued, "and I don't ever want you to look back. Do you understand me?" I still couldn't get any words out, but I nodded. She pulled me in and held me tight.

I eventually told Carlos the story too—the summer before I left for Lincoln. He had trouble accepting I was gay then and didn't talk to me about it for months. He came around about a year ago. We still don't talk about it much now.

As for George, I returned to the park several times, hoping to see him again. He never showed.

As chance would have it, I spotted him with his family at a fireworks celebration in Center City this summer past. He was standing with his arm around a boy that must have been his son—who looked about my age. George had picked up a couple of pounds, but he still looked good. I don't think he saw me, and I didn't wait around for him to.

★

"So, there you have it, my Christmas story of mystery, intrigue, and drama, all wrapped up in a pretty holiday bow," Antonio said.

Karen, who had stayed by Antonio after hugging him earlier, embraced him again. I stood and walked over, wrapping them both in my arms. None of us said a word. We stayed there for a moment, silently supporting our friend.

"Okay, okay," Antonio said finally, swatting us away. "Go catch your bus or your train or whatever."

"Oh, hold on!" I exclaimed, remembering the gifts I still had. I retrieved the bag from the door and brought it to them.

I handed each of them their gift. "As per the instructions written on the box, do not open until Christmas, and I mean not a minute sooner." A thought popped into my head.

"Wait here, both of you. I gotta make a quick call."

Antonio rolled his eyes.

"Actually, I need to make one too," Karen declared with a thoughtful look. I darted out, not waiting for her, and raced downstairs to the dorm pay phones.

When I returned, I wasn't at all surprised to learn Karen and I had done the same thing: rescheduled our travel plans so we didn't have to leave until later in the evening.

We ganged up on Antonio, convincing him to let us go home with him that afternoon. We helped him pack and caught the bus to his place. His mom blinked with surprise when we all showed up at her door, but she invited us in warmly, adapting her supper plans to include an extra two places.

We met Carlos, too, when he got home from school. Both he and his mom seemed extra pleased Antonio had brought us home. I'm betting it had been a long while since he'd had friends over.

After a warm supper, Antonio's mom pulled out photo albums of the boys when they were younger. The Savileo living room grew loud with good-natured laughter that night, at both brothers' expense.

Finally, when Antonio had had enough, he corralled me and Karen out the front door. He rode the bus with us to Thirtieth Street Station. We hugged Karen tightly as we dropped her off at her gate. At my gate, Antonio struggled to hold back his tears. I hugged him, kissing him quickly on the cheek. We wished each other a Merry Christmas and I boarded my train.

★

Years later, Antonio revealed to me that our visit had been the first step toward him regaining his love of Christmas. I'm blessed to have had the chance to help my closest friend that night.

Part Three

The True Meaning of Friendship

Interlude Nine

A Generational Surprise; I'm Not Alone

Christmas vacation was three weeks of lounging around the house being spoiled. Momma had her baby boy home, relishing in the fact he was still alive and kicking—literally.

Christmas Day was the usual runaround: getting ready for all the relatives and accompanying brood of children who were about to descend upon our house for our yearly dinner and good ol' extended-family bonding. Momma and Dad spent the morning fussing over who was doing what. Nina and I spent time hiding household items we didn't want little hands meddling with.

Family started pouring in around two in the afternoon; the parade didn't stop until four. Passing through our front door was a steady stream of grandparents, aunts, uncles, cousins…and food!

Since this was my first semester at university, I got asked repeatedly the same set of college questions from all my long-lost relatives. (With each retelling, though, I left out the incident in the park. I was trying desperately to put it behind me, and a room full of well-meaning but nosy family members would not help with that.)

Everyone we expected had arrived and we were about to sit down to eat when there came a knock at the door. Dad gestured to me, and I went to see who it was. I opened the door to find a tall, handsomely dressed gentleman standing on my front step, with a big grin on his face. He looked like my dad, but I just couldn't place him.

As I looked closer, though, it hit me. A smile blazed across my face as I realized this was my uncle Cameron—Dad's younger brother, whom I hadn't seen in close to twelve years. "This is the Dawson residence, isn't it?"

I laughed. "Yes, it is!" I followed that with, "You're my uncle Cameron, aren't you?" He smiled even wider in reply.

"Yes, I am. But help me out here: you're not my little nephew Desmond, are you?"

"Yes, I am," I confirmed with a lopsided grin. Before I knew it, he'd grabbed my hand, shaking firmly. He looked me up and down, and I couldn't help doing the same. At that moment Mom came around the corner.

"Who is it, dear?" Before I had a chance to answer, her eyes lit up and she shrieked. "Camy!!" Momma flew into her brother-in-law's arms, hugging him fiercely. She stepped back and hit him on the chest. "Why didn't you let someone know you were going to be in town?" Without waiting for a response, she yelled into the family room, where Dad was tending the fireplace, "Cal, Cal!"

My dad rushed around the corner and his face lit up just as much as Momma's had. My parents rushed my uncle into the living room, where Nana, Pop-pop, and the rest of the family were gathered. Upon seeing her son, Nana screamed as loudly as Momma had.

You see, Uncle Cameron lived in France and rarely came to this side of the Atlantic. He's a professional model and an executive for *GQ* magazine's Paris division. His face and body can be seen monthly in their glossy pages. He's definitely the jet-setting uncle of our family.

As far as I knew, Cameron was single, with a passion for expensive cars, clothes, and women. Whenever we saw him on television, beautiful women always surrounded him. He's the uncle every nephew dreams of being. It was great having him here for Christmas. How long and where he'd stay was on everyone's minds.

We got through dinner with lots of laughs and old stories about Momma, Dad, and especially Uncle Camy. After opening gifts and sharing in Momma's eggnog and delicious desserts, it was time for most everyone to go on their way—doggy bags in tow.

Nina, Vinny, Nana, and I helped Momma clean up while Dad and Uncle Cameron continued to catch up on old times. Poppop napped in the recliner by the fire. As it got late, my mother popped the magic question.

"So, Camy, where are you staying, brother dear? Now, you'd better say *here* because I ain't listening to you say 'the Hilton' or 'the Sheraton,' all by yourself on Christmas night!"

"Why, of course I'd love to stay here, sis," Uncle Camy said with a twinkle in his eye. "If you have the room?"

"We've got a guest room with your name written on it; bed's already made!" Mom smiled. "As for me, I am turning in. It's been a long couple of days." She hugged and kissed each of us, then headed upstairs.

My siblings and I eventually headed toward our respective rooms while Dad and Uncle Camy continued to catch up. I was about to switch my light off when I got a yearning for another glass of eggnog. As I came down the stairs, I overheard a conversation through the open door of Dad's study.

"So, Camy, I've loved catching up on old times, but I know you better than that. Something is up; what is it?"

"C'mon Cal! Why would you think I was here for any other reason than to see my family?"

"Past history maybe?" A moment of silence fell, during which I didn't move a muscle.

"Okay, so I'm not here for just a visit. Is that what you wanted to hear?" I heard Uncle Camy sigh. "I needed some time away from Paris and everything happening there. Especially the mess I'm in right now."

"Is this something I'm going to need a drink for?" Dad asked.

"Probably. Fix me one too?" I heard the clinking of glasses—Dad was pouring two fingers of his favorite whiskey into crystal tumblers, no doubt.

"You are about to become an uncle," Camy said after they'd had time to take a first sip.

"I see. Who's the lucky woman?"

"Now that's where it gets a little sticky."

"It's always a little sticky, isn't it?" Dad retorted. Camy ignored him, carrying on with his explanation.

"It's a child that neither you nor I can afford to acknowledge."

"Oh, Camy…I'm afraid to even ask what that means," Dad said, taking an audible sip of drink.

"Well, big brother—it's not a pretty story."

"I am all ears and slowly losing patience."

"Okay," Camy said dramatically, "I'm doing the publisher's wife, and she got pregnant."

"The publisher of your magazine? Roberto Haver?" Dad's voice rose in frustration. "What the hell were you thinking? What was *she* thinking?"

"Oh, it gets better, I'm afraid. I am doing the old man too." There was an explosive sigh—Dad's, most likely.

"Shit, Camy! Have you fucking lost your mind?"

"I didn't think so at the time, but now I'm not so sure."

"How do you know the baby is yours and not his?"

"Because she told me. It's like this, Cal: Roberto and I got involved a couple of months before I started doing his wife. During this time, he told me he thought he was impotent. He just didn't get aroused when he was with his wife. But I guess that wasn't the case, 'cause he sure got real hard when he's with me. But he's kinda small."

"That's far too much information for me, Cameron."

"Sorry. Well, anyway, when we started our relationship, it ended up helping him at home, with his wife. Then I met *her* at a company party, and man, is she a looker!"

"Hooker? Did you say she's a *hooker?*" Dad's voice climbed an octave.

"No! Come on, Cal; I said looker, not hooker. Well, the day after that party, she invited me to the house for cocktails. I never assumed we'd be alone, so of course, I agreed. When I got there, she greeted me in this see-through negligee, with a black lace bra and G-string underneath. Believe me—when I saw this, I wanted to run."

"Oh, sure—I bet your Adidas were smoking from trying to run...*toward* the bedroom!" Dad chuckled at his own joke, taking another sip of whiskey.

"Well, anyways. It was pure heaven. She's like a cougar in bed, and afterward, we really clicked." Uncle Camy paused—likely taking his own sip. "I've juggled this husband and wife team for the last six months. It was challenging, but I was handling it.

"Then last month, Isabelle—that's her name—and I were having champagne and strawberries in bed, and she announces to me, '*Mon cheri*, you're going to be a papa. Isn't that wonderful?'" Camy's voice approximated a sexy French maid—doing a pretty fair job.

"I nearly choked on my strawberry, Cal, because earlier that week, I was relaxing with Roberto after sex on his yacht when he says to me, 'Isabelle is pregnant, and it isn't mine.' Of course, at the time, I didn't seriously think it was mine either—I figured Isabelle was playing the field. I asked him, 'What makes you think it's not yours?' and he says to me, '*Mon ami*, if you haven't noticed, I shoot nothing but blanks.' Cal—this whole thing is killing me!"

"*I'm* already dead, Camy—just bury me now," Dad said sardonically.

"So, anyways, I decided I needed a break. I told Roberto I wanted a long overdue vacation to the States. That's the best part of doing the big guy: as long as you're keeping him happy, you can have the world."

"Too much information again, Camy."

"Yeah, sorry. So, there you have it: an all-expenses-paid vacation for a month. Just long enough for him to miss me and expose his wife's infidelity."

Silence fell on the study, and I inched forward to peek in. Dad sat there with his hands over his mouth, his gaze far away. He rose and poured himself another glass of whiskey. Then he began lecturing. Oh—I knew this version of Dad very well. He went on and on lecturing his younger brother, as I'd heard him do to my own brother and as he'd done to me countless times before.

It wasn't my lecture, though, so I zoned it out—not a huge feat, considering how shocked I was from all I had heard. I sat down on the steps behind me, reviewing what Uncle Camy had revealed. *Wow, and I thought I was this freaky accident of nature…come to find out it's running rampant through the family!*

I heard Camy interrupt Dad's sermon with "I need a place to stay, big brother, until I can figure out what I'm going to do." Silence fell in the study again.

"A place to stay…" Dad sighed. "You know I can't say no to you. You can stay here—that way I can keep an eye on you!"

I peeked forward again to see the two brothers hugging and slapping each other's backs.

"You seem to always be there when I need you, bro."

"Indeed, I do. Millie and the kids will enjoy having you around. Just don't have any shit follow you here. You got me?"

I sensed the end of the conversation, easing back up the stairs before they could see me, eggnog forgotten.

I lay in the bed a few minutes later, staring at the dark ceiling. *I wonder how long Uncle Camy has led this dual life? Am I destined to be like him? Could I even talk to him about what I'm going though?* Reality set in and I decided it would be best for all of us if I kept this part of my life a secret for a while longer.

★

Christmas vacation also included spending time with Angel.

Over the term, she and I had continued to bond through phone calls and letters in the mail, which only took a few days to go back and forth. I wrote to her every other day, even if nothing more than a couple lines. I loved getting hers because there would always be a brand-new poem written in each one.

As well as everything else she excelled at, Angel aspired to be a poet. Her poetry was beautiful. She had a way of capturing thoughts, and as you read it, you instantly understood the message within.

They say sons marry women like their mothers. Angel, beyond a doubt, had the characteristics I loved most about Momma, but she was her own woman too. As we shared more and more of our dreams, thoughts, and desires (even if it was long-distance), I grew to know what a truly strong and caring person I had found.

Angel and I made plans to spend Christmas Eve and the first day of Kwanzaa together. We decided not to try to do Christmas Day between houses, figuring this would overly complicate things.

I went over to Angel's place on Christmas Eve, and we exchanged gifts. The night before Christmas was a big deal in her house; that's when they opened their gifts. Her family spent Christmas morning in church, then went over to her grandmother's house. Coming from a close-knit family myself, I understood the pressures upon her to follow tradition.

The day after Christmas, I took her to breakfast at a local diner; then we caught a midmorning train into New York City. Angel loved to simply walk and window-shop. We walked from the Christmas displays at Macy's and Gimbels straight up town to Rockefeller Center in time enough to see the tree light up at dusk.

I loved being with this young woman. We still had so much to share despite having spoken and written to each other all term long. It was just better in person. I found it very easy to be totally honest with her too. And so, at one point during the day, I broke down and told her about the guys in the park—the whole unedited version. Angel didn't ask a single question; she just hugged me. "I'm so glad you're safe."

I wanted desperately to know what she thought about these feelings I had for men, but I didn't want to drive her away either.

Back home, my dad began calling Angel "the mystery woman," as he had yet to meet her. I checked with Momma, then invited Angel to dinner that Friday night. Being my mom's baby boy, I knew she'd pull out all the stops for me—and did she ever. Dad and Vinny spent the days leading up to Friday teasing me and play-punching me in the shoulder, dumb shit like that. As for Nina, she couldn't figure out what all the fuss was about.

I managed to completely avoid our house guest that week. However, I knew Uncle Camy would be at dinner that Friday, and I wasn't sure how I felt about that. I don't know why, but after his conversation with Dad on Christmas night, my uncle gave me the willies.

I picked Angel up on Friday afternoon and warned her to expect the unexpected. I knew everyone would want a piece of her. Sure enough, Dad took her off my arm the minute we walked through the door, relegating me to the kitchen to help Momma.

When we sat down to dinner, I suffered through being the brunt of Vinny's jokes. Angel laughed along with him but came to my defense too. Beautifully poised, entertaining, and funny, she really was the whole package.

After supper, Angel, Nina, and I did dishes, talking about recent movies and music. Clearly, my sister was really taken by her, just as my folks were.

But something else happened beneath the surface of Angel's debut. Throughout the evening, I felt Uncle Camy's eyes on me. I tried very hard to play it off, but it annoyed the fuck out of me.

Nevertheless, it turned out to be a great night at the Dawson house. Princess Angel had come and conquered the royal Dawson family.

On the way to her house, she and I decided to stop for a walk along the beach. We were having an unseasonably warm December that year—it was well into the sixties. As we strolled arm in arm, we didn't say much. I think we were both reflecting on how the evening had gone. We stopped at a bench, and finally Angel spoke.

She started by telling me about the family she dreamed about having. As I listened to her, I discovered I wanted exactly what she wanted. What's more, I realized I was falling in love with her.

And, from out of nowhere, I popped the question.

I took Angel's hand and knelt on one knee, right there on that December boardwalk.

"Look, Angel, you may not think this is the time; damn, I'm sure you're probably not even ready to be asked a question of this magnitude, but baby, I know what I feel is true and I know what I have to do. Angelique Janelle Ferris, will you marry me? Not today, not tomorrow, but when you are ready to.

"I want you to know I'll never lie to you, 'cause I would never want you to have a reason not to trust me. I will be your champion, loving and protecting you till death do us part. I want to have children with you, a little girl with a big smile and pigtails, as beautiful and charming as her mother. And if it's okay with you, I want a little boy who is just as awkward, smart, and quirky as his dad.

"Angel, baby, I'm madly in love with you, and I can't think of anyone else I'd rather spend my old and gray years with. I await your answer, my beautiful African princess."

Angel raised me up to the bench next to her and took a short pause before she gave her reply.

"Desmond Cameron Dawson, I would love to marry you, when you are truly ready to have me and *just* me. I have never felt so comfortable with a brother or his family as I do with you and yours. But I listen to *everything* people tell me, even when they are not using words.

"Yes, I know you are madly in love with me because I am just as crazy in love with you. However, there is another life-style calling you, and that's an issue I never want to come between our love. With that said, I want you to take the time you need to explore that lifestyle and resolve your feelings about it. Likewise, there are issues I need to resolve within my life too.

"We both have work to do before we come to this point. But I'm *not* rejecting you, my prince. I will marry you if—after you go through what you must go through—you come back to me as straight and truthful as you are tonight."

I reached out, took her by the shoulders, and drew her lips to mine. I kissed her passionately to seal our pact. I drove her home, turned the car off in her driveway, and held her in my arms as we listened to Jean Carne and Dexter Wansel on the radio. I wanted this feeling to last forever. I escorted her to her front door; she reached up and kissed me good night.

"I love you, Desmond Dawson," she whispered, slipping inside her house.

I drove home feeling euphoric. I'd found my soulmate! I explored my feelings, realizing that it wasn't at all about sex or lust with Angel—it was about the person she was and what we meant to each other.

When I arrived home sometime after midnight, I figured everyone had gone to bed. I headed for the refrigerator for another helping of Momma's peach cobbler and a scoop of Breyers Vanilla Bean ice cream. As I pulled the cobbler out and kicked the door shut, I jerked, finding my uncle standing right in front of me.

"Shit! Uncle Camy, I thought everyone was asleep!"

"Sorry, my boy—I didn't mean to startle you. I couldn't sleep. I decided to come downstairs for a nightcap; I was in your dad's study when I heard you come in."

"You want some?" I extended the dish of cobbler to him, trying to cover my discomfort. "It's the best peach cobbler on the East Coast!"

"No thank you. I think I stuffed myself to the limit tonight."

I went about making myself a bowl while he sat down on a stool and watched me.

"That's a very nice young lady you have there," he began after a minute of silence between us.

"Thank you," I said simply.

"The good ones are hard to find. I hope you hold on to her for a while."

"I'm way ahead of you, Unc."

"I'm just saying, Desmond—don't be like me. Here I am, thirty-eight years old, knocking on forty, and I'm still looking for the right woman." I nodded but couldn't help thinking, *Well, if you didn't fuck everything with a slit or a dick, maybe you'd have found her.*

"I'm sure, with the number of women you know, Uncle Camy, there's got to be at least one good one in the bunch?" I smiled at him, and he gave a small chuckle. Silence fell for another minute; then he spoke again.

"Look, Desmond—your mother, sister, and I have just about worn New York and Philadelphia out this past week. I don't think we've missed a single fashion show or specialty boutique, along with eating ourselves silly at every hot spot in both cities! I was wondering if you and I could spend a bit of time together. I want a chance to get to know my nephew a little better."

I replied through a mouthful of cobbler and ice cream. "Sure. When did you have in mind?"

"Well, you tell me; I don't want to steal any time from that beautiful young lady of yours." *There'd be no chance of that,* I thought.

"Well, Angel's due back at school the start of next week. Maybe we could spend some time then."

"I'd really like that." There was a lilt to his voice that spoke of additional layers to what he'd said. What those layers were, exactly, I couldn't figure out. He yawned and stood up. "I'll let you finish your dessert and you let me know when exactly you'd like to bond, okay?"

"Sounds good, Unc. Good night." I watched his back as he retreated into the dark house. *Man, did that feel weird.*

I didn't quite know how to deal with how Uncle Camy made me feel. I was sure of one thing, though—I wasn't going to let it affect the rest of the time I had with Angel. I'd deal with him after she'd gone back to school.

On New Year's Eve, Momma, Dad, Vinny, and Uncle Camy attended a black-tie affair in New York City. Camy—being a famous male model—always got invited to big designer parties. This particular one was by Halston, and Momma was very excited to be going.

On one of their excursions to the Big Apple, Nina, Momma, and Camy found this breathtaking white gown with very fine beads all over, cut low front and back, and with a very sexy split up the side—very "Ebony Fashion Fair." Camy had insisted Momma buy it for the party, and she looked absolutely stunning.

Nina had a couple of her girlfriends at the house that night for a sleepover. To their great dismay, Angel and I were to be their chaperones for the evening. We made out pretty well; Nina and her friends baked chocolate chip cookies and pop-corn, making sure to pass us a share to keep us from nosing in on their slumber party activities.

Angel and I settled on the sofa in the family room, playing chess and watching Dick Clark on the television. One of the things I most liked about Angel was the fact that we never argued. Sure, we disagreed about things, but we never raised our voices or fought. We said what we had to say and that was it.

That evening also brought us to the discussion of sex. Well, *I* brought us to it by doing the "man thing" and asking *when*. Angel, in turn, did the "woman thing" and said when she was ready, I would know. She had more to add, though.

"Look, Desmond, I love you more than words can describe, honey, but I won't be one of your many conquests. When you come to me, I want to be the only one, your till-death-do-us-part one. When that time comes, I will do for you whatever it takes to keep my man satisfied. I hope you will do the same for me."

"You can count on that, baby!"

We brought the New Year in with a toast and a heated petting romp in my room, away from teenaged-girl ears. Around one in the morning, I woke Nina and told her I was taking Angel home. I got back right before Vinny, my folks, and Uncle Camy arrived home. Momma and I had a late-night drink and gossiped about who she'd rubbed shoulders with at the party.

During the last few days Angel had before going back to school, we hung out at each other's house or went shopping. Momma and Dad were back to work, Nina kept busy with her friends, and Vinny had gone back to law school. Angel and I bumped into Uncle Camy periodically around the house, and he even took us to lunch one day.

Angel left on a dreary Sunday, which dropped me into a deep depression. I missed her fiercely, and it hadn't even been a day. I had another week at home to wallow in my loneliness. Surprisingly—or maybe not—Uncle Camy came to my rescue.

The Tuesday after Angel left, I wandered into the kitchen, thinking everyone was out of the house. But there was Uncle Camy, perched on a stool, enjoying a cup of coffee and a newspaper. As I poured myself a cup, he looked over at me and said, "So, how can I put you out of your misery during the duration of your time home? You're my last victim." I smirked and got myself some cereal. He tried again. "Your parents told me they have a membership to a private health club. Would you mind taking me? That's if you're not too busy?"

I thought for a moment, then nodded. *Maybe that's what I need—a good workout and some time in the sauna.* "Okay. Sounds like a plan, Unc. Give me a few minutes to eat and get dressed, then we'll go."

The club was about a ten-minute drive from our place. Except for a couple senior citizens, we were the only ones there. I jumped on a treadmill for twenty minutes, lifted some weights for a bit, and played a game of handball with Uncle Camy. I learned he was a very competitive player; he gave me a run for my money. Game point went back and forth until out of nowhere he made this incredible hit that had me flying across the floor, missing the ball and landing on top of him.

We both laughed so hard I thought my sides would burst. That's when I became aware that I was lying on top of his tight, sweaty body. For a random instant, I thought to myself how very comfortable it felt being on top of him. In a quick flash of eye contact, I knew Camy felt the same way. I broke our gaze and quickly rolled off him. We lay there, side by side, breathing heavily for a minute or so. I rolled to my feet and fetched the ball.

"You wanna hit the dry sauna?" I asked, avoiding eye contact.

"That sounds heavenly."

As we undressed, I continued to avoid looking in his direction. As soon as I was ready, I grabbed my towel and made a beeline for the sauna. Sitting in the sauna, I rested my head against the wall and closed my eyes. The door opened a few moments later, and I cracked one eyelid open to see my uncle stroll in. Uncle Camy had a bodybuilder's physique. He stood in front of me, removed his towel, and proceeded to lie down on the bench beside mine, closing his eyes. I couldn't help staring at his well-sculpted body lying next to me.

His eyes snapped open, catching me in the act of gazing at him from his torso to his thick thighs. I shut my lids tightly but knew I'd been found out. Camy cleared his throat.

"So, have you acted on these feelings, or are you just a voyeur?"

"Wh…what? What do you mean?" I stuttered.

"Are we going to pretend you don't have feelings for men?" he asked simply. I didn't know what to do, so I jumped up and bolted. I was in and out of the shower before Camy emerged from the sauna. By the time *he* had showered and dried off, I'd dressed and rushed outside, only then realizing I had nowhere else to run, seeing as I was his ride home.

I watched him exit the gym and walk toward the car, praying he would drop the whole matter. *Yeah, no such luck.*

"So, is this going to be the extent of our outing?" He settled into the passenger seat beside me. "Me, asking invasive questions; you, avoiding answering them?"

I avoided answering him.

"Okay." Uncle Camy sighed, gazing out the front windshield. "Can we do lunch, then?"

"Will there be further interrogations? Should I contact my lawyer?" I hated how petty I sounded.

"Oooh, you've got a bit of diva in you! That's good."

"I think we've done enough bonding for one day, thank you. Can I just take you home?"

"Look, Desmond, I'm not trying to pry into your life, but I wouldn't be a very good uncle or godfather if I didn't speak to you about a thing I know a lot about." I felt his eyes on me, but I couldn't bring myself to meet them. "Listen: if it will help knock down that brick wall of yours, I want you to know that I'm bisexual. There, I'm outed."

Well, that's old news. I found that out a week ago. Aloud, I said, "Is that supposed to shock or impress me?"

"I'm not doing such a hot job of reaching you, am I?"

"Nope! I can't say you are!"

"Do you know I would have died and gone to heaven if I'd had an older man to talk to at your age about the shit I was feeling and going through? *Damn*, I couldn't even bring myself to talk to your father—my only brother—until my late twenties. Even then, he wouldn't tolerate any details." Camy rubbed a hand over his head. "Can't you see, Desmond—I only want to be there for you! What do you say—can we call a truce and go have some lunch and talk?"

I reflected for a moment. *It would be nice to get some things off my chest*, I realized. "Okay, look—I really don't like people I barely know and who equally know nothing about me in my business. Likewise, I certainly don't need a snitch reporting back to my parents. So, here are your choices: what I say to you stays between us. If I find out it's gone further, you can forget about ever talking to me again in this lifetime." I looked him straight in the eye, holding my gaze steady until he nodded.

"You've got yourself a deal." We shook hands and drove to the Blue Lagoon Diner for lunch.

While I ate, Uncle Camy talked. Eventually, I worked up the nerve to add in my own experiences. Once the seal had been broken, you couldn't shut me up. I held nothing back. We swapped stories back and forth for the rest of lunch.

Toward the end, I started to gain an appreciation for what Camy was doing for me. By opening up to me, he'd laid the groundwork for me to open up to him. Now that I felt comfortable and safe talking to him, a great weight lifted from my shoulders.

From that day until the end of break, he and I spent most daylight hours together, doing anything that caught our fancy and talking the whole time. The day I left to go back to school, Uncle Camy rode down with us. Right before they turned around to head home, he got me alone in my dorm room for a moment. He predicted something for me that I would never forget, up until the very moment it came to fruition.

"Desmond, once you go all the way—and I don't mean the petting and mutual relief parties you've been having—once you fuck or are fucked by another man, your sexual and emotional life will never be the same again. So be sure it's what you want before you take that dive.

"I love you, nephew. If you ever need to talk, you have my number; call collect. I'll be there for you." We hugged and I thanked him for everything. We walked down the stairs and to the car where everyone waited. He smiled, winked, and climbed into the car. I waved goodbye, not realizing I'd be seeing him again in a few months.

And, sure enough, Uncle Camy was true to his word about being there for me. Every time I reached out to him by phone, he was there for me, guiding me through some pretty tough situations.

Interlude Ten

Roses Are Red...

The first evening the whole group was back together, we met up in Karen's room to share our holiday stories. I told them about my uncle Camy showing up and how we'd enjoyed a bonding of like souls. I explained my apprehension and fear of being called out and how he had laid those fears to rest.

Antonio started by thanking Karen and me for putting Christmas back on the map for him and his family. After we left that evening before the break, he and his mother had a long talk about what went down with his father, about Antonio's lifestyle, and about his issues around Christmas. His mother admitted she'd blamed herself for not leaving his father before it got as bad as it did.

Afterward, Antonio, his mother, and his brother pledged to heal the hurt in their home and bring back the Christmas they remembered and loved so fondly.

We learned that Phillip's mother had reentered rehab and he would not be returning for the spring semester. He had spoken to Brian over the holiday and was pretty torn up about the situation. He'd come to the realization that—as the oldest child—he'd have to get a job and look after his brothers and sisters.

Karen waited until we were all done relating our stories, then dropped a bombshell.

She'd been tutoring this football jock named Melvin throughout the fall term. He'd met her in a shared English course and told her if he didn't maintain a C average, he would lose his scholarship and possibly be put out of school. He begged Karen to tutor him, and she reluctantly agreed.

Surprisingly, after about a month, they found they had a lot in common. He would invite her to his games and she, in turn, would drag us along.

It seemed that on Christmas Eve, Karen received two dozen mixed red and white roses and a card that read, "To My Temple Sweetheart: roses are red and white, and I love to gaze into those eyes that sparkle like the stars at night. The last few months we have spent together have made me realize I want you to be my sweetheart forever."

The girls screamed and snapped their fingers upon hearing this news; Karen screamed along with them. She told us how she and her new guy had spent every waking moment together for the remainder of the holiday.

Melvin Weston was a linebacker for the Temple Wolves. Apparently, he was a damn good ballplayer: big and mean looking, but gentle on the inside. Seeing him and Karen together, you could understand why they just clicked. He gave her room to be her bossy self, and she waited on him hand and foot.

The rest of us reasoned it was only a matter of time before Karen and Melvin acknowledged what we had already figured out.

After we talked ourselves dry, we proceeded to play ump-teen games of spades before calling it a night. Brian and I walked to our rooms together. Before dropping me off at my door, he popped the question.

It seemed since Phillip wasn't to return this term, the school had given his spot in the dorm to another freshman starting that winter semester. Brian's new roommate was a white guy from Virginia named Barry Leamen.

"You want to swap rooms, Desmond? Be my roommate?" Believe me—I jumped at the opportunity!

The next day Brian and I talked to Kyle, who in turn talked to the director of housing and swung the move for us. It didn't take us long to move "Leave It to Beaver" and "Dennis the Menace" together into my room and me into Brian's. This was perfect. Being here placed me around the corner from Karen and just below Antonio's room.

Brian and I didn't have as much in common as Phillip and he did, but we related on a spiritual level. He went home to go to church every weekend, depending on what we were doing as a group. He had asked me several times during the fall if I wanted to go with him to West Chester, but because of every-thing that had happened—what with my courses and the trial—I wasn't able to find the time.

This term, though, I had no legitimate excuse. Plus, I felt as if I needed a spiritual element back in my life. So, the last Sunday in January, I decided I would go with him.

Second semester a bunch of us decided to take a journal-ism class together—the first of many shared courses within our majors. Karen's new beau was in the course with us; the two of them were like glue, pressed together hip to hip. And, believe me, they both had hips for days.

Another new face joined the group. Jean Claude Lefebvre hailed from Quebec, and like Antonio, he was an interesting mix of cultures.

That first day, we all had lunch together with the new guy, at Antonio's insistence (which was weird because most of the time Antonio couldn't be bothered with people outside our group). It didn't take much to figure out there was something going on there. I observed the two of them during class and at lunch. They had their own private conversation going on without a word spoken between them.

Jean Claude (or JC, as he quickly became to us) told us during that first lunch that his father was Black and his mother was from France. They had met during the Second World War when his father had been over there fighting as a young private in the Canadian army. His father's family was part of a community of ex-slaves that had migrated to Eastern Canada right after the Civil War.

We also learned that JC enjoyed running and cycling; Antonio quickly invited him to join us for our daily run.

It was near the end of lunch that we discovered what I'm thinking Antonio had been hoping from the start. JC became very quiet, looking down at his plate. Something was wrong, and as usual, our resident mother, Karen, noticed.

"What's up?"

He raised his head and looked at each of us in turn. "Does anyone have a problem with me being gay?" A spray of soda came flying across the table as Antonio choked and gasped for air.

"That one's our resident queer, JC," Karen said calmly, gesturing toward Antonio, "or should I say our resident drama queen." We all fell out laughing. "You can see what *he* thinks of that."

To which Antonio replied (once he'd wiped his face), "And she's the neighborhood bitch! Welcome to the inner circle, JC; you're in good company here."

What caught my attention during the entire exchange was the look on Melvin's face. I had a suspicion Karen hadn't told him Antonio's preference for men. To be confronted with a second openly pronounced queer; well, let's just say Melvin looked like he'd eaten something nasty.

We finished our lunches and headed out. Antonio paired up with JC; I knew Antonio was preparing to move in for the kill.

After that first day of school, we met up again for supper. I was waiting in the dorm lobby when Antonio and Karen walked up together. I knew by the look on Antonio's face he was quite satisfied with himself—I could only imagine why. To the contrary, Karen was noticeably upset. As we set out, Antonio seized the moment to pluck her nerves. "What's up with you, PMBT (premenstrual bitch 'tude)?"

"It's personal, asshole."

"There's nothing personal about any of us, dear. The look on your face is an open letter of distress; spill your guts, bitch!" Surprising both of us, Karen erupted into tears, right there on the street.

"Melvin and I had a huge fight," she explained between sobs.

"If all you had was a fight and you have no visible signs of scarring—discounting the fact that maybe he's all scarred up— count your blessings, baby. Believe me, there are many more fishermen where that one came from. All you gotta do is spread your legs and let them get a whiff of that fish thang." Antonio pantomimed the act he was recommending. "Real menfolk can smell that scent for miles. They'll come running from all directions, trust me. Let's eat. Oh, no pun intended, dear."

Karen just gave him the finger, crying some more. Clearly, Antonio wasn't helping the situation. "All right, Antonio, crazy glue your lips and let Karen tell us what happened," I said.

She wiped her face and began to talk with a shuddering breath. "Right after we left from lunch, Melvin got all quiet on me. He didn't say anything all the way to class. Normally, I can't get him to shut up. So, I asked him what was wrong." She sniffled. "At first, he said nothing, and maybe I shouldn't have pressed him. But you know me—I can't let anything go, so I kept at him until he finally broke.

"He asked if I had any other friends who were gay. Jokingly I said, 'In the closet or out?' Well, he got angry and started yelling. He said, 'Are all your fucking friends faggots?'

"I was so shocked I didn't say anything for a few seconds. Then I said, 'One or two maybe, but what's that got to do with anything?'"

Antonio interrupted her. "Oh, baby. It's time to drop that motherfucker; he sounds like a real homophobic dick to me." I shot a look in Antonio's direction; he had the good sense to play-zipper his mouth. Karen wiped at the tears that continued to flow, her words starting to tumble over one another.

"He started yelling at me, calling me a fag hag. He told me if I wanted to continue to date him, I'd have to get rid of the fairy squad. Then he stormed off. I was so upset I ran back to the dorm. I didn't go to any of my classes this afternoon—I just couldn't!"

I put my arms around her and held her as she erupted in a fresh round of sobs. Antonio couldn't resist, blurting out, "Well, fuck him if he can't take a joke; he wasn't that good of a catch anyway."

Karen wheeled around from my chest and fired back.

"You've got all the answers, don't you, Antonio? I guess your philosophy is fuck 'em and leave 'em, ya HO! I'm surprised your dick hasn't fallen off from overwork!"

"Oh no you didn't, bitch!" Antonio said as he twisted his neck, clearly about to start in on a bitch war. I stepped between them, giving Antonio yet another stink eye.

"Pull your claws in, tigree, and shut the fuck up please; this is serious, so act accordingly." He looked around me and sneered at Karen, who gave him the finger again. "Now look, you two, I'm not a cat fighter but I can pretend." I raised my hands like claws and started to make hissing sounds at both of them. They looked at me like I'd lost my head. But it had served its purpose—for a moment no one spoke. "There we go. Okay, you two—kiss and make up, then go back to your respective corners."

Happily, they both decided to back down, because I wasn't sure what my next move would have been. I needn't have worried. To Karen's and my great surprise, Antonio apologized.

"You know, we're not used to seeing you so vulnerable, girlfriend. I'm sorry—I thought poking some fun at you would loosen you up. I guess I was wrong. You're falling in love with this jerk, aren't you?"

"I won't admit to that, but I really do like him a lot," Karen said. "But why does he have to be such a dickhead?"

"Look, Karen," Antonio explained. "Most people aren't as comfortable as you are, dealing with gay guys. Damn—most of them would like to see us dead. Like my dad."

"I know. But I thought Melvin was different. He seemed so sensitive and down to earth. He isn't like most guys I've known. He's considerate, kind, and gentle."

"Oh, yeah, the gentle giant," Antonio sneered.

"Look," I cut in, hoping to stave off yet another yelling match, "I think if you give him time, he'll come around."

"For once in his life, Desmond has a point," Antonio said. "Look, if he cares about you, he'll come to his senses and apologize. You can take that to the bank."

"Thanks, guys; I hope you're right."

"So, now can we go eat?" Antonio asked, gesturing to the cafeteria. He and I put our arms around Karen and escorted her in.

During dinner, we managed to cheer Karen up some more. I worried, though, that as soon as she got to her room, she was going to fall to pieces again. Sending Antonio on his way, I convinced her to go for a walk with me around campus. It was my turn to call her out. "Karen, there's more to this than you are admitting, isn't there?"

"What makes you say that?"

"I know when my friends are in trouble. It has become my specialty." She rolled her eyes at that, but then made an admission.

"Antonio called me on it, but I couldn't bring myself to admit it…" She paused, the tears beginning to fall. "It's true, Desmond—I'm in love with Melvin! There, I said it! And I know what you're going to say!"

"I'm not sure you do," I countered. "But go on, finish what you were going to say."

Interlude Eleven

Karen's Story

I've had plenty of brothers hit and score on me. I've learned, well, how to hide my true feelings. I've learned, too, that being a pretty, voluptuous "big girl," not many men take me seriously. A lot of them will give me play just to rock my ass, and I know this.

And if it looked good to me, I went along with it. If it was less than adequate, I sent them packing. But it still hurts when you finally lower your guard and let one of those no-good motherfuckers in.

(Karen's words began to crumble as she started sobbing again. I guided her to a bench and held her until she got herself back together.)

There was this guy, Peter Miller; he was my first love. I was a sophomore and he was a senior. He was on the wrestling squad—all big and handsome. I never thought he knew I was alive. But one day he stopped me after geometry. He needed better grades in order to stay on the team and graduate. Same old story: I understood all the theorems, angles, and shit, and he didn't.

He was one smooth operator. He came up to me at lunch after class and asked if he could sit with me. Believe it or not, I was pretty shy back then; I couldn't believe he was talking to me, much less asking to eat lunch with me. He chatted, told jokes, and made me feel good. He worked for over a week tearing my barriers down. Then he asked me if I would help him in geometry. I was so happy to have someone like Peter Miller paying attention to me that I would have done pretty much anything for him at that point.

We never met up in school; instead, we went to his house or the public library's private community room. His mom was very sweet and always treated me nicely. This went on for all of wrestling season and straight through to February. I went to all his matches and watched him wrestle, but never talked to him there. He didn't want anyone to know a sophomore tutored him, so we kept our "relationship" on the down low.

It made me jealous to see all those senior girls hanging all over him in the hall and at his matches. But I *knew* I meant more to him than they did. He told me things when we were alone—some of his innermost secrets—and I shared mine with him.

One day during our tutoring session, Peter's mother had to take his younger brother to the doctor and left us there by ourselves. I didn't think anything of it, because he had always been a perfect gentleman when we were together. About twenty minutes after she had gone, he offered me a soda and invited me up to his room to show off his numerous athletic awards.

In his room, I was reading the plaques on the wall when he turned on his stereo and moved up behind me. I began to get very nervous and uncomfortable. I turned to him and suggested we go downstairs and finish our homework. He reached up and started to rub my shoulders. I wanted to push him away and run down the stairs straight out of his house. But a tiny part of me wanted him to go even further.

I started to pull away, but he firmly held my shoulders and drew me closer to him. Before I could react, he leaned down and kissed me on the lips. I jerked away in surprise. He smiled. "No one has ever kissed you before, have they?" I thought about it for a second.

"Yeah, my dad has." He laughed at this and I glared at him, asking what was so funny. He took me gently by the shoulders again.

"I meant, no other boy."

I admitted that, no, I hadn't been kissed. He pulled me in closer again and started kissing me once more. This time I didn't pull away. I put my arms around his muscular shoulders. I was French-kissing—for the first time in my life! His tongue explored the inside of my mouth and I welcomed it openly. We stood wrapped around each other for what seemed like hours. My body began to yearn for more, but in my mind, I was a *good* girl. And good girls weren't supposed to be tempted by boys. Certainly not while unchaperoned in their room.

Peter stopped kissing me and grabbed my hand. He led me to his bed. I pulled back, deciding to draw the line. He looked at me questioningly.

"Are you okay?" I looked into his dreamy milk-chocolate eyes, wanting very much for this to be okay, wanting to join him on his bed. Somehow, though, the good girl in me prevailed.

"I can't do this with you."

"Do what?" he asked.

"I can't sleep with you."

He smiled at me. "I don't want you to."

"Then why are you trying to get me in your bed?"

He looked into my eyes. "I thought we would be more comfortable there."

"That's okay; I'm comfortable right where we are," I insisted.

He resumed kissing me again and my legs immediately got all wobbly. He started to guide me toward his bed again, but the good girl was now firmly in charge. I pushed him onto his mattress, turned tail, and ran. I stopped long enough to grab my coat before escaping from his house. I heard him calling, but I didn't stop running until I made it home.

I ran up to my room, not even stopping to talk to my mother. I locked myself in and lay in bed amongst my stuffed animals. What had happened at his house kept going around and around in my head.

About an hour later I heard the doorbell ring. I jumped up and ran to my door to listen. I heard Peter's voice and my body began to tremble. A few moments later my mother knocked on my door. "Karen? Karen, baby?" she called.

"Yes, Mom?" I answered faintly.

"Are you all right, honey?"

"…Yes."

"That was Peter. He dropped your books off. He said you forgot them at his house." I opened the door slowly and looked out. "Are you sure you're all right, baby? Did something happen? Do you want to talk about it?"

"No, Mom. I'm just a little tired."

She kissed me on the forehead and told me to wash up for dinner. I was very quiet at dinner and went to bed immediately after. My dad came up later that evening after he got in from work and sat next to me. As he ran his finger across my cheek, I awoke.

"Hey there, baby bear, I missed my hug and kiss when I got in. Are you feeling okay?"

"Yes, Daddy." I hugged him tightly, overcome suddenly with emotion. He hugged me back, not saying a word. When I finally let go, he said, "Wow, I haven't gotten one of those in a long time. Are you sure there isn't anything you want to talk about?" I shook my head and lay down, acting as if I was going back to sleep. He stroked my cheek again, leaned down, and kissed me. "I'm here if you need to talk, baby bear." I yawned and nodded.

When he walked out and closed the door, I hugged my favorite bear just as tightly until I fell into an unsettled slumber.

The next morning, I woke early, showered, dressed, and was eating breakfast by the time my parents came down for their morning coffee. My mother felt my head and cheek. "Well, you're not warm." She searched my face for an explanation of my mood. I gave her a look she and I had shared regularly over the past few years. She sucked in a breath and said, "Oh, I understand." She looked at Daddy and winked. Even though my period *was* coming on, it wasn't what was wrong with me. But I was glad it gave me an out. I finished my breakfast, kissed my parents, and went on my way.

That day, I did everything in my power to avoid Peter. I didn't fully understand why—embarrassment maybe; a fear of what I felt about him perhaps; some intuition that needed listening to? I just knew there was more to him than I could put my finger on.

When I saw him coming in one direction, I went the opposite way. During our geometry class, I wouldn't look at him. Right after school, I packed up my books and set off across the school grounds without looking back. I thought, *Okay, I made it through the day. Maybe he'll just leave me alone and find someone else to tutor him.*

I was almost off school property when, from behind a tree, Peter popped out and had me blocked. He grabbed me by the shoulders—as he had done in his room—holding me securely in front of him.

"Let me go! I… I…" I found myself not able to finish my sentence.

He looked me straight in the eyes and said, "Or you'll *what?*"

"I've got to go home! My mother is waiting for me; we have to go to church this afternoon!"

"I don't believe you. I think you're afraid to face me and afraid of your feelings for me. So, I'm not going anywhere until you tell me why you keep running away from me."

By this time my stomach had tied itself in knots, and I could hardly breathe. Then I just let it all come out. "Look, Peter, I don't know what type of game you are playing, but I'm not the one."

He let me go, running his hand over his head. "So you think I'm playing some type of game, do you? Are you so insecure that you believe I couldn't actually be attracted to you?" He gave me a look of utter confusion. I bet he'd never had a girl reject him before.

"No! I don't believe you're interested in me. I think you figured I was going to be so taken in by the great *Peter Miller persona* that you could slip into my pants and I'd be grateful for it. Well, forget it! I may not be as experienced as those other girls you date, but I'm not stupid!"

He turned away from me, just as quickly turning back. "I thought you were different. I thought you really saw me for me, and not that I was just some stupid jock. If you don't think any better of me, then I guess you really didn't know me after all." It looked as if he was about to cry.

I'd misjudged him. *Really* misjudged him. Maybe what I thought was a play to reel me in as another one of his trophies was actually a sincere attempt to take our relationship to another level.

He continued, "Look, Karen—if all I am to you is just someone you feel sorry for and you tutor me out of pity, then don't bother; I'll find someone else. Maybe there isn't a real person under that brain after all. Maybe what everyone says is true; maybe the only thing you are capable of loving is your books!" He gave a bitter shake of his head and stormed away.

Had I really just hurt the one person outside of my family who really loved me for myself? I felt a pit in the bottom of my stomach. "Peter!" I ran after him, grabbing at his arm. "Please stop! I'm sorry! I was positive you were only using me! I was afraid of how you made me feel when you kissed me yesterday. And if I hadn't left when I did, I wouldn't have been able to control myself!" I laid it all out there for him, explaining feelings that I, myself, had only now become aware of.

And yet, he still looked hurt and rejected.

"What can I do to make it up to you?"

He stared at me with those sad, chocolate eyes and asked, "Do you really mean that?"

"Yes!"

He got a faraway look for a moment before saying, "Do you think you can just be my friend and help me through geometry…and let things take their course?" I smiled, relieved beyond imagining.

"Yes! I can do that!" We both laughed; then he leaned in and kissed me right there on the street where everyone could see him. I was on cloud nine and rising.

For the next two weeks, things were great. Our work sessions took on a totally different flavor. He spent most of the time staring and smiling at me while I tried to stuff some knowledge into that thick skull of his. I knew I was falling in love with what I *thought* was the first sincere boy I had ever met.

The senior prom was coming up in six weeks, and I expected Peter to ask me. I imagined in bed at night what we would look like out on the dance floor. I even fantasized about him being crowned king and me being crowned his queen of the prom. (The only problem was that the queen of the senior prom had to be a *senior*.)

Still, even after several weeks, he didn't seem to want our relationship out there where his friends could see it. He said they'd hassle him about dating a sophomore, and he didn't want to have to punch someone's lights out for insulting me. And at the time, I was okay with that.

We made out on a regular basis after that afternoon. I was sure I was going to lose my virginity to him the night of the prom. But when was he going to ask me? Didn't he know a girl needed some time to prepare for such an event? I decided if he didn't ask me four weeks before the date, I would come right out and ask him myself.

Surprisingly, on the Wednesday four weeks before the prom, he asked me if I would meet him at a party being thrown by one of the varsity cheerleaders that coming Saturday. Finally, I'd be recognized by his friends as his main squeeze. I shrieked with excitement, not wondering why he wouldn't just pick me up so we could go together. But I didn't care. I was about to become a part of the in-crowd, something I have always dreamed about.

My mother was happy to hear I was getting out of the house on a Saturday night. She always nagged me about staying home and studying all the time. Not that she didn't think studying was important, because good grades and education were number one in our house. I guess she was glad to see me going out for a change.

All day Friday I was a nervous wreck. I couldn't focus on school; I was so excited about going and worried about what to wear. My friends thought I'd lost my mind. Now, I hadn't actually told them about where I was going or that Peter and I were a thing. I wouldn't tell them now, because I wanted the big reveal to take place at the party, guaranteeing everyone would be talking about it on Monday: that I, Karen Stewart, was Peter Miller's main squeeze.

Peter and his boyz had business that afternoon, so we weren't getting together. He kissed me at one of our secret make-out spots and told me how much he was looking forward to Saturday night. I imagined he was excited because he was also going to ask me to the prom while at the party.

As I left school, one of my classmates stopped me. Trevor Gilson was someone I rarely talked to, but I knew he was one of the smartest boys in the sophomore class. He told me he needed to talk to me in private. I couldn't understand why he didn't tell me right there, but he'd always seemed harmless, so I let him walk me to the public library.

On the way there, we passed by a park. He asked me if I minded if we sat down so he could tell me what was on his mind. I agreed. He seemed really nervous, so I asked him if everything was all right. Truth was, he was beginning to scare me.

"No, Karen, everything is not all right. In fact, I have something very serious to tell you."

"Okay, well, tell me already!" I urged.

Trevor inhaled deeply, then began. "I have a gym class with Peter and a couple of the other wrestling guys."

"Okay…" I said, a slight tingling crawling up my spine at the mention of Peter. *Why would Trevor be talking to me about him?*

"We were all in the locker room today—I stood on one side of the lockers; Peter and his crew were on the other. I'm guessing they didn't know I was there, or maybe they didn't care."

"Care about what?"

"I overheard them talking about the party tomorrow night. Peter was telling his buddies that he was going to win the bet."

I grew tired with all this and stood up. "Look, I don't know why you think I care about what Peter Miller and his friends have to say in the locker room. It really isn't any of my business, and if all you got me out here to do is gossip, then I'm not interested."

Trevor jumped up and blurted, "The bet was about you!"

I froze, my heart suddenly beating really fast. "What did you say?"

"The bet was about you." Trevor dropped his eyes to the ground.

I sat back down onto the bench, urging him to tell me more. It seems Peter and his teammates had this wager that he couldn't fuck anything but airheaded girls. He'd bet each of them twenty-five dollars that he could bed a smart girl and even get her to fall in love with him. Part of the dare was that he would go all the way with her before the senior prom.

"You're the mark, Karen—the smart girl he's chosen to sleep with to win his bet. It's all going down tomorrow at LaRonda's party. Her parents are out of town for the weekend. There's gonna be alcohol and weed at the party… Peter said he was even gonna bring a date-rape drug to make sure you don't back out at the last minute."

We sat facing each other in silence for the better part of a minute. Part of me didn't want to believe a word Trevor was saying. I wanted so desperately to call him a liar. But another part of me had put the pieces together long before this and had been waiting for some confirmation of my suspicions. Yeah, I *knew* Trevor was telling me the truth.

Tears started streaming down my face; seeing this, Trevor reached for my hand. I jerked it away, though, unwilling to accept his pity.

"I know you have no reason to believe me, but I couldn't let them hurt you."

"Why not?" I asked him. "You don't even know me. Why would you even care?"

Trevor blinked; it was his turn to look as if he were about to cry. "I'm gay, Karen. The guys in the locker room suspect it and always find some way of making my life a living hell. I just...I didn't want to see a nice person like you get hurt, the way they've hurt me." Admitting his secret to me must have been too much for him; he shot to his feet and started to walk off.

"Trevor!" I barked, stopping him in his tracks. I gestured for him to come back and sit, softening my voice. "You didn't have to tell me what they've done to you. I've seen and heard what his friends do to people like us. I've told Peter how mean his friends are. He made me believe he wasn't like them."

As I said that, the tears we'd been holding back now rolled freely down our faces. He pulled a hanky out of his pocket, offering it to me. "Here, I think you need this." I looked at it and raised an eyebrow. He chuckled through his tears. "Don't worry—it's clean. My mom gives me a fresh one every day." I thanked him, wiped my face, and started to cry some more.

After our tears had subsided, reality set in. "What am I going to do?" I mused. "I feel like such a fool." Trevor opened his arms to me, and I leaned into his chest. His empathy unleashed another round of tears.

"Well, crying about it isn't going to solve anything. Girl—you need a plan, and if you need some help, I'm in. It's about time that crew got a taste of their own medicine."

I squinted at him. "What can I do to get back at them?"

He lifted my face with his hand and asked, "How adventurous are you?"

"What did you have in mind?"

Trevor told me how he'd had a crush on Peter since grade school. The two boys had played together as young neighbors, slept in the same bed at sleepovers, and were the best of friends for a while in middle school. When Peter was in ninth grade, he finally worked up the courage to tell Peter about his feelings for him...and another secret he'd told no one else.

"I told him I'm an intersexual."

"Interested in sex, yeah—I got that," I replied.

"No—I'm intersexual."

"What's that?"

"I have both sets of equipment," he replied, pointing to his crotch. I took a moment to process this. A word popped into my head.

"You're a...*hermaphrodite*?"

"They don't call us that anymore," Trevor replied testily.

"Oh. Sorry. I didn't know."

"That's okay. Anyways, I told Peter this. He called me 'queer' and told me never to come close to him again. He started telling everyone I was gay, and he led with constant harassment from that day forward." Trevor's eyes narrowed. "I've been waiting for a moment like this for *years*."

His plan was simple: I was to go to the party and play along right up to the part where Peter took me to a room for sex. I had to make sure I watched for when Peter slipped the ecstasy in my drink, then distract him while switching my drink with his, making sure *he* was the duped one instead of me.

I was to let him think I'd let him fuck me and follow him into a dark room, where I'd switch spots with Trevor.

Coincidentally, Trevor and I had a lot in common—he was a big boy, we both had short curly hair, and we were the same size, right down to our breasts. Trevor would bring his Polaroid camera that I would use to take pictures after I switched spots with him.

Once Trevor was in the bed with Peter, I'd flip on the lights and take as many pictures as I could. I'd then scream so that people would come running, especially his friends. They would catch Peter in bed with Trevor, and our revenge would be complete.

"It's a pretty risky plan," I said. "You stand to get hurt if things don't work out in our favor."

"Honey, there's nothing more they can do to me that would hurt more than what they already have. Plus, it's time for me to lose my virginity…and who better to lose it with! I don't care what people think—after graduation, I'm outta here." It was public knowledge around town that Trevor was gay (though no one knew about him being intersex, likely due to Peter not really understanding what Trevor had told him); after graduation, he planned to leave for a life in San Francisco, where his type was more accepted.

We shook hands, and I hugged him for being so brave. It felt right. We weren't only doing this for our honor; we were doing this to send a message to bullies and snakes like Peter.

Saturday night came, and everything went according to plan. I arrived at the appointed hour, dropping Trevor off in some bushes nearby. As the party became more and more crowded, he slipped in totally unnoticed.

Peter—high as a kite—was all over me, like Trevor told me he would be. I watched him like a hawk out of the corner of one eye and witnessed him slip the pill into my second bottle of beer as he brought it to me. I'd already "drank" one beer (I'd poured it out in the bathroom and filled it with water) and was acting like the drunk girlfriend.

After passing me the spiked beer, he gestured for me to follow him. He led me upstairs, shouting over his shoulder he wanted a bit more privacy. I caught the signal he gave his friend we passed on the stairwell, chuckling to myself.

We came to a corridor with five closed doors along it. We checked the first two rooms, finding them occupied—couples going at it hot and heavy inside. The third room turned out to be empty, and we slipped inside.

Peter walked up to the bed, set his drink on the nightstand, and attacked me with kisses. A minute or so into his mauling of me, I pushed him off and suggested we have some more beer. He agreed wholeheartedly, and I quickly snatched at his beer on the small table. He was already so high he never saw me switch his drink with mine.

We clinked bottles—"Bottoms up!" he declared—and we set to chugging our drinks. Or, at least, *he* did. He didn't notice I wasn't actually drinking at all; he was so busy trying to finish his and get back to business.

As he swallowed the last swig, I took his bottle, set both of them back on the side table, and suggested he take his shirt off. He absolutely relished the thought. As he began to fumble drunkenly with his shirt, I dashed over and cracked the door open. Trevor had been waiting (he'd followed us) and slipped in discreetly. He passed me the camera, then tiptoed farther into the room.

I switched the light off, plunging the room into almost total darkness. Peter grunted, and I quickly explained I was taking my clothes off, but I wanted it dark. He snorted an affirmative from inside his shirt, and I whispered to Trevor to remove his own clothes as my eyes adjusted to the dim light.

"Oh, baby!" Peter moaned, still yanking at his shirt. "I'm so drunk right now! Take 'em off quick—I'm hard and in the mood!" In any other circumstance, I would have slapped a guy silly for talking to me like that; instead, I gestured at the dark silhouette of the disrobed Trevor to climb onto the other side of the bed.

Peter sensed the movement of Trevor sitting down and went in for the kill.

I saw their two black silhouettes become one and heard them kissing passionately. *I hope this is everything Trevor dreamed of and more—it's a one-shot deal!*

Fifteen minutes into their lovemaking, I heard voices at the door whispering, *"This is the room!"* At this point, Peter was breathing heavy and thrusting away on top of Trevor. The door opened slowly, and a guy's hand appeared, fumbling for the switch. The moment light flooded the room, I started snapping pictures.

Peter had Trevor's legs in the air and was fucking him, with both of them panting in ecstasy. Trevor had on some sort of underwear that held his penis flat but exposed his vagina. Peter blinked over at his buddies by the door and chuckled. Obviously, he'd been expecting them. Trevor grabbed Peter's head, pulling it down for one last kiss. What a perfect picture.

Peter and his cronies made the horrific realization of who he was in bed with in the very next moment. It was as if they'd stumbled upon a plague victim. Peter shrieked, rearing backward, hiding his quickly deflating dick behind both hands. His friends started yelling and cursing in dismay, retching and staggering backward, even as Trevor quickly and subtly covered himself up with the bedsheet.

I cackled in delight, still unnoticed off to one side, snapping picture after picture, catching a good one of Peter covering his withered manhood, yelling *"NO!!!"*

All the ruckus had attracted attention; a gaggle of people had come to the door, jeering and laughing. Finally, Trevor rose up, bedsheet wrapped about him under his armpits. He leaned toward a dazed and drunken Peter, stealing a final kiss from his cheek. He turned to the crowd gathered at the door and declared in a loud voice, "He's a great kisser…but what a *small* dick!"

Peals of scandalized laughter rang through the room as Trevor and I—arm in arm—made our escape, not stopping until we'd slipped outside to the dark street. With nothing but the sheet wrapped around him, Trevor started the car and off we went. An hour later, when we finally crashed (me in my bed; him on the floor of my bedroom), we were still laughing.

"What was it like?" I couldn't help but ask as we both started to drift off.

"Incredible," came Trevor's immediate response. Then he added, "I wonder what it would be like the other way…"

"The other way?"

"Yeah. Both parts work, you know," he explained. I blinked in the darkness. It wasn't something I could even imagine.

That Monday, as I predicted, the gossip chain was hot.

Worried about Trevor's safety, I kept a close eye on him all day. Sure enough, right before lunch, he was at his locker when Peter and his buddies cornered him. They slammed his locker door shut and Peter got right up in his face.

"I'm gonna fuck your ass up, Trevor!"

"Well, you already did," Trevor replied, leaning toward Peter and whispering in his ear. "But that wasn't my ass." He winked at Peter, who snarled and reared back to slug him. At that point I rushed in, getting between both boys.

"If you lay a hand on him or bother him anymore this year, Peter, I'll go public with the pictures," I threatened.

"What the fuck are you talking about, Karen?" Peter said, taking a single step backward.

"That's right—back the fuck up, brother. You see I'm not as naïve as you and your buddies thought. I knew all along you had other intentions, and the shit blew up in your face. So, if I were you, I'd let it go, 'cause I have Polaroids: you and Trevor fucking; you and him French-kissing; your buddies cheering the two of you on. Here's two for proof."

I flipped open my notebook and there, in full color, was one of Peter fucking Trevor, whose legs were up in the air, and another with Trevor's legs wrapped tightly around Peter's torso. Both pictures showed Peter's and Trevor's faces clearly, and on one, you could see the faces of the same buddies who stood beside him now, smiling and cheering. They all leaned in to get a good look, backing away and looking a bit sickly when they recognized themselves.

"So, what'll it be, partners? Fuck with either one of us and I will go to your folks and the coach with the whole story. Who wants to put their college scholarships on the line?"

Peter looked me in the eye with pure hatred. "You think you're slick, bitch? All I need to do is take those pictures and fuck your fat ass up. Then what will you have?"

"You know something? You really are a dumb fuck. I liked these pictures so much I made duplicates, which are safe at home right now!" I threw my head back and laughed, then got serious again. "The next time you make a bet, you'd better be sure it's one you can win." A crowd had gathered as we talked. "And, by the way," I said, addressing Peter *and* the crowd, "Trevor's right: your dick is so small it wouldn't have even made me break out in a sweat." That brought a round of laughter from all the girls who'd hovered around us.

"You better watch your back, you fat dumb bitch!" Peter snarled, even as he pushed at his partners to back off.

"Ooh, I'm *really* scared, you tiny-dicked punk!" I felt a hand on my shoulder. I turned to see Trevor's face lit up with a wide, happy smile. The girls around me slapped me five as they went on their way, saying "Way to go, girl!" We had done it. I hugged Trevor and told him he had a real friend for life.

Peter and I never spoke again. Trevor told me they would pass by him and sneer, but they never did anything. I found out later that all the girls he'd duped into having sex had shunned him like a leper from that day forward. He didn't go to his senior prom, likely realizing his reputation had been ruined. He had gotten everything he deserved.

As for me, I became a new person after that experience. I lost my virginity my senior year on *my* terms, and I had no regrets. Matter of fact, the brother I chose packed a magnum and he knew how to use it. The only thing missing from that relationship was love. Sure, I liked him and all, but I didn't feel any more than that.

★

Looking back, I realized Peter's lines and moves were intended to draw me in to his ultimate plan. My desire to be loved by a man other than my dad blinded me. What's clear then and now is it was all about making me another notch on his belt. When I was with Peter it was always about what he wanted, when he wanted it. My inclination was to keep him pleased and he would always want me.

"Melvin, on the other hand, is different," Karen explained, bringing us to the present. "He is a simple and sincere type of guy. He respects my opinion on things. He's not afraid to reel me in when I occasionally lose it. And he's not afraid to admit when he's wrong. His Southern charm is as real as it comes. We love doing things to please each other. He's gotten into my mind, and I can't get him out.

"I didn't think he knew my body existed until Christmas vacation, but now that he has"—Karen gulped, turning several shades of red—"let's just say he is *very* passionate…and so caring! He goes out of his way to make me happy in bed. He does so much to make me feel good. Oh, Desmond, I just *know* he's a keeper!

"And I don't want to lose him over his inability to see people for who they are instead of what they are. I know he's got to work through this, but I want him to do it with me instead of without!"

I nodded, realizing I was seeing a new side of my friend. "Have faith, Karen. I know what it means to be in love. If it's right, he'll come around. You wait and see."

We finished our walk, returning to the dorms well after it had gotten dark. I kissed Karen on the cheek and walked with her down the hall to her room. I knew her next couple of days were going to be tearful... If Melvin *didn't* come around, I was worried Karen would put up a wall that would be next to impossible for the next man to break down.

I hoped her instincts were right about this one.

Interlude Twelve

One for All and All for One

The next day came and went, and Melvin totally ignored Karen's existence. Each class they had together, he totally blew her off. She became more despondent as the week went on. Our attempts to get her to forget him failed miserably.

Antonio wanted to catch the brother in a dark corner of campus and beat his ass. He kept saying, "A good ass whooping would do that boy some good! Lemme at him!" I wholeheartedly agreed with him but knew that wouldn't help Karen.

Two weeks went by without any movement from either side. Karen would cry herself to sleep at night, and Melvin studiously avoided us. I tried several times on my own to talk to him—when he wasn't with his football buddies—but he wouldn't give me the time of day.

The following week, Antonio got a lead. He'd met this football player who was on the down low, getting some from guys in the baths in town. A friend of Antonio's hooked the two of them up. The football player—after learning he and Antonio went to the same school—panicked and made a deal to tell Antonio what he wanted to know in exchange for not outing him.

A day later the guy told Antonio what he'd found out. It seems this guy and Melvin were teammates, so it was natural for him to ask Melvin about Karen. Antonio learned exactly what we were hoping to find out: Melvin was miserable without her. He was having trouble eating and sleeping. Melvin even told his teammate Karen was the type of girl he wanted to marry and have a family with someday.

"I showed him an extra good time as a thank-you," Antonio let me know at lunch the next day. "That's the last time I'll see him, though. He's not that great in the sex department…probably should have stuck with women."

Well, we now knew Melvin was the guy Karen hoped he was. Now we just had to figure out how to get the two of them together long enough for them to sort things out. I knew we had to resort to drastic measures.

That night, I sat Antonio down to brainstorm. Needless to say, that was a chore in itself. Also, I had to endure all types of name-calling from Antonio, from "matchmaker" to "worrisome busybody" to a "meddlesome fool."

"I might remind you you're the one who gave up some booty to get us the intel we need."

"Oh, it wasn't me whose legs were up in the air!"

Finally, we cooked up a plan that couldn't fail. At least, that's what I kept telling Antonio. The first step was to recruit some of the inner circle.

Myling was studying to be a sports broadcaster and interviewed college athletes for the university newspaper. Her part in this was to call Melvin and tell him she wanted to interview him for this month's issue. The article she was developing was about the pressure athletes faced maintaining their grades, their game, and their scholarships. Melvin was only too happy to take the bait.

Myling told him she wanted to have some photos done while they conducted the interview. She proposed they take a walk in Fairmount Park and do the pictures there.

That's where Dianna came in. She happened to have a project for her photography class and would convince Karen to be her subject for photos she would take…coincidentally in Fairmount Park. Karen—despondent as she was—agreed to help Dianna with her project.

Antonio—obviously—knew Fairmount Park very well and picked a spot where we could throw both Karen and Melvin together at an appointed time—a spot where they'd have nowhere to hide.

Lastly, I collected money from everyone to purchase a limo ride and a gift certificate to a small café-style restaurant in Center City.

Everything went according to plan.

Melvin met Myling in one of the park's parking lots, and they began to walk and talk. From the other end of the park, Dianna started out with Karen.

Myling and Melvin reached Antonio's clearing, indicating this would be a fine spot for some photos.

As the other two approached that same spot, Dianna prepped Karen for what shots she wanted to take. The two girls entered the clearing, with Karen coming to a dead stop.

Melvin and Karen stared at each other from across the open patch of woods. Karen was quicker than Melvin at putting the pieces together.

"This has Desmond written all over it. Where is he?!" She spun around in a circle, looking for me. I decided the jig was up, so I dragged Antonio out of the bushes where we'd hidden.

As we emerged, Melvin shouted, "What the fuck is going on here?" Myling filled him in with a mouthful of her own.

"We're Karen's friends and we *aren't* all gay!"

"And, even if we were," I threw in, approaching Myling from one side, "do you have any idea what it means to have true, loyal, and trustworthy friends you can turn to in good *and* bad times?"

Antonio had circled around to him from the other direction, adding his own two cents. "We don't care much for bigots! We hate it even more when people hurt the friends we love."

Dianna brought it all home by saying, "We don't care what the two of you do after this, but we love Karen and will do what it takes to see she stays happy. So, let me tell you one thing, Mr. Weston: you better get over that narrow-minded thinking of yours and have a heart-to-heart with our friend Karen here. And, after you talk, if you can't see it in you to treat her right, then leave her the fuck alone and go about your business. Karen—if this dude is who you really want, here's your chance to tell him what's on your mind."

We had them surrounded. They looked at each other for a moment more before Antonio made his timely remark. "Well, if you are waiting on your assholes to talk, all they can do is blow out funky air. My suggestion would be to use your mouths."

Melvin looked around at all of us, settling finally on Karen. "You have some very special friends."

"I know," she admitted. "I can always count on them to have my back. So, what do you suggest we do now? Continue to ignore each other, or go somewhere more private"—she glared at each of us in turn—"and talk this out?"

"I'll talk," Melvin said.

"Good. Sounds like a start to me," Antonio piped in. Before he could add something that would ruin the moment, I jumped in.

"And, seeing as you want privacy, we conveniently have another surprise for you. Back at the main parking lot, there's a limo waiting to take you both to dinner and, from there, wherever you want to go."

"But remember, Cinderella and Prince Charming: you only have three hours!" Antonio interjected, unable to stop himself.

"All right, team, our job is done here," Dianna said.

"It's now up to you guys what you do! We're out of here!" Myling said, crossing over to Karen and giving her a quick kiss and hug. The rest of us followed suit; once Karen was hugged-out, we left the couple alone in the clearing.

We hoped it would all work out for the best. Little did we know what the long-term effect of getting them back together would be…

We didn't see either one of them at all the next day and were on pins and needles, wanting to find out what had happened. That afternoon, we each got a call from Karen asking us to meet her in her room at 9:00 p.m.

When I arrived at her room that night, everyone else was already there. Karen and Melvin were sitting on her bed, Melvin's massive arm wrapped around her shoulders. We all broke out smiling at one other, realizing our plan had worked. Melvin cleared his throat.

"I'm gonna start. Um…I have some apologies to make. And I'm not quite sure how. I can't apologize for how I was brought up, for the values or beliefs that have been instilled in me. Why, shit—those are the things that got me here!

"What I can apologize for is not trusting my instincts about a person I have fallen in love with." Melvin rubbed his nose with the back of one hand. Needless to say, when the word "love" came out, our mouths dropped to the floor. Karen's face beamed.

"What I saw yesterday were true friends who went out on a limb for one of their own. I have many buddies on the team, but I don't know if they would have done what you guys did for Karen. Look—I don't know how I feel about two men or two women doing it. For the longest time, I thought it was disgusting. Why? Because I was told it was. Will I ever be comfortable around some of you guys? Only time will tell.

"But, as long as you are a friend to my baby, I won't ever disrespect you again. She is too important to me to lose over dumb shit like who her friends sleep with." He leaned over and kissed Karen on the cheek, squeezing her close within his muscular arm. The girls hugged Karen; Melvin rose and shook each of the guys' hands, drawing us all in for a quick chest hug.

"I have a good feeling I know whose idea this was," Karen said, "and I want to say thank you to everyone who participated. And, now that you all know I am all right, don't let my doorknob hit ya where God split ya. I've missed too much quality time with my man, and he's still making it up to me. See ya in the morning."

We all left happy with what we'd engineered but wondering where their relationship would go from here. Antonio turned to me as we got out into the lounge area.

"Damn, boy—we didn't do so bad back there. But I tell you, I'm long overdue for a piece of ass, and the piece I want has been put on hold for too long because of all this shit. It's time I got busy."

"I'm sure you won't have any problem getting your groove on," I replied, wondering if JC knew what was in store for him. "Just take it slow; I'm all out of fairy and matchmaking dust." He laughed and started off toward his room.

Before I got around the corner to go to mine, I heard a familiar voice calling my name softly. Turning, I saw Karen leaning on the wall nearest her hallway. I waved and walked toward her. When I came up to her, she threw her arms around my neck and planted a kiss square on my lips. Stunned, I didn't know what to say when she finally released me from our lip-lock.

"I don't know which way you're going to end up going, Desmond, but whoever gets you is going to be a very lucky person. I know this was your doing, and I want you to know you have a friend for life. Thank you."

Before I could say anything, she put her finger to my lips, smiled at me, and walked off. I couldn't help but smile at her receding form. *Yeah, we did do good.*

Interlude Thirteen

A Call to the Dance Floor;
Finding My Way

After helping Karen and Melvin work through their issues, it was time for me to work through my new roommate situation, as well as some concerns of my own.

Brian was a real mellow type of guy. Not much seemed to bother him and he always kept a positive outlook about campus and world issues. (He and I were always reading the campus and local newspapers and often discussed the news items in them.)

Each Friday morning, his bags were packed and by the door so he could catch the bus home to West Chester the minute his last class finished. I enjoyed having the room to myself all weekend. I could study whenever I wanted, listen to my music, and if I was ever inclined to hold wild sex parties, well, I had no roommate to chase away when the action went down. Too bad there was no such action happening up here.

Antonio and I still ran together in the evening, but with a new partner. Antonio wasn't as interested in our workouts as much as he was in "working out" with JC. In the rare moments I did get Antonio by himself, all he would talk about was what he and JC had done. It was obvious he'd fallen heavily for this guy. I suspect what attracted Antonio to him at first was how JC seemed to hold him at arm's length. It drove Antonio crazy that he could barely get a kiss out of the guy early on in their relationship. Which no doubt pushed him on in his pursuit to bed him.

I didn't want to be a cock-blocker, so I found other things to occupy my time. I figured this would give them room to develop whatever it was they were going to develop. At least that's what I told myself.

Of course, Antonio sensed my distance and confronted me with it one day in my room. "So what the fuck is the matter with you?" he said in his usual abrupt tone.

I, in turn, kept things nonchalant. "There's nothing wrong with me; what's up with you?"

He looked at me and laughed. "Oh, son—now we're going to play the bitch game? 'Oh, I'm fine, there's nothing wrong with me, I just have my finger up my behind, waiting for my turn.'" He shook his own finger at me. "You can talk that dumb shit with other folks, prep, but I know yo ass! I've seen it with my own eyes: a nice plump one, as a matter of fact! So, do us both a favor and drop the act. Tell me what's going on!"

"It's simple, Antonio. *You* have someone you are pursuing; *Karen* has got her man back... I know where that leaves me. I'm not cut out to be the third wheel, and I'm not going to start being one now. So, I decided to back off and give you guys some room."

"So, who the fuck told you I needed some room instead of my best friend?!" Antonio fired back.

"Look—JC's clearly got you working hard. You don't need to add babysitting me to the mix," I replied.

"Oh, so now I'm your fuckin' nanny, am I? Funny—I don't remember applying for the job! Furthermore, where are the health and fringe benefits that go along with that job?"

"And there you go with your smart-ass comments. I'm being serious, Antonio!" I was starting to have trouble maintaining my nonchalance.

"Don't hand me that shit, Desmond—I'm not one who decided to get attached to someone three hundred miles away. I'm not the one who can't face the fact he's interested in men and won't do something about it. This self-imposed monogamy is *your* doing, and it's driving me crazy.

"My suggestion," he continued, "is that you need to deal with reality: you are interested in men. And, afterward, you need a reality check: you gotta go out and do something about it! Didn't Angel give you a way out? Didn't she as much as tell you to go out here and find what is right for you? Bro—do it!

"And if you still feel the same way about her afterward, you *know* she'll consider your proposal! But you're not going to find what you are looking for sitting alone in this dorm room every weekend. You've got to put yourself out there for someone to at least notice you're available!"

I sat quietly, thinking about what Antonio had said. Part of me wanted to be angry at him for saying or even suggesting it, and the other part sat knowing he was right. I sighed and looked up at him.

"I don't know. I'm not you, Antonio; I don't know if being with a guy is really right for me."

"How will you know if you don't give yourself a chance?"

"I wouldn't know where to start. How do I get gay guys to notice me? Where do I find them? Do I pick up the Yellow Pages and look under 'Gays—single and looking'?"

Antonio chortled. "Ooooh, good one! I've never tried the Yellow Pages!"

"And there you go again—how come you can't be serious?" I said sternly.

"All right, Miss Thang, don't get your dick tied in a knot. I can't tell you where to look. Finding someone is half being in the right place at the right time and half acting on instinct. Every gay person has something called gaydar—you ever hear of it?" I shook my head. "Oh, yeah, you just get a sense from the way a person is looking at you, or a slight brush up against you, if they're interested."

"Okay, so I'm supposed to grow antennas out of my head and receive these gay radio signals," I said in a snarky tone.

"*Now* who's not being serious?" Antonio admonished. "Actually, you know what, Des? I think I *can* help you out. Did you ever sneak into a bar in that prep town you live in?"

"I didn't have to sneak in. Legal age in Jersey is eighteen, remember?"

"Well, excuse us Pennsylvanians for not being as progressive as you, Jersey Man. I did my share of underage sneaking into places, and I know all the spots. I think you and I need to hit the city this weekend. It's time to bring yo ass out of that walk-in closet." He looked me up and down. "You game? Fuck it—you're game. Just get yourself ready. We're doing this, tomorrow night."

Antonio grabbed my face and planted a kiss on one cheek. "And now I've gotta go work on JC; it's time to bring his ass out too. I'll see you at dinner."

After Antonio left, I sat on my bed wondering what a bar full of men would be like. *Am I ready for this?* And was he right—was I hiding from my true self? What about my commitment to Angel? I felt as if I was cheating on her, even contemplating this. Did she really expect me to go out and see other people, especially men? And what if I liked it—what then?

This was beginning to blow my mind. I wanted to run Antonio down and tell him to forget it. But the better part of me calmed down enough for me to realize it was time for me to come out of my safe zone. I *could* do this.

Saturday night came and there I was, standing in front of the mirror, wondering what the fuck I was about to do. A knock at the door jerked me out of my thoughts. "It's open!" Two strikingly butch guys dressed in jeans, cut-up sweatshirts, and sneakers moseyed into my room. They took one look at me and fell out laughing. "Okay, would someone please let me in on the joke?"

"Where do you think you are going, Dawson?" Antonio asked after he caught his breath from laughing. I looked down at myself, confused.

"I thought I was going to a gay club with you guys. But, from the way you're both dressed, I guess not?" That set them to laughing hysterically yet again.

"Look, bro, they might dress like that in John Travolta straight clubs, but where we're going, they *dance*. And, looking like that, you'll be holding up the wall all night long." Antonio started looking through my dirty clothes hamper. "Let's see…" He pulled out a pair of faded Calvin Kleins and tossed them at me. He proceeded to my dresser, where he pulled out an old Jets long-sleeved T-shirt that I only wore around the room.

Both he and JC surrounded me, pulling off my sweater, collared shirt, and slacks, and redressing me with the old, dirty stuff Antonio had found. Finally, I looked like a carbon copy of them. JC looked me up and down. "Damn, *mon gars*—if I weren't already into this guy, I might have given you some play!"

"Yeah, thanks but no thanks; I think your dance ticket is already punched."

"Okay, girls—now that we are done with the niceties, we gotta get going," Antonio declared. "It's eleven o'clock, and by the time we get into the down part of the city and find a parking spot we'll hit the clubs by about eleven thirty. The party should be just about starting by the time we walk through the door."

"How are we getting there?" I asked.

"Well, I'm glad you asked. It seems a certain someone has been holding out on us." Antonio turned toward JC.

"Okay, okay, let's not go down that road again," JC said. "I've got a car, Desmond."

"Oh no you don't; tell Des what type of car you have, my friend," Antonio prodded.

"Okay! My dad gave me his old Cadillac Seville convertible for my eighteenth birthday."

"Des," Antonio cut in, "this car is the joint!"

"So, what are we all standing here for? Let's go!" I pushed them both toward the door. As we got out in the hall, we passed Karen and Melvin. Karen narrowed her eyes, giving us a once-over.

"Okay, I'll bite: you guys headed out for pizza?" She held up a finger before Antonio could be his usual smart-ass self.

"Oh, let me take that back—I can tell from the look on Miss Thang's face over there"—she pointed at Antonio—"that you all must be up to no good.

"Desmond, watch yourself with him. I don't want to be getting an early morning call to come bail you out. 'Cause, honey—the only early morning call I wanna get is the one that'll be lying next to me!" She squeezed one of Melvin's butt cheeks, making him jump.

Antonio looked at Melvin with an arched eyebrow. "Be careful of wrong numbers; they can be a bitch." He made a face at Karen, which she returned in kind. Wanting to avoid more back-and-forth, I pushed Antonio toward the elevators.

"Don't worry, Karen," I said over my shoulder. "I'll keep us all out of trouble. I'll call you tomorrow afternoon and give you the details. See ya!"

The elevator opened, and I shoved Antonio through just as he was about to try to land the last word.

The ride into the city was great. We all sat in the front seat so Antonio could snuggle up to JC. As we rode down Broad Street, Antonio had tuned the radio to switch between 98.9 KTU and 105.4 WDAS. These were currently the two hottest Black radio stations in the city. When the Ohio Players' song "Fire" came on the radio, we all lost it, cruising down the highway, singing and dancing in our seats. I knew then this would be a night to remember.

As we reached Center City, Antonio put an arm around each of us.

"Okay, fellas—hold on to your dicks. It's party time!" From his pocket he pulled out a joint. JC and I exchanged a grin.

"Looks like we're getting this party started right!" We laughed as Antonio lit it up. We passed the joint back and forth, just cruising around, taking in the sights (aka—all the men).

Antonio had JC drive past Letters, at the corner of Twenty-Second and South Streets. There it was, in full Technicolor: gay Black men huddled up at the door, waiting for their turn to get in.

"This place is for you, Des—the clientele here is all preppy boys and old queens!" Antonio signaled to JC to look for a spot to park. "We'll stop here first; then I'm taking you to a more...extreme spot!"

I didn't know how to answer that, so I kept quiet. We were lucky to find a parking spot right there on South Street just as we finished up the joint.

We got out of the car as a group of brothers walked by. One very boyish-looking guy smiled at me as he passed. His eyes stayed on mine until he was quite a distance down the street.

"There you go, baby," Antonio said, clapping a hand on my shoulder. "You've been cruised!"

"What do you mean? What's cruising?" I said, watching the receding figure of the cute guy.

JC rolled his eyes. "You're kidding, right? With your phat ass and those good looks, you've never been cruised before? I don't believe it."

"Believe it, bro," Antonio said. "This is our brother's coming out party!" He leaned into me, and I felt the heat of his breath on my ear. "Look—play it cool. Don't jump at the first thing that comes your way, try not to come off anxious, and don't do anything that's going to make you feel uncomfortable. Basically, just go with the flow."

JC rolled his eyes again—this time at Antonio's advice. "Don't worry, Desmond—whatever happens, we've got your back. We'll keep an eye on you."

All of this reassured me; however, I still could not even conceive of what I was in store for.

We all had a buzz on as we made it into the bar. It seemed to me as if everyone turned to look at us. Antonio declared, "Fresh roadkill in the house!" which set JC to laughing. I had no idea what they were going on about.

Antonio led us to the bar, where we all ordered Budweisers. That seemed to be what everyone else was drinking. I turned my attention to the dance floor, marveling at the male bodies twisting and turning to disco music as a mirrored ball scattered shards of light over top of them.

With the joint and the beer in my system, I was feeling no inhibitions and itched to join all those men on the dance floor. Sensing this, Antonio leaned over and whispered something to JC, then grabbed me by the arm and led me to the floor. He made his way through the crowd of people, finding us a spot under the glimmering lights.

Instantly, we were swept up into the motion of the crowd, gyrating in sync with the music. I followed Antonio's lead, reproducing his moves as if I'd been born to dance. *Who said preppies don't have rhythm?* I didn't want to stop; it felt so good. I knew instantly this was where I belonged. It felt right. I felt like I'd arrived home.

Completely out of breath after the third song, we returned to JC at the bar. He had found a spot against the wall with a little ledge for our beers. "*Mon gars*, you looked pretty comfortable out there. Are you sure this is your first time? Inquiring minds want to know!"

"Piece of cake!" I said with a wide smile.

Antonio arched an eyebrow at me. "Well then, brother—you're on your own. Happy hunting." He grabbed JC by the hand, pulling him out to the dance floor.

I sipped on my beer, gazing around the room. Nothing but men, and most of them Black. It seemed strange to be in the majority for a change. As I swept my eyes across the open space, I caught many an eye. I smiled and kept scanning, trying to do as Antonio suggested and not seem too anxious. But I was—and getting more so by the minute.

What was supposed to happen now? I wanted someone to come up and ask me to dance, but then I thought, *Maybe I should make the first move?*

Antonio *had* said to use my instincts: they were telling me to wait. I decided to do just that, even if it took all night for someone to approach me.

An hour and two more beers went by, and even though there were plenty of people looking, no one had approached yet. Antonio and JC were still off doing their own thing. It was interesting to watch Antonio in his element. He had JC on his turf, and he was in a full-court press.

Suddenly, I caught the eye of this man. He looked much older than most of the other brothers who'd been cruising me. Like Antonio had predicted, my gaydar was in overdrive. I couldn't break the stare. And he wasn't breaking it either.

He reminded me of a young Quincy Jones, circa 1960s. I was still eyeing him when Antonio and JC came over to check on me.

"What are you still doing, hiding in the corner?"

"I'm waiting for someone to ask me to dance. No one has bitten yet."

Antonio clapped me on the shoulder. "Give it time, bro. You've got half the bar staring at you."

A bartender walked over, signaling to get my attention. "The gentleman over there would like to buy you a drink."

We all looked to where he pointed; it was my young Quincy Jones guy. I almost shit in my pants. Antonio nudged me until I spoke up.

"Um...sure! Another Bud, please."

The bartender smirked. "A polite one! You wait here, chicky—I'll bring that back with a kiss!"

As he moved off, I looked over to the older gentleman, nodding a thank-you. He returned that with his own smile and nod. JC leaned in and whispered, "Play this one cool—he's got class...and probably money!"

The bartender returned with the Bud, and I tipped him a dollar. He rewarded me by blowing a kiss my way. I looked across the bar again, only to find my guy had vanished.

"Do you want to come dance with us?" JC asked. They were getting their groove on, and I didn't want to spoil their time, so I sent them back out onto the floor.

I nursed my latest drink for a while, wondering if I'd somehow driven my guy away. *Maybe I shouldn't have let Antonio talk me out of dressing up.* A hand dropped onto my shoulder and I turned with a jerk. The older guy stood there, with a brilliant smile on his face. He was even more magnificent up close. I extended my hand. "Thanks for the beer!"

"You're very welcome," he said, taking my hand. He had a strong, warm grip. "Where are your friends?"

"I sent them on the dance floor. Are you here with anyone?"

"No, I'm here by myself. Might I interest you in a dance?" he said; it didn't quite sound like a question. Trying to quiet my anxiety, I took a slow breath before agreeing. He held out his hand, which I took with a grin, and he led me to the dance floor. I was feeling light-headed, basking in the feeling that someone had finally asked me to dance.

We danced through several songs, gazing into each other's eyes and smiling. After the fourth song, he put an arm around my shoulders and leaned in close. "It's warm in here; would you like to step outside and get some air?"

"Sure!" I said, remembering Antonio and JC. "Just give me a moment to let my friends know where I am."

"I'll meet you outside," he said, walking off.

I found Antonio and JC on the far side of the dance floor and told them what I was doing. Antonio became serious, pulling me close.

"Whatever you do, Des, don't get into his car. Keep it right outside the door."

"Thank you, Mom." I winked and headed for the exit before he could say any more.

I stepped out the door, finding him by the curb, smoking a cigarette. He extended his pack of Bensen and Hedges 100s as I approached. "Would you like one?"

I didn't smoke, but I wondered if I should accept just to look cool. I thought better of it, shaking my head. "No, thank you. I don't smoke."

"Good. It's a bad habit. One of these days, I'll consider giving it up." He replaced the pack in his jacket. "My name is Rick. What's yours?"

"Cameron; Cameron Da—" He cut me off before I could finish announcing my full name.

"No last names; it's better that way." Obviously, we were both thinking the same thing. I figured if this guy was a loser, at least he wouldn't know my first name.

But curiosity got the better of me; I wanted to hear his reasoning, so I asked, "What do you mean by that?"

"It's sometimes better if you don't," he said abruptly.

"If that's your choice…" I felt a bit uncomfortable now. We made small talk about the city, sports, and films. Nothing heavy. As we were talking, I could tell he wanted to ask me something and wasn't sure how to. So, I said finally, "Okay, Rick—small talk is good, but I can tell when there's a burning question on someone's mind. What's up?"

He arched one eyebrow. "You don't beat around the bush, do you, young man? I like that."

"I'm glad you think so. But you still didn't answer my question."

"All right! Pin me to the wall! Here it is, Cameron: I'm looking to get a little *something-something* tonight. I was hoping you and I could get to know each other a little better." His offer sent a shiver of anticipation through me. *I'd definitely like to have a little* something-something *with him!* My morals got the best of me, though (or was I just chickenshit?).

I looked him square in the eyes. "Hey, man, you are terrific looking and I'm enjoying talking with you, but—"

He interrupted me yet again. "Ah. Here comes the letdown line: 'You're too old for me; maybe there's someone out there closer to my age.' I've heard that one more than once."

"So, besides your other sterling traits, you're a mind reader too?" I said snarkily. "No—what I was going to say, Rick, is I'd like to get to know you a little bit better before I follow you home. I mean, who knows—you could be a rapist or a mass murderer! And what would I look like, going home with someone who just bought me a drink? Sorry, buddy; I don't get taken that easily." Wanting to finish on a positive note, I added hastily, "That's not to say I don't want to see you again!"

He looked me up and down, a wry smile lighting his face. "You know something about instincts. As I was watching you this evening, I knew you were different from a lot of the brothers who come in here." He sniffed, flicking his cigarette butt onto the street. "I tell you what, Cameron: I believe we are destined to meet again. I know we'll eventually connect on your terms. You won't spend the night with me? All right. But how about letting me have one more dance?"

Without waiting, he put his arm around my shoulders and led me back into the bar.

As we approached the dance floor, Donna Summer's "Last Dance" started to play. Rick pulled me in close; I wrapped my arms around his shoulders. Our torsos were pressed together; as we swayed, I sensed both of us getting aroused. *Man, have I blown my chance?* I wondered. Part of me wanted very badly to take back everything I'd said outside and let him have me right here. The sensible part of me—the one I'd have to face tomorrow morning—knew I was doing the right thing.

I was determined to enjoy this dance, though. As we moved in sync with the music, we hustled to the beat as if we'd been dancing forever. As the music ended, Rick twirled me around, wrapping his arms around me from behind. I looked at him over my shoulder, and we both smiled.

The lights came up and a groan swept through the bar—the dancing had ended for the night. Men started to funnel out. Antonio and JC found us lingering on the dance floor. The two of them were totally blasted—I'm sure they instantly forgot Rick's name the moment I introduced him to them.

"JC, give me your keys, bro," I insisted as Rick and I steered those two toward the exit. When we got to JC's car, we poured him and Antonio into the back seat, where they collapsed onto each other, instantly grinding and making out. I predicted Antonio had a 100 percent chance of bedding JC tonight.

I closed the door and turned to say good night. Without warning, Rick pulled me in close and French-kissed me right there on South Street. After a moment of shock, I melted into his arms and returned the kiss. Again, I felt like a fool for resisting his advances—this was one hot brother!

When he finally turned me loose, he said in a voice thick with passion, "See what you'll be missing tonight?"

Without missing a beat, I smiled and said, "If it's destiny, baby, you'll get another chance."

He laughed aloud as I sauntered to the driver's side of the car and climbed in. I lowered the window and our eyes met, as they had that first time earlier this evening. He leaned over, resting his arms on the car door.

"Hopefully, we won't have to wait long for destiny, Cameron." Rick straightened and saluted me as I pulled away. I watched him in the rearview mirror until he disappeared from view.

On the drive to the university, I could still feel the touch of Rick's lips on mine. I reflected on the long stare we'd last shared and the feel of his body pressed up against mine during that final song. The scent of his cologne had rubbed off onto me, and I breathed it in deeply. A question burned in my mind: *Will destiny bring us back together again?*

I could only hope and pray it would.

Part Four

The Spiritual and Physical Ties That Bind

Interlude Fourteen

Saving Souls

Early the next morning, Rick came to me in my dreams. I felt the rippling muscles in his stomach, the smooth texture of his face, and the warmth of his lips—lips that explored my naked body with wantonness. I tasted the sweet elixir of his tongue as it discovered the inner walls of my mouth. I heard his pleasure: the moans, the groans, and the snickers. I shuddered as his hands caressed my chest, and his teeth grazed my nipples, enticing them into hardness.

He worked downward, caressing, fondling, stroking, and devouring my manhood until I released the tension that built up inside me, and with a scream of ecstasy, I came.

I was awakened by a shake of my shoulder and a voice calling, "Desmond, Desmond, are you okay?" I opened my eyes to find Brian looking down at me in alarm.

"Yeah, yeah, I'm okay. I was just, ah, having a weird dream, that's all. What time is it?"

"It's 6:45; Sunday morning, bro. I'm on my way to take a shower and head home."

I leaned up on my elbows, painfully aware of my hard-on outlined by the bedsheets. "Shit—I didn't wake you, did I?"

"No man, I was getting dressed when I saw you tossing and turning, then all of a sudden you screamed. That must have been some dream." He squinted down at me. "What did you have to eat late last night?"

"What do you mean?"

"Well, whenever I eat something that doesn't agree with me, I generally have nightmares," Brian explained.

"Oh, well, maybe that's what this was," I replied, relieved to have an excuse, while painfully aware of the true reason. If Brian were to see the sticky mess I felt in my underwear, I'm sure he would have known the truth too.

"Well, I'm glad you're all right." He paused for a moment. "Hey, by the way, what are you doing today?"

"Nothing really," I admitted.

"Great, how about riding down to West Chester with me and going to church?"

I kept telling myself I wanted to go with Brian to his church; this was a perfect opportunity, given what happened last night. Some spiritual guidance was exactly what I needed today.

"Sure, why not? A change of pace will do me some good."

"Great, I'll see you in the shower in a few minutes. We have to catch an 8:00 a.m. train if we want to make breakfast at my house before church." Brian left the room with a big smile on his face while I lay there in the afterglow of my dream, feeling wet and sticky down there.

I dragged myself out of bed, took my shorts off, stripped the sheets, and threw them all in the hamper. I remade the bed and was out of the room before Brian had finished his shower. As I entered the men's shower room, I heard him singing his favorite gospel tune.

Maybe I do need saving from myself this morning, I thought, because all I could hear in *my* head was Donna Summer's "Last Dance."

We made it to the station just before eight. During the train ride, I got to learn a bit more about my new roommate.

Before coming to Temple, Brian had spent two years working in the ministries at his dad's church. He also told me about some of the church folks I would meet that day.

He talked a lot about this one woman, Sylvia Mason. She was thirty years old, the superintendent of the church's Sunday school, the youth choir director, an elementary school teacher, and a mother of three beautiful young children: Brandon, Carley, and little Othello.

From the way he talked about her, it was obvious he loved helping her with the many responsibilities in the church, as well as being a surrogate uncle to the children.

We arrived in West Chester forty-five minutes later and made the five-minute walk from the train to Brian's house. He'd called his mom from school to let her know he was bringing a friend along; when we got there, she'd put out quite a spread. We had a choice of eggs, sausages, bacon, grits, biscuits, waffles, pancakes, orange juice, milk, and coffee. Let me tell you, this woman could cook. From the quantity of food, I was surprised Brian and his family weren't three hundred pounds each.

It turned out we weren't the only folks over for breakfast. A steady stream of deacons and stewardesses passed through for a bite before service, which explained why Brian's mom had made so much food.

Before the crowd started coming through, I had a chance to enjoy an intimate breakfast with him and his folks.

Brian's parents were really cool—not what I'd expected. His dad was down-to-earth and very knowledgeable about many things. His mom was good ol' Southern peach charm—gracious, encouraging, and motherly, and perpetually asking if I had enough to eat or if I wanted her to fix something different. They were a very close-knit family, and I understood why Brian rushed to get home every weekend.

Like clockwork, we were out of the house by 9:55 a.m. and walked next door to the church. Sylvia Mason—the woman Brian spoke very highly of—was at the door, greeting the children and parents who dropped them off.

Sylvia was the type of woman both little boys and big boys alike fell in love with at first sight. She was a beautiful bronze color and had curly reddish-brown hair that fell two inches below her shoulders. She had thin eyebrows and long thick lashes, which accented her seductive light-brown eyes. She stood about five feet five inches tall and likely weighed no more than a hundred and five pounds. She was exactly what you'd envision a schoolteacher to look like—one admired by her students, young and old.

As Brian introduced us, Sylvia shook my hand and smiled, sending a warm tingle through my body. It was clear why he adored her.

By her side was an equally beautiful little lady. With Shirley Temple curls, a pink-and-white pinafore dress, and black patent leather shoes, she was absolutely adorable.

"Brian!" the little girl screamed when she saw him, launching herself into my roommate's arms. I guessed this was Carley, and if I hadn't known Mrs. Mason was married, I would have sworn she was Brian and Sylvia's love child: the three of them looked like a picture-perfect family. And believe me when I tell you—she had a lot of Brian's features.

"Where are the boys?" Brian asked. Sylvia gestured toward two young kids playing in the grassy yard next to the church; Brian went over to see them. When Brandon saw him, he rushed over, his two-year-old brother, Othello, toddling after him. The boys greeted Brian warmly, as if he were their father or favorite uncle. Brian greeted them with open arms. I could tell he loved them as much as they loved him. Matter of fact, within moments, children who couldn't wait to greet him had him surrounded.

Brian taught Sunday school to the four- to six-year-olds; Sylvia taught the seven- to nine-year-olds. Brian's assistant was home with the flu, so I stepped in to help with cutting and gluing duties. The Sunday school classrooms were side by side; throughout the morning, Sylvia and Brian went back and forth, exchanging materials and plenty of smiles.

Sunday school ended by 10:55 a.m.; the musical prelude started up at 11:00 a.m. Ten minutes later, the processional began, and the church was in full tilt from that point onward. Six-year-old Brandon and soon-to-be-four-year-old Carley sat with us; we were directly behind Sylvia and the youth choir. I began to wonder if there really was a Mr. Mason. He was certainly nowhere in sight. I figured I would save that question until after service had finished.

Incidentally, the reverend's sermon turned out to be very pertinent to my life at that moment. I'm guessing it was probably the same for a lot of his parishioners too: "Looking for

Love in All the Wrong Places." As he spoke of what you might pick up in bars, I wondered if he'd been hiding somewhere in Letters the night before, witnessing my debauchery. Nevertheless, the message I took from his sermon was God loves you first and foremost, and He has a plan that always includes love.

Brian's dad spoke for twenty minutes, keeping us enthralled the whole time. Even before the service wrapped up, I was hooked and knew I'd be back. It felt like my home church, and the congregation had welcomed me with open arms.

That afternoon, the reverend and Mrs. Harris, Sylvia, and a whole host of stewardesses helped in the soup kitchen. Brian and I chipped in too. Our task was to prepare meals for Reverend Harris to take to the sick and shut-in. After four hours of hard work, Brian and I had just enough time to catch a quick bite, then rush to the station for our 5:00 p.m. train to school.

I slept from the moment I boarded the train until we pulled into the Thirtieth Street Station. As we rode the L train to the dorm, Brian and I talked about his father's sermon.

"It really made me think about my life," I admitted. Brian nodded thoughtfully, clearly lost in thoughts of his own. I had an inkling of what it might have been about. "Hey, where was *Mr.* Mason today?"

"Fred?" Brian blinked, drawn out of his reverie. "He's the owner of one of the country's leading Black magazines, *Menage Noir.* It's a really busy job, so sometimes, he stays in the city for a few days."

"They've got a house in the city too?"

"An apartment. Well, apartment*s.* Mason's mother passed away a couple years ago. She owned a big row house that had been subdivided into four units. Mason has actually offered to let me and a couple friends rent two of them at the end of this school year."

"Your own apartment?! Where is it?"

"It's only a block away from the main campus."

"That's perfect! Are you going for it?"

"I told Mason I'd consider it," Brian said, but I saw from the look on his face Mr. Mason wasn't one of his favorite characters. "So, you coming back home next week with me?" Clearly he wanted to change the topic.

"I'd love to," I said, meaning it. "I'm thinking I'll probably come up on Sunday mornings and ride back with you in the evening?" Brian immediately cheered up at my announcement. I knew he'd always wanted more of his friends to share in the experience of his faith; I was glad I felt comfortable enough to do so. "Why, hell," I told him, "I might even convince Karen, Melvin, Antonio, and JC to come with me!"

I stopped for a second, considering something. *Might as well ask him straight up...* "Do you think your folks are ready for Antonio's lifestyle?"

Brian looked at me wryly. "With all the men in our choir who are gay, I can't imagine they wouldn't be!" And we both fell out laughing.

We got to our room, and I immediately gathered up some books. I needed to go to the library. On the way, I headed to Antonio's room to see if he wanted to go with me. Sure enough he was there, and not to my surprise, so was JC. Also not surprisingly, neither of them had clothes on. Clearly, JC had finally succumbed to Antonio's advances. *Or maybe JC has Antonio right where he wants him?*

"I'll probably meet you there later," Antonio insisted, though I expected he was having too good of a time to stop.

As I walked to the library, my mind wandered to Rick. *Am I looking for love in the wrong places?* I wondered, thinking back to Reverend Harris's sermon this morning. What if our meeting *was* destiny? Or what if that was just a pickup line he used to get brothers in bed with him?

And what about my relationship with Angel? Throughout the events of the past twenty-four hours, I hadn't thought once about her. Now, though—thinking back to Mrs. Mason and her children, I knew I wanted to have family much like hers one day.

This was too much to worry about right now, though; I needed to focus on a literature paper and calculus homework for tomorrow morning. There would be plenty of time to let my mind ponder these thoughts later in the week.

Interlude Fifteen

A Funny Twist of Fate

February gave way to March; by now we'd been going to Letters on Friday and Saturday nights, then to Brian's church on Sunday, for three weeks in a row. Midterms were coming up in a week, followed by spring break, so I made sure I got everything I needed to get done during the week, freeing up Saturday and most of Sunday for the new routine.

Like I promised, I talked the gang into attending Brian's church service and helping out with Sunday school. To save money on train fare, JC offered to drive if we chipped in for gas.

Brian's mom loved every minute we were there. She couldn't stop feeding us. Interestingly, Melvin made her the happiest; he had a wooden leg she could keep pouring food into.

Friday and Saturday nights at the club, I waited for destiny to do its thing, to no avail. There were other guys who hit on me, but they didn't have the juice Rick had. I'd dance a couple of dances, write phone numbers on slips of paper, then deposit them in the nearest garbage can as I left.

Several of those nights, Antonio took JC and me to other clubs in the area. I always hoped we would run into Rick at one of those spots, but again, I faced nothing but disappointment.

The Sunday night before midterms and right after we had returned from West Chester, Karen and Antonio ditched their better halves and took me out for coffee and dessert. It was Karen's turn to read me.

"Okay, honey, I am tired of seeing your long face dragging across the ground around here. If I have to beat it out of your little hussy ass, you're going to tell me what's wrong with you." Before I had a chance to open my mouth, she added, "Listen, Desmond—you can't put all of your hopes on one encounter. I don't care if it's destiny or not. Oh, and by the way—that's the dumbest, lamest line I have ever heard." She clicked her tongue and gave one of her famous hand flicks.

I turned to Antonio. "Is there *anything* you didn't tell her?"

He returned my look with a perfectly straight face. "Yeah, I didn't tell her about the wet dream you had the morning after you met him." Finally, his face broke into a smirk.

"Thank God for small favors," I replied, heavy with sarcasm.

"You're welcome. As I once told Karen, and even though you have the scent of rare beef instead of fish, the advice is still the same: there are many more cowboys out there who are looking to wrestle and lasso themselves a piece of rare meat. Just look at the one I snagged."

"But let me remind you, Des," Karen cut in, "there's still your relationship with Angel. How am I supposed to act around this woman next week knowing you are trying to fuck around with some man on this end?" I blinked away from her direct look. She had a fair point.

We planned to go to Washington, DC, over spring break to hang out with Angel and a couple of her friends, sightseeing and clubbing. She was house-sitting for her cousin who had business in California for the next ten days. Angel had cleared it with her cousin to have us all stay there. Convenient, seeing as we were all on limited budgets.

Angel and I also decided we would celebrate my birthday the Friday of spring break, and I would leave Saturday morning for Jersey to spend the remaining time with my family.

"Look, Karen," I said, not liking having to explain myself, "I know it's going to be a bit awkward, but Angel did tell me I needed to find out what side of the fence I wanted to be on before she would even consider marrying me. So, that's all I'm trying to determine."

"Well, if I can give you advice I first heard from a very well-known minister: a bird in hand is better than two in the bush. You know what you have with Angel, Desmond; why would you want to risk that on something unknown?" Again, she had a point. But I had a good answer for her this time.

"I risk every day by not knowing if I'm really gay or not. I can't keep hiding these feelings I have for men. If they're real, then I owe it to Angel to find out before I ruin her life."

"I couldn't have said it better, Miss Thang," Antonio quipped.

"I just think you're playing with fire, Des. You are going to get burned if you aren't careful. Especially following behind Mrs. Thang," Karen added, showing Antonio her tongue.

"I have no use for that, bitch; you're not my flavor," Antonio retorted, giving her the finger.

"And what am I supposed to do with that? It wouldn't even tickle my stuff!" Karen said, with an arch of her eyebrows, and added, "Oh—wait; were you showing me how big you are?"

"All right, you two!" I interjected before Antonio could get another word out. I was in no mood for their bickering. "Let's change the subject. What are you couples going to do when I go home after my birthday?"

"Melvin and I are going to continue down to Virginia Beach," Karen said. "His coach rents cars for all the guys through the university. They had to damn near sign away their lives to get them, though—promises not to drink or get speeding tickets and to be back on campus by Sunday night. The penalty for breaking any of those rules could mean their scholarship. So, you better believe my baby and I will be taking it slow."

"JC and I are going to drive up to Canada to visit his folks. He's promised to show me all the best sights." Antonio grew quiet for a second. That was unusual enough for me and Karen to pay close attention. "Honestly, guys, I haven't felt this grounded with someone since George. I hope his mama likes her new son-in-law…keep your fingers crossed for me?"

"I'm really happy for you, Antonio," Karen said. "JC is a really special guy and he's lucky to have someone, a very special someone like you."

Antonio looked under the table and around his chair as if he had lost something. "Who said that?!"

"BITCH!" Karen barked with a charming smile.

"No, really, Karen, thank you. That means a lot to me."

We paid the bill and walked to the dorm together, smiling and laughing all the way to our rooms.

Around ten that night–an hour after I'd settled in—Brian arrived from West Chester. He never came back that late, normally catching a train that got him here well before supper.

He seemed bothered by something, almost as if something had spooked him. He didn't say anything as he hung up his coat and unpacked his clean laundry. So, in my usual role as dorm mom, I asked pointedly, "What happened?"

"Nothing," he replied, not even turning to look at me. "Everything is okay; it's just fine. I'm going to take a shower, okay?"

I recognized an I-want-to-be-left-alone tone when I heard one. "Okay, but if you need to talk—and I mean about anything—I'm here for you, right?"

He climbed out of his clothes and wrapped himself in a towel before heading for the door. With his hand on the handle, he turned back. "You mean that, don't you?"

I looked at him directly. "You can take that to the bank, Brian. I'm here without blame or judgment."

"Thanks, I needed to hear that." Then he left for his shower.

A half hour later, he still hadn't returned. I walked to the showers to check on him, hearing the water running and that same familiar song he always sang. This time, though, his singing held a certain melancholy. I walked back to the room and did some reading until he finally came back. Again, without saying anything, he pulled on some pajamas, climbed into bed, and closed his eyes.

A few minutes passed before he turned over and asked, "Des, are you busy next Saturday? I know you guys are planning to head to DC after church on Sunday, but did you have any plans for the day before?"

I'd intended to hit the clubs one last time before spring break but decided to let him think I was undecided. "Just packing and stuff. Why? Do you need me to do something for you?"

"Well, I was wondering if you…" He trailed off, taking a deep breath. He looked as if he wanted to cry. "I was wondering if you would go to a birthday party with me in West Chester Saturday afternoon. We wouldn't have to leave here until you were packed and ready."

"Sure, man—not a problem. Whenever you want to go, I'll be ready. Just say the word. Whose party is it, if I'm allowed to ask?"

"It's Carley's fourth birthday party," he answered in a thick, sad voice.

"That'll be a blast," I said with enthusiasm, though wondering at his tone. "Matter of fact, I know just what to get her. I'll pick it up from the city this week."

"That'll be great." Brian sniffed. "Hey, Des?"

"Yeah?"

"Thanks for being a real friend."

"No problem, buddy, right back at you."

★

I finished my midterm exams by Thursday, leaving me a day to sort some things out before the weekend.

All week long, Brian moped around the room, clearly still bothered by something, though he didn't seem able or willing to share it with me. I didn't press it, because I knew we didn't have that type of relationship yet. But I knew someone who did.

I combed through my stuff and found Phillip's home number and address. I called the number, but it wasn't in service. Antonio told me what L-trains and buses I needed to take to get to the address Phillip had left us. And so, on Friday, I decided to go on a journey. I got up early and set out for the first stop.

Waiting there was none other than Antonio.

"What are you doing here? Don't you have an exam today?"

"Yep—this afternoon at four. So our asses better be back here by 3:00 p.m., Florence Nightingale."

"Okay. But you didn't answer my first question: what are you doing here?"

He looked me up and down before answering. "Look, the section of Philly you're heading to is pretty rough. So I've decided to watch your back while you do this errand of mercy you're on. Now shut up and get on," he said, signaling to the bus that had pulled up. I smiled, giving him a play punch on the shoulder as we started on our journey to find our missing friend, Phillip.

When we got to the address, Antonio's description of the neighborhood was right on point. As we walked up to the brownstone building, I saw graffiti painted over the walls and sidewalks; most of the spray-painted messages weren't exactly the type I'd choose to decorate my house with. There was garbage strewn everywhere too. At the base of the front steps, a bag lady sat beside her shopping cart full of what looked like junk. I knew what I thought of as *junk* was probably all she had in the world.

We walked up three flights of stairs until we got to the apartment I had listed on my card. From inside the apartment, a television blared loudly. We were also met by the sound of children screaming and an adult woman screaming right back at them.

I was afraid to knock.

Seeing this, Antonio stepped forward and pounded on the door for me. A screeching voice called out, "*Who the fuck is it?*" A shiver ran through me. *What have I gotten us into?* Again, Antonio was there to rescue me.

"It's Tony, Ms. Garvey!" he called out in a street voice I'd never heard him use.

There was (relative) silence for a moment; then the voice called out again, "Tony who? What the fuck do you want with me? Go away, I don't know anybody named fuckin' Tony!"

"Ms. Garvey, would you please open the fuckin' door? It's Antonio Savileo, Phillip's friend from Temple!"

Silence fell again as I tried to get my head around what was going on. Footsteps approached and we heard locks being turned. The door cracked open with the chain still attached. The face that looked out at us was something straight from a ghetto movie. Phillip's mom was supposed to be thirty-five, but this woman looked closer to fifty. With a cigarette in her hand and puffing smoke like a chimney, she smiled, showing a mouthful of rotten or missing teeth.

"Oh, hello, Tony! I haven't seen you around these parts in a long time. You're looking *real* good!" She leaned forward, noticing Antonio wasn't alone. "Who's your friend?"

"This is Desmond."

"Ooooo, he's a good-looking one, too!" she declared, passing her eyes all over me. "Are you fucking him?" My eyes popped open and I started to choke.

"No, ma'am; he's just a friend."

"Shame. He looks like he'd be a good fuck." She took a long drag, leering at me still.

"Okay, Ms. G—enough. Where can we find Phillip?"

"Why do you wanna know? You wanna fuck him too, now?" She laughed, which turned into a fit of coughing.

"Ms. G, stop shittin' around. I've gotta be at the school by four and I need to see Phil. Is he working?"

"You're no fun, Tony."

"No, ma'am, I ain't. Can you just tell me where we can find him?"

"All right, all right—don't go getting all white-boy on me!" She picked something out of the gap in her teeth. "He works at the Chinese laundry down the street. What time is it now?"

I looked down at my watch. "Eleven o'clock, ma'am."

"Oooo, he's got a sexy voice. You sure you ain't fucking him, Tony? Bet he's got a nice ass on him too. Turn around for me, sweetie!" She swirled her finger in the air. Antonio gripped my shoulder, preventing me from doing as she asked—as if I was about to.

"Which laundry, and what time does he get a break?"

"It's the one on the corner; they give him a fifteen-minute break around eleven thirty."

"Thank you, Ms. G. We'll see ya 'round, eh?" Antonio turned to leave.

"Nice meeting you, ma'am," I said, falling in behind Antonio.

"Same here, sweetie. And look—if he won't fuck you," she said, her voice raising to a shrill yell, "you come back here and I'll give you a whirl! And tell Phillip to bring me some cigarettes!" I couldn't get down the stairs fast enough.

I didn't say a word until we were on the street. As we hit the last step of that brownstone, I turned to Antonio and said, "Remind me the next time I get a bright idea not to act on it."

"Ms. G's harmless," he replied with a lopsided grin. "She was so high I don't think she'll even remember we came by."

We got to the laundry, but rather than go in the front, Antonio took me around to the rear of the building through an alleyway. There on a crate sat Phillip. His face lit up when he saw us, and he leaped up to give us a handshake and a hug.

"Tony! Desmond! What the fuck are you guys doing here? Did you go up to the house?"

"Yeah, we stopped there first," Antonio said, rolling his eyes.

"Man, was Mom all tore up as usual?"

"She's just the way I remember her, Phil."

"Yeah, yeah, yeah. You know she still talks about you all the time? Saying what a nice young man you were? And she always adds, 'Too bad he's queer; I could have fucked the shit out that handsome boy.'" He and Antonio laughed; I didn't know how to respond to that.

"She asked me if I was fucking Desmond. Matter of fact, if I remember correctly, she told me maybe I ought to fuck you so you'd loosen up on her."

"Yeah, yeah, yeah. No man or boy will be flipping this ass over unless I'm dead first. And I ain't planning on going anytime soon." He coughed, oblivious to the irony as he took another drag on his cigarette. "So what brings you fellas way out here?"

"It's Brian," I interjected, happy to be directing the conversation to why we were here.

"He's not hurt, is he?" Phillip asked, rising to his feet. "Did somebody hurt him?"

"No, man—it's nothing like that. He just hasn't been himself since he came back from West Chester this past weekend. You know Brian is the mellowest guy we know. Nothing ever seems to bother him. But whatever went down at home has him wandering around, looking like he lost his best friend."

"Oh. West Chester. That explains a lot." Phillip nodded sagely.

"So, you know something?" I urged.

"Yeah, I know a lot. More than I want to. Brian's my dawg, and I hate to see him going through the hell he's going through there."

"So what is it? Is there anything we can do to help?" I asked. Phillip took a drag, looking at me.

"Look, Desmond, I know you mean well and all, but leave this situation alone." He exhaled slowly, a cloud of smoke obscuring his features for a moment. "Man, I wish I could be there right now. A couple of games of hoop and some dawg talk and I know he'd be all right.

"You want to know something? If it weren't for Brian, I might not be here today. That boy's got the Spirit in him and he knows how to use it. He kept me from ending my life and my mama's too. No joke, Desmond," he added, seeing the look on my face. "I had a gun literally to my mama's head and I was gonna blow it the fuck off, and then I was gonna do me. True.

"All of a sudden, there's a knock at the door—the second before I was gonna pull that trigger. We always keep the door locked, but after that knock, it just flew open and there he was, standing in the doorway."

"Brian?"

"Brian," Phillip acknowledged. "He talked me down from using that gun, then got me out the apartment. We walked. For the rest of the day. We walked, talked, and prayed.

"When I say that boy has the Spirit within him, I know what I'm talking about." He took a short drag of his shrinking cigarette. "Man, I wish I could get back down to his church these days. Back when I was there, it was as if all the shit here didn't exist. Fuck, I barely make enough to keep us going these days, though.

"But you know something? Since that day, I'm at *somebody's* church, here in the city. Every Sunday." Phillip stood and flicked his butt away. "Brian entrusted me with a secret that I plan to take to my grave. I owe him that much. So, sorry, fellas, I can't help you. It's time for me to go back in."

"Okay. So you won't tell us Brian's secret. Fine. But how about doing him a favor?"

"How do you mean? Man, I don't have a lot of time, with the job and home…" He trailed off sadly.

"Can you get off Saturday and come to the university early?"

Phil thought for a moment. "Yeah. I think I can. Matter of fact, I know I can. These chinks owe me a hell of a lot of time; it won't be a problem."

"Ah, shit," Antonio said, wrapping his arm around my shoulders. "You got something up your sleeves, boy, and I know it's got Karen and me written all over it!" I just smiled, silently confirming his suspicion.

"What you got in mind?" Phillip asked.

"Brian asked me to go with him to this birthday party on Saturday, and if I know the host like I do, a few extra party crashers bearing gifts won't be a problem."

"Who's the party for?" Phillip asked.

"There's this little girl Carley at church who absolutely adores Brian. When they're together, they're inseparable."

Phillip's face became a mask, but it was obvious he was thinking something.

I gave him a puzzled look. "You know Carley?"

"Yeah, I knew her from when I used to attend Brian's church. That girl loves him a lot." He took a deep breath, his gaze far away for a moment. "Okay," he said finally. "I'll be there."

We shook hands, hugged, and parted ways. Antonio and I got back to campus with enough time for Antonio to study a little more for his midterm. For my part, I got on the phone and charmed Momma into putting another hundred dollars in my bank account.

Later that night in the dorm lounge, I asked JC if he minded driving to West Chester on Saturday and hanging out at a three-year-old's birthday party. He gave an inquiring look to Antonio, who sat at his side.

"Don't look at me! Just tell the man yes. You know he's going to convince you to do his bidding no matter what."

"Okay, yeah," JC agreed. "You're gonna owe me for this," he added to his boyfriend. Antonio gave him a lewd wink.

"Believe me, baby, paying up will be my pleasure!"

Everything was set. I just hoped this would be the magic formula to heal whatever ailed Brian. Matter of fact, I was praying on it.

Saturday morning came and I prepared for my trip to DC. The whole time I was packing, Brian sat in his chair with his eyes closed. He was either willing the morning to pass more quickly or he was meditating. Either way, I was fairly confident he had no idea what I'd hatched.

A few minutes after I finished packing, a preplanned knock came at our door. I did my best to act surprised. "Who's that at this time of the morning?"

Without opening his eyes, Brian answered. "It's Phillip."

I turned to him, expecting to see a grin on his face, letting me know he was wise to my plans. But he just sat there with his eyes still closed. Confused, I went to the door. Phillip stood there, right as planned. Finally, Brian moved, springing to his feet and meeting Phillip mid-room.

"Yo, dawg!" Phillip exclaimed as they hooked hands and did this funny choreographed greeting in the middle of the floor. I wasn't sure what I'd unleashed.

"Yo, man! Something told me you were going to be here this morning! I just knew it!" Brian drew his friend in for a tight embrace.

"I know you did, bro. You and I got it like that."

"Well, I'm sure glad somebody around here 'got it,'" I said in puzzlement as I closed the door.

"Don't bother shutting it," Brian said.

"Why not?"

"Because Antonio and JC are right there," he replied.

"No, they're—" I met resistance as someone pushed at the door. Antonio and JC sauntered in, smiling.

"How did you...?" I stuttered. Brian smiled at me for the first time in over a week. Then he turned and greeted the two newcomers. I blinked, wondering what I was missing in all of this.

"Are you guys ready to go?" Brian asked as he reached for his coat.

"Wait a minute, nobody move!" I put my hands out to stop all action in the room. I looked Brian dead in his eyes. "How, how, *how* do you know we are all going somewhere?"

Brian laughed—another first in over a week. "Isn't your posse always with you whenever you do this stuff?"

"This *stuff*? Okay—what's going on here?"

"Man," Antonio said, clapping me on the shoulder, "I think this vacation came just in time for you—you're losing it!" I looked over at him; he was smiling, but not in a conspiratorial sort of way—he clearly didn't know what was going on any more than I did. Phillip came to the rescue.

"Look, Desmond, there are some things best left unexplained for now. Just know my dawg here"—he wrapped an arm around Brian, who stood there quietly—"knows shit before it even happens."

"What? Like a psychic?" I looked at Brian, but he remained impassive.

"I dunno what it's called," Phillip admitted. "All I know is, that shit used to freak me the fuck out. Until we got to know each other better, that is. Now I just accept that's the way my boy is. Take my advice and do the same."

Brian said nothing, only giving a little shrug. I wanted to go deeper into this, but I knew this wasn't the time. It was almost noon, and if we were going to make a one o'clock party, we needed to get on the road.

I coordinated gifts for everyone and made sure Phillip had money to get home. As we all started pouring out the door, Brian grabbed me by the arm. We waited until the others were down the hall a bit.

"Thank you, my friend. I know what you went through to pull this off, and I am grateful. Some things in the universe are destined to happen: our paths crossing—yours and mine—was one of those things. We got here because you always follow your heart. Keep doing that, and it will never lead you astray." He pulled me in close, embracing me tightly. I swore I felt this warm tingling sensation pass between the two of us.

"Desmond, if ever you need me, no matter when or where, I'll be there for you," he said into my ear. I admit to feeling a bit freaked out. Maybe Antonio was right: I probably needed to take a vacation. I patted Brian's back uncomfortably, after which we joined the other three by the elevator.

The ride to West Chester was lovely. It was unseasonably warm, so JC put down the convertible top. We sang and horsed around the whole way there. As we drove into town, Brian got quiet again, but I witnessed Phillip whispering in his ear and his whole demeanor came back to its happier self.

The Masons lived right on the edge of town in this fabulous development, which sat next to a country club and golf course. Massive and all white, the house sported a four-pillared carport out front to receive guests. As we pulled up, two valets approached the car, opening the doors for us. As we walked to the house, we were welcomed by a gentleman of African descent dressed in a three-piece suit. "Good afternoon, Mr. Harris. It's always a pleasure to see you."

"Thank you, Obotuo," Brian replied. "These are my friends: Mr. Desmond Dawson, Mr. Antonio Savileo, Mr. Jean Claude Lefebvre…and of course you remember Mr. Phillip Garvey, don't you?"

"Ah yes, Mr. Garvey, the…expressive young man." The Masons' majordomo arched his eyebrow at Phillip.

"Watch it, Oh-butt-yo; remember the last time we matched wits," Phillip said with a mock snarl.

"How could I forget, Mr. Garvey? The memory of it is etched in my mind forever."

"And don't you forget it neither!" Phillip added.

"Yes, sir! Mr. Harris, the other party guests are outside in the gardens. If you'll follow me, I'll take you out there."

"Thank you, Obotuo."

As we were walking through the house to the backyard, Antonio whispered excitedly in my ear, even as JC whispered in his. We'd never in a thousand years imagined that sweet Sylvia Mason lived like this.

As we approached a row of tables that had been set out in the gardens, a lady was there waiting to receive our gifts; Brian, however, declined to give his up.

Farther in, we spotted Mrs. Mason. She was talking to a small group of people dressed in their Sunday best, seemingly out of place for a birthday party. I wondered if one of them was the mysterious Mr. Fredrick Mason.

Sylvia kept gazing over toward the children, who were riding a merry-go-round that must have been rented specifically for the day. She looked as if she'd rather join them than carry on with her conversation.

When she spotted us, she waved, excusing herself to those around her. She strode quickly over to us. At the same time, up on the merry-go-round, we heard a squeal—Carley had spotted Brian and was waving madly. He smiled, waved back, and blew her a kiss.

From behind us, a voice bellowed out. "Gentlemen! So nice of you to come!"

I turned toward the voice, coming face-to-face with my worst nightmare: Rick. I froze, staring at his widened eyes—no doubt a match for mine—before he cleared his throat and rolled on.

"Hmm...bit of a frog in my throat there." As he coughed again, he moved in beside Sylvia, placing a hand around her petite shoulders, turning his gaze to Brian.

I felt Antonio's breath, hot on the back of my neck. "Thaaaat's Rick, isn't it?" he whispered into my ear. I was glad he was there; I felt as if I might collapse on the spot.

While I tried to wrap my brain around finding Rick here, Carley jumped off her wooden horse and came running up to Brian, her Cinderella dress flowing behind her. She leaped at him; Brian caught her without breaking the staring contest he was in with Fredrick Mason.

"*Uncle* Brian, my daughter is madly in love with you," Rick declared, deadpan. "What is a jealous father to do?" He laughed humorlessly. Brian gave him a frosty smile.

"Don't worry, *Dad*. A little girl's first love will always be her father." Brian kissed Carley on the forehead and looked into her eyes, adding, "Happy birthday, little princess."

"Thank you, Brian!" she declared, wrapping her arms tightly about his neck. He squeezed her back, then set her down. She went running over to a clown making balloon animals for a group of children. We all watched her go; then Brian spoke again.

"Mr. Mason, let me introduce you to my friends." Rick nodded, redirecting his attention to us. "You remember my old roommate, Phillip Garvey?"

"Yes, of course. Good to see you again, sir."

"My pleasure as well, Mr. Mason," Phillip replied.

"Gentlemen, I'm going to stop you right now before this 'Mr.' stuff gets out of hand. Call me Fred, please. There are very few formalities in my house. My wife, Sylvia, and I try to live a simple existence amongst all this stuff."

"Give me the fluff and fanfare, thank you," Antonio blurted out, and everyone around him had to laugh.

"And who might this gentleman be?" Fred asked.

"Mister—I mean, Fred, this is Antonio Savileo, and that's Jean Claude Lefebvre. They're friends of mine from the university. And, finally, I want you to meet my new roommate and my dear friend Desmond Cameron Dawson."

Hearing my full name made me stop and look at Brian for a moment before extending my hand to Fred or Rick or whatever the fuck his name was.

"It's a pleasure to meet you, *Fred*. You and Mrs. Mason—Sylvia—have a beautiful home here. Thank you for inviting us." Our eyes met as they had that night at Letters. He looked as majestic and charming as he did that evening. I was worried I might lose it right there on the spot.

"Well, thank you. It's...*Desmond?*" Rick cocked his head to one side.

"Yes," I admitted, feeling a flush come on. "It's Desmond, Rick—*Fred!* I mean, Fred...Fred*rick*." *Shit!* Rick was playing it cool, though.

"Please, Desmond—you must get my wife to show you around before you leave. I get the impression you're a man who appreciates fine things."

"Yes, I do. Thank you, sir. I'll be sure to ask her." We both smiled courteously at each other. Then he turned his attention to all of us.

"Well, gentlemen, I have been told by my daughter and my wife that it is their day and I'm not to be shared with anyone else." He put his hand next to his mouth as if to whisper to the four of us. "I don't think they meant you, though; it's the stuffed shirts over there they don't want me mixed up with." He laughed and we joined in politely. "Please help yourselves to some food and drink, and if there is anything you don't see out here that you want, let Obotuo know and he will get it for you. Enjoy."

Rick (*Fred! I gotta call him Fred!*) strode off, and Brian made his way over to where Carley was watching the clown do his balloon show. Phillip followed right behind. Antonio and JC each grabbed me by an arm and led me toward the bar.

"Nice recovery—'*Rick—uhhh…Fred!*'" JC mocked under his breath.

"Quite the slip, Miss Thang!" Antonio admonished. "Please tell me your man—Mr. Fucking Rick—doesn't live in this big shit-ass mansion? We're gonna wake up from this fantasy, realizing it's some sorta nightmare?!"

"I wish I could tell you something, Antonio, but I'm just as lost in space as you are. What I don't understand is, does Brian know Fred and I have met? If so, what fuckin' game are the two of them playing?! Did you see the tension between them? There is something going on here in sweet tranquil West Chester that no one is talking about." I looked around at the picture-perfect scene around me. "And if I'm a pawn in their chess game, I want to know what the rules are."

"Well, maybe you ought to start with our star player over there: Brian Harris." Antonio directed our attention to Brian and Phillip, who were standing behind Carley as the clown presented her a balloon poodle. "I think he owes us all an explanation, and now is as good a time as any. Don't you agree, partners?"

"Baby, I'm right there with you," JC agreed.

"But wait," I said. "On the chance Brian doesn't know Fred and I met, let's not put that piece of information out there. Let's let Brian tell us what is going on." JC and Antonio both nodded their approval of the plan.

We got a drink from the bar and walked to where Brian and Phillip were playing with the kids. I gazed over at the boys and girls, recognizing most of them from church, when Brian turned and walked over to us.

"Okay, so you all want to know what's going on here?"

The three of us came to a complete stop, nonplussed at Brian's prescient comment. Antonio recovered first.

"You're damn straight we do."

"Fine, but not here. Let's take a walk." Brian took one step toward the house when a little body was there, pulling at his jacket.

"You're not leaving, are you?" Carley asked.

Brian bent down, looked her face-to-face, and said, "No, princess. I just have to take them to the potty. Will you excuse us?"

"Don't you be long!" she scolded, pointing a finger at him. Brian kissed her on the forehead.

"Scout's promise. I'll be right back." He extended three fingers to her, which she touched with three of hers. Then, after a quick hug, she ran to join the other kids.

Past the clown show, I glimpsed Sylvia and Rick (*Fred, damnit!*). He was conversing with some "suits," while she had been clearly watching the interaction between her daughter and Brian. She had a smile on her face, but it seemed be hiding a sadness behind it.

Brian led us toward the house, but as soon as we reached some tall shrubbery, he signaled for us to take a detour to another part of the yard. I took one last look toward the guests, catching Fred gazing at me. He winked and gave a little smile. I smiled back, feeling heat rise to my cheeks yet again. I rounded the corner and caught up to the group.

Farther along the shrubbery, we came upon a gazebo. We each took a wicker seat; then Antonio was on Brian to start explaining.

"Why do you have us out here in this vicious, hostile countryside? That man is serious business. And I think he suspects—like all of us are beginning to suspect—that you are having an affair with his wife." Antonio paused, clearly hoping Brian would speak up. When he didn't, Antonio added, "Inquiring minds would like an answer to the question: ARE YOU FUCKING SLEEPING WITH THE MAN'S WIFE?"

"Shhh, Antonio!" I hissed, glancing around the gardens for any nearby partygoers. He waved me off, staring Brian down. After a pause, we got our answer.

"No, I'm not at the present time sleeping with Sylvia Mason. But I am in love with her and her children." That silenced us for a good five seconds.

"Ah shit, you're dead meat!" Antonio said finally. "Why don't you just put a gun to your head and shoot yourself now! Yeah—it's obvious you're in love with this woman, and whether you're sleeping with her or not, everyone who knows you and sees you together are drawing the same conclusions that we are!" Antonio shouted.

"Antonio, keep your voice down!" I pleaded again.

"I know. I can't help it," Brian admitted. "I love being around her and the children. Sylvia and I get each other at a deeper level, you know? Plus, she's in a lonely marriage with a man who's a workaholic. She's told me he's never been mean to her. Matter of fact, he adores her, gives her and the children whatever they want—he's just an absentee husband and father. He cares more about his business than he does about his marriage." Brian leaned forward, lowering his voice. "He hardly ever has sex with her, for God's sake. She's to the point where she believes she's ugly and unappealing!"

"Damn—just tell the woman she's beautiful, give her a damn dildo, and tell her to learn to get her rocks off!" Antonio ranted. "She's got everything anyone in this world would ever want!"

"She doesn't have a real marriage or the love of the man she gave her heart and soul to. She's like this beautiful bird in a gilded cage, slowly dying of loneliness and captivity. Can't you guys see that?!"

"If she's so miserable, why doesn't she divorce his ass and walk away from all of this?" Antonio gestured to the manicured gardens around us.

"She can't. He won't give her a divorce," Brian said, his head drooping. "Mason won't allow the children to be a product of a broken home. He had her sign a prenuptial agreement binding her till death do they part!"

"What?!" I blurted.

"Yeah. The agreement can only be broken if he abuses her physically or is actually caught in the act of cheating on her," Brian explained. I pointedly ignored the looks I was getting from Antonio and JC. "If either of those things happen, Sylvia receives half of everything he owns. Likewise, if she is caught with another man in her bed, she will lose everything, including the children."

"Fuuuck…" JC muttered.

"So, you see, guys: she's trapped. I am her safety net. And because I'm the son of a very influential minister in the Northeast Conference, Mason would never publicly accuse me without solid proof."

"So, has she ever tried to find out if he is sneaking around on her?" I asked.

"Yes, she has hired the best private detectives Mason's money can buy. All of them have come up empty-handed. It seems all the man ever does is work and work some more. No one's ever been able to catch him with another woman. I guess he really is married to his business." Brian exhaled loudly. "You can believe what you want, guys, but I'm all Sylvia has. I'm the only one who doesn't see her as being a fool.

"I love her, and I know she feels the same way about me. If I could safely take her away from all of this and provide for her, I would. But I can't even take care of myself. As my faith is my guide, though, I'll find a way. I'll find a way out of this for both of us." Brian fell silent, and even Antonio had nothing else to say.

Finally, Phillip clapped Brian on the shoulder. "We should be getting back before they miss us."

"They'll keep their pants on," I said, holding up my hand. "I've just got one more question for Brian."

"You want to know why I asked you to come." He'd read my mind. Maybe *actually* read it.

"Yes," I admitted.

"Because you are the only person I know who could stand toe-to-toe with this guy. You've got intelligence, style, class, experience in the world...you name it—and he's got no more than you do," Brian explained.

"I dunno, Brian—I think he's got way more than me."

"No, Desmond—you have everything I wish I had in order to stand up to this creep. Yeah, he's got money now, but you know what they say—you can take the boy off the street...

You, on the other hand," Brian said, pointing at me, "were born naturally with all those gifts. And I've watched you use them for the good of others. Look what you did for me today, and I don't think you even know half of what you do."

I blinked at him, not knowing how to respond.

"Man," he continued, not waiting for a response, "you even have a classy name. Whatever your momma was thinking when you were born, she must have known you were going to be great one day. Shit, who thinks 'Fredrick Harold Mason' sounds important?"

"I do," Phillip interjected, a sneer on his face. "It kinda has a nice ring to it: Fredrick Harold Mason…like one of those faggot prep school punks!"

"Thanks for your insight, dawg." Brian sighed amusingly.

"Hey, I'm here for ya, bro."

"So there you have it, fellas," Brian said, wrapping up. "I just didn't want to face the lions without a couple of Christians behind me. Thanks for coming. If you want to leave now, I fully understand."

At that point we all sat there kicking the ground with our heads down. Brian got up and walked back to the party. Something urged me to run after him.

"Hey, roomie, did you mean all that shit about being intelligent, classy, and shit?"

"Okay, preppie," Antonio said, appearing at my side. "Put your ego back up in your head; it's beginning to leak everywhere!"

"Bitch!" I snarled, my pinky in the air. Everyone fell out laughing—even Brian, which was nice to see. Smiling back at him, I said, "What say we kick this party up a notch, roomie?"

"You got it, roomie!" Brian said. Then Antonio stuck out his arm.

"One for all," he boomed. Laughing, Brian, Phillip, JC, and I slapped our palms down on top of Antonio's hand.

"And all for one!"

We rejoined the party, kicking it up a notch as we agreed. JC and Antonio convinced Sylvia to allow for some music to be piped to outdoor speakers and started to boogie right there in the gardens. Carley squealed in delight at her birthday being turned into a dance party and joined in on the fun.

Off to one side, I managed to get myself to Rick's side, engaging with him and his business partners on their own turf—trading opinions on politics, the economy, and world events. I was proud of how well I held my own. Brian had been right. Without realizing it, I guess my interests while growing up and my privileged upbringing had prepared me to fit very well in this situation. This was my arena, I discovered, and I didn't back down even once during the several debates I got into that afternoon.

I know what you're thinking, but Rick and I didn't get a "moment alone," nor did we try to. We were amidst people the entire time. Plus, it was his girl's party.

But I felt his vibe—in the way he stood ever-so-slightly closer to me than the other men, how his gaze lingered on me just a fraction of a second longer...

I knew he could read my vibe too.

Despite the sexual tension between us, this guy had a lot of explaining too.

Or maybe he didn't?

Maybe I had simply been a way for him to get his rocks off that evening, if only from a kiss. Maybe that had been our one and only time together, and we'd be restricted to nothing more than political debates at garden parties from now on.

But no. *I've got something that intrigues him. I know Mr. Mason and I will be together again, sometime, somewhere, somehow…* There was more for us on the horizon; it was our destiny.

Interlude Sixteen

Just Palling Around

We left the party around six that night. Phillip decided to stay overnight at Brian's, so we dropped the two of them off there. JC, Antonio, and I were going to drive back to the city, intending to return the next morning for church.

So, with everything seemingly in order, Antonio took the wheel, JC snuggled up next to him for a nap, and I watched the world go by as we drove home. Antonio didn't speak the whole way back, though he did light up a joint—which I gladly decided to partake in. With sultry music on the radio, I let my mind wander into the abyss. It's what I needed; there had been so much going on in the past week I really couldn't focus on any one thing.

We got to the university around seven thirty, got some takeout burgers, and retired to our individual rooms. Well, JC retired to Antonio's room. I wasn't sure if JC had permanently moved in with Antonio or was just keeping his spot in Antonio's bed warm.

I'd wanted to talk to Antonio about what I felt but wasn't quite comfortable enough around JC to include him in the conversation too. Don't get me wrong—I thought he was a great guy; I hadn't built up with him the level of trust I shared with Antonio. So, I sat in my room, still high from the joint, devouring my burgers, staring at my four walls. Around eleven I figured I better get to bed so I wouldn't fall asleep during Rev. Harris's sermon tomorrow.

I was about to drift off when I heard a faint knock at the door. I thought I was dreaming, so I rolled over and tried to ignore it. Another knock came—more insistent, and a familiar voice called my name: Antonio. I opened the door slightly, and he came barging in with a bottle of Old Grand-Dad bourbon and two glasses. He pulled the chair from my desk up to my bed, turned my trunk down on its side to use as a table, and began pouring. "So, you ready to talk?"

"About what?"

"Girl, when the fuck are you going to stop playing this childish game? 'I don't know what you're talking about, Antonio,'" he said in a mocking voice. "Just be real with me!" He took a sip of bourbon.

"Fine—as soon as you do it too. I'm not the only one who gets evasive when asked a direct question, twin brother!"

"Okay, okay, you got me on that one. Anyway, cut the shit and tell me what you're gonna do 'cause, baby, I've got eyes. The two of you cats might have thought there were other people in your intimate chat today, but you and Rick—Fred—Harold—whatever the fuck his name is—were having a one-on-one all afternoon."

"Was it really that obvious?" I asked. Antonio arched an eyebrow, taking another sip. "Okay, okay. He had a real effect on me that night at the club, and now I learn he's this big, influential man... I'm not sure I'm ready for anyone like that."

"Bullshit!" Antonio swore. "If there's only one thing that Brian had the right idea about today, it was that Fred-Rick found his match. And I'm betting he will stop at nothing to find you again. What you better decide and decide quickly is whether or not you want to compete in the big leagues." I opened my mouth to reply, but he didn't give me a chance. "Bro, wait—I can see it in your eyes: of course you do! Well, I'm telling you, Desmond, you're gonna need someone with experience to coach you through this."

"Oh, and you're the one to do this?"

"Listen—I get this, brother. I understand why his marriage is basically over. Miss Sylvia can't keep up with him in the boardroom *or* in the bedroom! One thing about people at his level: they chew weak people up for breakfast and lunch, then use their bones as firewood to roast their dinner. If you go after this tiger, baby, you are gonna have to be in *control*. You can't succumb to the spoils of money."

"You think I should still go after him, even though he's married?"

"Sylvia is just what Brian said she is: a pretty bird in a cage, on display. She's got her beauty and personality going for her. Perfect as a showpiece on his arm. But our boy is looking for someone he can communicate with—on *all* levels. And he's gay on top of that. What he really wants is a strong man who will fulfill his hot, erotic sex fantasies."

I raised my eyebrows at this, a smile creeping across my tired face. This spurred Antonio on.

"Every time you climb into bed with this one," he said, his voice becoming more animated, "you've got to rock his world…but you gotta make him work equally as hard to keep you satisfied too!" That sounded good, but something was tugging at me.

"I dunno, Antonio. Maybe I shouldn't have anything more to do with him. I feel like he might be dangerous and a lot of people beside me could get hurt. Are you forgetting—he's got young kids as well!"

"Damn right, he's dangerous for you. But you're a danger to him too, and that's why both of you are interested in each other. You're the type of guy who will cloud his judgment and put him in jeopardy of messing up his game, losing it all because he has fallen in love with you."

"What?"

"Take my word for it, girl; that's part of the allure. But if you don't control this one, he'll control you and turn you into a wife.

"For most men cheating on their wives, it's all about the game. They don't worry about who will get hurt in the end; their main goals are to play to win and not get caught. Most of them have the sick notion they will never get caught. Matter of fact, they get bold and arrogant about how good they are. Those men are the ones who fall the hardest and lose the most.

"And when that happens to Rick, you have to know when to jump ship before it goes down."

"How will I know when?"

"Listen—I got your back. You know I do. And I can teach you everything I've learned on the street…" And here, Antonio hesitated. "But…you need someone who is a master player in this game. I think you know who I'm talking about." And I did. I needed Uncle Camy.

My uncle dealt with people like Rick on a daily basis; if he couldn't help me, nobody could. It was time to see if he would stay true to his word. It would be an added bonus if he agreed to keep this a secret too.

Antonio and I finished our bourbon in silence. He collected the glasses and the bottle, standing to leave.

"Hey, twin, come here," he said, looking down at me on the bed. I rose, feeling the room spin around me. Before I could fall, I felt his arms around me. Our faces were brought close together, and it felt only natural when our lips interlocked in a kiss.

You'll always be the man I truly want, I thought as our tongues swirled together. He kissed me long, hard, and passionately. It was only when an image of JC flashed through my addled brain that I stiffened a bit. He felt me resist and broke the kiss.

"Des, I love you like a brother and a real best friend." His voice was thick with emotion. "As long as I'm alive, I won't let anyone ever hurt you again. I made you that promise once, and I'm making it again." I nodded, hugging him tight and laying my head on his shoulder.

"Why couldn't it have been us?" The words slipped past my lips before I could stop them. Before giving him a chance to answer, I lifted my head and put a finger to his lips. "I know, I know—that wasn't our destiny. I know we have different roads to follow. But, like you, T," I said, using the name I called him when we were alone, "I won't let anyone keep me from protecting you. Wherever you may go, whatever you may get into, if you need me, I'll be there."

We kissed one more time; then he slipped out of my room. I climbed back into bed and was asleep before my head touched the pillow.

★

The next day, like most Sundays lately, Karen came banging at my door. "C'mon, Des! If you don't move your skinny ass, we'll be late!" Like Brian—on those rare times he stayed over on the weekend—Karen acted as one of the group's human alarm clocks. They made sure Antonio and I made it to church—and everywhere else, for that matter—on time. There were mornings where I prayed the two of them would oversleep so that I could too…but that had yet to happen.

This morning, to my dismay, she'd come to my door even earlier. We needed extra time to load the car so that we could head straight to Angel's place after visiting Brian and his family.

We arrived at the Harris household in time to enjoy breakfast with them. Karen was shocked to see Phillip there and couldn't wait to get him up to speed on Melvin.

During breakfast, we often had a chance to engage with Rev. Harris in a pre-sermon discussion about some topic one of us had been thinking of that past week. This morning, it happened to be me who posed a question: "Reverend? How does one choose the path they should follow?"

Well, Brian's dad took the topic and ran with it. He went so far as to pull out an old sermon he'd written on the subject a few years back. Everyone at the table became so involved in the conversation we almost missed making it to the church on time. We jumped out of our seats, helped Mrs. Harris clear the table, then rushed out to assist with Sunday school.

Normally, during his dad's service, Brian would sit with Sylvia's children and we would be right behind him. This morning, however, we walked into the service to find the whole Mason family taking up an entire pew—looking just picture perfect. We found Brian and Phillip sitting in the pew across the aisle from them. We all crowded into the same pew, with me sitting closest to the aisle. It just so happened Fred Mason was sitting on the end of his pew as well.

He smiled and nodded to me when we made eye contact; I returned the salutation. Throughout the service, my eyes kept drifting to him. I couldn't help it. And every time my eyes went over to him, I caught him looking at me. Antonio had been right: Rick was not ready to let me go. The game was on.

There was another unexpected twist in the morning's service.

As Rev. Harris prepared to deliver his sermon, he cleared his throat and said, "Please forgive me; I know I listed in your program this morning that I would be talking on the topic of 'Tending Your Fields,' but after having a conversation with some fine young folk this morning, I feel compelled to deliver a different message instead." I exchanged a look with Karen, who sat next to me. We knew where the reverend was going.

"So, my sermon this morning is called 'The Path We Choose.' Now, some of you no doubt remember that I have enlightened you with this topic before. However, this morning I'm going to take it in another direction.

"And, by the way," he added, gesturing down toward Sylvia and Rick, "it's good to see brother Mason with us this morning. We were beginning to forget what you looked like, brother, you've been working so hard! Even God rested on the seventh day, you remember!" The Reverend gave a gentle grin as his congregation chuckled at his joke. "I'm sorry, brother— I don't mean to embarrass you. I just love seeing a family worship together."

Fred smiled and waved. Rev. Harris continued. "Now, I'm going to keep picking on brother Mason for a while, only because I know he can stand the heat." He gave Fred a wink.

"Brothers and sisters, the path is laid out before you. And during your lifetime you will come upon many forks in the road. The direction you take at those points represents the power of choice God has given to man.

"But know this—no matter which way you go, God will be there, walking with you!

"Let me remind you of the parable of the farmer and his three sons." And the Reverend launched into a tale I knew very well from church sermons past. As his voice boomed throughout the lofty church hall, my thoughts drifted to the path *I* was about to take.

Stealing a glance at Fred and his family, I knew I was seeing a picture of what I desired for myself one day. This is how I imagined it would be with Angel.

But there was a fork in the road.

More and more I was intrigued by thoughts of being involved with Fredrick Mason. Despite his money and personality, he was a very handsome, well-built man. If I were to choose what man I'd have my first love affair with, Rick wouldn't be my first choice, but if I couldn't have the one I wanted, he'd make a good substitution. So, here I was, at the fork in the road.

Lord, all I am asking is that you walk and guide me through this.

Fred and Sylvia left directly after the service, so I had no chance to speak with him. The bunch of us stayed back to help Rev. and Mrs. Harris pack up food for the sick and shut-in. We shared a quick dinner with Brian, his family, and Phillip, then got on the road to DC.

As we drove, I stared out the window, letting the two couples have as much couple time as possible with a fifth wheel in the car. My thoughts turned to Brian and what we'd learned about him this past week. I couldn't help wondering if there was more he hadn't told us.

What else was he hiding, and why?

But it went deeper than that—what was this trick he had of knowing things before they were about to happen? And him talking about how this was my destiny? By this time my head had begun to hurt. I leaned my head against the window and shut my eyes.

When I opened them again, it was eight thirty, and we had arrived in Cheverly, Maryland, a suburban town about thirty minutes outside of DC. Angel had given us directions to her cousin's place, which we were able to find easily despite it being dark out. We pulled into the driveway, looking up at the house. The five-bedroom split-level home with a finished basement would be more than enough room for all of us.

We got out of the car, all stiff-legged, just as Angel opened the front door. Seeing her was like coming home again. No power plays; no games; no deceptions. She was the real thing and she was mine.

After making introductions, Angel showed everyone where they would be sleeping. She and I had gone over sleeping arrangements over the phone earlier that week, so there would be no surprises.

Karen and Melvin got one room; Antonio and JC got another. Angel had decided I'd have to sleep in my own room, and I was too tired at that moment to press her about it, so I dutifully dropped my bags in a cool, dark bedroom in the basement.

Angel's friends all lived in the area, so they were each staying at their own homes for the week; several were there when we arrived, however, ready for the night's festivities.

We'd decided to save money that week by chipping in for groceries and taking turns cooking the meals. Our first task was grocery shopping at a store about five minutes away.

Shopping with this crew was a real trip. Melvin had finally loosened up around us and turned out to be as big a fool as Antonio. They were like children in a toy store. I was too tired to play adult; luckily, the girls happily took on that role, keeping us boys in line as we loaded our cart down with food.

The next morning, Angel woke me up before the others, and the two of us fixed breakfast for everyone. While nothing like the spread Mrs. Harris put out on Sunday mornings, we didn't do too badly by everyone. Angel's friends Barbara and Flip, Barry and Cheryl, and her best friend, Georgette, had joined us; we were all seated around her cousin's enormous dining room table, coffee or juice—or an extra-large glass of milk for Melvin—in hand, trading life stories. I learned that college experiences seemed to be quite similar, no matter where you studied.

The next three days were hectic, trying to see and do everything each couple wanted to. We did manage to get a lot done, though. Monday, we visited the Capitol, the White House, the Lincoln Memorial, and the Washington Monument. On Tuesday, we went to the Smithsonian museums and a concert at Howard University. Wednesday, we finished up with the Arlington Cemetery and the National Zoo.

The really interesting stuff happened during the evenings, though. We all caught a movie together Monday night, going out for drinks afterward. Antonio and JC went out on their own Tuesday and Wednesday nights. (Needless to say, I wished I could have partaken in those escapades.) The rest of us went to Georgetown one night and the Harlem Theatre Company's show at the National Theatre the next.

As for me and Angel, we worked hard to make sure everyone had their needs met and had a memorable time. We were the perfect hosts.

At one point on Wednesday afternoon during a break between outings, Karen and Angel went off for what they called "girl time." The rest of us sat around playing board games or napped. I kept wondering what the two girls talked about for the two hours they were gone, but I figured I'd find out sooner or later.

Thursday morning came upon us quickly, and Angel and I helped everyone get ready for the next leg of their vacations. Karen and Melvin picked up the rental car his coach had reserved at nine thirty and got on the road to Virginia Beach. We finally pushed Antonio and JC out the door around eleven o'clock for what had to be at least a fourteen-hour trip up to Canada.

Next on the agenda, Angel and I cleaned the house. We stripped and remade beds, washed and folded all the dirty laundry, tidied up, dusted, and vacuumed. When we finished around six o'clock, we decided to treat ourselves to a nice dinner out.

I was exhausted but glad to finally have my woman all to myself. We cleaned up and walked to a nearby white-tablecloth restaurant for supper. On the way to her cousin's place, we visited one of those new movie rental stores, picking a VHS movie to watch on her VCR.

When we got to the house, Angel set me up on the sofa with a pillow, a blanket, and the movie and told me to relax. She said she had some other things to attend to. I offered to help but she convinced me to relax. Within fifteen minutes I'd fallen fast asleep.

Around eleven o'clock she woke me and snuggled up next to me on the sofa. With her, she had two glasses of wine. We drank and talked about our friends and how comfortable we were entertaining everyone together. We spent about forty-five minutes laughing and sharing funny stories about the different couples. We shared a look that lingered, and just like that, our wineglasses were on the coffee table and I'd pulled her close for a deep kiss. *What a wonderful woman I've found.*

We made out for a while longer; then she asked me if I was still tired. By that time, I had gotten my second wind and could have gone dancing till the wee hours of the morning. But Angel had other plans.

"Stand up, Desmond. Close your eyes."

"What?"

"Do you trust me?" she asked, taking my hand. I let her pull me to my feet and even let her turn me around. She wrapped something around my eyes, tying it firmly in the back. I laughed nervously but was game for whatever this was.

"Can you see?"

"Nope."

"Good." She took me by the hand and led me though the house, careful to tell me where to step and not to step. When we finally reached our destination, she whispered in my ear, "Don't open your eyes yet." She removed the blindfold, positioning herself against my chest, enclosing her arms around me. "Okay," she said. "Open up."

We were in her cousin's master bedroom, softly lit by dozens of votive candles. I had never seen anything like it before. Before I could say as much, Angel led me to the master bathroom, where more candles lit a steaming bubble bath in a huge Jacuzzi tub.

"I must be dreaming," I said finally. Angel smiled, taking my face in her soft hands and drawing my lips to hers. Her kisses moved down the curve of my chin, to the hollow in my neck, and down to my chest, which she exposed by unbuttoning my shirt. I let it slip off my arms and fall to the floor as she began to lick my chest hairs and suck my nipples, nibbling gently until they stood firmly at attention.

Her hands drifted down to my pants, unfastening them as she continued to kiss and lick down my stomach. She drew my pants and boxers down to my ankles, and I pulled my feet though. The steamy air in the bathroom caressed my exposed thighs and buttocks, even as Angel began to explore my pubic hair with fingers and lips.

A moan escaped my lips as she found my hardened member, teasing the tip with her tongue, tickling my balls with her fingers. In one quick motion, she engulfed my hard-on, my moan turning into a fevered shout.

I interlaced my fingers through her hair as we breathed in rhythmic harmony, moaning and groaning together with every eclipse of my manhood between her moist, warm lips, her tongue massaging my shaft as it slid through her mouth.

She withdrew, and I marveled as she stood slowly, letting my cock slide over her shirt—through her cleavage, over her smooth belly, coming to rest against the barely contained heat coming from the front of her jeans.

"Eyes up here, big boy," she whispered, catching my lips with hers as I lifted my gaze.

As we kissed, she began to remove her own clothing. I placed my hands over hers, gently moving them aside as I took over the task of unbuttoning her blouse. I slid it off her shoulders, where it fell to the floor as mine had done moments before.

Her luscious breasts exposed, I caressed them in the palms of my hands, lowering my head to meet this ripe fruit before me. I took each nipple into my mouth, sucking and biting it ever so gently. A cry escaped from her as she entangled her fingers in the curls of my hair.

Freeing one hand from the bounty of Angel's upper body, I unfastened the buttons that hid my ultimate desire. Her jeans slipped to the floor, and the aroma of her womanly scent filled my nostrils. I ran my hands over her lace panties, slowly tugging them down to her ankles. I took another deep breath of her womanhood, cupping her firm buttocks.

Audaciously, my tongue probed its way through her dark bush. Angel parted her legs, directing my mouth to the obscure reaches of her clitoris. Her moans grew more impassioned as my tongue flicked at her womanly folds, languishing in her juices. Her moaning peaked, and she drew me away suddenly, breathing heavily.

"Up," she managed between lustful breaths. I rose to face her eye to eye, knowing our night had come. I couldn't help but smile like a kid who stole candy.

Angel took my hand and led me into the tub.

It took us both a moment to adapt to the temperature, oohing and ahhing at the sensuous aroma of oils and soaps filling the air. Once settled up to our shoulders, we resumed kissing and caressing each other. We washed each other with the mountains of sparkling bubbles surrounding us, running our fingers through our hair, over our slick bodies.

The combined aromas of her hair, her body, and the candles had me completely entranced. We teased and played with each other in the water for what seemed an eternity, until she stopped, looking me in the eyes.

"Are you ready?" Angel asked in a smoldering voice. I grinned from ear to ear, nodding wordlessly. She led me out of the tub, where we took turns drying each other. We dropped our towels and embraced in another passionate kiss, my penis pressing impatiently against her yearning pussy.

I scooped her up in my arms, carried her to the bedroom, and placed her gently on the bed, then joined her. Our lips and tongues immediately went to work yet again. We showered each other's body with tender kisses and sensuous bites. She seized my cock with one hand, my body responding with a shudder of ecstasy. She shimmied down, replacing her hand with her warm mouth, sucking on me as if she couldn't get enough. Her wet pussy on my calf slid in tempo with her sucking; knowing her juices bathed my leg made my body quiver.

She left my manhood, her lips and tongue exploring regions below, giving attention to my thighs, knees, and ankles. Heading back up, her butterfly kisses reached my chest, making sure both nipples received firm attention, leaving each of them erect and alert with passion. Finally, she returned to my lips.

Hungrily I feasted in the fullness of her mouth. My tongue thrusting deeper and deeper as her body writhed against mine. Our embrace brought my rock-hard cock sliding back and forth between her buttocks.

"Hold on," she breathed, stretching a hand over to the night table. I breathed in the scent of her hair while she fiddled with the drawer. When she slid back on me, she held a condom.

Oh my God, I thought, *is this happening?!* She tore it open with her teeth; then, together, we got it rolled onto my rock-hard penis.

Raising her hips, she prepared to lower herself on me. I placed a hand on either buttock.

"Wait—are you sure, baby?"

"Yes!" she moaned, full of emotion, then sheathed my manhood fully within her. I gave a shuddering moan as I felt myself penetrate her pussy, even as Angel cried out sharply.

"Are you okay?" I whispered hoarsely, knowing instinctively I was the first to tap this treasure.

"I'm okay! Take me, Desmond."

And with those words I let her hips drop fully onto my member, bottoming out deep inside her sheath. I began to thrust my hips upward, getting into a rhythm of driving myself into her. Angel switched between whimpers and sighs as her body rocked back and forth in time with my thrusting.

She grabbed my wrists, pinning them down on either side of my head. I caught a look of fire in her eyes, which stoked the passion in me, and I pumped even harder into her. Bracing my heels on the bed, raising my pelvis, and hoisting her up on my thighs, I tore my hands free and grabbed her by the waist again. Her cries of pleasure matched my own—I knew her momentary pain had now turned to pleasure. She rode me like a jockey on a thoroughbred.

The tightening and twitching of her pussy muscles were bringing me to a peak sooner than I'd hoped for. I knew—for her pleasure—I needed to hold on longer. I flipped her over onto her back, placing her ankles on my shoulders. I withdrew for a moment, letting the crest of ecstasy settle a bit, then reentered her deeply, right to the root of my cock. She gasped, reaching a hand behind my neck.

"Oh, Desmond!"

I leaned in and kissed her roughly, our tongues slashing out at each other. A groan began deep in the pit of my stomach, mounting in intensity as I thrust into her over and over and over.

"ANGEL!" I shouted, the passion in me overflowing. My hard-on twitched even as her pussy tightened around it, and a powerful orgasm hit me. "Oh, Angel!" I cried again as I released my seed. In response, I felt a rush of warmth across my pubes and my balls as Angel climaxed too, releasing a waterfall of her own fluids.

We had reached our climax together in a splendid release of emotional love for each other.

Afterward, we lay panting, me draped over her. I was drunk with the scent of her—and almost spent of all energy. With my remaining strength, I turned her over once more, still inside her, until I lay on my back, and she was able to rest her exhausted body on mine.

We lay there quietly, holding each other, catching our breaths. I watched as one candle after another went out until only one remained. The last thoughts I had were how radiant the woman I loved was and how very special this night had been for both of us. I drifted off to sleep as that last candle sputtered out, a very satisfied man.

★

When I woke the next morning, my vision of loveliness was lying next to me, our limbs still entangled together. I smiled at her through a yawn, stretching like a cat. As I did so, her petite frame twitched, coming awake too. Our eyes met. There was one thought on our minds.

We barely left the bed that day, except to shower and eat before returning for more lovemaking. That night, though, we managed to get dressed up and go out for dinner.

She emerged from the bathroom, wearing a sexy spaghetti-strap sequined black dress and three-inch heels.

"Wow, you're beautiful," I said simply.

"You like it? Karen helped me pick it out. I take it you approve?"

"Oh yeah!" We laughed. "What else did she help you out with?" I inquired. She smiled mysteriously, giving me a small shake of her head.

"That's between us girls."

As for myself, I kept things simple, wearing my charcoal-gray Christian Dior suit.

She took us to Enjera, a five-star Ethiopian restaurant on South Twenty-Third Street, in the university district. It was magnificent. The food, music, and ambiance were only window dressing to my woman's beauty. At the end of dinner, the wait-staff brought out a birthday cake and sang happy birthday to me.

From her sleek black satin clutch, Angel withdrew a small box tastefully decorated with streams of ribbon. I opened it to find a gold-and-silver Citizen quartz watch with a diamond in the center of the face. I went to put it on, but she motioned for me to turn it over first. Engraved on the back were the words, *'To My One and Only True Love, I will be forever yours. Angel.'*

We danced after supper—the music was soulful and slow—then took a horse-drawn carriage ride through the old city.

It was two in the morning before we finally returned to her cousin's house. Sleepily, we undressed each other, sliding into bed, wrapping our arms about the other's naked body. Before I drifted off, I had something to share.

"My sweet Angel, I love you—deeply and fully. I don't ever want anything to come between our connection to each other!"

She answered with a long kiss, which communicated her feelings for me better than words ever could. As we kissed, though, I felt the slightest pang of guilt for not telling her about my feelings for Fred... *Why ruin this special moment?* I reasoned, blocking out thoughts of Fred Mason and settling in for a sleep with my girl in my arms.

I woke early the next morning to catch my train to Jersey. Angel came to drop me off. As I kissed her and boarded the train, emotions tugged at me, and I had to fight a burning sensation behind my eyes. Settling into my seat and catching sight of Angel through the window, it was clear her emotions had won out. She cried openly as she waved goodbye, until the train pulled out and she dwindled to a mere point in the distance.

I thought long and hard on the ride home about how I never wanted to do anything to hurt her. But Antonio's words kept running through my mind. Part of being a man is the thrill of the chase and the conquest of your bounty. I had conquered Angel but hadn't tired of the game... Yet another thrill: not to get caught in the act of chasing.

I knew what I felt with Angel was the real thing, *but* I had to determine if what I felt for men was also. I didn't think the "game" was over quite yet.

Interlude Seventeen

Turning Over another Decade

I was greeted at the Iselin Park train station by my anxiously awaiting mother. Dad and Nina stood off to the side, letting Momma get her hugs and kisses for her baby boy out of the way. It was all a little embarrassing, but I was home, in safe arms, so I put up with it.

On the ride home, I talked about Sundays in West Chester. I told my folks how I really enjoyed working with the Sunday school and about our talks with Rev. and Mrs. Harris. I mistakenly raved about Mrs. Harris's cooking, which earned me a motherly scolding.

"This woman's cooking is *not* better than your Momma's!" she declared.

"I know, Momma—no one's cooking compares to yours!"

"That's my baby boy, Calvin!" she said to my dad.

"I hear you, Millie."

Dad also told me Uncle Camy was in the States right now for a cologne ad and that he wanted to join us for my birthday meal. *His timing couldn't be better*, I thought, excited at the prospect of getting advice about my predicament.

When we arrived home, I went up to my old room for a moment of solitude before my birthday brunch began. I lay on my bed with my legs crossed and my hands behind my head, immersed in the nostalgia of my old posters, awards, and trophies. Something caught my eye; my dad stood at the doorway, a questioning smile on his face.

"You okay, champ?"

"Yeah, I'm okay."

"So how's it feel to be two decades old?" He laughed; I smiled.

"A little different but pretty much the same." Silence fell for a few seconds.

"You want to be alone." It wasn't a question.

"No—not if you want to talk," I replied nonetheless.

"I wanted to make sure everything was all right and that you were...over the incident."

"Oh." I hadn't thought about the attack and the trial and everything in some time. "Yeah, yeah—I'm okay with that. There's other things weighing on my mind right now."

"Anything you want to talk about?" Dad crossed his arms and leaned into the doorframe. I thought I'd keep everything for Uncle Camy, but here was my dad... He'd more than proven to me last fall that he was there for me too. I could trust him. I owed him the truth too.

"Yes and no, Dad. I need to have a man-to-man, with-no-judgment talk. Do you think you can handle that?"

"I think I can rise to the occasion." He was fighting a smile. "Just go easy on me when I begin to twitch and shake. They tell me it's something most parents suffer from." He grew serious then. "Do I need to close the door?"

"Yeah, I think so."

"Does it have anything to do with Angel and your time with her in DC?" he asked, taking a step into the room and quietly shutting the door behind him. "I'm guessing you two consummated your relationship?"

"Ah…yeah," I admitted, feeling a bit warm under the collar. "H-how did you know?"

"Oh, son—women aren't always the only ones who wear their feelings on their faces." Silence fell again, more awkward this time around. "So, how do you feel, now that it's happened?"

"You mean you're not mad or disappointed?"

"Why would I be? Son, you're a man now, and with that title come certain perks and responsibilities. Would I have liked for the two of you to wait until you were married? Maybe. I'm sure your mother will feel that way. But, for me, times are changing. Young people your age aren't waiting any longer. Matter of fact, there were people my age who didn't wait either, though not so many as nowadays.

"Is it wrong?" he asked, shrugging to himself. "Who am I to say? I guess I believe it's an individual choice. But back to my question: how do you feel?"

"I feel great!"

He laughed at that. "I can imagine."

"Dad, I really love Angel."

"I see that in your eyes."

"But how can I be sure she's the one?" I pressed. "There are so many other beautiful women out there; how do I know which one is the one for me? What if I make a mistake and find out later that maybe I should have...you know, shopped around?"

"*Shopped around*?! Is that what they're calling it these days?" He ran his hand across his chin. "Okay, son—follow me on this one. It's like when your momma's in the produce section of the supermarket. When she chooses a melon, have you ever noticed how she smells it, then shakes it, and finally thumps it a couple of times?" He mimed having fruit in his hand.

"She'll do this several times before she picks one. Now, I'm sure there are ten other melons in that pile she'd probably take. But she settles on the one that meets everything she's looking for." Dad waited for a second, gauging my reaction.

"So what I'm saying," he continued, "is you have to be sure you know what you are looking for *first* and then decided if a person meets the majority—if not all—of the qualities you want in someone you'll spend the rest of your life with." He arched an eyebrow at my silence.

"I don't know any other way to explain it, Desmond, except that you'll just know. Trust your instincts." He held out his arms, and I rose to hug him. "I have faith in you, son," he whispered as we squeezed each other tightly. "I know you'll make the right choice."

A knock came at the door. "Cal? Desmond, honey? Brunch is ready. Come on, fellas, before it gets cold." Dad opened the door to reveal Momma standing there in her apron and a dish towel in her hand.

"I just need to wash my hands, Momma," I said, kissing her on the cheek as I squeezed past. As I walked into the bathroom, I heard her ask my father a question.

"Melons? You were talking about melons?"

"It's a guy thing, dear. Let's go eat."

Just as we were digging into brunch, my brother Vinny arrived home from law school, his latest girlfriend Rachael in tow. Rachael had been hanging in there for close to a year now, and it looked as if she might end up as my new sister-in-law. Momma approved of her too, which was a first for Vinny's girlfriends. She sat the two of them down immediately and went out to the kitchen to get more plates.

The talk at the table revolved around Vinny and Rachael's school. They were both finishing up their degrees this spring. My brother wanted to take his law boards in the summer; Rachael planned to take the tests in September. We expressed how proud we were of both of them.

After brunch, I decided to go to the gym for a workout and swim, then come back for a nap before the dinner festivities that night. Vinny asked if I would mind having company, to which I gladly said, "No, I'd enjoy hanging out with my brother!" We grabbed some stuff and were off. Mom and Nina were going shopping and invited Rachael to join them. That left Dad to hold down the fort, which he never minded doing.

"I'll wait for your Uncle Cam to arrive. I'm sure he and I will find something to do."

Vinny and I lifted weights for an hour, played a round of racquetball, then cooled off in the pool. By the end, we were pleasantly exhausted and sat in the sauna, resting our tired muscles.

"Hey, bro," I began after a pair of guys left, leaving us alone in there. "Wanna hear some news?" Vinny looked up to where I lounged on the upper bench.

"Let me guess. You got your first piece of pussy."

"Damn!" I sat up straight. "How'd you know?!"

"Man, it's written all over your face. If that look of satisfaction gets any brighter, it'll fucking blind us all!" He laughed and punched me in the thigh. "So? How was it? Everything you thought it would be?"

"Fuck, Vinny—she blew me away. I couldn't get enough." I paused, adding, "I think I'm in love."

"Whoa! Hold on there, Junior, this was just your first; there's plenty more out there." He cocked his head to one side. "Hey, did Dad tell you the melon story?"

"Yeah! Oh, so you've heard that one too?"

"Yep—I think it's his favorite." We both fell out laughing. "Look, little brother, I'm not saying this isn't the one. But you have a whole lot of years of experimenting you can do before making a final decision. Give this newfound 'perk' a spin!" When I heard him quote yet another thing Dad had told me, I fell out laughing again.

"I guess while we're sharing, I got something to tell you too." It took only a single look at him to know what he was about to say.

"No way, man—you're getting—"

"Rachael and I are getting married," he finished for me, adding, "and I want you to be my best man." It took me a second to register what he'd just asked. When it did, I jumped up and cheered.

"Yeah! Yes, of course!" I stepped down to the lower bench and threw my arms around him. Two guys chose that moment to walk into the sauna, stopping cold when they saw two sweaty, unclothed men embracing. Vinny pushed me back slightly, even as I said, "This is my older brother! He's getting married!" Their confusion turned to smiles, and they offered their congratulations, shaking hands with him.

"Okay, stud," Vinny said after things settled down again. "Time for us to get out of here." We hit the showers, grabbed a soda, then jumped into the car.

"You mind if I tell everyone at dinner tonight about me and Rachael?" he asked as we drove to our place. "I don't want to spoil your birthday, but…"

"I don't mind sharing the spotlight, bro!"

We arrived home to find Uncle Camy had arrived. He and Dad were seated in front of the television, screaming at a Bulls vs Pistons game. It became evident quite quickly they were rooting for opposite sides. I didn't want to get in the middle of that, so I just said a quick 'hello' before heading upstairs to catch some z's before dinner. As I started up the stairs, Uncle Camy stopped me.

"Hey, Desmond—happy birthday, nephew!"

"Thanks, Uncle!"

"Let's talk after you get some sleep."

"You got it," I said, making my way up the stairs.

I slept deeply for two hours straight. When I woke, I felt like I'd flashed back to my childhood. Momma was seated on the edge of my bed, brushing fingers across my face. "Honey, time to wake up and get dressed for dinner." When she planned a big dinner like this one, she expected everyone to play their part and dress up nicely. "My boy's two decades old—a milestone! You gotta enjoy these when they come." I smiled up at her, receiving a kiss on my forehead before she left me to do my thing.

I stumbled into the shower, rinsing away the sleep, choosing a light-brown suit with gray pinstripes and a mock-turtleneck silk shirt. I looked down on my dresser, catching sight of my new Citizen watch, adding that to my ensemble.

It was quiet downstairs; everyone was probably watching television until Momma served up dinner. I stomped down the steps, adjusting my cuff so that my watch was visible, when a great roar of "*SURPRISE!!*" greeted me. I yelled out, stumbling down the last few steps as people poured out of every corner of my house to converge on me. It was everyone I knew—grandparents, aunts, uncles, cousins, friends, and neighbors.

I'm not sure how Momma did it, but Karen, Melvin, Antonio, JC, and Brian were all there as well, with goofy grins on their faces. *Someone's missing, though...* I looked around but couldn't find her anywhere—my Angel... As if thinking her name had conjured her up, she emerged from the kitchen, a picture of perfection. Dressed in a silky off-the-shoulder burgundy cocktail dress, she strode elegantly toward me, the sea of people parting before her. She came up to me, stood on tippytoes, and kissed me on the lips.

"Happy birthday, Desmond," she murmured as another cheer of laughter and applause rang out.

Momma was there then, at my shoulder. "Surprise!" I wrapped one arm around her, the other around Angel. This was a birthday I would never forget. Everyone I loved was there, and the surprises hadn't ended yet.

We all sat down for dinner—a feast to rival Momma's Christmas buffet. After dinner we all retired to the family room so I could open my gifts. While I was admiring a sweater one of my aunts had knitted me, the phone rang. Nina ran to get it, yelling to me from the kitchen that it was for me.

"Who is it?" I mouthed as I took the handset from her. She shrugged in her teenage-girl way, then scampered back into the living room. "Hello?" I said into the phone.

"Happy birthday, from a not-so-secret admirer." It was Fredrick. I was surprised to say the least.

"Hey man, thanks! Ah…are you in town, or…" I trailed off as my mother passed by with one of my nieces.

"I wish I could, but you and I both know that's impossible. I did send you a little something, though, and I hope you like it. Listen for the door; my driver will be there in the next five minutes."

"Wow, okay, that's great. Sorry you couldn't be here, but we'll talk when I get back, all right?" I was doing my best not to say anything too revealing, as I could tell prying ears were nearby.

"I hope so too, Desmond, but that will have to be your choice. Good night, enjoy your party." He hung up, and I stood there, staring at nothing for a few seconds.

"Des, come on!" came Karen's voice from the hall. She and Angel peeked into the kitchen. "Everyone is waiting for you to open the rest of your gifts!"

"I'm coming!" I waved her off; she took the hint and disappeared. Angel, though, came up to me and gently touched my arm.

"Is everything all right?"

"With you here, everything is perfect."

She beamed, leaning in for a quick kiss. We were walking back to the family room arm in arm when the doorbell rang. Before anyone could get up, I yelled, "Got it!" I pried myself gently from Angel's arm and darted to the front door. Sure enough, Rick's chauffeur stood there holding a small wrapped box.

"Good evening, sir. I am Mr. Mason's driver."

"Hi, yes, I remember you from Carley's birthday party last week."

"Ah, of course, sir. I have a package for you from Mr. Mason." He extended the box with one hand, then tipped his hat with the other. "Good night, and happy birthday."

"Thank you!" I said as I turned my attention to the limousine in my driveway. The windows in the back were tinted, so I couldn't see if "he" was in there. I watched as the car pulled out and drove slowly out of sight.

"Is everything all right, honey?" Momma asked, coming up behind me. "Who was that?"

"A delivery from a secret admirer, I guess," I murmured.

"Oooh! A secret admirer—aren't you the lucky one?!" *If only you knew, Momma…if only you knew.* I turned toward the house, giving my mother a kiss on the cheek. "You know something, Mom? You're terrific. I can't wait to see what else you have in store for me."

"So why are we standing here?" she replied, play-swatting me on the shoulder. We laughed and joined my guests in the family room. She didn't notice me hiding Fredrick's package in my inside jacket pocket.

With my family and friends around, I finished opening my gifts. Looking around at all the wonderful stuff and all the people who loved me, I couldn't believe how blessed I was.

I'd worked my way down to the last gift, thinking I was through, when Dad passed me an envelope. I looked at him, but he was playing his cards close to his chest. I shrugged, ripping the envelope open and pulling out the card. Written on the front was "Are you in need of a lift?" Drawn below the text was a cartoon character standing with his thumb out. When I opened the card, a Polaroid picture fell out. It was a photo of a car, with the words "maybe this will help" written in the white space at the bottom.

I immediately leaped in the air, screaming "Where, where, where is it?" Everyone laughed. Dad gestured to me to follow him to the side door. Opening it, he pointed to a beautiful brandy-colored Toyota Camry parked in the neighbor's driveway. With the other hand, he dangled a set of keys in front of me.

"That's mine?!"

"It is," he confirmed.

"Why is it over there?"

"We couldn't very well put it in our driveway—you'd have asked too many questions!" We laughed at that, and I threw my arms around him. Momma joined in, as did Angel, who'd followed.

"Can I take it for a ride now?" I asked.

"Absolutely not. You have candles to blow out and a cake to cut, and we need to get some folks on the road before it gets too late."

I pouted a little but then smiled. "Let them eat cake, for in the morning…" Momma and Dad rolled their eyes, leading us back into the house. I followed, my arm around Angel's waist.

Mom lit the candles on a beautiful red-and-blue sheet cake. As I made a wish, I grabbed Angel's hand and blew out the candles. "Damn, all but one," I said and blew out the last one. Mom, Nina, Karen, Rachael, and Angel helped serve cake, ice cream, and coffee to all the guests.

As everyone was eating and chatting, Vinny tapped the side of his wineglass. His moment had come. We exchanged a look; I gave him a nod and a wink.

"Excuse me, everyone, excuse me. Can I have your attention please?" He looked around nervously, his eyes coming to settle on his girlfriend sitting next to him. "First, Rachael and I would like to wish my little brother health, love, and many more happy birthdays in the future. Second, with Desmond's permission, I'd like to thank him for allowing us to steal a little of his thunder to make an announcement." Drawing a deep breath, he motioned Rachael to stand next to him and took her hand. "Rachael and I plan to get married this summer."

An uproar of congratulatory cries and applause rose, though none louder than Momma's.

"Oh my God, a wedding!!" She leaped up, tears already streaming down her face. She rushed over to my brother and his girlfriend, encompassing both of them in a hug.

On that high note, we began to pack up all the relatives and neighbors, getting them off on their way before midnight. As for my friends, Momma had organized for them to stay overnight. She had some choice words for them, however, before assigning sleeping arrangements.

"Ladies and gentlemen, I don't know how you do things in your respective college dormitories, but here in the Dawson household, all single women will be sleeping in the rooms upstairs, and all the gentlemen will be made comfortable in the basement. There's a bathroom and shower down there with plenty of sleeping bags and blankets. Oh, and I will be patrolling the hallways." She was about to turn back to tidying up the dining room when she remembered something.

"Antonio and JC: it'll be separate sleeping bags for the two of you!"

Antonio and JC blinked in shock for a moment before responding in unison, "Yes, ma'am!"

As we moved toward our respective sleeping quarters, Momma came up to me and asked me if I would yield my room to Uncle Camy. I smiled and agreed gladly.

Vinny, Melvin, and I escorted Rachael, Karen, and Angel to their assigned rooms, under the watchful eye of my mother. As we were climbing the stairs, I overheard Angel whispering to Karen.

"I wanted to thank you for our talk," she said, leaning her head in close to Karen's.

"How did things go?" Karen whispered back. Angel just smiled at her.

"What are you ladies discussing?" I asked nonchalantly. They both turned to stare at me.

"Women talk," Angel replied, sharing a giggle with Karen.

"All right! Five minutes, dears," Momma announced as we reached the upstairs hallway. "Then I want to see six big feet returning down those stairs and carrying on all the way down to the basement!"

"Yes, Mom!" my brother and I chimed as Melvin nodded vigorously.

I got Angel to her assigned room and kissed her good night. She pushed me away playfully when things became a little heated.

"Your mother's rules," she reminded me, waving me out and closing the door behind me. I smiled to myself, heading to my room to grab a few things. Remembering what I'd hidden in my jacket, I shut the door partway, pulling out the gift from Rick. I undid the silver ribbons and tore through the thick wrapping paper. Underneath was a black leather case. Opening it, I discovered a white-gold ID bracelet engraved with my name on the front in a beautiful, unique script. On the back was inscribed one single word: "Destined." A cold shiver ran down my spine.

"From someone special?"

I must have jumped four feet straight in the air before turning to see my uncle standing there in the doorway. "Shit, Uncle Camy!" I hissed, trying to keep my voice low. "Don't *ever* do that!"

"Sorry, nephew—the door was cracked, and I didn't see anyone else in here, so I thought it was all right to come in."

"Next time, please knock and announce yourself just in case, okay?!" I demanded.

"All right, all right—my apologies! I didn't realize this was a private affair."

"It's not." I immediately felt bad for jumping down his throat. I put a hand to my temple, looking over Camy's shoulder to make sure no one would overhear us. "Remember that offer you made? To be there for me? Well, I'm calling that chip in."

"I see. That sounds serious. And if that gold bracelet has anything to do with it, I believe I arrived just in time." We both stared down at Rick's gift for a moment.

"It does." I swallowed. "I don't think we'll have time tonight, but I need to desperately have that conversation with you before either of us get out of here tomorrow."

Uncle Camy nodded. "No problem, kiddo. I'm not due back in the city until Monday morning. We'll find time tomorrow." Emotion poured through me like a dam breaking. I threw my arms around my uncle.

"Thank you!" He laughed, hugging me back tightly. I made sure he was properly set up in my room, then headed to the basement and my sleeping bag.

Everyone settled in for sleep, and within half an hour, the basement was filled with the sound of Melvin's and JC's contented snoring. Unfortunately, it was also keeping me awake.

I got up and tiptoed my way past the bodies, sneaking up to the kitchen. In my pocket lay Rick's leather box and bracelet. I sliced myself another piece of birthday cake, sat at the counter, and stared at the open box as I munched away. From the gloom came a hoarse whisper.

"It's from him, isn't it?" I almost fell off my stool, turning to find Antonio staring at me from the top of the stairs.

"If another person creeps up behind me today, I'm gonna shoot them!" I hissed. Antonio ignored my warning.

"That was him on the phone after supper, wasn't it? And at the door—that was his delivery?" He pointed at the black leather case in front of me. I nodded.

"Yep. His driver dropped it off. I think he was in the limo out front, but I couldn't tell." I fingered the bracelet, tracing my name.

"And so the game begins," Antonio said cryptically as he walked toward the leftover cake. "May I?" I gestured for him to help himself.

"You might as well cut me a slice too," Uncle Camy said, appearing from the hallway. "And what game are we talking about?"

"Damn! Don't any of you queer folk sleep in this house?" I asked.

"So you are the infamous, all-knowing, all-seeing Uncle Camy," Antonio said, looking my uncle up and down.

"And you are the equally flamboyant and heroic Antonio Savileo?" Camy parried, returning the look. Antonio shrugged, bringing a smile to my uncle's face. "Pleasure to meet you!" He extended his hand, which Antonio grudgingly accepted.

"Likewise, I'm sure."

"Would the two of you please stop it?" I whispered, shaking my head at their verbal sparring.

"So this game of yours, it sounds very interesting. Whoever 'he' is, looks like he's got some money to throw around," Camy said, coming to inspect the bracelet.

"Believe me, 'some' doesn't begin to describe this guy's wealth," Antonio said over his shoulder as he poked a finger in the icing around the edge of the leftover cake.

"Get a plate," I instructed my friend before adding, "He's married with three small children."

"Oh dear," Camy replied.

"And we're sure Brian, Des's roommate, is involved with his wife," Antonio added.

"We're not sure about that!" I said.

"Blinders, blinders! Danger, Will Robinson!" Antonio waved his arms about like a robot. "Take those damn ugly rose-colored glasses off your face before I smack them off myself!"

"Whatever."

"Well, this definitely sounds like my type of party. Do tell me more," Camy declared as he fished a fork out of a drawer and set into the cake next to Antonio.

"Okay, here's the shortened version Unc: I meet this guy in a bar—"

"*Gay* bar," Antonio clarified.

"Okay—*gay* bar, and we make a connection. He wants to take me home with him, but I flatly refuse."

"Good move," Camy said through a mouthful.

"…And then I don't see him again for weeks."

"Meanwhile," Antonio cut in, unable to let me tell the story, "Desy's roommate convinces him to attend his church every week in godforsaken West Chester, PA."

"West Chester, you say? I can't wait to hear how these details are connected."

"Patience, gurl!"

"Antonio! Keep your voice down! Anyway, I start going to church every Sunday, dragging the crew with me. Every week, we witness Brian playing husband to this fabulously beautiful woman and father to her adorable little girl."

"And the father?"

"Yeah—we learned he's this workaholic, nonexistent father. Well, just last Saturday I got invited to the little girl's fourth birthday party."

"But the invitation doesn't come from her mother!" Antonio cut in yet again. "Nope—it's from our lonesome heart, wannabe husband, Brian! And this guy"—he pointed at me— "drags all his boyz along with him!"

"All right. The plot thickens. Continue."

"Well, when we get to the party, their house turns out to be this huge mansion. The kind with butlers and maids and chauffeurs…we're talking many, *many* dollar bills! So, we walk in and try to play it cool, when all of a sudden, workaholic dad arrives on the scene. And it just so happens to be the same guy who wanted to bed me at the club three weeks before!" Finally, Uncle Camy was left speechless. He just stood there with his mouth wide open while Antonio giggled at his reaction.

"Listen to this," he said after he finished laughing. "Desy, here, tries to play the guy off but instead turns him on even more! Meanwhile, lonesome-hearted roommate Brian swears to us he's *not* boning this man's wife but plays the violin song of how she wants out of her marriage but can't, because of the prenuptial agreement that says she'll lose everything, *including* the children!" Still lost for words, my uncle just shook his head.

"This guy is Billy Dee Williams all over," I said. "I'd be lying if I said I didn't want to get involved with him…but now I'm confused. The girl I love finally fucks my brains out—"

"Wait, what?!" Antonio interrupted.

"Come on, Antonio; keep up!" I taunted him, pleased to have something over him. He glared at me and I smiled back sweetly. "Yeah, she did! But, anyways, Mr. Mysterious is no longer mysterious. And, just to put icing on my cake, tonight he calls to wish me happy birthday and sends his chauffeur to my door to drop off his love gift. And yes," I add, holding up my hand, "I want to get into his head and his pants, without becoming one of his boy toys. I want to be in control! So, there you have it. The cut-to-the-chase version of this wild story in its entirety: finished."

"Well. You young men certainly know how to get caught up in drama, don't you?" Uncle Camy put a hand to his forehead, squeezing his temples. "You know what? I'm going back to bed; you two have made my head hurt." Camy took two steps toward the hallway.

"Wait! You mean that's it? You're not gonna help?" I said in a panic.

He came back to me, planting a kiss on my forehead. He did the same to Antonio before addressing both of us in a low voice. "Yes, I'm going to help. But not tonight. I have to sleep on this one, Desmond. I'll have an answer for you in the morning. Deal?"

Relieved, I nodded. Antonio shrugged, sticking a finger back in Momma's cake. Camy smiled and waved, heading up to my room.

Antonio and I finished up our late-night snack and tidied up. Without a word, he closed the box to my new bracelet and placed it in the pocket of my robe. He took me by the hand, leading me back downstairs. Our sleeping bags were on either side of JC's. Antonio shook his boyfriend to interrupt his snoring; then we all went back to sleep.

The next morning, Momma got up early and fixed breakfast. When I finally dragged myself up the stairs to show my face, I heard her mumbling to Dad, "I know my cookin's better than *hers!*" *Oops…* I thought. *Probably shouldn't have said anything about how well Brian's mom cooks…*

After eating (and letting Momma know how much I loved and appreciated her food), I helped my friends from Temple load JC's car for the trip back. Once they were on the road, Angel and I took a ride in my new car, swinging by her parents' place for a bit before she caught a ride with Vinny and Rachael back to DC.

When I got back, Uncle Camy suggested we go out to the diner for a coffee and a chat.

"Okay, nephew. I gotta say, you've found yourself in quite a pickle here." He was drinking coffee, black; I was nursing a soda but still felt the aftereffects of all the sugary foods I'd eaten the day before. "I'm not overly pleased with the road you've chosen to take, but then, everyone has the right to make his or her own mistakes."

"So, can you help me?" I asked, wondering suddenly at the pickle he himself was in with his boss and boss's wife. *A discussion for another time, given that he doesn't even know I know…*

"Yes. Of course I will. My first bit of advice is this: be careful when getting mixed up in rich, powerful circles. I've been there, Desmond. The rich are not people to toy with lightly." He took a sip of his hot drink. "You've got an advantage, though: you've got what it takes to hold your own with them. You'll be able to deal with the best of them. As long as you're careful."

"I will be."

"I know—you've got a good head on your shoulders. You take after your father in that respect." He winked at me. After fiddling with the handle of his cup for a few moments, he nodded and added, "I've got an idea of what we can do. Give me a few days. I'll call you—probably Tuesday evening—to firm things up. Until then"—he pointed a stern finger at me—"do not accept any offers from this Fredrick until after we've had a chance to talk again!"

"Agreed!" I said, happy to have someone like Camy on my side.

★

Finally, the time had come to head to Temple. Momma and Dad stood watching as I packed my new car, fully ready to leave by around four. Dad had already purchased a parking sticker and secured me a parking space in the student garage.

"A car is a big responsibility, Desmond. Don't take any unnecessary chances with it."

"Yes, Dad," I said, leaning in for a bro hug. I gave Momma a kiss, climbed in my new car, pulled out of the driveway, and waved to them as I set off for school.

I rode down the parkway, listening to WDAS. Thoughts of Angel swirled through my head—hopes for a family and how to get there despite all odds. *If my destiny is to have this interlude with Fredrick Mason,* I thought, *then so be it. Bring him on.*

I had a solid plan for my life now; my goals were clearly set before me.

At this particular fork in the road, I'd chosen my path. May God walk with me.

Part Five

Check and Checkmate

Interlude Eighteen

A Game of Seduce and be Seduced

When I arrived at my dorm room, Brian was seated on his bed, reading the bible. He was looking more like the brother I'd come to know and like. After some small talk, I couldn't resist asking him about what happened after we left last Sunday.

"Mason took Sylvia and the kids to Disney World on a whim." He sniffed. "But they came back early due to his work, Sylvia told me. I hooked up with her on Friday—I guess the vacation had been a wash, because Mason spent more time checking in with the office than with the kids in the park. Sylvia ended up taking them to all the attractions by herself, and they only saw their dad for meals at night." We both shook our heads.

"There's something going on in that relationship," I told Brian. When he arched an eyebrow, I added with a wink, "You're not the only psychic in the room!" He chuckled and turned back to his bible. I unpacked my stuff, then headed out the door to visit with Karen and Antonio.

"Thank you for saving Sylvia and me, Desmond," my roommate said to my back. "Whether you know it or not, you're making our lives a little bit easier."

I froze. "Ah…I'm not sure what you mean, but you're welcome." Just when I made a joke about being psychic, he had to go and show me the real thing. I knew he had a…*talent*, but he was letting me see just how aware of stuff he really was. It was eerie, almost as if he could see into our future and was moving chess pieces across a game board.

But tonight wasn't the time to figure out my roommate and his abilities. I needed to check in with Karen and Antonio.

\#

True to his word, Uncle Camy called me at 9:00 p.m. that Tuesday.

"I'm in New York right now, but I'm clearing my calendar for the next week and a half. I'm coming to stay in Philly tomorrow. Your schedule during the day is yours, nephew, but between the hours of 8:00 p.m. and midnight, you are going to be my student."

"What does that mean?" I asked.

"It will become very clear after the first night, Desmond," he assured me. "Now, have you had any further contact with this Frederick fellow?"

"No. Is that strange?"

He laughed through the phone. "No! It just means the game has begun. Be patient. I anticipated this play." It was all very confusing for me, and I admitted as much.

"I'm not sure I can handle this."

"Listen, nephew—if after this week and a half you still feel this way, don't pursue him. Tuck your tail between your legs and run." He ended our conversation with these words of encouragement: "But I know you can handle your business. And may God help that son of a bitch if he tries to use or hurt you. 'Cause when I get through with him, he will know he's been played by a Dawson. We Dawson men play to win."

That night I lay in bed, praying silently that I would be strong enough to face what lay ahead of me. I prayed that I would be smart enough to protect my heart and wise enough to finally figure out what my most authentic sexual identity was.

I met Uncle Camy promptly at 7:00 p.m. the next night at the Thirtieth Street Station. To my surprise he was not alone. With him were three handsome, well-built gentlemen, each in their twenties: a brother, Malcolm; an Indian, Rajasham; and a Frenchman, Claymont. We left the station and headed for the Peninsula Hotel on City Line Avenue. Uncle Camy had reserved a four-bedroom suite with all the extra luxuries you could imagine.

For the next ten days, Uncle Camy would be my teacher; his three companions, my tutors.

We talked the first night about sex, love, and the gay life. Each one of my uncle's companions took turns sharing their experiences. Uncle Camy told me to pay close attention to each gentleman's story, as they had each been where I intended to go.

"I chose them because they have certain talents in the art of making love to a man," he said in a private moment between the two of us. "They will help you understand how to catch and keep the richest fish."

The three of them were all models for the magazine my uncle worked for; by night, they were all callboys for rich gay clients. And, like Camy said, they each had their own specialty.

Rajasham, for instance, excelled in the art of sensual body massage. With the right exotic oils, his hands became lethal sexual weapons. He knew how to first bring a man to a state of complete relaxation, followed by teasing him toward an earth-shattering orgasm.

Claymont had honed his mouth into his weapon of choice: kissing and fellatio were his battlegrounds. A single kiss from him would rouse a man to full erection; his tongue was a master of licking and probing a man to ecstasy; his teeth, weapons of pain that brought nothing but pleasure.

Last but certainly not least was Malcolm, whose previous down-low life in the hood had taught him the art of a good fuck. From his bulge, he was clearly packing a long, thick one. The first thing he told me was, when you fuck a man, you want to be in control. It wasn't about how hard or how long it was; it was the intensity of the fuck—whether fast or slow. Once fucked by a master, a man would become a kept monkey on a string for life.

So there it was: three masters, who were to be my tutors for the next ten evenings. How far would their training take me? Only time would tell. To be honest, I was quivering in anticipation of what was to come.

While Malcolm, Rajasham, and Claymont were to work on the physical aspects of my training, Uncle Camy would school me on the intellectual side of dominating a man.

He'd prepared by collecting all the information he could on Fredrick's life. Rick's rags-to-riches story was common knowledge; however, information on his personal life was pretty scarce. Uncle Camy had connections to the gay underground, though, and through them, he was able to glean a bit more on Mr. Mason.

Rick had been very discreet with his affairs, but there were a few ex-paramours who were willing to kiss and tell. One young man in particular—a brother named Jerrod—was willing to tell all for the price of an expensive dinner and a good fuck. Uncle Camy was willing to oblige him.

I was immensely grateful to my uncle for his sacrifice and contributions to my education. I could only imagine how much money he spent on me over our ten nights together—surely no less than fifty thousand dollars. (For one, I knew his models didn't come cheap. Though they were friends, they were on "assignment" and demanded top dollar!)

Camy's training didn't take place in a classroom; we went shopping and ate out while we talked. There seemed to be no bottom to his wallet. We first talked about what made you most appealing to another man. How your dress and your manner of speech said a lot about who you were.

And, speaking of dress, Camy purchased a tuxedo, a pair of suits, a week's worth of casual outfits, jewelry, and trinkets he said I'd need to meet Fredrick on his level.

"Never be controlled by another man's gifts or money," he said. "You can accept gifts from him, but make sure that's all they ever are. Never take anything that would require something from you later on down the road. You are your own man, nephew. Not some for-rent boy toy.

"You're not arm candy either," he continued. "You're an individual in your own right—carry your head high and keep your self-respect intact. Always."

He told me about private men-only clubs and resorts. These were spots where rich gay men could escape to, to partake in the joys of gay sex and companionship without being exposed to the judging eye of the world.

"They're secret, exclusive meeting places for older men and gigolos—younger men and boys...lavish weekend getaways where *anything* goes." He got serious for a moment. "If you get invited to one of these—whether by Fredrick or anyone else—you *must* let me or someone like your friend Antonio know where you'll be! Promise me this!"

After Camy wined and dined Fredrick's ex, Jerrod, he reported to me that Rick did indeed attend some of these getaways but didn't seem to engage in the group orgies that took place there.

"Apparently, he's more inclined to play the game of conquering a single lover, taking advantage of the solitude and intimacy these settings allow." He also learned Rick was an avid tennis and racquetball player and enjoyed working out at his private health club. Mr. Mason was an intellectual man who had a natural thirst for knowledge. As the owner of a magazine, it was only natural he read all the major newspapers and kept subscriptions to all the major magazines as well.

Rick owned a private jet, a chauffeured limousine, and several pieces of property around the Eastern Seaboard and co-owned a small Caribbean island.

The personal aspects Jerrod revealed of Fredrick provided the icing on the cake for me. This young man had been his lover for three years, during a time when Rick had been amassing his fortune. Jerrod described Fredrick as a dark and powerful man. He had a way of staring into your eyes hypnotically that left little room for resistance. He used this skill in his business and his personal relationships alike.

Apparently, Fredrick acted on his gut and made spontaneous decisions that could leave you out in the cold, your feelings trampled on. Jerrod explained Rick had a dual personality, ranging from a slippery serpent to that of a stealthy panther.

In terms of his love life, his greatest need was for a lover to submit absolutely to him. Jerrod recounted how the demands Fredrick made of him during their relationship were severe. Ultimately, the young man hadn't been strong enough to deal with his intensity, almost becoming totally consumed by it. Jerrod wasn't able to play the selflessly devoted lover; when Rick found out that Jerrod was seeing another man, he became insanely jealous and finished the relationship on the spot.

"I coulda been seeing a woman, and he wouldn't have cared, though," Jerrod reported to my uncle. "He tolerated his lovers seeing women because he lived with the same battle himself."

Up until that point, though, Frederick had given Jerrod his complete devotion as a dominant lover. He displayed his intense commitment through his wallet and within the bedroom.

As difficult as he was to get along with, Frederick was equally hard on himself. He could be overly intuitive at times, which left him vulnerable to hurt. He punished himself whenever he thought he'd shown weakness among his business associates and would rant about anyone whom he could not dominate through his force of will.

And, at the core, Fredrick was incredibly fearful that the web of lies and deceit he'd spun about him would one day come crashing down, leaving him alone and adrift. That is why he would never leave Sylvia, why he lavished such an extravagant lifestyle on her. She was, and would always be, his security net.

Uncle Camy and I sat in a booth at his favorite steak house, reflecting on all the things he'd learned from Jerrod.

"This is not a man to be played with lightly, nephew," he said, looking me deep in the eyes. "Look where it got Jerrod— he's a broken young man now, unable to get any older men to look at him anymore."

I nodded, savoring an oaky red wine Camy had selected for us.

"But," he added, "play it *right*—gain his confidence, show him you can match him in wits and in bed—then you will become a powerful person in your own right. You'll be a young man to be respected, as the confidante of such a powerful man." The thought of that made me giddy—and it wasn't just the wine.

I also learned a lot about my uncle in the days that followed. His own training was based on many years of dealing with rich men and learning some of these lessons the hard way.

"My first lover was much like Fredrick. He was rich and influential and loved the game. He taught me much of what I'm telling you now, though there was a lot I had to learn on my own."

★

My evenings with Camy and the guys were an exotic dream. Never in my wildest imaginings did I think there were so many aspects to receiving and giving pleasure. The first time I witnessed my tutors disrobe and perform sexual techniques on one another, I almost left in shock and embarrassment. *But how else am I going to learn how to satisfy my tiger?* I reasoned, then settled down to watch.

It wasn't all watching, either. After a few initial demonstrations, I became an active participant in the training. Uncle Camy cautioned the guys, however, that a demonstration of anal sex, with me on the receiving end, was *not* to be part of my training. That would be a physical experience I would have to wait to enjoy. As for me fucking one of my trainers, though? That was totally acceptable, and believe me—the high achiever in me went for an A plus!

Our time together had almost come to an end; Uncle Camy and each of my tutors had shown and taught me everything I needed to know to win the favor of my king. It was now time for me to put what I had learned to work.

The five of us spent our last Saturday morning together in the health club exercising and getting complete makeovers. I enjoyed a massage, facial, manicure, and haircut. We dined leisurely through the morning and early afternoon on room service. At our midafternoon luncheon, Uncle Camy announced we would be attending a very special party that evening—a black-tie affair. I had a feeling this was my coming out party.

Uncle Camy's personal valet, Bartholomew, had flown in the night before and was assigned to help me get ready for the night's soirée. He consulted with me on every item I would wear that evening, right down to my silk boxers. He was pretty cool and easy to talk to; I just could not get into him calling me "Master Desmond."

I got confused when he asked me what I wanted to wear the next day and then proceeded to pack an overnight bag for me, but I resolved to go with the flow—I trusted whatever Uncle Camy had in store for me.

I emerged from soaking in my room's jacuzzi to find Uncle Camy and my tutors were nowhere to be found.

"Bartholomew, where'd everyone go?"

"They've gone on ahead, Master Desmond. You'll rejoin them at tonight's affair. I'm to escort you on this final leg of your journey. Here." He passed me a carefully folded note on thick stationery. "Your uncle asked that I give you this."

Dear Desmond,

Well, nephew, my friends and I have given you all the tools you need to pursue your Mr. Mason.

Your outing tonight will give you an introduction to the life you are about to become a part of. I have the utmost confidence that you will impress; after all, you are a Dawson.

We have flown ahead and will meet you there. I left Bartholomew behind to assist you with everything you might need. You can confide in him. He won't steer you wrong.

With all this training, I hope you also take time to reflect on this way of life. Once you start to play this particular game, there is no turning back.

Your mentors and I will be looking out for you this evening. As I promised you before, all you need do is ask and I will always be there for you.

By the way—tonight will be the perfect time to put all that French you learned at school to good use; you'll know when to use it. Practice with Bartholomew this afternoon; he's well versed in the language.

Love you,

Camy

Bartholomew helped me dress while we conversed in French, as Uncle Camy had suggested. A limousine would be waiting for me at the front entrance of the hotel at 5:00 p.m. to take me to Philadelphia International Airport.

"I'm taking a plane? Where exactly *is* this party?" I asked Bartholomew in French as we rode in the limo.

"A jet is waiting to fly you to upstate New York, Master Desmond. Another limo is waiting for you there to drive you to Chaverton Manor."

"Is that a club?"

"Non. A private residence. On the books, this is a business party being given by your uncle's publisher."

"Business party? Am I expected to do business?" I asked, only half joking.

"The gentlemen there will bring companions, who will be your age. You'll be announced at the entrance as an unattached young man, which means you may be approached by any number of older gentlemen."

I sat back, reflecting on that.

"You are to use all you were taught by your uncle," Bartholomew continued in French, "and be very careful of how far you let any man take you. It will be up to you how to proceed." He patted the overnight bag he'd packed for me. "Whatever you decide, you will be prepared."

"What about my stuff at the hotel, if I decide to…*stay* overnight?"

"Your belongings are being transported to your dorm room. When you decide to return, the plane will bring you back, and Alex, here"—he gestured to the limo driver—"will drive you to the college." The driver made eye contact with me in the rearview mirror, nodding. I nodded back.

When we arrived at the airport, the limo taxied right up to a private Learjet hangar. I had never flown on a small jet like this before, so it was quite an experience. The main cabin was laid out like a living room, with plush white leather seats and a wet bar stocked with top-shelf liquor. There was wall-to-wall shag carpeting on the floor. *A boy could get used to this kind of thing.*

At takeoff the pilot announced our flying time would be approximately one and a quarter hours. Bartholomew provided me with a drink and some hors d'oeuvres.

I sat, quietly preparing myself for what was coming next.

The sun had long set by the time we landed in Albany. Another limo sat waiting outside the plane. Bartholomew fussed over me one last time, reminding me to call the pilot by midnight with my intentions. He handed me my overnight bag and a small envelope with flowing gold script, sealed with wax—my invitation to tonight's affair.

"*Bonne chance, jeune homme,*" he said, extending a hand. "I won't see you again after tonight."

"Merci, Bartholomew," I replied, shaking his hand. "Thank you for everything this afternoon."

On my own in the back of my second limo of the day, I peeled open the invitation: a panel card with a gold crest and the words, *"The pleasure of your company is most humbly requested at the Chaverton Manor."* On the back were the details of the soirée:

Monsieur Desmond C. Dawson

You are cordially invited to Monsieur Roberto Haver's "Male Extrava-ganza"

At

The Chaverton Manor

1257 Chaverton Drive, Albany, New York

Hors D'oeuvres and Cocktails at 8:00 p.m.

Dinner Will be Served at 9:00 p.m.

Attire: Formal

The mansion sat on an out-of-the-way road up in the hills. The driver turned onto a paved driveway and stopped at a security post. My identity confirmed, the wrought-iron gates swung open, and we drove up a winding laneway lined with trees adorned with white twinkling lights. I could make out more lights—from a large house at the top of the hill.

The driver pulled up to the front entrance of the home: a magnificent mansion in the federal colonial style, rising up around the surrounding glow of trees. A footman rushed over and opened my door, welcoming me.

I walked slowly up to the open front door, where a valet took my coat and scarf and directed me through a foyer to a staircase that overlooked a sunken great room. I looked down at the stunning architecture and interior design of the hall. I was greeted by a herald, to whom I handed my invitation. He turned toward the ballroom and announced in a booming voice, "Mr. Desmond Cameron Dawson." He pointed out the host to me, and I thanked him.

Everyone turned to look when the man announced me; the room grew abuzz with whispers.

Woodpeckers pecking at my stomach, I made my descent. I threw my shoulders back and schooled my features into what I hoped portrayed seduction and allure.

I took each step slowly, walking up to the elderly gentleman I'd been directed to. He had a bronze tan, silver hair, and a very distinguished manner. At his side was a familiar and very welcome face: Uncle Camy.

"Bonsoir, Monsieur Dawson. It is a great pleasure to meet you." The host greeted me in French. "I am Roberto Haver."

"Bonsoir, Monsieur Haver. The pleasure is mine," I replied in the same language. With a broad smile, he pulled me in for a kiss on either cheek. "You have a beautiful home," I added in a sexy baritone for his ears only, "matched only by your handsome appearance."

Mr. Haver laughed and turned to Uncle Camy. "You are full of surprises, Cameron. You never told me your nephew was so conversant in French!"

"He's a Dawson; why wouldn't he be?" Camy said with a broad grin.

Monsieur Haver turned to me. "Please, *mon ami*—call me Roberto and make yourself at home. The entirety of my house is open to all my guests this evening. If you choose to spend the night, I will have one of my men prepare a room for you." He gave me an appraising look, then turned to Uncle Camy. "You know, Cameron, if I'd met your nephew at the same time I met you, I would have had you both."

"I don't think your heart could have withstood the two of us," my uncle replied with a wink at me.

Mr. Haver chuckled, draped an arm over my shoulder, and led me farther into the ballroom. "*Viens avec moi,* Desmond; let me introduce you to some of my guests."

As we crossed the room, I was assailed with appraising looks, nods, and curious smiles from all directions. I spotted Malcolm, Rajasham, and Claymont in the crowd, each attached to older men.

Monsieur Haver had introduced me to a small group of gentlemen when I felt an arm slip around my waist. I swiveled, coming face-to-face with a very handsome young man dressed in a burgundy smoking jacket. He had a European air to him, amplified by his continental French accent.

"*Mais, Beau-père* Haver, you are—as usual—keeping the best prizes for yourself!" In my ear, he added, "I couldn't resist noticing how incredibly gorgeous you are." He took my hand, kissing it lightly. "*Je m'appelle Jon Miguel Haver et je vais te coucher avant de la fin de cette nuit.*" He had a sexy smile and a sexier voice, but I wasn't going to bed with anyone just because he said so.

"Monsieur Cameron Dawson, *à votre* service. The night is still young—there's no telling how it might end." I gave my own sexy smile, gently retrieving my hand.

"Jon, I think you have been checked," said a very familiar voice as yet another hand settled on my shoulder. "If anyone is going to enjoy Mr. Dawson's undivided attention for dinner and dessert—and hopefully breakfast—I intend it to be me."

I turned to look Fredrick Mason square in the eyes. "Roberto," I said to our host, "I didn't realize I was on the menu as an appetizer, main course, and dessert!"

"Ha! It didn't take long for the vultures to circle," Roberto remarked.

One of the household staff announced dinner was about to be served. Roberto held out his elbow to me. "I don't remember the chef listing you as one of the entrees, but I would be flattered if you sat next to me."

"Of course," I said graciously, taking the proffered arm. Looking over my shoulder, I added, "*Je suis désolé*, but it looks like I am spoken for, for dinner. Who knows what will be served for dessert, though?" I smiled and let Roberto lead me away.

As we walked out of the ballroom, I took a deep breath. *I wonder how I've done so far?* I assessed what my next move should be. It seemed Fredrick did not want to be upstaged by Jon Miguel; I figured I just needed to be patient and see what their next moves would be.

The dining room was a massive affair. Large round tables were arranged loosely around a gleaming hardwood dance floor. A five-piece jazz ensemble sat off to one side, already playing soft dinner music. To the other side were French doors leading to what looked like an indoor arboretum.

There were black place cards arrayed around each table, much like the invitations we had each received. Each table was set with fine bone china plates, golden silverware, and French crystal flutes and goblets. In the center of each table were imported black lilies in cut crystal vases.

I found my place card to the left of Monsieur Haver's. It seemed as if—willing or not—I had already been chosen by our host as his arm candy for supper. I was relieved to see Uncle Camy's name to Roberto's right. Next to mine was Jon Miguel; across the table from us was Fredrick's name. I started to feel like nothing that was to happen tonight would be by chance. Malcolm, Rajasham, Claymont, and their dates were all close by at adjacent tables. I knew dinner would prove to be a very interesting experience.

We settled at our seats, and servers materialized immediately to fill our glasses with sparkling white wine. They served a salad next, followed by warm crusty breads with exotic-tasting vinegars and oils to dip them in.

I felt Fredrick's eyes on me constantly.

Next to me, Jon was proving to be a nuisance; I had to repeatedly return his hand to his own lap rather than mine. Each time I did, I caught Fredrick grimacing with displeasure.

Midway through dinner, Fredrick seized his opportunity and invited me to the dance floor. The band was playing a slow instrumental piece; Rick took me in his arms, and we began to sway slowly back and forth. As we danced, he whispered into my ear, "This was an unexpected surprise."

"This isn't our first 'unexpected' surprise meeting," I said with a sly smile.

"I've never seen you at any of these functions before now. Or was it that I did not have my radar fine-tuned?" He arched an eyebrow.

"Maybe I wasn't old enough to hang out with the big boys, or maybe I wasn't interested until now." We kept dancing for a few moments; Jon made a suggestive gesture in our direction.

"If that asshole puts his hands on you one more time, I'm going to break his fingers," Fredrick declared.

"I don't think that would be such a good idea. If you did, he wouldn't be able to play with himself!"

"Switch seats with me for a few moments. I guarantee I'll have him off your case with little to no bloodshed," Fredrick insisted.

"And what makes you think I need you to do that? Last time I checked I could take care of myself."

"I am sure you can. I just think I can do it better. I don't like sharing you with anyone else."

I leaned forward and whispered in his ear, "Mmmm…it sounds like you're the jealous type. Be careful, or else I might have to make a run for it."

"The last time I kissed you, you didn't run very fast. I don't think I have anything to be worried about."

I laid my head against his chest, breathing in his musk. I closed my eyes, remembering our first kiss. Feeling his arms around me triggered the memory of our first slow dance at Letters and how taken I'd been with him. His strong arms pulled me in closer, and I felt him grow hard at the increased intimacy.

As the dance ended, he took my hand and led me through the French doors to the arboretum. On the way, we grabbed two glasses of champagne. Glancing back at our table, I caught Jon throwing a concerned look our way, which brought a smile to my face.

We walked through the foliage of exotic plants as we sipped our drinks. No words passed between us, and I wondered what he was thinking. The path opened into a clearing with a handful of wicker love seats. Rick motioned for us to sit together in one of the seats. I grew impatient as he uttered not a word but sat with his legs crossed, body turned toward me. Finally, he spoke. "I know what you are doing."

"And what might that be?"

"You're trying to drive me crazy."

I smirked. "I hope it won't be a short trip; that would spoil all my fun."

"See—you are nothing but a tease. That could get you into serious trouble."

"Oh, *I'm* the tease in this game? Let me remind you of a certain birthday gift," I said, leaning closer into him.

"That wasn't a tease; it was a gift of friendship." I didn't believe him for an instant. "Did you like it?" he added, inching his legs close to mine.

I decided to change tactics. I pulled back.

"It was very nice. I was especially intrigued by the inscription on the back. Let me see, what did it say?" I unfastened my cuff link to reveal his bracelet sitting above my shirt cuff.

"You're wearing it?" He sounded pleasantly surprised.

"Why of course; why wouldn't I?"

"Wait a minute, did you know I would be here?" he inquired. For a second, I thought about telling him I did, to see where that would lead.

"I didn't," I admitted finally. "And I am not going to say I wear this often; that would only inflate your head. Let's chalk it up to coincidence."

"So, what *are* you doing here?"

"I could ask you the same thing," I shot back. "Are you following me? You told me before you could find me anytime you wanted to. What's to say you didn't ask Monsieur Haver to invite me? A week ago, I received a hand-delivered invitation," I lied, watching his reaction closely. "Know anything about that, Mr. Mysterious?"

He shrugged, running a hand over his hair. "I'm afraid I can't take credit for this one. I received a hand-delivered invitation as well. Followed by a call from Roberto to come out and talk business. I was conversing with friends when you appeared at the top of the stairs. Your arrival captivated me and everyone else. Seeing you, all I could think was a heavenly angel has entered the ballroom." He placed his hands on my shoulders, pulling me in close. Then his lips were on mine, and we kissed softly.

By some unspoken agreement, we found ourselves standing, wrapping our arms tightly around the other. Our kissing became more ardent, more frantic.

"Desmond? Oh, Desmond?" came an unwelcome voice. "Where are you hiding, you *gorgeous* creature? It's Jon Miguel!" His timing could not have been worse. Then again maybe it was perfect. I didn't want Fredrick to think I was going to drop my pants for him right there.

Rick ended the kiss, his lips twisted bitterly. "I'm going to fuck that bitch up if she doesn't leave you alone!"

I looked at him sternly, a palm planted firmly on his chest. "Don't; I can take care of myself, thank you. Chill out and let me handle this." He held my gaze for a moment before his eyes softened. He shrugged, gave me a peck on my forehead, then walked in the opposite direction from where Jon's voice had come.

A few seconds later Jon emerged from around a tall potted palm tree.

"There you are." He smiled unctuously. "What are you doing out here by yourself? Are you all right, my little flower?"

I glared at him, but he smiled, oblivious to what I was thinking.

"Mon Beau-père was worried about you, *cheri*. I told him I would find you and make sure you were well taken care of."

"I am fine. But you know what? I could really go for some dessert!"

"Magnifique! They are serving it now. I'll escort you back so you don't lose your way." He winked suggestively, extending his elbow. "Beau-père has arranged some entertainment for our enjoyment during dessert. This being your first time here, I am sure you won't want to miss it!"

"You're absolutely right. This being my first visit, I'm taking it all in." I accepted his arm.

"Hopefully, it won't be your last." Jon winked as he guided me toward the dining room. I looked at the foliage, spotting Fredrick through a large green frond. I smiled at him, giving a subtle nod.

As we returned to our table, Uncle Camy caught my eye. I gave him a noncommittal shrug, sitting down in my chair. Moments later Fredrick emerged from the arboretum, taking a loop around the room, finishing at his own seat. His gaze bore into me, a lusty, possessive look that made my dick stir in my pants.

Meanwhile, our host had moved to the center of the hall. "Mesdames et messieurs," he announced, to laughter, given that there were no women in the crowd, "prepare yourselves for a dance extravaganza." He waved his hand, and the rumble of drums began to sound from around the room.

I heard a commotion toward the main doors; twisting around, I caught sight of a stream of scantily clad men loping in. At a drum signal, they released their manhoods from their codpieces. My eyes were overwhelmed by the sight of big ones, fat ones, skinny ones, all of them longer than you could believe. As the dancers twirled among us, gasps and cheers rose, spiking when one of the performers chose an attendee's lap to sit upon.

The smell of lust hung heavy in the room. Everyone was eating up this human dessert…all but one man. He had eyes only for me. Even in the midst of this human buffet, Fredrick's stare bore into me; *his* lust, he directed only in my direction.

At one point, a now thoroughly inebriated Jon Miguel had affixed his lips to the nipple of one of the dancers, even as a second one had begun disrobing him. *He's a good-looking guy without his clothes on*, I had to admit. If it had not been for Fredrick, I might have been more inclined to accept his advances.

Gradually, the dancers began pairing off with guests, leading them off to private corners and darkened rooms throughout the mansion. I was silently relieved when Jon got dragged off by his two; it was nice to know his attention would be diverted for the rest of the night.

I waved off a few of the dancers, looking around for Fredrick, but he was nowhere to be found. *Did he go off with one of them?* I checked my watch, shocked to discover it was almost midnight. I needed to let the pilot know *soon* if I intended to fly back to Philly that evening.

Uncle Camy saw me from across the room. He waved and walked up to me. "Are you all right?" he asked, seeing my expression.

"Unc, if this is the way you live, I can't imagine you ever being bored with life." I shook my head ruefully.

"Yes, this is one of the perks." He followed my distracted gaze around the room. "If you are wondering, I noticed your friend slipping out the main entrance a few moments ago."

"You mean he *left?*"

"It would appear so. Do you two not have something planned for this morning?"

"Nope. We kept getting interrupted by that horny puppy dog, Jon Miguel."

"Ah, yes, Roberto's stepson." Camy chuckled. "Roberto was hoping the two of you might have…*things* in common."

"Be sure to thank Roberto for me," I said with a sneer.

"Well, it's partly my fault too. I encouraged it, figuring it would frustrate Mr. Mason and make him want you more. From all the staring he did this evening, I'm guessing it worked."

"Oh, it worked. Better than you can imagine. I hope not to my detriment." I sighed. "What do I do?"

Camy checked his own watch. "It's just before midnight; there's a plane to catch, but you need to decide now."

I looked around and sighed once more, making up my mind. "This was an amazing experience, and I don't know how I will ever be able to repay you, but I'm going to call it a night." I laughed when a funny thought occurred to me. "Can you imagine what Cal and Millie would say if they knew what went on here and what we've done all week?!" Camy gave a low hiss. "Yeah—don't worry, Unc—this is one adventure they *won't* be hearing about!" I laughed again, with him joining in—albeit a bit hesitantly. "Thanks for everything, Uncle Camy." I kissed him on the cheek, and we shared a big hug.

"Love you, nephew. Be patient. You've hooked your fish. Time to reel him in, *slowly*. That one's a fighter and he's not going to give in easily." We walked over to where Roberto stood, watching the pairings-off with a smile on his face.

"Leaving so soon, young Dawson?" He asked.

"Yes, sir. I wanted to thank you for the wonderful evening."

"So formal?" he asked. "Come now—it's Roberto. You are family now."

"Thank you, Roberto," I said with a smile.

He kissed me on each cheek. "*Mon jeune ami*, the man who captures your heart will have truly found his pot of gold." I smiled and hugged him once more.

Camy saw me up the stairs. At the top, I turned and swept my gaze across the ballroom below. I caught sight of Malcolm, Rajasham, and Claymont, giving each of them a wink and a nod.

At the door, a footman helped me with my coat. As my jacket settled on my shoulders, the reality of tonight's experience settled on my mind. *What an incredible evening I've had...*

I stepped out into the brisk night. I waved to Uncle Camy; he reassured me the pilot would be standing by at the airport. I wondered if my uncle was disappointed I was not staying... *Nah—I'm pretty sure he understands.*

As I stood there in the cool, pre-morning dark, awaiting my limo, a voice called from my right.

"Desmond."

I turned to see Fredrick leaning against a pillar. "I thought you were on your way home."

"Are you disappointed I'm still here?" he asked.

"I'm not sure…" I responded, playing coy.

"Well, that's certainly not the answer I wanted to hear." He stepped closer. "I couldn't stand not being near you and watching that bitch trying to make time with you."

"How could he, with you staring at us from across the table?" My limo drove up. "Well, I guess this is a missed opportunity for both of us. This is my ride." The chauffeur came around and opened my door.

"I take it you are not staying locally?" Rick asked.

"No. I'm headed to the airport."

"Well. How convenient. I also am headed there. Do you have room for one more in there?"

I struggled to hide the smile that wanted to spill across my face. "Hmm…it seems you're in luck. But won't you miss all the night's activities?"

"I was hoping we might continue the activity you and I had started." A sly grin crossed his face.

"That's a little presumptuous of you, sir," I said. His grin erupted into a bark of laughter.

"I suppose it is. But I figured, no harm, no foul."

I climbed into the limo, gesturing for him to come in after me.

"Straight to the airport, Mr. Dawson?" the chauffeur asked after he'd gotten in his seat.

"Yes, please."

On the way to the airport, Rick and I spoke as if we'd known each other a long time. When his barriers came down, he became very easy to talk to, much like the person I had met at Letters that evening months ago. As we talked, a thought struck me: he reminded me an awful lot of Angel. He made me feel comfortable and he made me laugh—much as Angel did when we were together.

As we approached the airport, the driver buzzed and asked Fredrick where he wanted to be let off. He looked at me and told the driver to give us a few moments.

"I won't be denied another moment of your beautiful smile and the essence of your sweet lips." His voice was thick with barely contained lust. "All I want to know is, will we be taking your plane back to the city, or mine?"

"Again, that's awfully presumptuous on your part, don't you think? Who said I was ready to surrender myself to you?"

He reached for my face and drew my lips to his. All I had learned from Claymont would come into practice now. I returned his kiss with every part of my sensual being. Fredrick paused with his eyes closed and took a deep breath.

The chauffeur buzzed again. "Sir?"

I responded, looking deep in Fredrick's eyes, "Mr. Mason will be flying back with me."

The chauffeur answered, "Very good, sir."

Fredrick picked up the phone next to him, glancing at me. "May I?"

"Of course."

He dialed in a number and began to talk. "Nelson, I will be flying to the city with a business associate. You may head home without me. I will see you bright and early in the morning." A pause filled the space between us for several seconds. Then, looking deep into my eyes, Rick replied, "Well, I'm sure mine will be most enjoyable."

Interlude Nineteen

Twist and Turns—What Do I Do Now?

Our flight home was a tantalizing mix of erotic conversation, locked lips, and mutual sexual gratification. My French and Indian tutors had taught me very well. With the use of my mouth and hands only, I brought Fredrick repeatedly to the edge of climax until at last we both exploded together.

We arrived at Philadelphia International Airport, exhausted and nestled in each other's arms. The jet came to a full stop, and we found our limos outside, waiting to whisk us off to our final destinations for the night.

Fredrick kissed me one last time before we rose from our seats. A contented sigh escaped from him.

"So where do we go from here?" he asked, stroking my cheek.

At the risk of ruining the mood, I replied, "You tell me. You're the married one."

He looked at me without expression for a moment. "Yes, I am," he admitted finally. "Does that bother you?"

"I don't know, should it?" It was my turn to pause for a moment before I answered my own question. "Yes, actually, it does bother me, on several different levels."

"What might those levels be?"

"Well, let's start with the fact that you have kids at home. Next, my roommate cares a lot about your wife and children; in my mind that make me a home-wrecker. Last but not least, if we carry on with this affair, I don't know if I'll ever be able to look your wife, my roommate, or even myself in the face ever again." I took a deep breath, looking anywhere but at Fredrick. "Sooooo…is that enough levels for ya?"

I'm not sure where that all came from, but it felt good to get it off my chest. I walked over to the plane's bar and poured myself a drink. Before I could take a sip, Fredrick came up behind me. He put his arms around me and laid his chin on my shoulder.

"I know all about your roommate and my wife…but this isn't about them; it's about us. But if this makes you too uncomfortable, there's nothing we did this evening that would prevent us from going our separate ways at this point."

I froze. "Is that what you *want*?"

"No," he said immediately, "it's not. But, whatever this turns out to be, wherever we take this physically and emotionally, I won't be with someone who will harbor regrets. That's not healthy for either of us." He turned me around by the shoulders to face him. "Let me ask you this, Desmond: isn't there someone in your life who'll be hurt by us being together? I can't imagine a man as sexy and intelligent as you *not* having either a boyfriend or a girlfriend."

I didn't say anything for a moment. The feel of his strong hands rubbing my shoulders prevented me from thinking clearly. "There is someone," I admitted finally, "and I love her very much."

"So, there you have it. I also love my wife very much. But I love being with men discreetly. The thing is, with all the men I've been with, I haven't found a single one who makes me feel the way Sylvia does."

"So, what are you telling me, Fredrick?"

He put a finger to my lips. "I'd really love it if you'd call me Rick. 'Fredrick' is the business mogul. 'Rick' is the person with you right now, the person close to you."

I kissed his finger, closing my eyes. He replaced his finger with his lips, and we made out again, slowly, gently. I wrapped my arms about his neck to stop myself from falling.

"I want all of you, Desmond Dawson," he whispered. "Your lips, your body, your mind, your soul...the total essence of your wonderful manhood. And I want your love." He kissed me one last time, then stepped back. "If you are not able to give me those things, then I will leave you alone. I won't call; I won't pursue you. Hopefully, we will remain friends, and if I can help you in any way, all you have to do is call."

Rick reached into his jacket pocket and pulled out a gold case. He pressed a button on the side and the case swung open. He pulled out a card, then handed it to me. "This is a number that very few people have. And now you have it. I hope you will use it when you are ready." He turned, gathered up his things, and headed for the door.

Then, out of nowhere, a scene from my favorite old Bob Hope movie crossed my mind. I smiled. "Hey, Rick, thanks for the memories, guy."

He looked at me, returning the smile. "I'm hoping we'll have many more encounters, and I'll be able to bank some more!"

"Do you expect those encounters to be sooner or later? Because with you, Mr. Mason, I'm never quite sure when or where we'll just 'run' into each other!"

"Well, we seem to have a unique way of landing in each other's backyard; I expect it will be soon." He blew me a kiss and disembarked.

I watched him walk down to his limousine. He looked at the plane one last time. Seeing me, he saluted and climbed into his car. As the limo pulled away, the pilot walked into the main cabin and asked if that would be it for the evening.

"Yes, that will be all, thanks."

"Did you have a successful trip, sir?"

I smiled as I gathered my things. "This trip was what you'd call a life-altering experience…and I survived it."

"I'm going to assume that the smile on your face means you enjoyed yourself too?"

"Yes, you can assume that it does!" I agreed. We shook hands, and he saw me off the plane and down to my ride.

On the trip to the dorm, reality began to set in again. On one hand, I was still reeling from my experience that night; on the other hand, an odd sense of despair was settling in.

I'd finally connected with Rick, and there seemed to be real possibilities for a long-term affair. I felt like I was now in the driver's seat. But there would be consequences to taking this trip. I pulled out the card he'd given me, wondering if I should save it or rip it into tiny pieces and toss them out the window to scatter along I-76.

I decided on the former course of action, tucking the card back in my pocket.

We reached my dorm around three in the morning, to utter stillness. The driver removed my bag from the trunk, then came around to open my door.

"All trips must come to an end, sir," he said, perhaps sensing my mood.

"You're probably right, Alex."

"If you ever need a ride, just call." He handed me the second card I was to receive that night. I smiled and nodded, fishing out a twenty to give him. We shook and waved goodbye. I walked to the dormitory door, picked up my overnight bag, and headed up to my room.

As I rode the elevator to my floor, I felt myself crashing as the events of the past twelve hours finally took their toll on my body. I had made my debut in the world of men who loved men. I was in the throes of an affair with a married man. God only knew what the morning would bring. But, before that happened, I needed sleep.

I opened my room door, dropping my bag onto the floor. I undressed without thought for my finery, tossing everything into a pile. I flopped onto my bed stark naked, belatedly thankful Brian had already left to go home for tomorrow's service. I shifted onto my back, sighing deeply.

Suddenly, I became aware of an ache in my loins. To my surprise, a part of me had not yet been worn out. I reached down, grasping my rock-hard erection. With a shrug and a chuckle, I began to stroke myself. My mind drifted back to the events of the plane ride. My pace quickened as I relived Fredrick's caresses and kisses. The memory of how I'd pleasured his body brought me quickly to the edge, and with a single, sharp groan, I exploded in climax.

I settled back, coming down from my release, breathing deeply, feeling my heart pound in my chest. Completely exhausted now, I was asleep in seconds.

Interlude Twenty

I Got Your Back

No sooner had I fallen asleep—or so it seemed—than there came a sharp knock at my door.

"Desmond? Desmond, are you in there?" *Why is she knocking at this time of night?* my tired brain wondered. "Let's go, sweetie!" Karen yelled through the door. "It's seven o'clock. We've got to get moving!"

I rolled out of bed and shuffled to the door, becoming aware of the sticky mess on my belly. I opened it a crack, peeking through. "Hey, Karen—can I take a rain check this morning?"

"On one condition," she agreed, bringing her face close to the door crack. "You give me the skinny on where you've been and what you've been up to this past week and a half. 'Cause I know you've been up to no good!"

Another familiar face pushed himself into view. Antonio.

"Forget church, bitch!" he exclaimed, pushing my door wide open and waltzing in. I scrambled about to find something to cover my nakedness. "We want the whole enchilada—

olives and pimentos too! JC and I will even treat you to break-fast."

"In that case I'll let Melvin know it's a stay-at-home party with sausage and eggs on the menu!" Karen added, trying to catch a peek of my junk.

"Hold on, guys," I exclaimed, wrapping myself in bed covers, "no offense to your other halves, but if I tell this story, it's just between the three of us, okay?"

Antonio and Karen exchanged a look and a shrug. "Not a problem for me," Antonio declared. "Let me take care of my man's morning needs and I'll see ya in about two hours."

"*Two* hours?!" Karen laughed. "It takes me less than half that long to satisfy *my* man!" I shook a finger at Antonio to ward off any retort; he laughed and obliged me. "I'll leave Melvin out of this on one condition," Karen bargained. "Desmond—you have to call the Reverend Harris and his wife and make up a good Christian lie as to why we won't be there today."

"Fine!" I agreed, more to get them out of my room than anything else.

To my surprise and relief, Brian answered the phone. "Hi, Desmond! How was your trip?" I blinked, stuttering wordlessly. I hadn't yet told a soul about my invitation to upstate New York last night—I'd barely had time to prepare for it myself before being whisked off in that private jet.

"How did you know I went away? Actually, never mind. Of course you know!" *This is Brian, our resident psychic, after all.* He laughed through the phone.

"Well, you've been disappearing every night for the past two weeks. When I asked Antonio, he said you were hanging out with your uncle. And yeah," he added, "I sorta *knew* too."

I smiled at his partial admission. "Well, I had a *really* great time. And I'm sorry—I shoulda left you a note or something."

"Apology accepted," Brian said. "I'm just looking out for you, brother!"

"Look, that's why I'm calling. I'm really beat from my trip, and I was wondering if you could make a good excuse for us not coming to church this morning. Everyone is gonna hang close to the campus today."

"I figured that might be the case, so I took the liberty of telling my parents I didn't think you guys would be coming in. I told them everyone was busy preparing final papers and projects. Mom was disappointed, but she told me to tell everyone she expected to see you guys next Sunday; ditto from Dad."

"I'm gonna miss your dad's words of wisdom today," I admitted, meaning it.

"I'll tell him that; he'll appreciate hearing it. And when I'm back, I look forward to hearing about your trip to Albany." *How did he...? Damn him!*

"Um, okay—I'll fill you in on all the gory details." I doubted Brian would want to hear some of the finer ones, though.

"Awesome. Hey, Des?"

"Yeah?"

"I'm glad you had the opportunity to tame the lion. I hope it was everything you thought it would be. See ya when I get back?"

"Yeah, man, I'll see you tonight." I hung the phone up. Brian had really laid the spooky psychic shit on heavy. I think it was time for us to set some boundaries with what he was "allowed" to know...or at least reveal.

I napped for another hour, then headed for the shower. As I soaped up, I pictured Rick's hands and lips on me as they'd moved across my smooth bare skin. The hot water soothed me, and I sighed at the pleasant memories.

Karen arrived at exactly 9:00 a.m. with Antonio in tow. We set out for one of our favorite breakfast spots: the IHOP on City Line Avenue. We chose a quiet booth at the back, where I shared the whole story of my past week and a half.

I told them about my evenings with Uncle Camy, the training my instructors had given me (the condensed version—clearly, Karen was not feeling the whole hands-on approach they'd taken), and about the black-tie party. I described the magical feeling of being a prince for a night and about reeling in Fredrick Mason.

Karen nodded slowly but looked at me with judgmental eyes. Antonio, on the other hand, couldn't stop slapping me on the back and congratulating me on a job well done. (I had no doubt Antonio would be wanting the low-down dirty edition later on.)

"So, at any point during your fling," Karen said, making the last word sound dirty, "did you even think about my girl, my sista—Angel?!"

Before I could give my answer, Antonio jumped in. "Bitch, can't you let the boy just revel in his sexual excursion without dousing him with reality?"

I didn't know how to answer Karen's question, because—quite honestly—I *couldn't* remember whether Angel had crossed my mind at all during these past two weeks. I'd been entirely absorbed in the pleasure of my newfound life…but I couldn't tell Karen that. So, I lied.

"Karen, even with everything that happened, she barely left my mind." I held her gaze, long enough for her to miss Antonio's dramatic eye roll.

Karen bought it. Or she had decided to let it go, for now.

After being grilled over breakfast, I returned to my room for a well-needed nap. Yet again, seemingly as soon as I fell asleep, there came a pounding at my door.

"Who is it *now*?!" I groaned.

"A package for Mr. Desmond Dawson?" came a solicitous voice I didn't recognize. *Shit!* I scrambled out of bed, stumbling as I pulled on a pair of shorts and yanked the door open. A handsome delivery guy stood there; he gave my shirtless body a quick once-over before his eyes snapped up to my face.

I suppressed a grin, announcing, "I'm Desmond." I felt my dick shift in my shorts; it had been slightly hard when I woke up.

He nodded, handing me a clipboard to sign. I signed it and handed it back to him, making eye contact. He held the look as he handed me the package.

"Thanks," I said; he nodded again.

"I'll see you around." He turned and walked off.

"Hey!" I called out. He stopped, looking back at me expectantly, the hint of a smile on his face. "Lemme see if I have a couple bucks for a tip."

"Oh." He shook his head. "Thank you, but that won't be necessary; the sender included my tip." He waved and carried on toward the elevator. Of course, who should get off as the doors opened but Antonio. He gave a low whistle at the delivery boy, then saw me standing at my door mostly naked. His eyebrows shot up.

"Who's the Mac Daddy?" he asked, tossing a thumb over his shoulder as he strode into my room. "'Cause that boy's got some buns on him!"

I laughed and shook my head. "Your gaydar can really pick 'em, can't it?"

"Damn straight—that's why I'm a Diva with a capital *D*." I rolled my eyes, closing the door and turning into the room.

"My gaydar also told me there was more to your disappearance than you let on this afternoon, bitch," he added. "So what say we first examine the package you just received, then you can give me the uncensored version of your 'Tale of Two Men'?"

"Deal." I settled on my bed, inspecting the box. "It doesn't say who it's from, but I can make a pretty good guess."

"Baby, you don't even have to waste time 'guessing.' Get it open!"

I pulled a small card from an envelope affixed to the box and read it aloud:

Like the brightest star's light in the middle of night,

your beautiful smile illuminated our evening flight.

Just as the moon and the stars fade in the early morning light,

so ended our unforgettable night.

I sit in anticipation of my star's return.

Missing you, 'R'.

"Damn!" Antonio swore. "He's sweet on you! You sure you didn't give anything up last night that you want to let your sista know about?"

"Honey, I was a lady to the bitter end, thank you very much."

"Then, child—you got a whole lot of explaining to do!" Antonio pulled a chair over to my bed, sitting so that we were knee to knee. I couldn't get the paper off the box fast enough for him. "If this is the way you open Christmas gifts around your house, I'm surprised y'all aren't still there."

"Enough, Mr. Smarty. Keep fucking with me and I won't open it at all."

"Oh, you'll open the package, bitch, or I'll rip the shit off my damned self!" We both fell out laughing.

Inside the box was another card. As I dug underneath, I found a Phillies baseball cap, a small Phillie Phanatic doll, and two keys: one gold and one silver. I glanced at Antonio, who gave me a quick shrug. "What does the note say?"

Opening this card, I read aloud again:

Desmond, enclosed please find a complimentary pass for you and as many friends as you care to bring to this year's Phillies opening game.

If you choose to accept this gift, there will be an offer for you at the end of the game. Make sure you have both keys with you; they will be how you'll communicate your choice to me.

If you choose to accept my offer, this will be a new opportunity for the two of us to get to know each other even better. If you choose otherwise, that will be a signal for me to go back to the drawing board and try something new.

I hope you will keep the source of this gift private. I know you'll agree that discretion is the better part of valor.

Until we are together again, 'R'.

I lowered the note, grinning ear to ear. The room fell quiet; Antonio was in one of his rare silent moods, waiting for me to say something first. I stuffed the note in the band of my shorts, fell onto my pillow, and whooped loudly into it. When I sat up for air, Antonio was smiling too. He reached over and placed a hand on my shoulder.

"Get up, boo—put your sneakers on; we're going for a run!" he declared.

"What? Why?"

"'Cause you gonna work enough energy off so you can focus and give me the full, unabridged version of what led up to this." He pointed to the box at my side.

We met outside and started jogging. For a good five miles, we said nothing, running in companionable silence. In my head, I tried to order my thoughts, making sense of the whirlwind events that had taken me so far in so little time.

Finally, the run wore us out. We grabbed some bottled water and picked a bench outside the student union to cool off on.

Once I'd caught my breath, I retold Antonio everything—from picking Uncle Camy up at the train station to Rick's final kiss goodbye on the plane.

By the end of my story, Antonio was silent for the second time that afternoon. Even during the story, I'd gotten nothing from him but raised eyebrows and single-word murmurs.

We went up to my room, where I finally turned to confront him.

"What's up with you? Why am I getting nothing but grunts and farts?"

"What do you want me to say?"

"I want to know what you're thinking!" I exclaimed.

He crossed his arms and sighed. "I don't *want* to say anything," he explained, "but I know you'll go bitch on me if I don't, so here goes: I'm somewhat happy for you...*and* jealous of you at the same time."

"Okay..."

"You've landed in the best of all worlds, Desmond! This Fredrick, or Rick, or Fred, or whatever the fuck his name is, has *everything*. And now it looks like he'll soon have you. Plus, there's no dickhead father in your way to ruin things for you." He held up a hand to stop me from interrupting. "I know—this situation still has its issues, but if you look at what he could do for you..." Antonio paused. "I know what's coming next too: you're gonna fall in love with this asshole...that is, if you haven't already?!" He looked at me closely, but I kept my features schooled. "My fear, Des, is he's gonna break your heart real bad. And I know in my soul there's nothing I can say that will get you to walk away from this situation."

A lump caught in my throat. "*Give* me a good reason, Antonio. Give me one and I'll dump him tomorrow."

Antonio stalled, blinking at sudden tears in his eyes. "I can't, Des—I *won't*. This is your chance to find out if this is what you want for the rest of your life."

He sniffed, wiping his eyes with the back of his hand. "This guy's a man's man—the kind of guy I *think* you're looking for. I can tell you, though, he's the worst type to get involved with. You deserve more than he's capable of giving. But you gotta find this out for yourself!"

"Antonio—" I reached for him.

"No! My problem is I love you, Desmond. I love you way too much to watch you go through this. So, there's my dilemma!"

"What are you asking me?" My voice fell to a whisper.

"Nothing! I am not asking you anything. We shouldn't be looking for love here. I've got Jean Claude; you've got Fredrick Mason."

"But…"

"Don't worry, bitch," he said, clearing his throat. "It's not like I'm going anywhere. I'll be there for you through it all. Like I always am," he added—not without a touch of bitterness.

I paused for a moment, collecting myself. I looked into his eyes—eyes that loved me unconditionally. "I tell you what: you keep on being you and looking out for my back, and I'll work on protecting my heart. Deal?"

"Yeah, brother, straight up! I got your back!"

We walked to the door. Antonio turned and pulled me in for a tight hug, hiding his face in my shoulder. I squeezed him tightly to me, comforted by the love we shared for each other. I felt a quick kiss on my cheek; then he whispered, "Good night," and was out the door.

I watched him walk to the elevator as I leaned on my doorframe. *How different things would have been without JC or Rick in our lives...*

Shaking my head, I turned to my room.

Fantasies, friends, and foes to come...how do I choose between them? I wondered.

Only time would tell.

Acknowledgements

What happens to a dream deferred...Always believing it will come true, visualizing it, watching it finally come to be.

First and foremost, I give honor to my God, my Lord and savior Jesus Christ for Desmond's story. You planted the seed of this story, you led me to the fruition of this novel, and you supported me spiritually throughout.

To my parents, whose love has guided me, protected me, and brought me to this point in my life. Your love was always unconditional, and you supported me in all my life's endeavors – artistic and otherwise. You were my biggest cheerleaders. I know you are looking down on me favorably.

To REMJ, who taught me the meaning of love and commitment. Your continued belief in my talents have fueled me to pursue my dreams with fervor. You will forever hold that special place in my heart.

To Gary Hurtubise, whose vision, understanding of my characters & story, and literary guidance helped me prepare my novel for submission and publication.

To my friends Lorenzo "Tony" Fletcher III, Robert M. Manson, Jr., Anthony Hook, Alvin Cooper, Eric Booker, Tony King and Kharlos Panterra, for their enduring support and encouragement. Your insights, belief in my talents, (when my own belief waned) and kicks in the pants were what I needed. Love you guys.

To my children, grandchildren, brothers, sisters, nieces and nephews, whose love continues gets me through the rough times. Our accomplishments are a testament to strong family values.

Finally, to my fans who have watched me grow, embraced my works and have always been in my corner. Thank you!

About LBJ Harris

LBJ Harris was born on October 1, 1958 in Neptune, New Jersey. He is one of seven children born to civil rights leaders. His mother chose his first name because it was unique, as she knew her baby would grow to be.

When he was seven years old, his parents moved the family to an all-white community, to ensure he and his siblings received a good education, and to guarantee their safety against opponents of their parent's civil rights work.

Harris knew from an early age that he loved performing on stage. Throughout his early years and young adulthood, he performed in church choirs, his high school band, and in the high school drama club. Upon graduating from high school, his love of the arts led him to West Chester State College in Pennsylvania.

In 1979, Harris earned his Bachelor of Arts in Speech, Communications and Theater. While at college, he worked for the Three Little Bakers Dinner Theatre as a performer, lead dancer, and stage designer. His set designs and acting roles earned him major acclaim in local newspapers.

In 1981, he moved back to New Jersey where he formed a two-man performing duo, a joint company KapSig and eventually his own company, 'Le Noir Cabaret Repertory Theater Company'.

Harris would move to writing, directing and producing originally written musicals for his local community as founder of Le Noir Cabaret. Those works included: 'Moments in Love', 'An African American Musical Review', 'SIBONISO', 'Anna Mae', and 'Ashbury Cove'.

Harris and his theatre troupe toured his musical SIBONISO in 1994 at the newly renovated Paramount Theater, Asbury Park, NJ, and at the Carver Community Center in San Antonio, Texas.

In 1989 Harris chose to become a single father, adopting the first of his four children. He elected to place his arts career on hold after the arrival of twins in 1998. Over the next 15 years he focused on raising his four children and one grandnephew.

In August of 1999, while completing a second Master's Degree in Education, Harris saw the birth of one more child: his novel, "When Love Calls Your Name". He finished the manuscript in April of that next year, though ultimately shelved it, along with a number of other unpublished works.

After his youngest two children graduated from high school in June of 2014, Harris chose to return to the stage. That October, he appeared in the ensemble cast of African American men entitled, "Messages from Men: Machismo, Magen, Mirth & Maturity" at the Cape May Playhouse. He wrote and performed an original piece, "Letter to My Children", in dedication to his children.

With a renewed yearning to pick up his career where he left off, Harris anticipates publishing his first fiction novel, "When Love Calls Your Name" in the fall of 2021.

Facebook
www.facebook.com/LBJHarris

Pinterest
www.pinterest.com/LDKollectons

Twitter
www.twitter.com/Lbj_harris

Connect with NineStar Press

www.ninestarpress.com

www.facebook.com/ninestarpress

www.facebook.com/groups/NineStarNi
che

www.twitter.com/ninestarpress

www.instagram.com/ninestarpress